THE TWO CHIEFS OF DUNBOY

THE TWO
CHIEFS OF DUNBOY

A Story of
18th Century Ireland

By
J. A. FROUDE

Edited with a Foreword by
A. L. ROWSE

1969
CHATTO & WINDUS
LONDON

Published by
Chatto & Windus Ltd.
40 William IV Street
London W.C.2

*

Clarke, Irwin & Co. Ltd.
Toronto

SBN 7011 1566 1

Original edition first published 1889

This edition and Foreword © A. L. Rowse 1969

Printed in Great Britain by
Northumberland Press Limited
Gateshead

CONTENTS

CONTENTS

FOREWORD

AFTER Macaulay, Froude was the most brilliant writer of all the English historians of the nineteenth century. And, for myself, I prefer Froude's style—more supple and subtle, more flexible and poetic, expressive of varied shades of feeling, not so declamatory and rhetorical, if less structural and firm. Froude's was the sensibility of a later, more complex, generation, as also of a more sceptical temperament, a mind less cocksure of itself. Nevertheless Froude was the one historian to compare with Macaulay: when the first volumes of his history of England in the sixteenth century came out, the instinct of the Victorians was right in acclaiming him as the only comparable successor to the great historian of the seventeenth century.

Though they were both significant figures in the public life of their time—Macaulay more so, as a professional politician —their careers and fates were very different. Froude was the child of the Oxford Movement, youngest brother of one of its leaders—of whom Newman formed expectations; but the young man lost his faith, and was subsequently rescued from scepticism and despair by the positive charge that Carlyle's personality gave out in its prime. Some tincture of scepticism, however, always remained underneath Froude's Protestant positiveness—nothing sceptical about Macaulay: it is one of his gravest defects.

Macaulay became enshrined as one of the nation's worthies, if in the temple of Whig deities; his statue in the ante-chapel of his college, Trinity, venerated at Cambridge, his tradition carried on to our time by his great-nephew, George Macaulay Trevelyan. Froude was badly treated by his university of Oxford; his early autobiographical novel, *The Nemesis of Faith*, burnt in the hall of his college, Exeter, by the Sub-

7

Rector; made to resign his Fellowship, persecuted all his days by the official spokesman of the Oxford History School, the horrid Freeman, who lay in wait for every volume of Froude's *History* as it came out; never an honorary degree. Lord Salisbury did impose him on the university as Regius Professor at the end of his life: it killed him. As the candid Bishop Stubbs wrote of Froude: 'he is a man of genius, and he has been treated abominably.'

The truth is that Froude fell among all the stools—it is a part of his enigmatic, living interest. The child of the Oxford Movement became the great historian, and defender, of the Protestant Reformation. The earlier Liberal became the Imperialist, historian of the Elizabethan seamen, recorder of empire-building achievements in the West Indies, South Africa, Oceana. This offended Liberals and Little-Englanders, as his work was a constant offence to High Churchmen. Like Carlyle, he was out of sympathy with both political parties (who can blame him today?). An Imperialist, he was yet opposed to Disraeli's pro-Turkish policy: Froude's sympathies were pro-Russian, with the oppressed minorities of the Balkans and the Near-East. The closest friend and disciple of Carlyle (too much so!), his biography, one of the best biographies in our literature, created a storm of controversy as insufficiently sympathetic to the Master, and this embittered Froude's last years.

Perhaps it is not surprising that every one of Froude's major works sparked off a controversy—it may be that he was a trifle naïvely candid, he was certainly disobligingly truthful. But he was a man of original genius, who did not fit into conventional people's categories and pre-conceptions. And the result is that —a best-seller in his own day, whose works sold in hundreds of thousands (second only to Macaulay among historians)— every one of his books is alive, tingling with life and vigour, with poetry, prejudice and sense. Of all the great Victorians, he is the one who most demands proper and competent appraisal, bringing sympathetically before the public for its attention and enjoyment.

Apart from the famous case of the biography of Carlyle, the work of Froude that created most controversy was his big book in three volumes, *The English in Ireland in the Eighteenth Century*, published 1872-1874. This was to be expected: Ireland was the storm-centre of British politics in the later nineteenth century, Irish historiography was a free-for-all, and nobody could say anything about Ireland that was not immediately controverted, and perhaps controvertible. It was not that Froude was unsympathetic to the Irish; indeed, in his ambivalent way, he was emotionally attracted by the Irish, understood all the quirks and crannies of the Irish character, their strengths and their weaknesses, but he did not believe in their capacity for self-government as things were in his day— nearly a century ago. His biographer, Herbert Paul, wrote: 'he would have done anything for the Irish, except allow them to govern themselves.' But, then, Herbert Paul was a Gladstonian Liberal.

Actually, what Froude thought was rather subtler and more provocative. He thought that the Irish would not show themselves worthy of self-government until they fought for it. (Here was Carlyle's Teutonic doctrine of force, of Might making Right, in a highly relevant and dangerous context. Froude had no liberal illusions about the role of force in history.) In a sense the Irish took him at his word: Ireland has now celebrated the half-centenary of the Easter Rebellion as the decisive act towards independence.

Froude was influenced by the Teutonic-superiority nonsense so prevalent among nineteenth-century historians—the superiority of the Anglo-Saxons, the inferiority of the Celts, etc. How could he escape it, the closest associate and follower of Carlyle, chief purveyor of the German-inspired rubbish? The surprising thing is that Froude did not have more of it: it does not bulk so large as with Freeman and Green and Stubbs, it does not take such an absurd and exaggerated form as with his brother-in-law, Kingsley. I have, however, reduced its obtrusive expressions in this book, and cut down his reflections on the Irish character.

The Two Chiefs of Dunboy was published in 1889, fifteen years after Froude finished *The English in Ireland*, of which it is in some sense a parergon. His latest biographer, Professor

Waldo H. Dunn, thinks that the novel was written slowly at different times over a number of years—I find no indication to that effect—and that it had been in Froude's mind ever since the History to write it. It has not been observed, however, that the story arose in Froude's mind from the fusion of two episodes from *The English in Ireland*, which are to be found in volume 1, Book III. The story, that of the two chiefs, the Catholic Irishman and the Protestant Englishman, Morty Sullivan and Colonel Goring—the expropriated chieftain and the colonizing intruder in occupation of Sullivan's ancestral lands—is in its main outlines a true story of the 1750's. Colonel Goring was, in fact, an upright revenue-officer, John Puxley, bent on doing his duty with little aid or encouragement from the government in Dublin, who was waylaid at a forge on his way to church at Glengariff and murdered by Morty Sullivan and his companions. The murder was then revenged by Puxley's nephews, who ran Sullivan down to his lair and burned it over his head. But Froude has woven into the story the character and career of the sinister informer, Sylvester O'Sullivan, from actual episodes that took place thirty years before.

Anyhow, Froude has magnificent material to hand and a rattling good tale to tell. He was singularly well qualified to tell it. Froude knew Ireland and Irish types well, from earlier years when he spent time there, and in later years when summer after summer he used to rent Derreen on the Kenmare River from his friends, the Lansdownes, for the shooting and fishing, the open air life on the mountains and in those waters. There are splendid descriptions of the scenery—in that Froude was Macaulay's superior; he was a good sailing man, and knew the inlets and bays, the reefs and coves, like the back of his hand. He naturally understood the Calvinist type of Colonel Goring, a Cromwellian born out of his time in the latitudinarian days of the eighteenth century. Then there is the politics of the time. Many popular writers could do the former, but few would have the sense of politics, of the political issues, the sheer political understanding to portray the latter. Here the historian stood the novelist in good stead; it made a strong combination.

FOREWORD

Much as I enjoy the seascapes and the seamanship, the excitements of gun-running on a cove at night or a sea-chase, I admire even more the confrontation of the stern Calvinist, Colonel Goring, with Primate Stone, the *rusé politique*, the Laodicean, portrayed as Epicurean and aesthete, who ruled Ireland from his palace in Dublin. Froude gives a far richer and more perceptive portrait of this political ecclesiastic—a kind of English Cardinal Fleury or even Dubois—in the novel than in the History. How Froude and Carlyle, who liked simple men of action, hated the type! It all makes for dramatic conflict, enriches the scene, deepens the effect: a great deal of the history of the time, of its social life, is woven in.

Why, then, was this distinguished novel not more successful?

For one thing, the historian overbore the novelist in it. The original is too long and discursive; the historian is bent on explaining everything, instead of leaving the event to tell its own tale. I have pruned and pared the historical disquisitions in which so many of the exciting events were embedded. Froude called his book a Romance, but there is no love interest in it: it is very much a man's book, like Scott's or John Buchan's. There are three women in it, but only one is anything more than a lay-figure—Morty Sullivan's sister, with her passionate hatred of the English driving him on like a later Mrs. Erskine Childers or Countess Markiewicz, a Mrs. Despard or Maud MacBride. (Froude knew his Ireland.) A modern would have made more of the emotional relationship between Morty and his friend Connell—that Froude understood such things is evident from his reference to the handsome Stone, when young, as having been reputed the Duke of Dorset's Ganymede.

I have not altered a word of the text—except the wording of the translation from the Irish of Connell's touching farewell to Morty, the night before his execution, in the last lines of the book. The story can now stand out, free from accretions, in all its visual vividness and exciting episodes—the duel between Morty and the Colonel, the gun-running at night, riot in Dublin, the sea-chase, the murder at the forge, the burning of Morty's lair over his head. One recalls that Froude's junior, Robert Louis Stevenson, found his formula with *Treasure*

Island, in 1882, seven years before, and that the 1880's saw the flowering of his work, the revival of the historical romance. The elderly historian was not above learning from his juniors, and his story would make a splendid film today.

A. L. ROWSE

Chapter I

MR. BLAKE'S BUSINESS

ON the right bank of the Loire, two miles below the town of Nantes, there stood in the middle of the eighteenth century the extensive premises of the firm of Messrs. Blake and Delany, Irish exiles who had been naturalized in France, and were carrying on a large business there as merchants and ship-owners. The relations between the great countries of Europe were generally unsettled. The normal condition was war. In the intervals of nominal peace the seas continued insecure. The traders had to depend upon themselves for the defence of their property. Their ships went armed, and the yards where they were fitted out wore the appearance of naval arsenals. The river side, where their establishment was carried on, had been embanked for several hundred yards; the ground had been levelled, large warehouses had been erected over the water, and barges and larger vessels lay at the wharves and quays below them to be loaded and unloaded by projecting cranes. Rows of solid stone buildings ran up over the area behind, shaded by acacias and chestnut trees.

At the time when our story opens, business was in full activity. Large ships were moored alongside the jetties—others, evidently belonging to the same owners, were anchored out-side in the river, whose white painted but weather-stained hulls showed that they had returned from distant expeditions in the tropic seas, while coasting smacks, sloops and luggers spoke of a trade near at home which could be no less considerable.

Mr. Blake, the chief owner and manager, for Mr. Delaney was but a sleeping partner, furnished an instance—one among many to be observed at that epoch—of what an Irishman could do when transplanted from the land of his birth. His father had been a gentleman of property in the county of Galway. He was a Catholic and a patriot. He had fought at Aghrim,

13

and had caught St. Ruth in his arms when the fatal cannon shot which killed the French General decided the fate of Ireland. He had retired upon his property, when the campaign was over, being protected as he supposed by the Articles of Limerick and Galway. But these Articles required the consent of Parliament; and receiving that consent only in a mutilated form, they proved but a weak defence. His estates were forfeited, and like so many of the bravest of his countrymen, he fled to France, became an active officer in the Irish Brigade, rose into favour with the French Government, and won fame and rank in the wars of the Low Countries.

His son, Patrick Blake displayed talents in another direction, which opened to him a more promising career. He showed a practical aptitude for business. His patriotism was as ardent as his father's; but his eye was keen, and he discerned that there were ways of assisting Ireland's cause, in which he could combine his country's interest with his own. He became the agent of the Irish Brigade. He set on foot the organization for recruiting the young Catholics who were impatient of English rule, collecting them under the name of Wild-geese, and bringing them over into the French service to learn their trade as soldiers. He was employed in dispatching and recommending the French officers who were sent over from time to time into Galway and Kerry to keep alive the national hopes.

While thus engaged he discerned, in the unfortunate commercial policy which destroyed the Irish woollen manufacturer, an opportunity for disorganizing the Irish administration, of combining all classes and all creeds there, peasant and landlord, Catholic and Protestant, in a league to defeat an unjust law, and while filling the pockets of his countrymen to build up his own fortune at the same time. Irish wool, at the opening of the last century, was supposed to be the most excellent in the world, and commanded the highest prices in the natural market. The English woollen manufacturers, afraid of being beaten out of the field if the Irish were permitted to compete with them, persuaded the Parliament to lay prohibitory duties on Irish blankets and broad cloth, which crushed the production of these articles. Not contented with preventing the Irish from working up their fleeces at home, they insisted that the Irish fleeces should be sold in England only, and at such a price as would be convenient to themselves. The natural price, which the French were willing to pay, was three or four times higher—and the effect was a premium upon smuggling, which no human nature, least of all Irish human nature, could be expected to resist.

Blake was the first person who saw the opportunity of developing it into a system, and combining interest with patriotism. He was so successful that, before the century had half run its course, four-fifths of the Irish fleeces were carried underhand into France, in spite of English laws and English cruisers. Irish lawlessness for once had justice on its side, and flourished like a green bay tree. Patrick Blake became the wealthiest merchant on the Loire, and his gains were sweetened by the sense that they were the spoils of the oppressors. The wool cargoes were first paid for in specie. The amount of gold and silver carried out of France in consequence, drew the attention of the Government. The remedy was easy. The business had only to be further extended. The vessels that had brought the wool returned loaded with brandy and claret. The revenue suffered a further wound, and the corruption and demoralization spread from farm-house to castle. Neither Peer nor Squire cared to pay duty on his Bordeaux or his Cognac, when he could have his cellars filled for him at half price, if he cared to ask no unnecessary questions.

His business brought Blake into a secret and confidential correspondence with men of all ranks in all parts of Ireland. His vessels continued to carry the Wild-geese. Being famous for speed, they were chosen by the bishops and unregistered priests whose presence in their own country was forbidden by law, and who had therefore to avail themselves of irregular opportunities. Transactions of this kind passed into politics. His relations with the Court of the Pretender had continued. When the French Government wished to disturb England at home, it was through Blake that they communicated with the disaffected Irish Catholics. He became involved gradually in the conspiracies and intrigues of the time, and when Charles

Edward went to Scotland in 1745, Patrick Blake not only provided the brig in which he sailed, but himself accompanied the Prince to the point where he landed, and fetched him back again after his defeat, at the end of his wanderings in the Highlands.

In the midst of his disappointment at the conclusion of the peace, he could console himself with perceiving that year by year the Protestant Establishment was growing weaker, that the fast-spreading anarchy was more fatal to English authority and influence than the bloodiest defeat in the field, that slowly but surely his own people were recovering their hold on their own land.

The shipyards and the buildings connected with the working establishment covered several acres. At one end of them, and divided from the business premises by a high wall and a plantation of trees, was Mr. Blake's own residence. It was a solid *château*, designed and erected by himself, on a scale which corresponded with the position which he had arrived at. From the central door, a wide flight of steps led into a garden two acres in extent, which stretched down to the river, and was divided by straight gravelled walks. The beds were brilliant with flowers, exotics many of them, brought home for him by intelligent captains of his own ships. American aloes, then strangers in Europe, flung up their tall yellow spires, oleanders waved their pink and white blossoms in the wind, acacias of all kinds threw patches of shade upon the paths.

On the river side the garden was bounded by a terrace, which extended along the entire length of it from end to end. This terrace was Mr. Blake's favourite walk, commanding as it did a fine view up and down the Loire.

Chapter II

A QUESTIONABLE VISITOR

ONE morning, late in the summer of 175–, the owner of
this wealth was pacing the terrace with some impatience,
watching the movements of a brigantine which had just come
in with the tide from the sea, and was taking up her moorings
some two hundred yards distant from him. He was a strongly
built old gentleman, with a face seamed and tanned by work
and weather—but otherwise apparently little the worse for
the sixty years which had rolled him along his busy life-way.
A whistle hung round his neck by a cord, in which the thumb
of his left hand was mechanically slung. In his right was a spy-
glass, through which he was rather anxiously examining the
deck of the brigantine, as if he missed something which he
expected to find.

The crew of the vessel had brought her sharply round to the
buoy. The topsails were clewed up; the mainsail lowered, and
a boat was dropped from the davits. A rough-looking seaman
stepped into the stern-sheets from the gangway, and was rowed
in to the stairs, at the head of which Blake was standing to
receive him.

'You are late, Dennis,' he said, as the man came up to meet
him, 'you are late. We looked for you three days ago. You
have a heavy cargo I see by your water-line, but where are
your passengers? French officers that were coming back with
you? I see nothing of either.'

'Well, your honour,' answered the man whom he had called
Dennis, 'I don't know in the world what has come to the boys.
The could water has got into the hearts of them. I suppose it
is the peace that done it. After Fontenoy, as your honour
knows, they were as plenty as swallows in the Spring.'

'Hum!' said Blake. 'You have only your lading then. And
what has delayed you on your way?'

THE TWO CHIEFS OF DUNBOY

'I'll tell your honour how it was,' Dennis answered. 'There was a gentleman along with me, that was afraid if the English saw him it might be a little unpleasant.'

'You have one of the holy bishops with you—or one of the fathers that are on the mission? You should have brought him on shore, that I might pay my respects to his reverence.'

'A bishop or a priest is it,' laughed Dennis. 'A mighty quare Father of the Church Mr. Sylvester would be making. I thought best to leave him where he was till I had seen your honour, but you shall see and spake with him yourself. The gentleman had rason to think that if the British Government had their hands upon him, there would trouble come of it.'

'I suppose I know who you mean by your Mr. Sylvester. I have seen honester faces than his in my time, and I could have spared the sight of him again. We shall learn by-and-bye what brings him here just now. But how are matters going in Galway?'

'The country is well enough—never better. The houghers have made a clean sweep of Sir Walter Talbot's cattle, and the Scotch drover that came in and took the land that's on the lakes has found a bad bargain. The King's writ has not yet run in Connemara. Devil a Sheriff's officer has served a warrant in the land your honour came from, and never shall, please God.'

'The Protestants have hold of the estates for all that,' said Blake, gloomily, 'and are likely to keep them for all that I see to the contrary.'

'They have lost the hould on Galway town anyway,' answered Dennis. 'Barring the Mayor and Aldermen that has to swear that they are Protestants when they take office, and sure they mane it no more than your honour would, there are not half a dozen of the heretic blackguards left in the place, that is the truth; and for the Acts of Parliament, they just laugh at them. We are doing well, by the mercy of God, and we will see the day yet when your honour will have your own again.'

The prospect of changing his French *château* for what was left of his ancestral castle on Lough Corrib either seemed to Blake more remote than his officer expected, or perhaps in

18

itself not particularly desirable. He was contented to know that the English were falling back into their usual policy of weakening their friends and attempting to conciliate their enemies, and did not pursue his inquiries. He turned abruptly to another subject.

'This passenger of yours, Dennis, this Sylvester, I must see him, but I would like to know what he is after. The last time he was here, he had come from Paris to beg a passage home. He had been in trouble in Dublin, he told me, for bringing back some of the college lads out of heresy to Holy Church. This was his story then, and the fact of it was that he was employed by Walpole, the English Ambassador in Paris, to spy into our trading business, and supply the Castle with information. He had a protection in his pocket at that moment in case a Government cruiser fell in with him.'

'To hear him talk, you would suppose that there was no truer Irishman in the four Provinces. If he tould lies it was for the good cause, and for one lie that he tould your honour he tould twenty to them in Dublin. But I don't like the looks of him, and that is the truth of it.'

'You don't like informers, Denny. I don't like them either. No good cause was ever served by lying. He that is false to one is false to all, that is my experience. Let a man once take to it, 'tis like the whiskey. He never leaves it after. If I might take my way with the fellow, I would ship him off to the plantations in Martinique. How came he in Galway?'

'It was not in Galway I fell in with him at all, your honour. Your honour was expecting Wild-geese. As there were none in Galway I looked into the Kenmare River as I went by. I thought may be there would be a flight of them in at Kilmakilloge. Not a feather there either, but I found Mr. Sylvester O'Sullivan in a wild way about the old place at Derreen, and about the brother of him, Macfinnan Dhu. Sure it is mighty proud they are of their family thim Sullivans, come of the giants that was before the great Flood they say, and if anything goes wrong with the last of the race they think the world is coming to an end. Well, there is something going wrong with Macfinnan Dhu just now. I could make little out of his talking, but any way Mr. Sylvester prayed me for the love of God and the Saints to take him over where he could have speech with Morty Oge, him that was with the Prince. He said he was in Paris.'

'If he wants Morty Sullivan,' said Blake, 'we can pleasure him that far. Morty is in Nantes at this moment, and will be here at breakfast tomorrow. If he is of my mind he won't believe too much of what Sylvester may say to him. Keep your man under hatches, till I send for him.'

Chapter III

MORTY O'SULLIVAN

IN a small but handsomely furnished apartment in the
château, two gentlemen were sitting the next morning, engaged in earnest conversation; one of them Mr. Patrick Blake,
the owner of the establishment, the other a spare sallow-com-
plexioned man, with short black hair, slightly grizzled, square
features, chin clean shaven, a heavy moustache, which hanging from the upper lip concealed the mouth, and the hard
grey eyes of the dark Celt of the south of Ireland. His age
might be forty or a little over. The lines of his face were firm
and peremptory, as of a soldier, or of someone accustomed to
command. It might be unsafe to guess at his calling, but it
was easy to see that he was a person of consequence, able,
resolute, prompt alike with mind and hand, and one whom a
prudent person would sooner have for a friend than an enemy.

They had finished breakfast and had drawn their chairs to
the window, which opened on a balcony and overlooked the
garden and the river. A long telescope stood between them on
a brass pedestal. They had been examining through it a singularly beautiful vessel which was lying in the tideway at half-a-
mile distance. She was three hundred tons burden and had
been originally a brig, but Mr. Blake had discovered that the
fore-and-aft rig gave advantages in working to windward which
were of supreme importance when speed was the first consideration. She was called a trader, but that trade was not her
only business might be inferred as well from her general
aspect as from the gun-slides, which were plainly visible through
the glass, upon her deck. The most ignorant landsman could
have seen at a glance that she was meant for mischief. She was
laid up, as it was called; but her paint was fresh and her spars
were scraped and varnished. An active crew could probably
fit her for sea in a few days, or even, under pressure, in a few
hours.

21

'You have decided then,' said Blake in a tone of disappointment, and at the close of what had been a long argument. 'There the vessel lies for you and you will not take her, and you decline my offer. When the *Doutelle* was a brig, no ship of her size in the English service was a match for her, either running or in a wind. The world is before you, and the world's enemy to prey upon. You can serve your country, and you can make your own fortune too. Speak the word, and never rover sailed out of the Loire with such a ship and such a crew as I can furnish you with. The strength of England is in her commerce; strike her there, and you strike at her heart. Had I your years, Morty, by the Saints in glory! do you think I'd be dragging out my life over ledgers and bills of lading, when I might be making a name for myself as a hero, and breaking the merchants' houses in London by the losses I'd bring them to? By my soul, I'm half minded to go out myself, old as I am!'

'I'd be sorry for your sake, Mr. Blake,' said his companion, 'to see you off on any such errands. You are doing very well as you are. You are breaking a larger hole in the English Exchequer every year with your wool and brandy trade than ever I could do with the *Doutelle*'s guns. Your place is where you are, and long may you live to fill it. But there is a question I'd like to ask you. This peace that they have made at Aix! will it last, think you—you will be better acquainted with the ways of the politicians than I can be.'

'It will not last,' answered Blake passionately. 'It cannot last. It is only a breathing time, and but half that. They will be fighting again before the ink is dry on the signatures. Here at home there will be war once more before five summers have gone round, and in the storm that is brewing, that proud Island will have the feathers plucked out of her at last.'

'But five years! Here is peace but just signed; and you want me to hoist the Black Flag in the old *Doutelle* and go to sea as a pirate, in the hope that when five years are gone the French Government will look over my small irregularities for the harm I may have done the English, let me keep my plunder, and perhaps give me a commission. That is the plain meaning of it, and piracy is not so reputable a calling as it used to be.

But peace is peace, and business is business. Suppose I take a West Indiaman, what am I to do with her—where am I to sell the cargo, how am I to get rid of the crew?'

'The sea is deep,' replied Blake coolly, 'and dead men do not float with proper ballast. Send the ship to the bottom and the crew along with her. If you are across the Atlantic, they will buy the cargo of you at Martinique or Hayti, and ask you no more questions than you please to answer. If you are this side bring it here; or ye may carry it to Ireland, if you will.'

'My friend Blake,' answered Morty, 'you are a bold man, and a sanguine, but your position and mine are not precisely the same. You will risk your vessel. If you lose her it will not break you. I, as you well know, should go into the business with a halter about my neck.'

'Sail under the French flag, and never fear that you will be in trouble for it. I tell you again, the peace won't hold, and you yourself will help to break it.'

'And swing in chains myself on a Deptford gallows,' said Morty, 'for that is what your pirate work ends in, and a fit end it is. Times are changed, my good friend. Buccaneers don't conquer kingdoms any longer and get thanked by their sovereign. Your pirate now is a public enemy. To call him a patriot does not alter his character. I have been proclaimed traitor in England, for joining the Prince, and there has been a price set on my head; but, though I made a mistake, I did nothing which dishonoured me as a gentleman and, at my age, I don't wish to begin.'

'And what do you intend to do with yourself, most excellent Morty, since you will not take my offer? You give up the Stuarts—you will not fight the English on your own account—and you know very well that an open rebellion in Ireland, just now, is impossible. France and England will fight again by-and-bye, perhaps to-morrow, perhaps not for four or five years. How is it to be meanwhile? Shall I take you into my counting-house and teach you to mend pens and keep ledgers?'

'No, no. I am a soldier, and I shall follow my own trade, as my betters are doing. Lacy offers me a place on his staff, in my old army. Lally is going to India to help Dupleix and will take me with him, if I like. In America, as you tell me, there is work going on, or again, there is the Don, willing to engage any number of us. These are opportunities. I can choose my own employment, and we shall be doing best service to our own country and to our own cause, by earning fame and credit under the great Catholic powers.'

'You stand much upon your honour, Morty Sullivan,' answered Blake; 'and it would be unfitting in myself to be blaming you for that same. Honour is a fine feather when it is not draggled, like the plume in my old hat here. By the same token, there is one of your name, and small credit is he to the family, if all tales are true, that is at this moment in Nantes, and is asking to see you. Dennis, the master of the brigantine, yonder, brought him over from Kenmare. He is in bad favour in the town, about some informing business. I don't properly know the rights of it. I told Dennis to keep him on board, to wait your convenience, for fear harm should come to him. If you please, they shall bring the fellow on shore.'

'A Sullivan from Kenmare?' said Morty, 'and to see me? Who, and what is the man?'

'Sylvester is what he said was the name of him when he came to me some years back, and that is what he calls himself still.'

'Sylvester O'Sullivan! Sylvester the Scholar! Why, he must be my own kinsman—my father's first cousin; he that taught me Latin when I was a boy at Derreen. What know you of him, that you speak so coldly?'

'It is some ten years now,' said Blake, 'since he was here look-ing for me. He told me he had been a teacher in Dublin. He had fallen into trouble under the laws against the Catholics, and had been in danger of his life. He had since been in Paris. By that time, he supposed all would be forgotten, and they would not be thinking of him any more, so he wanted a cast back to see his family. Dennis, yonder, took him to Valencia. The lads came on board to hoist out the brandy casks, and as Mr. Sylvester was shuffling about among them, he dropped a paper on the deck. Somebody picked it up, and it was found to be a pass from the English Minister at Paris. The next I heard of my gentleman was that he had been caught sending a letter to the Castle, telling all that he had learnt about our trade down there, and who the persons were that were concerned in it.'

'Any story is good till you hear the other side,' said Morty. 'I will believe that a Sullivan has been selling his country and his soul when I have it proved to me, and not sooner—let alone one so near in blood to the chief of the clan. Sylvester had a long head of his own, as I remember him; and it will not have grown shorter upon him with age. Sylvester will have come to speak with me about my poor mother that is gone. He'll be bringing me some word from her, it is likely. God rest her soul!'

Chapter IV

TWO OF A CLAN

A WHISTLE from the window summoned Dennis from the stairs below the garden. Receiving a brief order, he paddled back to his vessel, and presently reappeared, bringing his guest, or his prisoner, for he more nearly resembled the latter, along with him. The look of the man as he was introduced into the room, entirely justified the ill opinion of him which Blake, notwithstanding Morty's protestations, evidently continued to entertain. He was an undersized, mean-looking being, perhaps sixty years old, and he appeared more abject than he really was, from the manner in which he carried himself.

'Well, Mr. Sylvester,' said the merchant, 'so here you are again. You are a cunning old fox, but you may run your head into a noose once too often. Do you remember the last occasion when you were in this room?'

'I do, and well, your honour, and a beautiful room it is. And good your honour was to me that same time.'

'Good was I,' said Blake, 'and what are you I'd like to know? You came to me with a fine story of all ye'd done and all ye'd suffered for your country. You wanted me to send you home to Kerry, to your family there, and all the while there was black treachery in the heart of you. You were an informer, man, and had sould yourself to them in the Castle of Dublin.'

'Your honour speaks nothing but the truth,' said the man, 'so far as the truth is known to ye. Sure enough I had the bit of paper Mr. Walpole giv me, if it is that ye mane. I'd be none the worse for such a thing if the magistrates got hold upon me, as it was like they might with the errand I had taken upon me. But the way of it was this. I was wanting to go home to my own people, and there was a stir just then about the trade, and the Danes' treasure, and the Wild-geese, and the French going over; and they were saying in Paris the English would be

26

sending the red-coats to sweep the country clear of the whole
of us, and I thought I would be useful *deceaving* them a little,
and making distrust between them and the gintry like.'

'That might suit with ye as a rogue's trick,' said Blake, 'but
if that was what ye were after, why did you not speak plainly
to me? I don't believe ye. There was that letter ye wrote from
Killarney to the Castle. How do you explain that? telling them
how ye had come over, and how the cargo was run.'

'Sure and if I tould them,' said Sylvester, 'here was never a
word of truth in the whole story I tould them. It was little they
could learn from me, clever as they might be; and as to speaking out to your honour, there is an old saying that one may
keep counsel, but never two, and I thought maybe some of
them Paris people might be asking ye questions about me, and
your honour would not tell what ye did no know.'

Blake looked at the wretched being, hardly knowing whether
to laugh or be angry.

'And how about your turning Protestant?' he asked, 'and
forsaking the faith ye were born in? One of my own people
saw you in Killarney church, swearing away your religion before the Archdeacon.'

'Sure and if I did, your honour, there is no sin in telling a
lie to a heretic.'

'So you mean you were lying all round?' said Blake. 'You
gave information and it was false, and they paid you money
for it which you put in your pocket?'

'Indeed, and I did, your honour, and where is the harm for
the good cause? I went back to live at my old place, and it is
a little reward that I had from the Castle to send them word
when the boys were abroad. Never a lad came to hurt or a
cargo to be taken for anything they ever learnt from me, and
the money was good anyway. But your honour is making me
speak out mighty plain before strangers,' and he looked uneasily at Morty, in whose face contempt and disgust were
strongly mixed with interest.

'Have no fear of my friend,' the merchant said. 'What is the
business which has brought you over?'

'I was wishing to spake a word with a relation of my own,'

Sylvester answered. 'Your honour knows him. Morty Oge, I mane. Him that went with the Prince. They say he is in Paris, and I supposed may be your honour might help me to the sight of him.'

'Morty Oge is not in Paris,' replied Blake. 'He sits there in front of you.'

Sylvester started as if he had been shot. The dull listless manner disappeared. The decrepit figure quivered with life. The eyes fastened hungrily on the face before him as if he would read every line of it. For a few seconds he doubted, then flung himself on his knees and clasped Morty in his arms.

'It's himself,' he cried. 'It is my own boy, after all these years. The Saints preserve us! Who ever saw the like of it? But speak to me, Morty. Speak to me that I may hear the voice of ye, for you are strangely changed.'

'Twenty years have changed us both,' Morty said, 'but your kinsman it is, or all that you will ever see of him; by the same token you'll remember how you taught me my Classics on the old rock at Derreen, and carved the sundial in the stone for me that will be there to this day; how you tied the brown fly for me that caught the big salmon in Glanmore Lake, when I was a small spalpeen no higher than my leg.'

'It is—it is his very self,' sobbed Sylvester, devouring Morty with eyes from which the tears were running. 'Twenty-five years! and you look so grand and powerful like, and you have been in the wars with princes and the generals; and your own mother, that is in glory, wouldn't have known ye till ye spoke; and now you are given back to us, and the Blessed Virgin will bring ye safe home.'

'Home?' said Morty. 'Well, I don't know. I have need of my head for my own uses, and there is a price upon it since that Scotch business. I am much attached to my countrymen, but if they like nothing else that is British they like British gold; they might serve me as they served the Desmond.'

'I won't say, your honour, but such things there may be in Ireland. It comes of having the Saxons among us. They are infected like with the plague, and honest men catch it of them. But your honour will be as safe in Kerry as in the King's palace at Versailles, and safer, too, if all tales are true; and oh! Morty, you are sorely needed. It is broken-hearted we are for the want of you, and yourself the chief of the name. If ye stay longer from us the last Sullivan will soon be gone out of Tuosist.'

'Not while Macfinnan lives and reigns at Derreen,' said Morty, 'and he would be a bold lad that took the lands in Kilmakilloge, if they put Macfinnan out. And sure they can't put him out. He holds under the lease, and he had a son, I heard. They called him Mick. He will be growing into a man by now.'

'Indeed, then, that is what we fear Mick will never grow into, at all at all. Macfinnan is well enough but Mick was changed at the cradle, or there is water in the heart of him where blood should be. He is a stout youth to look at, but he goes about the woods hanging the head of him, or whistling to the seals or the like, and never a stroke in his arm for play or anger.'

Morty laughed. 'You see, Blake,' he said, 'an O'Sullivan must do credit to his breeding or they won't acknowledge him. His father must send him over to me. I will make a man of him yet.'

'You're mistaking me, entirely,' Sylvester said. 'If that was the worst of it, we'd do yet, but there is a black purpose against the whole of us. Ye will mind the colonies of Protestants old Sir William Petty set along the Kenmare River. He was trying to plant Kerry as they planted the North, and fine work we had to clear them out again after Sir William was gone.'

'Well, and what of it?' said Morty. 'They were got rid of, and there was an end. They are not coming back, I suppose?'

'Indeed, but they are, and the Divil's work in the train of them,' Sylvester answered. 'There is to be a new Colony, and either the Colony will clear the Irish out, or the Irish must clear the Colony out again, and this is what I'd be wishing to speak to ye about. I'll tell you how it is. When Sir William's people went out they gave the Macfinnans back the glen with the lase for the three lives. Well, the ould Macfinnan, he that had the *lase* first, your grandfather that was, got a ball through his body at Mallow races. Your uncle, that was the next, your

29

mother's brother, shortened his life with the whiskey. Then came Macfinnan Dhu, that now reigns, may the Lord spare him to us! but he is growing old, and has not long to remain. Your uncle was troubled in his conscience for the oaths that he had sworn, and when my cousin came there were fines to be paid if the lase was renewed, and the money was not over plenty with him. The people were talking that the laws would be changed, and he would have his own back again, and where would be the use of his calling himself a Protestant, when in a few years they would be all gone out of the Island? So he put it off, and let the time go by, and now what does the ould Earl do?—that is Petty's son they have made a Lord of—but sends word that when Macfinnan dies and the lase falls, they will take the place into their own hands.'

'And what does the Earl want in Tuosist?' said Morty. 'Has he not lands enough in England? Has he not tens of thousands of acres among the lime-stone pastures of Meath and Dublin, that he grudges the Sullivans the rocks and bogs of Kilmakil-loge? Will he plant his wheat-crops on Knockatee or make a deer park in Glenrastel and Glenatrasna? Poor man! It is a short life any Earl's steward would have at Derreen.'

'I have nothing to say against that,' Blake wearily answered. 'But your story is as long as the big snake whose tail was in Gougaun Barra Lake when his head was going out of Cork harbour.'

'We have come to the tail now, and that is where the sting is you will find. You have heard belike of the great Annesley law case, that made the fortunes of half the lawyers in the Four Courts. Lord Annesley had the lands that reached from Bantry out to Dursey Island, with a deal besides elsewhere. He died and left a son, but the brother of him took the estate, for he said the boy was a bastard, and he had him kidnapped and sold as a slave in the American plantations. He comes back fifteen years after and claims the lands, and it was up and down, one Court saying one thing, and another another, till the Counsellors had eaten the worth of it, and the little that was left came to be divided.

'The best part of the Bantry estate went to Mr. White that

you will have heard of. The lands at Berehaven and Dunboy Castle, your own place, Morty, and the home of your fathers, fell to one Goring, a relation of the lord that was gone. But he was a harmless creature. He just let things go as they were, and no one had a word to say of him good or ill, till four years ago he died, and Dunboy fell to his brother, the Colonel.'

At the name of Colonel Goring, Morty and Blake exchanged glances of some surprise, and listened with increased interest as Sylvester continued:

'The Colonel (he was captain then) was in the same regiment with Colonel Eyre, and as like they were as a pair of sparrow hawks. They were at Culloden together, and when the Duke sent Eyre to Galway, Goring went with him, and fine work they made between them, restoring order as they called it. The English had the fright on them, and, by-and-bye, when Goring gets the Berehaven Estate, they told him he was to do the same work down there. So they made him a revenue officer. They gave him a power of men under him, with command of a hundred miles of the coast; and who but he was to make a sweep of the whole country? Ye will mind yourself how it was, Blake, four years back. Never one of your vessels could be seen off the coast, but what Goring would be looking out with his boats and his English divils along with him. And the worst was what came to your own flesh and blood, Morty, for Dursey Island was part of the property that came to him. The old Castle was standing at that time on the Sound, and 'twas there your own mother was living, and your sister with the child she was left with when her husband, Donnell Mahony's son that was, died. The Colonel put her out under pretences that she was sheltering the smugglers there, and he must have the Castle pulled down; and they had to go in the winter storms to the ould place at Eyris, and that is all that is left to you, Morty, of the lands that were your fathers'. There your mother died, God rest her soul! and there your sister lives now all alone with her boy; and a rough place it is for her that was bred like a lady, with the wild lads that come and go there.'

Sylvester had no longer to complain of want of attention in one, at least, of his hearers. Morty was hanging passionately upon his words.

'My mother!' he muttered between his teeth. 'Strange,' he said, 'that this same man should cross my path again. He it was who caught me and Sheridan, and would have shot us; and he now reigns at Dunboy and makes war on women and children! Why is the wretch alive? Why have none of you put a ball through him?'

'The Colonel is a crafty lad, as well as a bould one,' said Sylvester, 'and it is none so easy to reach him. He had a dozen men with him up to last year from a man-o'-war that is at Kinsale. He is at the ould devilry again, bringing in Protestants to live among us. The Parliament changed the law, and they can stay now, worse luck! He has found copper in the mountains; mighty fine they say it is; and he has fetched over great gangs of miners from Cornwall who dig the copper for him, and are settled about the place. They are making money, too, and there are so many of them that they are not safe to meddle with at all. The gentry about Bantry are just mad, for they have lost the market for their fleeces, and they have no claret in their cellars. But what does the Colonel care for that, so long as he is doing the Lord's work, as he calls it. And I have not told ye the worst yet.'

'You have told me bad enough,' said Morty sternly; 'but go on with the rest.'

'Well, you will mind the shape of the long strip of land that runs down from Kenmare to the Durseys. The mountain line that is in the middle of it parts the counties of Cork and Kerry. The streams on one side fall into Bantry Bay; on the other, into the Kenmare River. The Colonel's lands and the Earl of Shelbourne's lands meet on the ridge; but because they are in two counties, and the authority is different, the boys slip across the borders when trouble rises. The Colonel saw that he could never stop the trade as long as the boys had Glanmore and Kilmakilloge free for them. So he gets the ear of the old Earl that is in London—kin of blood they are, I am informed. He has tould him there is no English law in Kerry. He has minded him of what his father did, and the power of money that he made, and the Protestants that he put in up and down the river for the peace of the country. He tells the Earl how he has found the copper close by and handy, and if the furnaces are opened in Glanmore again, they can smelt it on the spot and make a brave trade. The Government had been complaining about the Wild-geese and the Rapparees, and the French coming and going. So the Earl has come into it, and he has sent the notice I told ye of, that when Macfinnan Dhu drops, the lase will not be renewed, and the agent will take possession of Derreen; and the bad work we thought we had done with will begin over again. So now you know how it is, Morty. It is for you to save us if you can; and if you fail us now and ill comes of it, you have had your warning. If you let the Colonel have his way, divil a drop of brandy will ye ever land again in Tuosist, Mr. Blake, or fetch a woolpack from the caves.'

Harder and sterner Morty Sullivan's face had grown as he listened to his kinsman's story. He was touched in his pride, for the English Colonel was in possession of the Castle of his ancestors. He had his own personal grievances in connection with the flight from Culloden, and Goring's share in the pursuit. Some fate seemed to force him into collision with a man who knew nothing of him, save as an outlawed follower of Charles Edward, yet at every step of his life was inflicting upon him wound after wound. He sprang from his chair and strode up and down the room while Blake watched the working upon him of a story which had come so opportunely to support his own arguments.

'You say this business is coming close upon us,' he observed. 'What ails Macfinnan Dhu? He is no older than myself.'

'We age quickly in Ireland, your honour, with the whiskey and the broken heads; and Macfinnan had his share in both, honest man. But indeed it is the thought of all this, and he the cause of it by his own carelessness, that is like to be the end of him. The Earl's notice about the lase came down the week before I left. No complaint had he to make of Macfinnan, who had always paid his rent like a gentleman. But the Earl said he was going to take up Sir William's colony again, and drain the bogs, and open foundries and fisheries and "benefit the

poor people on the property", as he was plased to call it. He
had all respect for Macfinnan Dhu, small thanks to him for
that same. No alterations were to be made in his life-time, and
as a token of his regard and esteem for his old friend, as he
called him, he begged leave to send Macfinnan a case of wine,
the best he had in his cellar.

'Macfinnan was in bed with the fever when the letter come.
Mighty ill he was at that time, and he calling for the whiskey,
and the more we guv him the worse it was with him, but when
the letter was brought, and the wine came along with it the
Earl spoke of, he up with himself with a spring as if he was
shot out of a gun. He flung his old cloak about him. Down the
stairs he went, and out at the door, and up the big rock that's
there with the sundial on it that Morty spoke of just now.

' "Bring up the basket," says he. Sure if it had been whiskey,
he would have been in no such hurry, for it is a sin to throw
good liquor away. But for wine, sure it is no drink for a man
at all, at all. "Bring it up," says he again. "Bad cess to you, what
are ye delaying for?" There were six dozen bottles in the
case. He out with the first. In a voice which ye might have
heard at Colorus, for Macfinnan had ever a wild cry in the
throat of him, he called the curse of St. Finian on the stranger
that was driving the Celt from the land of his fathers. Then
he smashed the bottle on the stone, and the red stain ran down
the side of it. Out with another, and then with another, till he
had finished the whole of them. We helped him down when
he had done, and if he had relieved his sowl, it seemed as if he
had relieved his sickness along with it, for he called for his
horse and his pistols, and he swore he would ride to Kenmare
and make onasyness for the agent. But we held him quiet that
time, and by-and-bye he grew faint-like, and the faver came
back upon him, and we got him to bed, and I tould him I
would take a cast over in Mr. Blake's brigantine that had
looked in from the sea, and I'd talk to yourself about it, Mr.
Morty, for they said you were in Paris. But by good luck I
have found ye here, and now you know the whole, and you
and Mr. Blake can see between ye which ye will be best able
to do.'

34

Chapter V

COLONEL GORING

AT the western entrance of Dunboy harbour, a mile from the village of Castleton, and at a little distance from the shore, there stood, at the date of our story, a manor house, or something between a manor house and a cottage, which formed an agreeable contrast with the usual forbidding aspect of Irish dwelling-houses. It was low, on account of the storms which in winter sweep round Bantry Bay with peculiar violence. The roof was of purple Valencia slate; the body of the building was constructed of the grey stone of the district, but was almost concealed by ivy and flowering creepers which covered the walls and clustered about the windows. A verandah stretched the entire length of the front, supported on wooden pillars, over and round which twined China roses, with occasional fuchsias, then newly introduced into Ireland. The back of the house was sheltered by a grove of large trees. Right and left, and scattered about the grounds, were young plantations of pine and oak, and lime and larch, which, if they had the luck to grow, would be protection from every gale that could blow. The lawn was brilliant with the rich green of the after-grass: a light fence, through which there was a gate, divided it from the beach; and beyond was a landlocked cove where a dozen stout fishing boats were riding at their anchors.

On the one side, on a rising ground, were the whitewashed barracks of the Coast Guard, with a mast on which flew the white English ensign. On the other, were a row of stone cottages of late erection occupied by a few West of England families, who had been tempted over by reports of the extraordinary wealth of Bantry Bay in every kind of fish. The long brown nets spread to dry upon the shingle, were sparkling with silver scales, for the herring had come in, and the pickling tubs were running over from the heavy catch of the previous night. A large, high island shut off the view of the open water. To the left, was the dark mass of Hungry Hill. To the right a range of heather-clad mountains, which fell in precipices to the sea, with creeks and hollows running up among them, fringed, when the tide was out, with banks of yellow seaweed.

Almost within gun-shot was a grassy promontory on which the ruins stood of the old Dunboy Castle, the confiscated home of the O'Sullivans, which was famous in Irish history for the splendid defence made there against Sir George Carew and an English army. The castle was then taken and destroyed, and had never been rebuilt. The lines of the fortifications were marked by grassy mounds, interspersed with bushes, and a flock of sheep were lazily feeding where the bones of the garrison lay a few feet below them.

Here lived and here reigned, in the Irish phrase, Colonel John Goring, whose presence and whose actions had drawn so much comment, favourable and unfavourable, in the two counties of Cork and Kerry. The house and the settlement had been erected and created by himself. For the first three years after his arrival, he had received some assistance from the Government. The French scare was then fresh, and he had been allowed a small sloop and a dozen men. When peace was signed, the sloop was withdrawn, and as the smuggling had been reduced till he had barely hands enough remaining to man a long boat. On the other hand the fishing station throve admirably; the mines in the mountains were of high promise; and thus, independent of the Coast Guard, the Colonel had men enough of his own who were ready always for any useful service when he found it necessary to call upon them.

It was a mild morning early in September in the same year, 175–, in which we have seen Morty Sullivan and Sylvester at Patrick Blake's *château* at Nantes. The windows leading into the verandah were open, and in the dark dining-room behind could be seen a second breakfast table, at which were seated the Colonel himself, with his lady and another person, a gentleman, either a visitor or an inmate of the family. Mrs. Goring may have been eight-and-twenty, with dark blue eyes, and regular features, just mellowed into mature womanhood.

COLONEL GORING

The Colonel was three or four years older. He, too, was tall and slender. His face, once strikingly handsome, had been disfigured by a sabre cut which, however, if it spoilt the symmetry of his features, had added to the manliness of his expression. Though he was not much past thirty, his chestnut hair was already touched with streaks of silver, as if life had brought anxieties already, which were leaving their marks upon him.

The third member of the party was less noticeable. He was a quiet, middle-aged man, dressed in plain black, perhaps a scholar, perhaps a minister, gentle mannered and low voiced, and answering when spoken to with a deference which indicated some kind of dependence. His name was Fox. That he was a clergyman of some kind, appeared from the address of a letter which the Colonel had just thrown across the table to him, with another to his wife. Before the Colonel himself lay a large heap, which had just been emptied out of the post-bag, a weekly luxury which his various duties compelled him to allow himself. The nearest post-office was at Bantry, and until the Colonel's arrival, the letters for Dunboy had lain there in the window till they were called for.

John Goring had been a boy of fourteen when his brother succeeded to the Dunboy estate. Inheriting from an aunt an independent property of his own, he himself had joined the army on leaving Eton. He had been distinguished on every occasion when the chance had been offered him. He had served in the Low Countries. He had been on the staff of the Duke of Cumberland in the Scotch Campaign. His especial friend and intimate had been Stratford Eyre, with whom he had been sent in pursuit of the insurgent Highland chiefs after Culloden. When Eyre was sent as Governor to Galway, Goring went with him thither, and it was while he was thus engaged that the news reached him of his brother's death, and of his own succession to the property.

He was well off, and a neglected estate on the borders of Cork and Kerry was more likely to be an expense to him than an advantage. His first impulse was to have nothing to do with it, and to pass on the uninviting inheritance to the next heir. But it was one of the occasions when English statesmen had awakened for a brief interval to the disorders of Ireland, and thought it necessary that something should be done. It was represented to Goring that if he wished to serve his country, here was an opportunity thrown especially in his way. The Government offered him the brevet rank of Colonel, with the command of the Coast Guard from Cape Clear to Dingle. Colonel Eyre strongly urged him not to refuse a position so exceptionally honourable and useful.

They were both convinced, from their experiences in Galway, that the contraband trade was intimately connected with the revolutionary disorder of the country, and that until it was checked in some way, no permanent improvement was possible. His own work, Eyre said, could be carried out far more easily and effectively if a brother officer on whom he could rely was co-operating with him in the creeks and bays of the South.

The revenue service had a bad name in Ireland. It was odious in itself, because it was an interference with an occupation which nine-tenths of the people regarded as innocent and praiseworthy. A revenue officer who did his duty generally came to a rough end. If he escaped, it was by dishonest connivance with operations which it was his business to prevent. Even Eyre's representations would not have overcome Colonel Goring's reluctance to meddle with so unpopular a calling.

It has often been observed that if a soldier falls at all under spiritual influences, the effect upon him is peculiarly strong. At that moment a religious revival was spreading over England and Wales. Whitfield and the two Wesleys were the leaders whose names were brought specially before the world. Colonel Goring was one of those who became sensible of the new impulse, and became sensible of it as a call to devote himself to anything which presented itself as a duty. He had always been what is called a religious man, in the sense that he believed that he could be called to account hereafter for his conduct. But his convictions had ripened from a consciousness of responsibility to an immediate and active sense that he was a servant of God, with definite work laid upon him to do. He carried his habits as a soldier into his relations with his Commander above. Under Cromwell he would have been the most devoted of the Ironsides.

By this test he had to try finally, when other considerations were exhausted, the question whether he was or was not bound to accept the Dunboy property. He had studied Ireland anxiously. He had observed with disgust the growing weakness of the Protestant settlement and the reviving energy of the Catholics. To him, an Englishman of the old Puritan school, the Pope was anti-Christ. He absolutely disbelieved that Irish Popery could be brought either by connivance or toleration into loyal relations with the English Crown. He did not like Penal laws. He knew that the relations of his own country with the Catholic Powers of Europe made the enforcement of such laws impossible, except spasmodically and uncertainly, and he thought that laws which were not meant to be obeyed were better off the Statute Book. But he was convinced also that Ireland could only be permanently attached to the British Crown if the Protestants were there in strength enough to hold their own ground. Cromwell's policy of establishing Protestant settlements South as well as North was the only rational one.

With these motives and with these purposes Colonel Goring left the army and settled upon the estate at Dunboy two years after the battle of Culloden. He had thus been established there for several years at the time when our story opens. Fortunately for himself, he was wealthy. He had property in England and property in other parts of the world, which made him independent of his Irish domain. He could carry out any rational plans which he might form without fear of expense. He was respected if he was not popular, for the gentry of the county were out at elbows and admired, in spite of themselves, a man who possessed what they suffered from the absence of. In all ranks in Ireland, from highest to lowest, everybody was hungry for something. Mendicancy was the universal rule. Goring wanted nothing, and such spoils as might be going he left to his neighbours to divide among themselves. He was superstitious. He believed himself to be living under God's orders, as a subaltern lives under the orders of his general.

Such a Providence befriended him signally soon after his

arrival. He discovered copper ore in the mountains in considerable abundance, and it seemed as if intended specially to encourage him in the purpose which he had in view. An experienced engineer from Cornwall having reported favourably on the surface indications, he brought over a company of miners —able, energetic workmen, who had been hearers of Whitfield, and shared in his own convictions. A large part of his land was unoccupied, but only required capital and industry to carry crops and cattle. To make his settlement self-supporting and independent of the Catholic farmers and peasantry, he invited Presbyterian labourers and artisans out of Ulster. He was confident that the coast fisheries could be worked to profit. Cornwall again supplied him with a dozen boatmen and their families. He had built cottages for them and provided nets and lines and all necessary tackle; and the common bond among them all was their religious earnestness, which not only made them a single congregation, but united them in a virtual brotherhood.

Among his tenantry Colonel Goring made no distinction between Catholic and Protestant. No well-behaved occupant was disturbed from his holding. Such as he found connected with the smugglers he resolutely expelled; the rest he protected to the best of his ability from the effects of their own habits and the customs of the country.

The colonists whom he had introduced, however, were his chief interest, for it was on them and on their well-being that he depended. They had joined him, not merely or principally for the worldly advantages which they might expect, but having been recently converted (as the phrase was) into a certain missionary enthusiasm, they were Protestants of an advanced type, inclining, as was generally found among the most impassioned and most earnest believers, into Calvinism and Independence. Colonel Goring personally had strong sympathy with these forms of thought. He had invited over a mildly eloquent Falmouth minister, the Mr. Fox who has been already mentioned, to help him. In this extemporized chapel the congregation collected on Sunday mornings and evenings, said their prayers without the help of a liturgy, sang their hymns together, and listened to Mr. Fox's exhortations. They were best pleased, however, when the Colonel himself would take the minister's place, and say a few plain words to them in a soldier's dialect—words which, if without ornament were absolutely sincere, and therefore going straight to hearts as sincere as his own.

One and another would drop in and listen to the Colonel's preaching. The peasantry, till they were taught better, saw no reason why their boys and girls might not learn to read and write from the Protestant master, and the priest of Castleton might have seen his sheep stray away from him, had not circumstances come to his help. He was interested himself in being on good terms with Goring, for he had been introduced from abroad, and might have been sent to prison, if Goring had pleased. The Colonel instead of molesting him invited him to dinner on holydays, and the priest was willing enough to go. So perhaps they might have continued, had the Colonel been no more than an improving landlord of Evangelical persuasion. Unfortunately he had other duties, which brought him into collision with the usages of the neighbourhood.

On his first arrival, when the war alarm was at its height, his activity in suppressing the smugglers was understood and allowed for. After the peace things relapsed into their natural condition. The anxiety in high quarters passed off, and local officials, like Colonel Eyre, in Galway, were given to understand that measures which irritated the people were no longer desirable. The revenue cutter was simultaneously recalled from Dunboy, the coastguard was reduced in number, and if the Colonel had been contented to look through his fingers while things reverted into their natural channels, he would have only done what was desired and expected from him by the general inhabitants of the country and by the chief authorities in Dublin.

His conception of his duty made such a course impossible to him. He thought that he had effectively put the smuggling down. He saw it suddenly revive while his means of contending with it were reduced. His letters to the Castle were at first coldly replied to, and were then left unanswered altogether.

The gentlemen in the neighbourhood held aloof in mild surprise that he was unable to do like the rest of them.

Colonel Goring failed to draw the distinction which he ought to have drawn between theory and practice. Finding the smugglers returning upon him, increased in numbers and audacity, and his own coastguard entirely unequal to encountering them, he drilled and armed his own boatmen, and as many of his other hands as cared to volunteer. With their assistance he again swept the bay, seized half a dozen cargoes, boarded and sank a large French lugger which had been deserted by her crew, and made himself more feared than ever. But his success was fatal to the popularity both of himself and his settlement, which came to be looked on as a Saxon garrison. Anger and ill-will took the place of the old friendliness. The priest came no more to dinner. Peasants from the village or the mountains were no longer seen at the chapel, nor Catholic child at the school. A few of the Colonel's smaller tenants remained grateful to him for former acts of kindness. Every one of them who wanted anything came clamouring for it, and was profuse in protestations of affection. But the Colonel had sorrowfully to feel that among his Catholic subjects he was rather losing ground than gaining it. Their master he might be as long as he was strong enough to hold his ground; they would fear and in a sense they would respect him. But they would not accept him as the friend which he had wished and hoped to be.

Colonel Goring, however, had seen too much of life to give way after a first disappointment. He was sure that he was doing right. Thus he went steadily on, careless what the world might say or do. He never quarrelled with his people about their rents. In such matters he was as indulgent as they had the conscience to ask him to be, and Irish consciences will ask a good deal. But any of them whom he detected in correspondence with the smugglers he persevered in sending inexorably about their business—among them the two ladies at Dursey Island, about whom Sylvester O'Sullivan had been so eloquent. He knew nothing of them. He knew only that their 'Castle' was the rendezvous of dangerous and desperate men, that the caves in Dursey Island were magazines of arms and stores.

Letters enough reached him after this, with a sentence of death in them. The officer who had preceded him at Castleton had been shot, and he was to be sent the same road. But the chance of a bullet does not stop a soldier from obeying his orders, and Colonel Goring had received his, as he understood it, direct from his Commander-in-chief. For the present he was fighting his battle single-handed, but he had been in correspondence with Lord Shelbourne. He had gone to London to see him in person, and explain his situation to him, and the Earl had been so impressed with what he heard that he had taken the steps of which the reader has been already informed, to revive his father's operations. Colonel Goring could look forward confidently and hopefully to the time when these engagements would be carried out. When a second Colony like his own was established a few miles from him across the mountains, the mines could be brought into fresh activity. A large trade would follow, and the wild spirits of Bantry and Kenmare could then be bridled effectively and for ever.

Chapter VI

DUNBOY

BUT we keep waiting the post bag and its contents. Throwing his wife the single letter which he found in it addressed to herself, and another to the minister, Colonel Goring had proceeded to attack the considerable heap which fell to his own share. The first which he took up was from his agent in London. He opened it with the nervousness that men often feel on receiving letters from their agents. The news they contain is generally important, and not always agreeable. His face, however, lighted up as he read. He looked across at his wife. 'Elizabeth,' he said, 'if you are not too much occupied with your own correspondent, I have good news for you about our estate in Jamaica.'

'What a strange coincidence,' she said. 'My correspondent writes to me on the same subject. She is a good, excellent woman, and she says that being "professing Christians", as she calls us, we have no business to own slaves, and that we ought to set them free. I think as she does, John. If any fresh profits have come from that quarter, I don't want to hear of them.'

'All good people are not of the same opinion on that subject,' answered the Colonel quietly. 'I have heard it maintained that the slaves on an English West Indian plantation are better off than the poor labourers of Cork and Kerry. God help them if they are not! But we need not argue about it. The estate is sold.'

'Sold?'

'Yes, sold. I told my agent that I wanted to get rid of it. He has found a purchaser, who gives me double what I expected. We can use the money in making our poor people here a little less miserable, and you and your friend can now denounce slavery as much as you please without reflecting on your husband. But here is better and better,' as he read on without

44

waiting for an answer, which might not have been completely acquiescent. 'The ore from the new shaft which we sent over to be analysed is declared to be the richest in Ireland. One of the largest copper merchants in Swansea is ready to smelt any quantity of it, if we can find vessels to take it over. But we have a way out of that. Hear what comes next. "I have seen Lord Shelbourne's solicitor and I have shown him the report of the analyst. He says the Earl remains determined to restore his father's furnaces at Kilmakilloge and recover his estate from the disorder into which it has lapsed. He waits only for the falling in of the lease, which cannot now be distant. The timber still standing in Tuosist will be amply sufficient to smelt all the copper which you can raise. On the death of the present tenant, which is reported to be imminent, the work is to be immediately proceeded with and, advanced in years as he is, the Earl hopes, before he leaves the world, to see the barony in the prosperous condition in which his father left it."

'What do you think of that?' the Colonel said, rubbing his hands. 'Here is a ray of sunshine in the darkness; and the West India money comes pat to the purpose. We will drive another gallery into the mountain, and find work for fifty more of the starving creatures in Castleton.'

Mrs. Goring's conscience might not have been entirely satisfied with the manner in which her husband had cleared himself of the guilt of slave-owning. But the results of the sale were to be well applied at any rate. The minister was delighted, and if he saw nothing amiss the harm could not be great.

Again the Colonel read over his agent's communication, making the most of what was agreeable before proceeding to his other letters, the contents of which might not be so pleasant. Then, with a grave face, yet struggling with a smile in spite of himself, he perused the next which came to hand. It was a solemn-looking packet, sealed with the episcopal arms of the diocese.

'This concerns you, Fox,' he said. 'It is from the Bishop's secretary; you will hardly believe it genuine. Listen.

' "His Lordship has heard with extreme concern that Colonel Goring has been setting an example of disobedience to the law, which his Lordship is unable to characterize in language sufficiently severe. His Lordship understands that Colonel Goring has introduced into his estate, from England, a number of persons calling themselves Protestants, professing opinions offensive to God and dangerous to the State; that he has erected a conventicle, attached to his dwelling-house, where these persons assemble for what they term Divine worship, that he has with him a minister, a follower of the Schismatic and Sectarian George Whitfield; nay, that on certain occasions Colonel Goring has himself assumed a preacher's office. His Lordship is informed, further, that Colonel Goring has opened a school for the instruction of the children of these persons, to which also other children of his Irish tenants are allowed access. Colonel Goring, as a magistrate, cannot be ignorant that, in so acting, he is violating the Canon Law of the Church and the Statute Law of the Land. His Majesty has, indeed, with the advice of Parliament, been pleased to concede a liberty of using their own forms of worship to certain classes of Dissenters from the Established Religion, but only under strict conditions, which, in the present instance, his Lordship cannot find to have been complied with. The Act of Parliament therefore permits no meeting-house to be opened for Divine worship which has not been licensed, either by the Bishop or the Archdeacon, or by the magistrates of the county in Quarter Sessions. No such license has been granted to Colonel Goring by either of these courts, nor, if the tenets of Colone Goring's congregation have been rightly represented to his Lordship, is it possible that such a license will be granted.

' "The opening of a school is an irregularity of a yet more serious kind. The education of children has been confided entirely to the care of the Church of Ireland. Under the Act of Uniformity, no school of any kind is allowed among us which is not under the direction of the ordained clergy.

' "His Lordship, therefore, while regretting the painful duty which his office imposes upon him" (Hang the fellow! what does he mean by painful duty? It is never painful to do a duty if it is a real one.) 'His Lordship, in short, requires me to shut up my conventicle, and send my people, if they choose to remain in Ireland, to their Parish Church—The doors and windows were broken out a hundred years ago, and there has never been service in it since—If no Church school is within reach, the children are to be sent to the Charter School at Cork, where they will be instructed in the principles of the pure and apostolical faith established in this land.

'"His Lordship trusts that Colonel Goring will comply at once with these directions, and spare the Bishop the necessity, which may otherwise be imposed upon him, of bringing the subject before the Primate."'

'Did any body ever hear the like?' Goring growled. 'I do believe Luther was right, when he said that Satan seemed sometimes to enter into these bishops as he entered into Judas Iscariot. They will be the ruin of this country yet.'

'John, John, don't talk like that,' said his wife; 'I can't bear to hear it. Why didn't you listen to me, and ask for the license? I was sure harm would come of it.'

'No harm can come of it. I have only to write to the magistrates. As far as doctrines go, we might all be members of the Church of Ireland, if there was any church for us to attend. And as to loyalty, our friends, the Presbyterians, showed something of it at Derry and Enniskillen. I don't mean Satan, really—I mean Ireland's Evil genius—say what you will.'

'Nonsense, John.'

'But it isn't nonsense. License, indeed! The Catholic priests ought to take out licenses. Not one in a hundred has a license, or is ever asked for it. There are 500 Protestant Chapels in the North, which have been opened under the Toleration Act. I don't know that in one instance there, either, a license has been applied for. The Law having been once passed, it goes as a matter of course—and, as to the schools, in every village there is some poor Catholic scholar teaching shoeless urchins, under a bridge, to read Ovid and Virgil. It is astonishing, by-the-bye, how well they do it. They may break the law, all the country over, and I must not have our poor boys and girls taught reading and writing, for fear I make rebels and heretics of them.'

'You must write to the Bishop, for all that, or I will do it for you,' said Mrs. Goring, as she rose and went out under the verandah.

'I'll tell him, what is quite true,' he called after her, 'that I had intended to build a little church at Glengariff for the Protestant families that are about there, and that I will do it yet, unless he worries me into turning Dissenter in earnest. Of course I will write to the Grand Jury, and I will see that you are put in a right position,' he went on, turning to Fox. 'They will be sending their police down and arresting you else. But you see what a stream we have to struggle against. I really mean it, about the Glengariff church. It will not cost very much, and I should prefer the old service for my wife and myself. Some of the others may like to go with us—and you, too, for all that I know. Wesley goes to church, I believe.'

'And I, perhaps, may apply to the Bishop for ordination,' said Fox, laughing. 'I believe I could satisfy him of my orthodoxy.'

'We will hear what the Primate thinks about it. I can spare the Bishop the trouble of referring to him, for I must go myself, one of these days, to Dublin, and I will hear what his Grace has to say. But it is a lovely morning—we have stayed in too long. I will just glance over the rest of my letters, and we will follow Mrs. Goring.' One only called for much attention. It was written in a hand which was evidently disguised, and ran as follows:

'Sir,

'I have not had the pleasure of seeing you since ye came to your Government at Dunboy—but I'll see ye once more before all is over, and set ye on your way off the stage to the Elysian fields. This is to give you notice that your coffin is making ready. 'Tis all your own fault, and—for the slaughter ye committed on poor people after Culloden fight—you'll be served as Lord Lovat's agent was. God be merciful to your soul.'

'Ireland again!' said he, throwing it down with a sigh. 'I am glad Elizabeth is not here. Don't mention it, for these letters

always agitate her. I have had so many that I have mostly
ceased to attend to them. They mean something or they mean
nothing. No one can say. But this is peculiar. Who here knows
about Culloden fight or Lord Lovat's steward? There is some
stranger about, and there is mischief in the wind beyond the
common. But come out now. It is my morning's *levee*. You have
never yet seen the genuine Irishman, and I can show you the
real article.'

On the lawn before the window was gathered a motley congregation of men, women and children, sitting crouched upon
the grass; the women in blue or madder-coloured cloaks, the
hoods drawn over their heads, rocking their bodies to and fro,
and moaning half-intelligible sounds; the men in tattered
coats, unbuttoned breeches and hats, once with rim and crown
and now with neither, the little ones bare-footed, bare-legged,
with ragged, uncombed hair. Each one of them wanted something of his honour or the good lady. All had their tale of
misfortune.

The nearest of them, an old man he seemed, but age and
youth were not easily to be distinguished, was sitting on a stone
step, sipping leisurely the remains of some liquid at the bottom
of a wine-glass.

'Why, Tim,' said the Colonel, 'I gave you the castor-oil two
hours ago. Not done with it yet?'

'Ah, your honour, the Lord be good to you for that same, the
blessed drink that it is. Would I be swallowing it all to the
onst? Sure it's drop and drop I take it, and I wish your
honour's health and long life to ye, at ache taste.'

'Your honour is a kind master, and you will be good to me,'
said the next. 'Your honour'll mind the little haffer ye giv
me the last fall. Och, it was a beautiful little haffer that she
was, and it has plased the Lord to take her to himself; and
what will we do with the rint day coming round and the
children crying for the milk?'

'Ah, thin, hould you tongue with ye for a discontented
crature as you are,' interrupted a fellow whose head was bound
up with a handkerchief. 'It is little the likes of you hav to
complain of, with the best landlord over ye that ever came to

49

Ireland, and himself direct upon ye, and none to come between. It is not one of your own tinants that I am your honour. Glad would I be for that same if it was the Lord's will with me. It is on Mr. White's land that I am, and it was hoping that your honour would spake a word for me, that I am troubling ye this day. Sure there is five that is between me and him. There is Mr. Darby that is in London that has the big lase, and the big lase is parcelled out to three more, and thim again to others before they come to us that put the spade into the ground; and each one of them all will have his profit before I'll find so much as a potato to put into the mouths of thim that belongs to me. I was thinking maybe your honour would tell Mr. White that if he would just dale directly with meself that's on the land, and would put thim interlopers out of the way, I'd giv him the double any way of what he receives from Mr. Darby, and better it would be for the both of us.'

'That is true for you, my man,' said the Colonel, 'but it is little I can do for you or Mr. White either. The land comes to us tied up in these leases. There is half my own that I can do nothing with. They will say there was no compulsion on you to take the farm. If you could not live upon it you might have gone elsewhere.'

'And where would I go, your honour? And where would we live at all except upon the land, and where would I find a bit of ground for me except in the place where I was born? They tell me if I have so much to pay I must work the harder. 'Deed then it is little encouragement we have to work when if I dry a bit of the bog they raise the price upon me, and he that farms the tithes comes and takes the tinth of the crops when the nine-tinths have gone already for the rint.'

'Which of them was it that broke your head for you, my good fellow?' the Colonel said. 'You seem to have got a bad hurt there.'

'I'd be none the worse for a bit of the plaister, your honour, and that is true, if the good lady would be pleased to help me to such a thing. We wint up in a turf-boat to Bantry, me and Bridget, that is my wife that's here;' he said, pointing to a big bony woman that sat on the grass near him. 'There was more of the boys with us. We had gone to see Mr. White's agent and learn if he would do us any good. And the agent was in Dublin, and we could not see him at all. So we had a taste of drink with the lads of the town, for we were tired after the long row. How it was I don't know, but they got disputing, and from that to joking with Bridget there, and she didn't like it, and she thought I was not standing up for her as I ought; and indeed what need for me? for there is not a stouter woman in the county of Cork, and it is nine children that she has, barring one that's with the Lord, for it's overlaid he was. Well, Bridget she got angry, and she whipped the stocking off the foot of her and dropped a ground apple into the toe. Och, but she laid about her that time, and the first person she hit was her own husband, and so your honour my head was broke, but troth, it is many times she has broke it, the darlin', and a good wife she is to me. The Lord receive her into glory.'

Goring took down the man's name and address, for there were many more petitioners waiting to be attended to, and then passed him over for his wounds to be looked to. He was the arbiter of all disputes in the barony and the universal doctor in all disease and accidents. Women had come to denounce each other for scandal-mongering—somebody's donkey had eaten a neighbour's cabbage—neighbouring cottiers were wrangling over their boundaries—babies had been changed in the cradles by the 'good people'—and the Colonel had to advise whether the changeling should be thrown into the sea or into the fire. The commonest demand was for medicine to cure ailments for which no cure was possible, as they had grown out of neglect and poverty. Croups, fevers, broken limbs, and wounds—the Colonel was to prescribe for them all. He had but to speak the word and it would be enough. They would hang a draught about their necks and believe the effect would be the same as if they swallowed it.

'You see these poor people,' Goring said to his companion when the lawn had been almost cleared, 'they know that I mean them well. They believe in me, and I suppose that in their way they have a regard for me. Yet of all the men you have seen here to-day there is hardly one who would not try to shoot me if he was so ordered by the secret societies! There is not one, man or woman, who, if I was killed by the smugglers, would help to bring the murderers to justice. They are taught from their cradles that English rule is the cause of all their miseries. They were as ill off under their own chiefs; . . . There is not a race in the world who would be happier or more loyal if they were governed with a firm and just hand. England has tried every other remedy. This, which is the only one which can succeed, she has never tried, and I fear she never will.'

Such comfort, help, admonition, as was possible, had been distributed to the various applicants, and they had been dismissed for the day. The women had fallen chiefly to Mrs. Goring, and her share of the morning's labour had not been the lightest. But the tongues were at last silent, and the owners of them had gone away, to return most of them with fresh complaints on the morrow. There lingered only a girl, barefooted, but neatly dressed, who had crouched patiently at the back of the rest, waiting till their clamour was over, as the Irish always do when they have a real sorrow.

'And who may you be?' said the lady. 'I never saw you before—you are a stranger!'

'I am called Moriarty, your ladyship. I am from Glenbeg, beyond the mountains yonder,' the girl answered in a low, modest voice.

'And what do you want with us?' Mrs. Goring enquired with interest, for this last petitioner was unlike any of the rest. 'What can we do for you?'

'Oh, my lady! Maybe I shouldn't be here, but where I'd go else in the wide world I don't know, and it's not for myself that I'm seeking you. My father—his honour the Colonel will have heard the name of him—has the farm at the head of the glen that's above Ardgroom. There is none but meself to live with him, and none but him to take care of me, for my mother is dead, the Lord be good to her soul! and my brothers are gone away beyond the seas, and we know nothing what may have become of them! And my father has got the sickness upon him, and he is upon his bed and he speaks never a word!

And Father McCarty came up from Eyris and give him the Blessed Sacrament and tould him he need come no more, for it was six miles away, and my father would soon be in glory. But that was two days back, and he is moaning yet, and he has been a kind father to me, and I'd heard speak of your ladyship and of his honour that there was none like ye. You'll know, maybe, what we should do, and you will give him back to us!'

The Colonel had by this time joined his wife.

'What is the matter with your father?' he asked. 'What does he complain of?'

''Deed, your honour, how can I know what is the matter with him? He just lies on his back and never spakes a word, but he puts his hand upon his breast and moans, and looks wild out of the eyes of him!'

'Does he take any food? What have you given him to eat? Perhaps he has swallowed something that has gone amiss with him!'

'Sorra bit of anything has passed his lips since the priest came,' she sobbed, 'and, indeed, there has been little in the house for either of us, since the drivers came and took the cows away, barring a few spades of potatoes that is left in the bog!'

'My good girl,' said Goring, 'I cannot prescribe for a sick man in such a state as you describe without seeing him. How far off do you live?'

''Tis eight Irish miles by the road, your honour, and it is a wild place and a wild track to it! And it is time I was on the way home, for I left a friend from a cabin that is not far off to watch if he wanted anything while I was away, but he can ill bear me out of his sight, and I must be getting back before the sun is under the hill. It is not for your honour to be putting yourself out for the likes of us that don't belong to you. I thought maybe ye'd give me something to take home with me that would do him good; but if ye cannot, God save your honour and your ladyship, and kindly thank ye!'

She gathered herself up, curtsied, and was going away, but she staggered after a few steps and sank again on the grass.

'God help them!' the Colonel said, 'I believe they are both starving! Take the girl in and give her something to eat. She has come all this way on foot this morning and tasted nothing. I will go to Glenbeg myself; it is but a morning's walk. A boy can lead a pony with a basket and food, and this poor young creature can ride.'

Faint as she was she again struggled to her feet and insisted that she was strong enough to walk and must set out at once. 'There was no need,' she said, 'for his honour to be toiling over the hills, and maybe he might meet with those he'd be sorry to fall in with.'

But she had overrated her powers. She was utterly exhausted, and was obliged with many tears to own it.

Rest and food were indispensable before she could even sit upon a horse, while if her father was to be saved, there was not a moment to be lost.

Goring, who by this time knew something of Irish character, discovered in her objection to his going that there was something which she had not told him behind. There was a shorter path to Glenbeg over the mountains, entirely solitary, with which he was perfectly familiar. In quieter times he had shot over the moors on the ridge, and knew every turn and point among them. The moors would be safer than the road, and walking would be safer than riding, as he would be less likely to be observed if dangerous people were abroad. He determined to go alone, taking his gun and dog with him, as if his object was but a brace or two of moor fowl. Putting a flask, with some sandwiches and restoring medicines, in his pocket for immediate use, he whistled to his favourite pointer and started up the hillside, leaving orders with a servant to follow on horseback with the girl by the road as soon as she should be able to move.

Chapter VII

THE SKULL AT THE CAIRN

I T was a glorious September morning, and still wanted an
hour of noon when Colonel Goring set out from his house.
Glenbeg lay the other side of the watershed, on the slope towards the Kenmare River, and the way to it was across the
dividing ridge. The scenery is treeless, and utterly wild and
desolate. After reaching the top of the mountain range, you
walk for miles among heathery moors and swamps, where the
streams rise which fall east and west into one or other of the
two bays. Half-a-dozen ragged peaks break the outline of the
range, buried in clouds in wild weather, on such a morning as
the present, standing sharp and clear against the azure sky.
From Lackawee, which is one of the loftiest of them, you look
immediately down upon Glenbeg Lake, two thousand feet
below you. Beyond it is Ardgroom Harbour and Kenmare
River, and far away the Killarney Reeks and the Purple Mountains and Mangerton.

Leaving Hungry Hill far on his right, Colonel Goring
ascended the brook which fell into the sea behind his house.
After climbing sharply for a couple of miles he reached the
cradle of the stream in a wide morass. The peat was dry in the
clear autumn weather. The air was fresh and delicious, and
perfumed with heather. On the banks, between which the tiny
rivulet trickled along, were patches of rich, green grass, where
sheep and cattle ought to have been feeding, but there were
no signs of either, nor of any human creature. Nature was left
alone in her wasteful beauty, and as there was no wind, the
silence was unbroken, save by the croak of a passing raven, the
sharp bark of an eagle, or the whirr of some old cock grouse,
whom the dog had scented out among the moss hags.

Goring's thoughts were so much occupied that more than
one fine point had been neglected, and the dog had looked

55

round in reproachful surprise as the bird, whose presence he
had indicated so skilfully, flew away unharmed. The Colonel
had been a famous shot in his youth. To please his poor companion he brought down a brace of birds as he walked; but he
was in a hurry and could not linger. He had crossed the bog,
and reached the hillside the other side of it. A few hundred
yards distant rose the highest point in all the neighbourhood,
with a cairn of stones on the top of it. He was examining the
shape of it, and speculating on the origin of its singular name,
Maulin, when he observed the dog questing round in a way
which showed that he scented something, but was not satisfied
as to what was before him. The dog stood, then broke his
point and ran on again in the direction of the cairn, then
stopped again, as if puzzled and uncertain. He supposed at
first that a pack of grouse might be running on in front, but
instead of carrying his head up as he would have done had
there been birds before him, the animal was snuffling uneasily
along the ground, but always making towards the top of the
hill.

The manner was so peculiar that Goring followed, curious
to know what it could be. As he advanced, a couple of ravens
rose just out of gunshot, apparently from among the stones of
the cairn. Another rising immediately after, he concluded that,
scanty as the sheep on the hills seemed to be, one of them must
be lying there which had come in some way by its end. He
turned, called the dog off, and was going on, when he heard
himself suddenly hailed by a human voice. From behind a grey
rock a few yards from him there stepped out a tall, slight,
athletic, active-looking man, who might be some five-and-
twenty years old. Eccentric as was the costume of the Irish
Squireens of the period, it was evidently not to them that he
belonged. He had a hat like a Spanish muleteer, a short,
braided jacket, breeches supported by a belt about his waist,
and light boots and leggings. He carried a gun upon his arm,
and looked like a sportsman—a gentleman and a foreigner.

Goring observed him with some surprise and some suspicion.
The stranger, however, seemed perfectly unembarrassed. 'Good
morning, sir,' he said in correct English, though with a slightly

foreign accent. 'It is a fine day among the hills. You have had sport? I heard your gun half-an-hour ago.'

'There are a few birds on the lower ground,' answered the Colonel, 'but not many. There is little game in this country to tempt visitors. You came this morning from Kenmare, I presume?'

'I came from the place where I spent last night,' replied the stranger smiling. 'I am on a mountain walk with my gun, like yourself. That is all which we at present know of each other. May I ask to whom I am speaking?'

'I am Colonel Goring, of Dunboy, sir, the principal magistrate in this district—for want of a better.'

'I supposed as much,' the stranger said. 'There cannot be two persons in such a neighbourhood so distinguished in appearance as I have always heard that officer to be.'

'Having told who I am,' Goring said, not choosing to notice the compliment, 'it becomes my duty to enquire in turn who you may be?'

'It matters little, sir,' the stranger answered. 'I call myself a foreigner. I was born yonder, I believe,' and he pointed to MacGillicuddy's Reeks, 'but I have passed most of my life abroad. I am here but for a few days, and am using my time to look about me in your mountains. In a week I shall be gone. This, perhaps, is information enough.'

'I am sorry to seem discourteous,' said the Colonel, 'but it is not enough, and since I have told you that I am a magistrate, you will understand why it is not enough. You carry a gun. Have you a license for it?'

'I have such license as I give to myself,' the youth coolly replied. 'In the country that I came from that is sufficient and must suffice here.'

'It will not suffice here, sir,' the Colonel said sharply. 'I must suppose that you are ignorant of the rules. No person is allowed to carry arms in this country who has not satisfied the authorities that he is entitled to carry them. The law requires me to insist that you give a fuller account of yourself.'

'The law may require you, sir,' the stranger rejoined, with the same mocking calmness. 'The law requires many things in

Ireland which it does not get, I am told. I may ask too, what law? Kerry law, I have heard, is to do no right and to take no wrong. We are in Cork now, I believe. The border is within a few yards of us, but we are on the eastern side. What the law is in Cork you may see a few yards from you.'

He pointed to the cairn. Goring looked and he saw, if it was not a dream, something like a human head projecting above the stones. The eye-sockets were empty; the skin and flesh were torn from the bones. The beaks of the ravens and the teeth of the mountain foxes had broken through the skull. Half the brain had been devoured and the rest was oozing down in a ghastly stream over the neck. Goring's nerves had been hardened on the battlefield, but a sight so horrid and so unlooked-for for a moment entirely overcame him. He recovered himself and sprang up the cairn. Through the chinks between the boulders he could make out the body of a man but lately dead, for the clothing was unsoiled and dry, and no rain had fallen since it had been placed in its present position. It was fast bound to a stake which had been driven into a crack in the rock and the stones had been heaped up round it.

'That, sir,' said the stranger, 'is, or was, two days since, what they call here a tithe proctor. The tithe is a tax which the law, of which you spoke, requires the Catholic peasants of this country to pay to a minister whom they have never seen, in support of a religion in which they do not believe. The collection of this tax being dangerous, the minister is content with half of it, which he enjoys in safety five hundred miles away. The proctor keeps the other half in return for the risk which he runs, and now and then, as you see, it goes hard with him.'

'Whatever else I see,' replied Colonel Goring, 'I see a dangerous person before me at this moment. A foul murder has been committed; I find you, sir, upon the spot, and by your own confession you know something of the assassins. There must be an instant inquiry, and I cannot lose sight of yourself. There is a poor man, a mile or two beyond this, in danger of death, to whom I am carrying relief, and I will not leave him even for this frightful business; you will have to accompany me, sir, and will then return with me to Dunboy.'

THE SKULL AT THE CAIRN

'I shall be sorry to disappoint you, Colonel,' the stranger rejoined, still with unbroken composure. 'My engagements and my pleasure require my presence elsewhere. I am armed, as you perceive, as well as yourself. You will choose whether you will hear me quietly, and then leave me to go my way, or take your chance of what you can get by violence. I tell you distinctly that of this man's death I knew nothing till last night. I came hither merely to see with my own eyes an example of Irish revenge. For the sick man you speak of, if you mean Moriarty of Glenbeg, you may spare your anxiety. Help has already reached him.'

Colonel Goring could not refuse a certain admiration for the coolness with which he was defied. But his duty was still plain. 'I choose nothing and I promise nothing,' he said. 'I must arrest you in the King's name.'

'It matters not,' the stranger answered. 'I will tell you what it is good for you to know. The old man whom you are on the way to visit has held the farm of Glenbeg for forty years, and his father held it before him. The rent they paid was light and the Annesleys, or whoever they were that owned the land, gave them no trouble. The estate passed to others. The Moriartys held by custom, and custom was forgotten. The occupying tenant's rent was trebled, and on such terms he could not live. The law allowed these things and the courts maintained them. He would have starved or have been driven out, but he found friends where the owners and the middlemen were content that he should find them. He found traders who would give him twice the market price for his fleeces. He dealt with them. He paid his exorbitant rent with the profits which he was thus able to make, and all went well again till you, sir, came into the country and ordered that the trade which had saved him should cease.

'This poor man could no longer meet the middleman's demands. His rent fell in arrears. For two years he paid nothing because he could not. The middleman, an attorney at Kenmare, seized his sheep and cattle. He struggled on with his oat patches and potatoes. On the top of all came the proctor, a month since, in the name of religion, swept off his crops, carried

59

away the poor furniture of his cabin, and left him, with his child, to perish. That natural justice, sir, which your laws set aside, would not allow such an act to go unpunished.

'There were persons, individually unknown to me, who heard what had been done. The instrument of legal tyranny had himself sought his occupation, and lived by the exercise of it. They concluded that such a wretch required to be dealt with. They caught him, it needs not to say how or where, they brought him hither, close to the scene of his crime, that they might make an example of him to the country round. They fastened a stake in the middle of yonder cairn, they bound him to it, and they bound his arms to his side. They piled the stones round him to his neck and left him with the eagles and the ravens.

'As for Moriarty, other friends, who had traded with him in better days, heard last night that he was dying of hunger. Relief was sent to him immediately, and it arrived soon after the poor man's daughter had gone for help to you. They were in time to save him, and you need have no further anxiety on his behalf. For yourself, sir, let me give you a friendly warning. I bear you no ill will, but there are others who do. I advise you expressly to go no further on your present errand.'

With these words, and politely touching his hat when he had done, the youth sprang lightly behind the rock against which he had leant while he was speaking. Goring darted forward to detain him, only however to see his late companion bounding down the hill like a cricket ball, and passing out of sight round a spur of the mountain. Pursuit was useless, and he was left alone to consider what he would do.

The stranger, he was satisfied, must be one of the officers of the French Irish Brigade who had come on a recruiting expedition. That a crime so audacious should have been perpetrated within four miles of his own residence, and almost within sight of it, was a frightful evidence of the revival of a lawless spirit. He connected it with the letter which he had received in the morning.

He forced himself to climb again to the top of the cairn and examine the condition of the being who had perished there.

60

Every detail which Goring could observe confirmed the stranger's story. The body was bound to a stake as he had said. The arms had been pinioned to his side. The flesh, though torn by the ravens, had not begun to decompose. At the utmost, life could not have been extinct more than forty-eight hours. He piled stones on the head to protect what was left of it till the remains could be carried down and buried.

The discovery ought immediately to be published. The loss of two or three hours however, was of no serious consequence, and Goring decided to go on first, in spite of the warning, to Moriarty's farm house. The danger with which he was threatened was itself inviting, for it implied that he might come on the traces of the murderers before the scent was cold.

Leaving the Cairn, with its horrid contents, he strode rapidly along the high ground in the opposite direction from that in which the stranger had disappeared. After walking for half an hour he turned the shoulder of Lackawee, and saw the peaceful waters of the Lough stretched out at his feet.

Beautiful it was as ever, the quiet islands at the mouth of the Kenmare River, dark and solid, and the far off Skelligs rising blue on the horizon as if shaped out of transparent mist. But Goring was too anxious now to think about the landscape. The cabin which was the object of his visit, stood on a green bank on an island formed by a river, which divided behind it, then joined again in a single stream, and flowed out into the Lough. It was eighteen hundred feet below him, but the slope was grassy and clear of stones and, partly sliding, partly running, he was soon at the bottom

The cottage itself was not superior to the ordinary Irish cabins. The walls were of mud, the roofs of thatch, half of which had been torn off by the wind. A hole in the middle of it blackened with soot served for a chimney, and a hole in the wall for a window. Glass it had none, and a wisp of straw was thrust into it to keep out cold and rain. The door had fallen off its hinges and lay on the ground. Outside were half a dozen small green enclosures divided by stone walls, where sheep and cows and geese had once fed, but all were now deserted.

Four acres of yellow stubble clean of weed, showed where an

oat-crop had grown and had been cut and carried. Four weeks since those oats had been yellowing for the harvest. The oats were gone, and the man who had taken them away was rotting on the hill-top.

In wet weather the cabin itself could only be approached by wading. The water was now low, and there was a line of stones which were dry. Looking sharply on all sides, for he could not tell who or what might be near, Colonel Goring stepped across, and went up to it. Not a symptom was to be seen of any living thing; the sunshine streamed in freely through the open door; he entered; a spinning-wheel lay overturned on the floor, with the fragments of a broken stool. There were ashes on the hearth, but they were cold. The scanty earthenware, the iron hook and kettle, which the poorest Irish household cannot do without, were all gone. At first it seemed as if there was not so much as a bed, for none could be seen, not even the rush heap or peat stack which occasionally serves for one, nor did it seem as if there was space for any second room. Looking carefully, however Goring discovered at last a latch in the inner wall. Lifting it he found himself in a narrow shed, into which light made its way feebly through the holes in the roof.

Here as his eyes grew accustomed to the darkness, he percieved a frame of boards nailed together and strewed with fern. This had been the old man's sleeping place, and there was a pallet in a corner for the girl who had come to him in the morning. But the bed was empty, the occupant of it was gone. Everything was gone. For any sign that could be traced, no human creature need have been near the place for days or weeks. Part of what he saw was easily explained; the small comforts, the bare necessaries of life, had been seized for the rent. But where was the old man himself, and where were those who had brought him help? The utter desolation was more startling to him than if he had found himself in a nest of Rapparees; for all that he could tell they might be hidden under the river banks, and might spring out upon him at any moment.

The pointer, however, which would scent the presence of man more easily than he could do, gave no sign, but looked composedly in his master's face. By degrees he assured himself that he and his dog were the only living creatures on the spot. And he presently found a partial clue to the mystery. There was a post on the shore with a chain, to which a boat had been attached. The chain was loose, the boat was gone, and there was the mark of the keel on the shingle where it had been run down into the water. The party who had brought the food had afterwards carried the old Moriarty down the lake, perhaps to be out of the way when enquiry came to be made into the murder.

What was he to do now?

The horse track from Dunboy by which the girl would be coming with his servant followed the shore to the bottom of the Lough. There bending to the left it had been carried up another valley, and by a lower pass through the mountains. He thought at first that he had better return this way and meet them. But he reflected that the persons from whom the stranger had warned him that he might be in danger had gone in that direction. They would be on the look-out for the girl, for they knew where she had been, and he could be satisfied that she would be taken care of. He concluded that his wisest course would be to go back by the way that he had come, and to send a party as speedily as was possible to bring down the body from the cairn.

Chapter VIII

THE END OF MACFINNAN DHU

A YEAR had passed over the settlement at Dunboy since the incident described in the last chapter, a year which had brought with it the ordinary vicissitudes of good and evil, but had made no distinct alteration in Colonel Goring's purposes or prospects. The event to which he looked forward as so important to his complete success had not yet taken place. Macfinnan Dhu's constitution continued to bear up against age and fever, and whiskey, and Lord Shelbourne's intended reforms at Kilmakilloge were not to be commenced till he was gone. The body of the man who had been murdered had been brought down from the mountain. An inquest had been held upon it, but no evidence could be had to identify the perpetrators, and the verdict found was against persons unknown.

The old Moriarty had reappeared after a time at his cabin, and with signs of improved circumstances. Cows again browsed upon his meadows and sheep upon the hills. The house itself was enlarged and comfortably furnished. But the suspicions which might have attached to his prosperity as connected in some way with the crime were dispelled, first by the priest who had visited him, and swore that at the time of the murder he was unconscious and was then supposed to be dying; and secondly, by the accidental discovery that his re-establishment on his farm under so much happier conditions was due to no one but to Colonel Goring himself, who had purchased the lease of Glenbeg and bought out the middlemen, and had taken the poor old man for his own immediate tenant.

Meantime his own settlement continued to prosper. The yield of the fishery was abundant. The fish houses on the Island were crowded with herring barrels, and the dried cod and ling stood in stacks upon the shore till French and English dealers came in for them. The mines proved richer and richer as fresh lodes were opened. They furnished employment to large numbers of the native Irish, and a kind of intercourse was still maintained, not wholly unfriendly, between the old inhabitants and the new.

But the unrest which always prevailed in the South of Ireland when there was a prospect of a French landing, was growing with alarming intensity. Peace was not yet avowedly broken; but the French and English were fighting in India and America, and the signs of the approaching war were visible on all sides. Privateers were known to be fitting out at Nantes and Rochelle, expecting their letters of marque. Vicious-looking craft, of various sizes, had been seen hovering about the Irish coast under French colours, anywhere between Cape Clear and the mouth of the Shannon. The Bantry smugglers had multiplied so fast that, without larger support than the Government allowed him, he found he would soon be unable to hold them in check. He had some information that muskets and powder had been landed in large quantities in Roaring Water Bay, and while he was straining his utmost to protect the coast, he was assailed by a hundred petty acts of persecution, each of which, if taken singly might have seemed an accident, but coming close together showed that a combined attempt was being made to drive him out of the country.

He had relieved the poorer tenants of the neighbourhood by buying in the ground leases; he provoked the resentment of the petty tyrants of the Baronies; and claims of all sorts and kinds upon his own property were started out of the ground under his feet. A claimant was even found for his own house at Dunboy, under some antiquated deed. He was entangled in a labyrinth of law-suits, each of which when it came on for hearing was found too flimsy to be sustained. But a worrying and exasperating correspondence with solicitors was no small addition to his other anxieties. Again and again he represented his situation to the Government in Dublin. He described the alarming revival of the contraband trade, the apathy if not the enmity of the gentry of the country to himself, and the organized persecution of which he was made the object. The hostility to him was due entirely to his resolution to do his duty; and he said plainly that without assistance, or at least without some open countenance from the Castle authorities, it would be impossible for him to hold his ground.

The ruling authorities alternated between panic and deliberate inaction. When frightened they were precipitate and violent. When the alarm passed off, or before it arose, they refused to be moved. The contraband trade they were content to let alone. As to war, it had not yet come, perhaps it would not come, and there was no need to be in a hurry. Colonel Goring's letters received no official answer. As he persevered in writing, it was intimated to him indirectly that the Customs duties formed a part of the hereditary revenues of the Crown. The Government in London, finding Irish constitutional liberty beginning to be troublesome, were contemplating the abolition of the Irish Parliament, and the carrying on the administration with the hereditary revenues alone. Patriotic Irishmen, therefore, ought not to wish that revenue to be too completely collected.

Whatever might be the cause of the apathy, Colonel Goring had to be convinced that he had nothing to look for from the powers at the Castle, beyond his half-dozen Coastguard men. The one hope which burnt bright in him was in his expected help from Lord Shelbourne, and here, too, it was not impossible that he might again be disappointed.

In spite of the rude treatment of the wine basket, the Earl could not be brought to disturb the last years of the old Chief at Derreen. No change was to be made till Macfinnan Dhu had been gathered to his fathers. The Earl himself was far advanced in years. His son, who was to have succeeded him, and resembled his grandfather, Sir William, had died suddenly. The heir to the great Shelbourne estates was now his sister's son, Lord Fitzmaurice, a scion of the old Geraldines, who was suspected of entertaining no favourable disposition towards aggressive Protestant colonies and, like the generality of the Jacobite Anglo-Irish gentry, preferred a Papist to a Calvinistic Republican.

Colonel Goring would have been more than mortal if he had not desired that Macfinnan should be the first to go, and leave the Earl time to set his plans in motion. For once fortune seemed to stand his friend. After being restored to vigour by his wrath, Macfinnan went back to the habits out of which his illness had imperfectly frightened him. After draining a pint of whiskey at a draught, in a bet with a neighbouring squireen, he was carried helpless to bed. In his life he had been an unwilling Protestant, to qualify himself to hold the lease of Tuosist. The priest, when he was in *articulo mortis*, set his conscience straight for him. His sin had been inconsiderable, for in his whole life he had never set foot inside a Protestant church. His spiritual affairs having been arranged, he called his son Mick to his bed-side, cautioned him to stand by the old place through good and evil, and drink and fight when opportunity offered, as a gentleman should do, and so made a good end, after the manner of his fathers.

A letter from the agent at Kenmare brought the news to Dunboy. The Earl's instructions to him, he said, had been to lose no time in entering upon possession. He proposed to go in person to Derreen, to show proper consideration for the family who were now to be removed. Several gentlemen of distinction would accompany him, at the Earl's desire, to give importance to his action, and he trusted that Colonel Goring himself would join their party, since he was likely to be so much interested in the future management of the property. The agent had decided, after some uncertainty, that the day of the funeral would, on the whole, be the fittest for their visit. It would be a sign of respect which was demanded by the custom of the country, and as evidence of an intention to deal generously in the change which was to be made.

Chapter IX

A CHIEFTAIN IS BURIED

THE death of Macfinnan Dhu made a sensation throughout Kerry. The O'Sullivans of Dunkerron, the chief branch of the old race, had been long gone. Their castle was in ruins. The water-spirits who had wailed in the moonlight upon the shore on the death of each of its inmates, had sung their last dirge when Elizabeth was Queen of England, and they had been seen or heard no more. Morty Oge, the next in rank of the family, had carried his sword into the service of the foreigner, and the Lord of Derreen was the last of their chiefs who had resided on the scene of their old dominion. The Earl of Shelbourne's intentions were no secret, and it seemed as if the curtain was about to fall over one more of the ancient Irish Septs.

Under any circumstances the last honours would have been paid punctiliously to a man who had been personally popular and who had filled so conspicuous a place. The revolution known to be contemplated had on this occasion called out a peculiar feeling. The smaller squires, the sons or brothers of some of the more considerable families in the country, the multitudes of Sullivans, for half the peasantry bore the name, and all the Catholic population of the adjoining baronies on both sides of the Kenmare River, decided to be present at the funeral, both out of natural respect and to show the dissatisfaction and jealousy with which they regarded the threatened return among them of English strangers.

Macfinnan Dhu was waked with the usual honours. The buckeens who had been his boon companions sate the night through drinking whiskey in the hall at Derreen, the coffin standing on trestles in the middle of them, with the candles burning round it. The blind piper in a corner played the *keen* of the O'Sullivans, and those who were not too drunk to listen professed to have heard the Banshee wail outside the window.

In the morning—it was again a bright September day—the grounds were early thronged with thousands of people who had gathered there by land and water. From Berehaven by the pass over the mountains, from Glengariff and Bantry, from Sneem, across the bay, and even from Killarney and Tralee, old and young had come together for a holiday, and for a patriotic demonstration. They had brought their food with them to spare the purse of the injured heir, and had distributed themselves in picturesque groups over the lawn and under the trees in the orchard. Stern old women, with features trenched deep with furrows and wrinkles, sat on their haunches on the rock where the dead man had broken the Saxon's wine bottles, smoking their short pipes, and mumbling over again the curses which he had thundered at him.

The old church of Kilmakilloge—church of the lesser St. Michael—where the younger branch of the O'Sullivans had been buried since the time of the Danes, stood on a grassy hill above the harbour, a mile and a half distant from the house. Who the lesser St. Michael was, how he differed from the Archangel, and what brought him to Ireland, local Irish tradition, for once modest, does not pretend to know. The harbour which bears his name is an inlet, two or three miles deep, on the eastern side of the Kenmare River.

A few hundred yards off was a pond, to which St. Michael gave miraculous virtues. A floating island rose once a year in the middle of it, and a bathe in the water, while the island was above the surface, made the lame to walk and the blind to see. Analogous advantages attached to a grave in the churchyard; and so considerable were these, that bodies would be brought from the adjoining Baronies to be put away there. The natives of the glen, jealous of their exclusive rights, would resist by force, and desperate battles were often fought on these occasions. So holy the spot was supposed to be, and so severe the competition for admission to it, that the space was fast filled. The peasant who secured a grave there was allowed but a few years of rest before he was dug up to make room for another. The grass was littered with the fragments of coffins, and skulls were piled in heaps against the chancel walls. The vault of the O'Sullivans alone remained sacred from disturbance, and was guarded partly by a railing and partly by the respect of the population.

Hither on this September morning were to be borne the remains of the chief who had just departed. The coffin, with his arms in silver upon the lid, was brought out and laid in a cart. The gentlemen, who had wound up their night watch with an ample breakfast, mounted their horses in the courtyard, and talked anxiously and earnestly as they rode round to take their places behind it.

'So here,' said the O'Donoghoe of Glenflesk, 'we are to see the last of the Sullivans. They have been a fine family, and there is a brave gathering anyway of them that would be present at the end. 'Twas said the agent was coming himself. May the Devil have the sowl of him!'

'A sore sight will the like of him be this day,' said a young McSweeney, 'and unless I brought a regiment of red-coats with me, I'd be careful how I showed myself among the lads, till the anger is out of them. What would he be here at all for, and he to drive the widow and the orphan from under the roof that sheltered them?'

'What says Mr. Sylvester to it?' the O'Donoghoe said, turning to an elderly man, whose boots and leggings, spattered with mud, showed that he had ridden fast and far to be in time for the ceremony. 'Will the boys fight, think you, Sylvester?'

'Fight is it?' answered the person appealed to, whose acquaintance the reader has already made at Nantes. 'And what would they be fighting for? Sure, the Earl is master, to do as he likes, and the King's Majesty, God bless him! stands at the Earl's back with the red-coats; only they do say a—'

'What do they say?' enquired the O'Donoghoe, to whom such effusive loyalty seemed too warm to be entirely sincere.

Sylvester did not care to finish his sentence, but another gentleman in the party finished it for him: 'It was rumoured in Kenmare last night,' he said, 'that the Earl in London was sinking, and that my Lord Fitzmaurice would have a word to say before this work went forward.'

A CHIEFTAIN IS BURIED

The conversation was cut short by a long, low cry which arose in front of the house, and a summons of the horsemen to their ranks.

The cart was already in motion, rounding the rock before the door, and two strings of women, one on either side of it, were chanting the dirge for the dead, their voices rising and falling like the notes of an Æolian harp, now hushed and low, now rushing up the scale into a scream of passionate despair. Immediately behind the cart rode the priest and the young lad who was so soon to be disinherited; after them followed the mounted gentry. In the rear, as the cart advanced, the particoloured crowd formed into a line which seemed interminable, Macfinnan Dhu being far on his way to his resting-place before the last of the mourners was clear of the grounds.

The road, after leaving the domain, followed the turns of the shore, amidst heather and bare rocks. From the point of a crag in the wood behind the house the whole train could be seen from end to end, winding its mournful way, while the cries of the keeners became fainter in the distance, swaying fitfully on the autumn wind. A string of boats accompanied the procession on the water, while others were seen streaming in from the sea. A large vessel of unusual rig and striking appearance lay in a cove at the harbour mouth. She had a French flag flying half-mast high, and a galley and a long-boat full of men were observed to leave her and pull in to the land under the church.

The women ceased to wail when the coffin reached the sacred ground. The priest put on his vestments and chanted the office for the dead, the multitude clustering silently under the broken tower of the desolate building, among the bones, buried and unburied, of vanished generations of men. One side of the iron rail which protected the vault of the Derreen family had been removed. The massive flagstone had been lifted off, and in the dark space below a dozen coffins were seen, side by side, mouldering into dust. All that remained of Macfinnan Dhu was passed down among the silent company. The priest pronounced his last blessing.

The crowd resolved itself into groups, which gathered over

the churchyard, each knot forming round some grassy mound, and bewailing afresh the kinsman that lay below. The gentry remounted their horses to return to the house, where there was to be a final feast before they departed to their homes, not, however, without throwing surprised and anxious glances at the party who had landed from the vessel, and had stood in a group by themselves during the ceremony.

These were a dozen seamen dressed like a crew of a man-of-war, and two officers with them in the French Naval uniform. The elder, and evidently the superior, was a short, alert, sinewy-looking man, in the full vigour of life, swarthy and sunburnt, with a foreign air and manner; the other several years younger, was tall, light and active, with a bright Irish face, curling chestnut hair, and laughing, humorous mouth. They were known, apparently, to more than one gentleman present, who lifted his hat in recognition, but they seemed to avoid immediate observation.

Dismissing their men, they left the burying-ground alone, and were presently joined by Sylvester O'Sullivan, who appeared to have some important communication to make to them. He had some scroll or letter in his hand, the contents of which—for it was sealed—he was describing to them. The spot where they were talking commanded a view of the mountain pass through which the road from Kenmare descended into the valley. Before they had concluded their conversation, a party of horsemen were seen coming down over the brow, and picking their way among the rents and holes which had been torn out of the track by the watercourses. Sylvester touched the elder officer's arm, and pointed to them with his finger. The officer nodded, and gave a brief direction to his companion, who sprang like a greyhound over the wall by which they were standing, and bounded down the grassy slope which led to the shore.

Chapter X

THE EARL'S AGENT

THE riders who had been seen descending the mountain road into the Valley of Kilmakilloge had reached the level ground at the bottom of the hill before they perceived the vastness of the concourse which the funeral had brought together. The agent had anticipated that the assembly would be large. Macfinnan Dhu's personal friends would be there, and the inferior gentry of the county might, perhaps wish to show respect to his memory. Among many of these the old chief had not been particularly popular. In his younger days he had been a fire-eater, and had been in many a quarrel which had left a feud behind it. Belonging, as he did, to the old blood, Macfinnan had held in small respect the Protestant adventurers who had passed into occupation of the land. But all scores were cleared by death; and the agent hoped that he might find a good many of them present, to whom he would have an opportunity of explaining publicly Lord Shelbourne's intentions.

He meant to take the occasion to impress upon them the precariousness of their own situation. They held their properties only as representatives of the English conquest. They were surrounded by a population who, however humble they might affect to be, regarded them as robbers and intruders, and were on the watch always for an opportunity of destroying them. In the event of an insurrection they would be themselves the first victims, and he meant to make them see that the presence of a thriving Protestant settlement at the most exposed and dangerous point upon the coast might be the surest safeguard to the whole of them.

These expectations were not encouraged by the aspect of the harbour and the valley. Irish nationalism was evidently

73

represented there in extraordinary force. There had been no design to remove Macfinnan Dhu's household till provision could be made for them elsewhere; but formal possession was to be taken of the premises and half-a-dozen men had been seen sent down by water from Kenmare for the purpose, who were to meet the agent on his arrival. It seemed doubtful whether, coming on such an errand, these persons could venture to approach the house in the face of such a display.

The agent's own party consisted of about twenty horsemen. There was a young Herbert from Killarney, a Mr. Denny from Tralee, a Blennerhassett, a son of Sir Maurice Crosbie, an Orton, and Colonel Goring, who had joined them at Kenmare. They wore their swords, Goring only excepted, according to the custom of the time, and each had a couple of servants behind him with pistols at their holsters, and musketoons slung at their backs. Colonel Goring was unattended and unarmed. His life had been often threatened—more than once he had been shot at, but he usually went about his business in the wildest parts of the country with no more defence than a walking stick. To carry pistols, he said, was to be tempted to use them, and might rather increase than diminish any danger that there was.

The agent, as the scene broke upon him, pulled up his horse and looked anxious and uncertain. Disagreeable surprise was written on the faces of the rest. Goring only appeared able to enjoy the brightness of the picture, the play of colours as the women's dresses shone blue and crimson over bay and shore, the hundred boats moving to and fro about the harbour, and the stir of animated excitement in a spot so silent and secluded.

'We'll find a warmer entertainment at the house than we looked for, Colonel,' said the agent to him, after a pause of three or four minutes. 'Rather warmth than welcome, so far as I can see. Better, perhaps, if we had waited for another day. I am not sure but what we should turn back. It is never wise to disturb a hornet's nest, and it is my belief that is what we should be doing if we went on. My lord will not be pleased if he hears that there has been trouble.'

'Turn back!' said Goring. 'Why, sir, they have seen you

coming, and all the country side will be set laughing at you. If you want respect from an Irishman, the worst thing you can do is to turn your back upon him.'

'You are a soldier, Colonel, and you think it is enough to command and to be obeyed. There are plenty in Ireland willing to command, but devil a one I know of that is willing to obey.'

'There is one law over all,' said Goring, 'and that is God Almighty's law. When you find out what His will is, and try to do it, things will begin to go well with you, and not till then, in my judgment.'

'What is the use of your talking like a preacher, Colonel?' answered the agent querulously. 'Sure, we all know that, but the law ye spake of is mighty hard to discover. The praste in the Chapel says it is one thing, and the parson in the Church says it is something else, and it is not clear to me that either the one or the other know what they are talking about. The Parliament is quarest of all, for they make laws for the honour of God, as they call it, and if the magistrate tries to put the laws in practice, it will be the worse for him, as yourself knows, Colonel, if ye would speak the truth.'

'By Heaven,' said Dick Crosbie, as his companions called him, 'I wish they would do one thing or the other—either execute the laws or else repeal them. Carry out the Popery Acts; in thirty years there will be neither priest nor Papist in the land, and the Protestants and the English can do as they will. Repeal the Acts and we'll be all friends together. As it stands, ye get all the ill-will for the making such laws, and ye lose the good they might do you if you put them in force.'

'You are wrong again there,' replied the agent. 'The Popery Acts are like the curb you have got on your second bridle there. By the same token it is not long ye'd remain without it on the back of the mare you are riding, for a vicious beast she is, or I know nothing of horseflesh. When the devil is not in her you can ride her easy on the snaffle, and let the curb hang till ye want it. But unless she knew it was in her mouth, Dick, she would have you off with your back on the ground before ye had time to ask where ye were. Let the people talk as they will, they understand that the Acts are in the Statute-book, and can be found there when we want them. Half the head tenants on the estate are Catholics at heart, and Catholics in practice, too, for they go to mass and have no fear of it. When they sign their leases I ask no questions that, maybe, they would not like to answer. If I chose to do it I might make them swear away their souls at the quarter sessions, but I look through my fingers, and they are careful how far they go, and so we get on together without quarrelling.'

'And this,' said Goring scornfully, 'is what you call governing Ireland, hanging up your law like a scarecrow in the garden till every sparrow has learnt to make a jest of it. You let the people laugh at it, and in teaching them to despise one law, you teach them to despise all laws—God's and man's alike.'

'You may think so, Colonel,' observed Mr. Herbert, a polished gentlemanlike man, who represented the county in the Irish Parliament, 'but, as our friend says, you do not understand Ireland. These are not the days of Oliver Cromwell. We cannot ride the high Protestant horse in this century, and God forbid we should. If wars or rebellion come we must be severe again; there will be no help for it; and war I suppose there soon will be if it has not broken out already; but as long as peace continues, gentleness is the only way.'

All this time they had been walking their horses slowly forward, the agent still doubting whether it would not be wiser to postpone his visit, when, by turning a corner, they came in sight of the mouth of the harbour, which had hitherto been concealed, and for the first time became conscious of the presence of the strange vessel. They halted again, this time all with a spontaneous start, for many years had passed since any such craft as this had been seen or heard of in the Kenmare River.

A landsman's eye could perceive that he had no ordinary trader before him, which had just put in from stress of weather or in want of necessaries. The immense spars, the tautly set up rigging and the unusual character of it, the many boats and the general smartness of her style, implied a crew too large for a peaceful merchantman. Though she was a mile distant, they thought they could see the gleaming of her polished guns. With what object could a French cruiser be anchored in these quiet waters?

Goring only had any key to the mystery. There had been no official declaration of war; but he had received recent notice that French privateers had been seen outside the channel; he had been directed particularly to look out for one which had come recently out of the Loire. Her destination was not known, but it was supposed she might be connected with some intended enterprise in Ireland, and a general warning had been sent to all the stations round the coast to be on the watch.

Goring could hardly doubt that the vessel which was lying quietly in Kilmakilloge harbour was the very one which had caused so much alarm. What could have induced her to venture so far up the estuary, and to have anchored so publicly and so conspicuously, was a mystery, but a mystery into which his office made it his duty to enquire.

Irish gentlemen are never wanting in courage. Lenient as they might be with the smuggling trade, they drew a sharp distinction between commercial irregularities and treasonable dealings with a foreign enemy. A French landing would imply a fresh civil war and a fresh fight for their lives. The agent calculated that among the Catholics who would be attending the funeral, few, if any, would be armed; for the law was strict in this respect, and they were shy of openly breaking it. The Protestant squireens would probably have their swords and pistols, and if there was to be a difficulty with the crew of the privateer, he believed that he could rely on them. At any rate, he was now determined to push forward and see what it all meant.

'We are taken by surprise, gentlemen,' he said. 'The extraordinary gathering here to-day has a further purpose in it than we know, and the coming in of this piratical stranger is in some way connected with it. There may be danger both to you and to me, but our duty is plain and I depend on you to stand by me. Look to the priming of your pistols, and we will ride forward.'

Chapter XI

THE DUEL

THE house at Derreen stood in an open space in the middle of the wood. The drive by which it was approached was a quarter of a mile long, and at the gate where it left the road was the invariable lodge which stood at the entrance of every Irish domain. The windows had been long broken, and were stuffed with rags. The thatch had disappeared from the roof, and the heather which had been laid on instead of it, was held in its place by stones and clumps of turf. The door was open, and there was no one to be seen, everybody who could walk being at the mansion. Two huge hungry pigs were in possession of the kitchen, and were routing about a cradle in which was a deserted baby. As the agent and his party rode past, Goring sprang from his horse, drove them out with his whip, and gave sixpence to a girl who was going by to watch the child till the parents returned. He mounted quickly again, and they went on.

The people coming back from the funeral were streaming up the drive. The greater part of them had already arrived, and were spread in all directions under the trees. It was like a race day at the Curragh. Boys were holding horses, or leading them round to the stables behind the house. The riders in their long coats and boots, with heavy hunting whips in their hands, were talking eagerly in excited knots. A rough tent or booth had been erected on the lawn, where the crowd were supplied with unlimited whiskey. But either the drink had not yet taken effect, or some other cause was keeping the people quiet. There was little merriment, not even a quarrel or, so far, a broken head.

An uneasy sense of expectation appeared to be sitting heavy on the whole assembly, as if some serious business or other had still to be transacted before the fun could begin. One small

group, which was conversing apart from the rest, drew particular attention. It consisted of young Mick Sullivan, a gentle-
looking lad, whose succession was threatened with extinction,
his cousin Sylvester, and the two officers in French uniform
who had been seen in the churchyard, and had landed from
the vessel in the harbour.

The agent and his friends were received as they rode up with
stern silence. When it became known who the new arrivals
were, there rose a sullen murmur like the moaning of the sea
before a storm. That any active resistance was deliberately contemplated to so formidable a person as Lord Shelbourne's
representative was not likely if it was possible; but the Irish
temper was inflammable, and there was no mistaking the
resentment with which the supposed purpose of his coming
was regarded.

The gentlemen alighted and gave their horses to their
servants, but yard and stables were already full. No disposition
was shown to take the horses in, and they were left standing
where they could find room. After an embarrassed pause of a
minute or two, young Mick—on whom the duty fell of receiving visitors at the house—came forward with a cold welcome.
The agent was excited and awkward.

'Mr. O'Sullivan,' he said, 'I am sorry to have arrived too late
to pay my last respects to the memory of your father. The estate
has lost the oldest of its tenants. It was my duty, it was my
personal wish, to attend when he was committed to the grave.
Business unfortunately detained me at Kenmare, but I am in
time to repeat in person the communication which has been
already submitted to you in writing, and which will have set
your mind at rest at to your future comfort. The earl's intentions towards you are of the most liberal kind, and your
removal from this place, whenever it takes effect, will be an
improvement in your station and fortune—nay, will be a subject of congratulation to yourself and to all who wish you well.
You have, I suppose, considered the paper which has been
submitted to you?'

The agent spoke firmly, though his voice shook a little, for
the dense knot of people who had crowded to hear him and

the intensity in the expression of their faces tried his nerves.

'Indeed,' answered the youth, blushing and hesitating, 'his lordship's orders have been left within, but your honour knows one can lose a father only once in this world, and it is a loss when it comes that puts other thoughts out of the mind. If ye will say your will I'll be ready to hear ye.'

'Speak up, man,' said a voice behind him. 'Don't be down-hearted. Speak up to his honour. Sure ye are among your own kin and there is none can hurt ye.'

'No one,' said the agent, 'means less hurt either to my young friend here or to any gentleman present than the Earl of Shelbourne, in whose name I am here this day. For forty years, as you well know, his lordship has left the old families on the land from Tuosist to Iveragh, and yourselves can say whether distress for rent has been ever heard of among you for all that time. Good friends we have always been and good friends I hope we shall remain.'

'The blessing of God be on you for that word,' said Mick gathering up his courage. 'If the deed and the word answer one to the other we'll have no more to ask. It is true for you, sir, my father was never distressed for the rent, for the rent, as your honour can tell, was always paid to the day. And what for now would the Earl be putting us out, as your paper speaks of, from the home where we were born and our posterity behind us?'

'My good fellow,' said the agent, a little pettishly, 'your posterity shall prosper after you, and you shall prosper too, if the Earl and I can help you, and how can you speak of your being put out when ye shall have the best farm in County Meath in exchange for the bogs and rocks of Kilmakilloge?'

'His lordship is mighty kind, and we are greatly obliged to him,' answered the youth. 'But the rocks and bogs ye spake of are where my fathers have reigned for a thousand years and more. Here we have lived. Here, if it please your honour and his lordship, we would like to remain undisturbed, and if ye will just lave us alone it is all that we will desire of ye.'

The audience hummed approval. 'Bravo Mick,' half a dozen voices shouted. 'That is the truth, if the Divil spoke it.' The

THE DUEL

agent feeling that, so far, he had made no progress, stepped boldly to the top of the rock and addressed them all.

'Gentlemen,' he said, 'we all know, for we are never tired of repeating it, that the Irish are the finest race under the sun. That is your opinion, and it is my own too, for Ireland is as much my country as it is yours. We also know, or if we do not, 'twere well we should, that under the sun there is no country where the inhabitants live more wretchedly, or where the soil is worked to poorer profit. This valley is now as barren as the rest, yet it has not been always barren, as some of you may perhaps remember. Time was, when copper was brought here to be smelted in thousands of tons. You may see to-day the channels which brought the streams to the water mills. You may see the pyramids of cinders left behind by the furnaces. Time was when there were a dozen boat-yards at Buna, and a hundred fishing boats, made and manned on the estate, brought cod and ling from Scariff, and turbot and soles from Ballinskelligs. On Colorus yonder stand the ruins of the fish houses, where the herrings were salted and dried, and were carried to all lands. There was industry, there was plenty, in the days of the Earl's father; and the Earl that now is would bring the good times back again. The land is his, and you are his children, whom God has given him. You desired to be left to yourselves. He consented, and you see what has come of it.

'Once more, therefore, he will put his own shoulder to the wheel. He will give you back a prosperity which you cannot create for yourselves. He will send again trained workmen of his own, and for every stranger that is brought among you, there will be work and wages for half-a-dozen of yourselves. These are his Lordship's intentions by you, and if you will do your part as he will do his, there will be a new world in Kerry from this day.'

The crowd listened, but they listened, most of them, with a half good-humoured contempt, the rest in sulky silence.

'Is it the old times he'd bring back again?' cried a wrinkled, weather-beaten old woman, who sat crooning on the step before the door. 'I mind those times. That was when the Protestant Saxons were here, the Divil mend them, who believed

81

neither in Saint nor Spirit, nor the Blessed Virgin herself. We were Papist dogs then, and lucky we used to think ourselves if they flung us an old bone to crunch. And what was the end of them? The storm came off the mountains, and the Divil came along with it, and carried them all away, thim and their boats and their money. Will ye fly in the face of God that made ye, and set up the like of them again?'

' 'Tis well seen, your honour,' said a decent-looking man, 'that each people in this world like its own ways, and little is the good that comes from forcing them. The English, don't we know it, are mighty and powerful; but we'd be better pleased if they would keep to their own island, and leave us to ourselves. We don't want any more Protestants down here, at all, at all.'

Mick had spoken no more, but someone whispered a word in his ear; he roused himself, and said:

'Your honour has not precisely told us what you are now purposing to do, and, barring the respect for my father, for which I thank you, we don't yet know exactly for what purpose you are here this day. But I'd be sorry ye should be without the hospitality of the house, and I'd ask ye to dine with us, if ye mean as well as ye say ye do.'

'There should be do doubt of that,' answered the agent, cheerfully. 'We have had a long ride, and we will take your offer and thank you. If ye'd order a feed for our horses, they would be none the worse for it, for there they stand, poor things. Good friends I hope we will always be, Mr. O'Sullivan, and as to my purpose this day, have no fear that I'd be disturbing you. You will stay where you are, and welcome, till we have a better place ready to receive you. The Earl's orders were that nothing was to be done hard or hasty.'

A blank pause followed this announcement, interrupted only by the sobs and cries of some of the women. In the midst of the general uncertainty, Sylvester O'Sullivan, who had kept, hitherto, in the background, now shuffled forward, with the abject manner under which he knew so well how to conceal his real feeling.

'Your honour will not mistake the poor boy,' he said. 'It is proud we are to see you yourself and the other gentlemen that are with you; and we are grateful for your kind intentions. The errand you are come upon might have been softed in our ears, if it had so pleased your honour and his lordship—but the Earl knows best, and when he gives his commands we are to obey. Sure it is distinction enough, and well we know it, for the like of us to live under his lordship's rule, and a good lord he has been to us these many years, the Saints be praised! If he is maning now to take the domain into his own hands, we have heard you tell us how all is intinded for our good.'

He drew back, as if he had no more to say—then, as if recollecting something he had forgotten:

'I have a bit of paper,' he said; 'it had like to have escaped me, which I was to give into your honour's own hand—maybe ye will cast your eye an it before ye lave your final orders with us.'

Notwithstanding Sylvester's affected humility, the agent thought he detected something insolent in his manner. The 'bit of paper' he supposed to contain one of the innumerable petitions which were thrust upon him when he went his rounds on the estate. He waited impatiently while the old man fumbled in his pocket. He was not a little surprised when it proved to be a letter, formally addressed to himself, and sealed with a coroneted coat of arms. He broke it hastily open, glanced over the few lines which it contained, and looked again at the seal with combined incredulity and uneasiness.

'How came you by this, Mr. Sylvester?' he said sternly. 'My Lord Fitzmaurice has employed a singular messenger. The date is yesterday. Do you know the contents of this letter?'

'Your honour, I was at Killarney last night, on a little business of my own,' Sylvester answered, 'and I thought I would just look round upon my lord, in the Castle, to learn if he had any commands. I tould him I'd maybe see your honour at Kilmakilloge this day—so he just wrote what you hold in your hand, and he sealed it up; and I rode back with it over the mountains to Sneem, in the early morning, to be in time for the boys that were coming to the funeral, to bring me across the water. 'Twas making haste I was, for fear I'd be disappointing you.'

'Gentlemen,' said the agent to his own immediate companions, and taking no notice of the malice of Sylvester's last words, 'Do any of you know Lord Fitzmaurice's hand? You, Mr. Herbert, must be familiar with it. With you, Colonel Goring, I know that he has communicated more than once. Look at this, and tell me whose it is?'

'The writing is Lord Fitzmaurice's, there cannot be a doubt of it,' they both said, without the slightest hesitation.

'Then, gentlemen,' said the agent, 'I will read the letter aloud. It concerns every one present, almost as much as it concerns myself.

' "The Earl of Shelbourne died in London four days ago. You will leave young Macfinnan in possession of Derreen till you hear further from me."

'Those are the words which are here written. How the Earl could have died four days since, in England, and the news be known yesterday at Killarney, remains unexplained. I had a letter from the Earl himself yesterday morning. It was dated a fortnight back and at that time he was in good health.'

'There was a whispering in the town,' said Sylvester, with an air of absolute innocence, 'that a pigeon had come over with a note at the leg of it, and that my lord was now King of Kerry; but it was no business of mine, and sure I thought his lordship would have told me anything it was fit I should know.'

'There can be no question that this is his lordship's hand and seal,' the agent declared. 'I can myself swear to it. And this being so, our business here, for the day, is ended. Macfinnan,' he went on, calling Mick, for the first time, by his title, and shaking him by the hand, 'if this news proves true, I give you my hearty congratulations. My Lord Fitzmaurice is a good friend to the old blood—for it runs in his own veins—and if it pleases him to continue me in the charge of this estate, you and I will have no quarrels, depend on that. I never yet, of my own will, disturbed a tenant—lease or no lease—and, with God's help, I never will. We will just drink your health in a glass of your father's claret, and leave you to your sorrow and your joy.'

84

THE DUEL

The good news flew over the ground from lip to lip. 'The ould Earl is dead—Glory be to God! The old Earl's out, and the new Earl is in. Long life to him, and long may he reign; for it is a good beginning that he has made with it. The last is gone of the English blood, and long may it be before another comes to trouble us. Fitzmaurice comes of the Geraldines —God bless him! He is the boy that will keep the Protestants off the backs of us, and the bailiffs and the revenue lads—bad cess to the whole of them!'

To the immense multitude the news that Macfinnan was to remain gave boundless delight, and even to the gentlemen who had come with the agent it was a relief, though they had been prepared to support him had it been necessary.

To Colonel Goring the defeat of his hopes was naturally a severe disappointment; but he was a man who had schooled himself to take Fortune's buffets and rewards with equal thanks. He could still do his own duty, and Providence would shape the issue. Meanwhile, another object required his immediate consideration. He had not forgotten the mysterious vessel in the harbour or his own obligation to enquire into her character. The news of Lord Shelbourne's death might have driven the recollection of her out of the mind of the agent. Goring's direct duty was to learn what she was.

The two officers who had been in the ring surrounding the young O'Sullivan evidently belonged to her, and in one of them he had no difficulty in recognizing the person whom he had met on the mountain above Glenbeg. Indeed, the man so little tried to conceal his identity that when he saw Colonel Goring's eye rest upon him, he seemed rather amused than alarmed, and replied with an ironical smile. It was to his companion however, that the Colonel's attention was directed most anxiously. He was sure that he had seen him somewhere, and after struggling with his recollections, he satisfied himself that the officer before him was no other than the Morty Sullivan who had been his prisoner with Sir Edward Sheridan after Culloden, who had escaped, and had made his way on board the Nantes brig which was waiting on the coast. O'Sullivan's name had been proclaimed, and a reward offered for his capture, dead or alive. He was known to have fought at Fontenoy before the expedition to Scotland, and to have been afterwards with the Prince at Paris. His name had been mentioned in connection with the privateer which Colonel Goring had been warned to look out for. In an instant the whole situation explained itself. Without hesitation he walked directly up to where Morty was standing.

'We have met before, Mr. O'Sullivan,' he said. 'I do not easily forget a face.'

'No one asked you to forget it, Colonel Goring, for that, I believe, is your name. If you have any doubt, you may look again. It will not be turned away from you.'

The sharp challenge and the prompt reply startled everyone. The move towards the house was arrested, and all stopped to know what next was coming. To most of the party present Morty was personally unknown, while Goring, if he was disliked, was feared and respected.

'Gentlemen,' Goring said, 'I must call for your assistance in the name of the law. The person whom you see before you is a proclaimed rebel, with a price on his head. He was with the Pretender in Scotland, was captured, and for a few hours was under my own charge. The strange vessel in the harbour I believe to be the privateer which I have been ordered by the Government to look out for. I suppose him to be her captain. I arrest him, and I require you all, on your allegiance, to prevent his escape.'

Ready as they were to throw difficulties in the way of the law when it merely interfered with the general license, the Irish squires were careful how they meddled in defence of criminals of a more serious kind. As long as it was a question of a duel, or a faction fight, or frauds on the revenue, or of informations under the Popery Acts, the Imperial authority interfered as rarely as possible. But a sharp line was drawn at rebellion. Those who were rash enough to take arms against the Crown, or were discovered to have been involved, however secretly, in any treasonable correspondence, were instantly crushed.

Morty, seeing them uncertain, sprang to the top of a rise in the ground.

'Arrest me! will you?' he said. 'Arrest me! that you may set my head on your Temple Bar, beside Kilmarnock's and Balmerino's. Then I must send for them who will put in bail for me!'

With a silver whistle which hung by a cord about his neck, he thrice blew a sharp, shrill call, and out of the wood on all sides there rushed out bodies of seamen, armed to the teeth with cutlass, dirk and pistol. They were under command of a third officer, seemingly French, who had the air of a gentleman.

'Go, Connell,' Morty said to his young companion, who was still at his side. 'Go, help de Chaumont to hold those blood-hounds in the leash, or we shall have the place turned into a shambles in a moment. You see those men,' he said, looking full at Goring, the agent and the rest. 'You see those men, what they are, and how many they are. Let but one of you lift a hand to touch me, and the soil you stand on shall run with blood, and not one of you shall leave these grounds alive. Privateer! Yes, I am that privateer, or sea rover, of whom you have heard something and may feel more if you choose to try. I am a French subject. To England I owe no allegiance, England has stripped me of my house and my lands, and while I live I will do what lies in my single arm on land or sea to pay back my debt. I am here to be present at the burial of my kinsman. I will go hence as I came. Meddle with me now, if you dare!'

Seeing themselves surrounded by sixty or seventy armed ruffians, and well aware that if there was any fighting the peasantry would take Morty's side, the gentlemen concluded that they would be held excused to the authorities for declin-ing an unequal struggle and taking him at his word. Goring himself saw that it would be useless to persist in the arrest.

'You have taken us by surprise, Captain Sullivan,' he said, 'and you have our lives in your hands if you please to murder us. I tell you none the less, and to your face, and in the face of these villains of yours, who, if any doubt remained, are evid-ence enough of your real character, that you are a rebel, a pirate, a murderer for all that I know—you have forfeited your life to the law as a felon, and you will come to a felon's end.'

'Whisht, man,' whispered the agent, aghast at Goring's words. 'Are ye mad that ye spake so? Will you have us all murdered? Sure if it's the divil himself ye will lose nothing by keeping a civil tongue in your head.'

Indeed it seemed as if Goring was wilfully provoking his fate. Morty bit his lips till the blood ran. Luckily, not many of his men knew English or understood what had been said, but they saw that their Captain had been insulted. They drew their cutlasses and unslung their musketoons. At a word from him, a shower of balls would have been their answer to Goring's threat. But it was Morty's object to avoid a quarrel with the gentry, many of whom in their hearts wished him well.

'Gentlemen,' he said, reining in his passion, and forcing himself to speak calmly. 'Colonel Goring tells me that I am a pirate, and that my life is forfeited. I will give him a chance to take it. For what I am, and for what that vessel is which I have the honour to command, I have no answer to give. I will answer, if called on, to my sovereign, King Louis of France, and to no other. But if Colonel Goring desires to know what has brought me back to these shores, when France and Spain offered me rank in their armies, and with them I could have fought in honourable service against our hereditary enemy, I will tell him that he is himself the reason. My quarrel is with him. Let us end it, and then if my presence on this coast is a danger to the rest of you, I will go; and you shall hear of me no more.

'It is not, sir,' he went on, turning direct to the Colonel: 'It is not that you would have murdered myself and my friend after Culloden. You were then but one of the myrmidons of the Butcher Cumberland. What you did was by his orders, and I do not hold the slave responsible for his master's brutalities. It is not that you are the so-called owner of the land of my fathers, in possession of my own Castle at Dunboy, which they defended till every stone which was battered down by Carew's cannon was paid for by an English life. But you have done worse. Like a coward as you are, you have made war on weak women: my mother, who, if all had their rights, would have reigned as a queen in these glens and mountains, my sister left a widow with her child, you drove them out both from the poor refuge which had been left to them in the Castle at Dursey. My sister, who was gently nurtured, has found shelter among kindly but rude seamen, in a cabin where you would not keep your own riding horse. My mother is dead. Her blood is on your hands, Colonel Goring, and I call you to account for it.'

Morty had not calculated without reason on the effect of such a speech upon the listeners who were hanging upon his lips. Colonel Goring was unpopular. He had come into the country as a stranger and an Englishman. The zeal with which he had discharged his office had made him more enemies than friends. With his Protestant enthusiasm there was no sympathy at all, and he was believed universally to have prompted the late Earl of Shelbourne in his intended measures at Kilmakilloge. He was conscious at the moment that he had not a single well-wisher on the ground, and that he must fight his own battle. He was not disturbed. He listened gravely, but with unbroken composure.

'Captain Sullivan,' he replied, 'your own language justifies the words which I used to you. You do not deny your identity. You cannot shake off your allegiance by abjuring it. You do not pretend that you are not at this instant in arms against your lawful sovereign. I did not know when I removed them that the ladies in Dursey Island were relatives of yours. I am sorry, as a man, for what they suffered, but the connection, which I now hear of for the first time, shews me that my decision was a right one. The castle which they occupied was the depôt of the contraband trade of Bantry Bay. They themselves abused the courtesy which had been extended to them on account of their station and sex. It was impossible for me to allow them to remain there. I offered them a comfortable home in a quarter where they could not be dangerous. They refused to accept it. If Mrs. O'Sullivan had been contented to live quietly on the Island, she would have met with every consideration from me. But if she chose to connect herself with practices which I was bound to repress, I am not answerable.

THE TWO CHIEFS OF DUNBOY

I did but my duty, and I would do it again.'

'Not answerable!' cried Morty furiously. 'By the living God, but you shall be answerable! You fight with women, and you are afraid to stand up to a single man! I might shoot you there where you are and who would blame me for it? But I will take no advantage. Step out upon the grass, here where we stand, and meet me man to man; you have your own friends about you to see fair play. Stand out, I say! I came back, when I had never thought to see Ireland again, to call you to a reckoning, and I will have it of you, or I will know why. Are you a coward, man, as well as a villain, that you hesitate?'

'You and I have crossed swords once already,' replied Goring with entirely unruffled coolness, 'and you know best who turned his back on that occasion. If I hesitate, it is because I doubt whether, as holding the King's commission, I can honourably exchange shots as an equal with a proscribed outlaw.'

Universal as was the practice of duelling in Ireland in every rank but the lowest—and there, too, the change was only from sword and pistol to the blackthorn—the agent felt that he must put in an appearance of protest. That such a scene should take place on Lord Shelbourne's estate, under his own eye, and without objection raised, might easily cost him his place. He reflected, besides, that if Colonel Goring fell, he might be charged with having allowed a Government official to be assassinated by pirates; while, if it went the other way, Morty's comrades would probably avenge him by a general massacre.

The more he reflected, the less he liked the prospect. 'No, no,' he said to Goring. 'You shall not. It must not be.'

No one could be more conscious than Goring that to fight a duel under such circumstances was altogether unbecoming to a person in his position. Independently of the religious objections which he could not forget, his office, his rank in the Service, the stand which he had made and was making against the relaxed habits of Irish society, alike forbade him to risk his life in open conflict with a pirate and a rebel. But in Goring, too, original sin was not wholly eliminated, and Nature will have her way on some occasions, even with the wisest. Morty

Sullivan had insulted him beyond bearing. He felt, besides, that if he was thought to have flinched when thus openly challenged his influence in the South of Ireland would be gone for ever.

Misinterpreting the composure of Colonel Goring's manner, and supposing that he was yielding to the agent's interference, Morty tore off his glove. 'Let me quicken your resolution,' he said, and he flung it in his antagonist's face.

Goring caught the glove in his left hand, and tossed it gently back.

'It shall be as you please, Captain O'Sullivan,' he said, 'and no time can be better than the present. Macfinnan will lend us his father's pistols. They have done duty on similar occasions, and may serve for this. Gentlemen,' he said to Herbert and Crosbie, 'you will kindly act for me on this occasion. See the pistols loaded and the ground measured.'

Never had there been such wild delight in the domain at Derreen, as was expressed by the crowd now assembled there, at the news that there was to be a duel. What bull-fighting is in Spain, what prize-fighting has been in England, that duelling was in the last century in the sister Island. It was the passion and delight of all orders, high and low. Men fought for something or for nothing, for honour, for revenge, or for the mere enjoyment of the sensation. They met, not in glens or woods, or solitary glades, but in the most public places which they could find, under the world's eye, where every one who pleased might attend. On the present occasion the flavour was the more exciting because the fight was to be on the old-established lines of quarrel between England and Ireland. Goring was the representative of the Conquest and of English authority. Morty Sullivan was a Southern Celt of purest breed, the lawful heir of Dunboy, if right was done him, in the eyes of almost all of the spectators of the scene.

The agent's alarm that if their captain fell the privateer's crew might become ungovernable was not unfelt by Morty himself. He had no expectation that the duel could have any such result. He could split a bullet on a pen-knife with his left hand, or snuff a candle at twenty paces without extinguish-

ing it. He intended to kill Goring, and was perfectly confident
that he was going to do it. But his honour required that the
meeting should not be misrepresented to the world. He would
not have it said that he had shot his enemy in the midst of a
circle of his own followers.

'De Chaumont,' he said, calling the young French officer who
had brought them up through the wood, 'march your men
down to the boats and keep them there till I join you. Connell
will stay with me. Gentlemen,' he went on, addressing two of
the visitors who, as experienced in such things, had volunteered
to be his seconds, 'I am in your hands. Twelve paces or six—
across a handkerchief if you prefer it? Arrange as you will, only
be quick. We are wasting time.'

The preliminaries were soon adjusted. Twelve paces was the
usual distance, and twelve paces was at once agreed on. Goring's
seconds proposed that the principals should fire together at the
signal. Morty's seconds preferred that they should fire con-
secutively, and toss for the first shot. Goring, to whom the
question was referred, told them to settle it as they pleased,
and it was arranged as Morty's friends desired. The ground
chosen was a level strip of lawn under some tall elm trees in
front of the windows of the house. The sun, for it was late in
the afternoon, had set behind the wood. The air was still, the
light shaded and even. The spectators fell back on either side
and stood in two rows, leaving a space clear between them,
open at either end.

There was no lingering over unessential formalities, for
everyone was anxious to have the business over. The combatants took their places and their seconds brought them their
pistols. In an Irish house the duelling-pistols were always in
order, as the honour of the family depended on them. Macfinnan had cared for his as if they were his choicest jewels, and
new flints had been fitted on the instant it was known that
they would be in demand. Morty Sullivan snatched his with
passionate eagerness. Goring seemed as little disturbed as if he
were at a shooting match. He took no notice of his antagonist,
but examined his weapon with much deliberation. He felt the
spring of the lock, glanced at the rifling of the barrel, and then,

having apparently satisfied himself, waited for the result of the toss.

It fell to Morty. He was to fire first and at his own time after the handkerchief was dropped. The signal was given. He paused a second or two raised his pistol, took deliberate aim, and then let fall his arm again, and scanned his enemy's body as if considering where he could hit him with most certainty of fatal effect. Then he raised it again with a vicious smile on his lips. His eye fixed; his arm stiffened and became rigid as the stock of a crossbow. He drew the trigger, the hammer fell and the pistol missed fire.

Angrily he cocked it again, again pulled, this time without waiting, and again there was no result.

'There is something the matter with your flint, sir,' said Goring coolly. 'You had better let it be looked to.'

With an angry flush on his cheek Morty flung his weapon to his nearest second, who readjusted the flint and returned it to him.

He fired instantly, but Goring's calmness had disturbed his nerve. His arm shook. The ball, which was intended for his antagonist's brain, passed through his hat, cutting away a hair or two on the way, and left him untouched.

It was now Goring's turn. With the same composure as before he again examined his pistol, as if to assure himself that he could depend upon it. He then, for the first time since they had taken their places, looked steadily into Morty's face.

'Captain O'Sullivan,' he said, 'you required the satisfaction of shooting at me, and you have had it. It is not your fault that you missed me, for you were deliberate enough. I might now save the hangman trouble. But your life is forfeited; it belongs to your country, and to your country I shall leave you. Fire at you in return, I shall not; but that you may know and that all here may know that your life is mine at this moment if I please to take it, do you see yonder bough at the top of the furthest elm, with a single yellow leaf at its extremity? Mark that leaf.'

He, in turn, raised his arm and glanced swiftly along the barrel; a flash, a shot, and the leaf cut off at the stem by the ball, slowly fluttered to the ground.

'Give us other pistols. Load again,' cried Morty furiously: but even the Irish crowd who would have been well pleased to see Goring fall, could not refuse their admiration for his courage, his forbearance and his skill. There was a cry that enough had been done; the seconds on both sides interposed; they declared the affair was over and could go no further.

Chapter XII

A NIGHT ON THE MOUNTAIN

THE scene which had taken place at Derreen was so little an exception to the common incidents of Irish life, that it would have passed as an ordinary occurrence, but for Morty Sullivan's appearance in the *Doutelle*, and the audacious language in which he had boasted of his position and his character. The authorities in Dublin Castle desired to hear as little as they could help of local irregularities in the remote counties of Ireland, nor would there have been reason to fear that in the present case they would shew more curiosity had it not been for the critical relations at the moment between the Courts of St. James's and Versailles.

The presence on the coast, however, of an avowed pirate and outlaw might attract inconvenient attention, unless it could be in some degree extenuated. The agent might find himself in trouble if he could not anticipate the accounts of others. He therefore hastened back to Kenmare to prepare and send off a report on the instant. He could feel easy that Goring, being of a free and noble nature, would not colour the matter favourably for himself. He could give his own version with the more confidence, as he could be assured that what he said would be what the Castle would most wish to hear.

'An incident,' he said, 'had occurred at a place on Lord Shelbourne's estate of no serious consequence, but which he thought he ought to mention. A gentleman of ancient family, a tenant on the property, had died, and the funeral had been largely attended. A vessel under French colours had put into the harbour for the occasion. The commander was a relative of the deceased, and his object in coming in had been merely to pay respect to his kinsman. Colonel Goring, of Dunboy, happened to be present, and it appeared that the Captain of the vessel and Colonel Goring had met previously under unpleasant circumstances. They recognized each other on the grounds. They quarrelled, and in spite of his own efforts to keep the peace, they had exchanged shots in a duel. But no harm had come of it. The French vessel had no other business on the coast, and had departed already or would depart immediately. He had thought of detaining her, and of arresting the officers, but he had an insufficient force with him, and an attempt at capture would have been probably ineffectual, and would have led to serious bloodshed.'

So wrote Lord Shelbourne's agent, according to the fashion of the time.

Morty Sullivan was equally impatient to be gone. He was savage with the accident which had robbed him of his revenge; savage with himself for having lost his nerve and having failed to repair it; savage above all with the man who had crossed his path so often, and always to get the better of him, and had now insulted him with his contempt.

He had the cargo of arms to put on shore, but an attempt to land them at Kilmakilloge in the midst of so much excitement and such a concourse of people, would be a public act of defiance, and might provoke and even cause a military occupation of the district. He decided therefore to land the chests two nights later at a spot at Glengariff, familiar to the local smugglers, to leave de Chaumont on shore to arrange for the reception and distribution of them, and himself meanwhile to stand off to the open sea as if finally taking his departure from the coast.

The festivities at Derreen were thus over at an early hour. The chief guests having taken their leave, the rest broke up before nightfall and went to their various homes, the wild cries from the scattered or scattering parties echoing among the glens in the twilight.

The friends with whom Colonel Goring had ridden down had left him. He had to make his way to Dunboy alone, and he felt that he could not be too quick about it. Of his encounter with Morty, so far as he had been himself in peril, he thought no more than if his horse had fallen, or if he had met with any other accident from which no ill had followed. But of the *Doutelle* and of Morty's presence on the coast he thought much and long. He must send instant notice to headquarters, and he must prepare his own station for a possible attack.

There were two roads from Tuosist to Dunboy, one a horse track, long and circuitous, by Ardgroom and Eyris, the other a foot track up the hollow of Glanmore, and thence direct over the mountains. This was the nearest way by several miles; but the whole country side had been set in motion by the funeral; many hundreds of people who had come from the side of Bantry Bay would be going home by this route. The O'Sullivans, who would be the largest part, bore Goring no good-will at any time, and would be in worse temper with him than ever after his treatment of their chief. Brave as he was, he did not care to expose himself unnecessarily. He decided that he would take the longest road, where he would least be looked for, but that he would leave his horse with a farmer whom he could depend upon, and would trust to his feet. He would thus be less liable to observation, and if attacked he could take to the mountains.

The day closed before he had disposed of his steed and had finished a hasty dinner on rye bread with a slice of salmon from the river. The evening was still warm and starlight. The moon would rise at midnight, but he hoped to have reached his home by that time, and so not to need it.

He set out briskly. The road for the first two miles led along the shore of the harbour. As he passed the mouth, he saw the white sails of the *Doutelle* as she drifted down the river with the tide. The boats had vanished, only far off could be heard the faint splash of oars, or voices calling across the water. When he had walked sharply for half-an-hour, the road struck inland, on a spur of the great mountain range which divides Glanmore from Ardgroom. In the entire solitude, and in the absence of any sign of other travellers besides himself being abroad, his pace gradually slackened, and his thoughts wandered through the incidents of the afternoon to the condition of a country where such incidents were possible.

Here had been an assembly of gentlemen of the county, the

representatives of English authority, collected together. An outlawed rebel had appeared in the middle of them, and instead of any attempt being made to arrest the man, he had himself been compelled, by popular sentiment, under penalty of forfeiting the esteem of his neighbours, to stand out and let the fellow shoot at him. So absurd it was that he laughed aloud at the thought of it. What sort of a country could it be where wrong was right, and evil good, and unreason reason? What extraordinary destiny condemned to failure every effort that was made to improve it?

Thus meditating, he had ascended a steep slope on the side of the mountain, and had come out upon a stretch of level ground, through the centre of which the road ran for a quarter of a mile and then descended into the valley beyond. On his left rose a precipitous wall of rocks which, in the gathering darkness, for clouds had spread on the sky, seemed as if they would defy the skilfullest climber to scale. On the right was a wide and treacherous peat-moss, which, even in daylight, it was unsafe to cross. In the distance was the pale glimmer of the sea, where the stars were still shining, and directly in the middle of the open space before him, showing black against the background of water and sky, were three massive stones, one upright, one leaning against it, and a third lying on the ground. They marked the spot where tradition said some old King of Kerry had fought his last battle, won his last victory, and had there been laid in the grave. Few persons cared to pass that way after nightfall; for in those days elf and fairy had not yet taken their leave, and the waywardest of these tricksey spirits held midnight revels at the warrior's tomb. Goring, who, though he did not disbelieve in such apparitions, let his meditations run on upon the line which they had been following, and had paused to contemplate a monument which so intimately fitted in with them, when he saw distinctly some dark object move behind the headstone.

He thought at first that he had disturbed a sheep from its night's lodging. Looking more attentively, he perceived it was a human figure in a woman's cloak, which was crouching on the ground.

Cool as he was he could not resist an involuntary start.

As the figure rose to its feet, he saw plainly that it had the semblance of a woman, and a woman of flesh and blood, dressed in the grey cloak of the country, and with the hood drawn over its head. In the faint light he made out a face and eyes, but whether the apparition was old or young, or a tangible reality at all, he could not satisfy himself. He was about to question her, when, putting her fingers to her lips, she said in a low voice, which he thought he had heard before:

'For the Lord's sake, Colonel, go no further down the road this night; ye were watched from Tuosist! There is a party of the Sullivans got the start of ye in a boat, and they lie waiting for ye at the foot of the hill! They swear they will have your life for what ye done and said to Morty Oge this day! They are beyont, at the turn of the hill. Speak low, or they'll hear ye!'

'And who may you be, my good woman?' said Goring, 'that you are here in this solitary place and at such a time?'

'It is Mary Moriarty, from Glenbeg, that I am your honour. Your honour will mind my father that had the hunger fever upon him last year, and was like to die, and your honour gave us help that day and bought the lase of the land, and saved the both of us, the Lord reward ye for it! I was at Derreen at the burying, and there was a dance after at the shebeen house at the river side, and I heard the boys talking about your honour, and how ye would never see Dunboy again.'

'You are a good, brave girl!' said the Colonel. 'But this is no place for a young maiden to be abroad in at this hour, when such wild lads are about as those you tell me of. There is more danger to you than to me!'

'Never heed me, your honour. Look to yourself, or they will be on ye, maybe, before ye know. They would never hurt a girl, bad as they are, unless belike they found I had been spaking with your honour.'

Goring, as usual, had no arms but a walking stick. 'Below the hill?' he said, 'how many of them are there?'

'There are ten or twelve at the lowest,' she said, 'let alone those that may have joined them on the way! I saw them from the bridge, as they went down to their boat. They have guns

THE TWO CHIEFS OF DUNBOY

with them, worse luck! I'd bid ye take the mountain if you could reach it. There is a sheep track up the crag, but ye could hardly find it in the daylight, let alone in the dark night!'

'I must go back, then,' he said, 'and take the other path through Glanmore. I have travelled that way often enough.'

'Ye can't travel by Glanmore neither,' she answered, 'for I heard Mr. Sylvester telling the Glin boys to be watching for your honour, and it will be the Lord's mercy, and no thanks to the ould villain, if he has not sent another lot of them to follow ye on the way that ye have come!'

The Colonel, though fearless of death, would not throw his life away without an effort to save it. He was reflecting what he had best do, when a whistle from the direction in which he was going was answered by another from behind. The girl's conjectures had been right. They were between two parties who were advancing from opposite sides, and in a few minutes would meet where they were standing.

The morass was impassible. They would have sunk in it before they had gone five steps.

'Quick, quick!' the girl said. 'Trust yourself to me, your honour! There is but one way, but I can guide ye, black as the night is. If it is bad for us to see it will be worse for them to follow.'

Goring glanced doubtfully in her face. Her father, as he knew, had once been connected with the smugglers. Was it possible that this girl could be in league with his pursuers?

'Let us go,' he said. 'But you must lead the way—it is as dark as a wolf's throat!'

'Quick, then,' she answered. 'Spake no word, and step as lightly as you can, lest ye set the stones rolling.'

The caution was easier to give than to observe. Her own feet were bare, and she moved as noiselessly as a cat.

A few yards of heather only divided the road from the foot of the cliff. At a distance it appeared to be a continuous wall. But it was cracked in the middle of a fault—one side had slid away from the other, leaving a chasm between them into which a *débris* of earth and rubble had fallen from above. The grass had grown over it, and there was thus a steep, narrow, green

100

slope running up for seventy or eighty feet between two walls of rock, which, however, approached gradually and finally ended in a chimney which could not be ascended. To go up the slope, therefore, was apparently to be shut into a funnel from which there was no exit. The girl, however, made directly for it, with the speed of a goat. The Colonel followed with more difficulty, but he was light of foot and active, and as long as the grass lasted moved as silently as his guide. In three minutes they reached the bottom of the chimney, and paused to recover breath.

They were but just in time, for as they turned round they could hear and indistinctly see that a number of dark figures already surrounded the monument, and were looking about them and searching the ground. They were sure that their intended victim had been on the road between them. He could not have crossed the morass. He must be somewhere concealed under the cliff. They speedily found the slope; a very short time would have sufficed for them to discover the object of their pursuit, had the opening in the rock been the *cul-de-sac* which it appeared to be. But where the slope ended, a horizontal crack ran along the face of the precipice on the western side. A narrow shelf had been thus formed, six inches wide, where the sheep crossed on their way to the lower ground, and where a man could go whose head was steady.

The Colonel's guide was familiar with the place. The passage was a mere ledge. The girl stepped along it without hesitation. The Colonel had to feel his way with foot and hand, but followed her without accident. Turning a projecting point of rock they found themselves on a path beaten by the sheep, which led out upon the face of the mountain.

Here they stopped again, for the Colonel to collect himself. As he was leaving the cliff he displaced a loose boulder, which rolled over the precipice and sent the shingle flying at the foot of it. The fall of the stone betrayed the direction of the flight of the fugitives. Shots were fired at points where they might be supposed to be, and a dozen forms were seen scrambling among the crags, and searching for the outlet from the funnel. One perhaps found it and tried to cross, for there was a sound of a heavy fall, and of a shout for help. Colonel Goring and his singular guide found themselves alone on the mountain. . . .

Unacquainted as he was generally with the Kerry side of the range, circumstances had made him at one time painfully familiar with the gorge which was called the Pocket. A mile and a half away, a wall of rocks stretches across, six hundred feet high, over which a stream falls in a series of cascades. Above this wall is what perhaps was once a lake, but it has been filled in, and forms now a smooth level meadow, completely shut in by the mountains. The soil of the meadow is and was in Goring's time exceptionally good. A solitary farmhouse stood in the middle of it, and there was no other human habitation within several miles.

Here had lived a peasant with a wife and maidservant, many cattle, and a few acres of oats and potatoes, a man well-to-do as Kerry then was, but of gloomy and solitary habits. It happened that a clerk from Goring's mine works absconded, taking a bag of money with him. He made his way through the hills, climbed down one night on the precipice, and, trusting to the sympathy of the Irish mind with delinquents of all kinds, asked and obtained a night's lodging at the farm. The farmer, tempted by the gold, killed him while he was sleeping, and buried him in a bog hole. Suspecting that he had been seen by the maid-servant, he threw her over the waterfall also, and pretended that she had fallen down by accident. The murders were discovered; the murderer was executed. Goring had been several times on the spot when the bodies were being searched for. He was confident that if his companion would but guide him as far as the farm, which had since been deserted, he could thence make his way alone.

The Pocket, after being the scene of so horrible an atrocity, had naturally borne an evil name. Not only did the farm remain untenanted, but no one willingly went near the place in the day-time, and after nightfall it was supposed to be left to spirits of darkness. Mary Moriarty, when he suggested this plan, showed marked unwillingness. She told him a story of a relative of hers who had gone there looking for the stolen money, which had never been recovered. He had seen smoke coming out of a peat bank, and when he went to look, he found a place for all the world like a whiskey-still, and a little creature no bigger than his hand stirring the fire. He offered her relative a sup of whiskey; he took it and found it was melted gold that he was swallowing. He came to himself with the pain, and he was in his own cabin by the fire-side, with the water from the kettle pouring on the face of him.

Finding Goring only laughed, she grew positive and angry. She could not find the place. He would lose his footing in the crags. The road below would be safer for his honour than that black, ugly glen. The more unwilling she showed herself, the more Goring felt that she had some reason for it beyond what she acknowledged, and the more determined he was to discover what the reason could be.

At length, finding that he was obstinate, she said, 'Well, then, I'll take your honour to the edge of the cliff, anyway. The moon will be rising by that time, and ye can look over and see what will be before ye. If ye like to go further thin, ye may take your own way.'

She set off up the ridge of the mountain, moving so fast that Goring had no breath to ask further questions. They reached the crest, and she flitted on before him, threading her way among moss hags and jutting rocks, and along the side of slopes so steep that a false step would have meant a roll of a hundred feet. At one point they descended into a shallow chasm, where was a tarn, in which the stars were glimmering and a lonely heron was making his midnight meal.

For more than an hour they had walked on at full speed, and Goring judged that, by that time, the point for which they were making could not be far off. His guide suddenly stopped at the edge of the ridge, and beckoned to him with her finger to come forward. She was on the brink of a precipice, which fell abruptly below her for seven hundred feet; at the bottom was spread out the broad, level meadow at the head of the Pocket Valley. The moon had risen on the shoulder of Knockowen, immediately opposite them; the pools of the river which stole slowly down the middle of the glen were glimmering in the golden light.

He was gazing at the scene, conscious of nothing but its extraordinary beauty, when she drew him back, and bade him follow her a few feet down, where they could stand with the rocks at their backs. For explanation she pointed to the deserted farm, and round it, looking carefully, he saw a crowd of figures in rapid motion. They were not more than a quarter of a mile from him, and, as he estimated, two or three hundred of them.

They appeared to have white shirts on; from the regularity of their movements, and from the short, sharp calls, like notes of command, which, in the silence of the night, were distinctly audible, their evolutions appeared to be directed by some kind of authority.

'As your honour belongs to the army,' she said, 'you will know what that means. Sorra be with them. It is the old work they are after again, and never good came to this poor country from the like of it, and never will. Your honour, I'm thinking, will hardly be willing to cross this glen, this night, in the middle of them?'

Goring had heard often of these midnight drills in the mountains. He had, himself so far, seen nothing of them, and but half believed the stories which had reached him. Here was the very thing under his eyes.

Perched high up like ravens, in a niche in the crag, the Colonel could see without danger of being seen, and could speak freely, being too far off for his voice to be heard.

'You knew what would be going on here,' he said, 'and that was the reason why you did not wish to bring me this way. How came they to trust you with their secrets?'

'Well then, I'll tell your honour. I heard the boys talking down at the dance, and they were saying how it was arranged that they were to meet in this place after the funeral.'

'You have done your country a good service, my girl,' he answered. 'This poor, misguided people are thinking of another rebellion, and they will only destroy themselves if they try it. The French are just encouraging them for their own purposes.'

'It is likely that is true, your honour. Never good came to

Ireland of them French officers, that I heard of.'

'They have officers among them down there who have been in some regular service.'

'Your honour is right in that too. Ye will have seen them young gentlemen that were with Morty Sullivan at Derreen this afternoon. There was Mr. Connell, that is fram Darrynane, across the water. He has been in Morty's company in the wars abroad for five years gone. And there was the other, a Frenchman. Connell has gone away with Morty in the ship he has. This one was left, and he is yonder. Morty was to have been here himself. He has slipped away out to the sea, that your honour may think he's gone; but he is coming back to land the chests, bad luck to him, and thin the French gentleman is to join him again.'

'Did the lads at the dance say when the arms were to be landed?'

' 'Twas the night after the next Morty was to come in. They were talking so I couldn't hear distinctly the place they agreed on. Some one said Glengariff. It was one he and they knew well enough, any way.'

At the end of an hour the evolutions ended. The men formed into a large circle and sang an Irish chant, of which the words were inaudible, but the sounds floated up in the night breezes and died in the gorges of the mountains. When it was over they all disappeared, as if they were unsubstantial as the phantoms they resembled.

'You and I must be going,' said Goring, 'and be quick upon our road, or the dawn will be upon us before you can reach your home. We will now make for the hills above Glenbeg. It cannot be more than two or three miles from us. I will see you to a point where you can look down at your father's cabin, and then we must part.'

The daylight had not begun to appear when they reached the point that Goring spoke of. It was still dark, and the girl could make her way into the valley without fear that she would have been seen in his company.

'I can never forget this night,' he said. 'God reward you, my brave girl, and make you happy, and never shall you or yours want a friend while I or my wife are alive. Before we separate, however, I must ask you two questions. I have asked your father for no information, but I desire to learn how, and by whom he was taken down the lake on the day you came to Dunboy to tell me that he was dying.'

'I'll tell you that, and no harm,' she said. 'It was some old friends of ours that had come to Ardgroom in a sloop the night before, from Nantes. They heard by chance how it was with him.'

'As I was on my way to see him,' Goring said, 'I met a man on the hill-top, whom I saw yesterday at Derreen, at Morty Sullivan's side. Was Morty Sullivan one of these friends you speak of?'

'He was not that. He was not here at all. It is Mr. Connell ye are meaning. He it was that came with the sloop, and the others with him. He went in the boat to Glenbeg. He gave my father what he needed. He left his men to carry him down, and went himself to the mountain. Your honour knows what you saw there.'

'I know. I know. Fearful wrong had been done, and it was fearfully revenged. Had Connell a hand in that business? He told me No.'

'He told you no more than the truth, but if your honour thinks you owe me any kindness for this night's work, you will ask me no more questions. If ye will take a poor girl's advice ye will be gone out of this country back to your own land ye came from. It was a good day for my old father that brought ye here, and there is many besides us that has cause to bless ye. But it will be a better day for yourself that takes ye away, for ye have ill friends here, and that ye have cause to know.'

Chapter XIII

THE GUN-RUNNING

THE dawn was breaking when Goring reached the Cork side of the mountains, from which he could look over Dunboy, and could see his own house among the trees.

There he found everything quiet. After the exciting scenes which he had passed through, the composure itself seemed unnatural. No news had as yet arrived of the incidents at the funeral. At his own house no one was as yet stirring, for when he reached it the sun was but just above the horizon. The men outside were going about their work, and he was himself so often out on night expeditions that his return in the morning created no surprise among them.

One of his fishing smacks had just come in from outside with a heavy catch of cod and ling. He directed two of the fishermen to take them in a boat to Bantry and dispose of them. He sent with them an Irishman in his service, on whom he could absolutely rely. He wrote a few words to the Admiral, which for security he sewed in the lining of the man's coat. He bade him make his way from Bantry across the country with all possible speed, and deliver the note into the Admiral's own hands either at Cork or Kinsale, at whichever port the squadron might be.

The boat dispatched, his next anxiety was to discover by such other channels of information as he possessed at what point Morty Sullivan would attempt to run his arms-chests. That the attempt would be made in a night or two he was convinced, as Morty would not venture to remain on the coast any longer. The time had been fixed for the night after the next, and an officer of the *Doutelle* had been left behind to take charge of them. Mary Moriarty had heard Glengariff mentioned, but the bay was wide, and the time was short. Spies were sent about to gather anything that could be heard. Watchmen went to the tops of the hills to keep a look-out towards the sea. The Colonel, having done all that for the moment he could do, swallowed a hasty breakfast, threw himself on his bed, and slept.

It was late in the afternoon when he awoke. Parties returning over the mountains from the funeral had meanwhile brought the account of the duel, with the rumour that the Sullivans had lain in wait to kill the master on his way home. They had failed, and were savage at the disappointment; but how he had escaped no one could say, nor, when it was ascertained beyond a doubt that he was in his own house, could anyone guess how he had got there. Morty Sullivan was on everyone's lip. He had been seen here, he had been seen there. He was coming into the harbour to destroy the master's own dwelling with his guns.

Among the many stories flying, the most credible was brought in by a sloop which had fallen in outside with a Scariff fishing boat. The Scariff men said that before daylight that morning, a large vessel with two masts and a strange rig had been near them in a calm. They had been on board her, selling their fish. She was full of men, who said they had a thousand stand of arms on board, and fifty barrels of powder. The country was about to rise, and they said the French were coming over and all the English were to be killed.

Colonel Goring had desired to be informed when the boat returned which he had sent up with the fish. Three men had gone in her, and one was to carry his message to Cork. It was with surprise and some uneasiness that he learnt that three had come back. On hastening to meet them at the landing place, he was relieved to find that his messenger was not one of them. The third man was a stranger, who had induced the boatmen to bring him down, by alleging that he had matters of importance to speak to the Colonel about.

These matters did not seem important after all. He was a carrier from Dunmanway, he said, and he traded in salt butter for the Cork market. His honour, he understood, was cheated by the Bantry dealers about his fish. The finest cod that had been caught for the season had been sent up that morning, and divil a right price at all had been paid for them. He would be glad to do the Colonel's business himself that way, if his honour would be pleased to meet him.

Harassed and anxious as he was, Goring would have turned the Dunmanway carrier over to his steward, but he gathered from the man's manner that he might have more to say, and let him talk a little longer.

Carriage, the fellow said, seemed mighty scarce in Bantry. The boys had been wanting his carts and horses for the next day, and for the life of him he couldn't tell what they were about that they should be taking them. Maybe there was work going on carting sea-weed, or the like of that. But for all else they had to do they might carry the sea-weed on their backs, the poor creatures.

Gradually, sentence by sentence, the Colonel drew out that the carts and horses were to be on the shore at the harbour at Glengariff on the night following. A vessel of some sort was coming up from the sea. A contraband cargo of some kind was to be run, and taken off into the country before daylight.

The man's story might be purposely misleading, but Colonel Goring was experienced in such things. It corresponded exactly with what he had learned already. Colonel Goring slept upon his problem, and woke the next morning resolute, with his plan settled in his mind. He sent for five or six of his people on whom he could best depend. He told them frankly that the South of Ireland was in a more dangerous condition than they had hitherto experienced. The peasantry of the mountains had been drilling in large numbers. He had himself seen them. He had learnt that arms were that night to be landed for them, and when these arms were in their possession the Protestants at Dunboy, with their wives and children, would be in considerable peril.

They were not only willing to go, but eager, and their comrades they said would accompany them to a man. Colonel Goring desired them to pick out thirty of their best and coolest shots. These, with the four coastguardsmen and himself, he thought would be sufficient. He charged them to mention the subject to no one, for if the slightest hint got abroad, warning fires would be lighted on the hills, and the scheme which he had formed would be defeated. At low water the *Doutelle* would have to anchor half a mile from the cove where he was assured the landing would be attempted. Certain reefs of rock would then be left dry which commanded the entrance to it. These rocks he intended to occupy after nightfall, and if no alarm was given, he believed that he could shelter himself among them unseen.

Often after sunset the larger boats went out with drift nets, or with long lines for skate and congers. No particular notice, therefore, would be attracted if two or three boats were seen to leave the harbour with eight or ten men in each. Two of the boats chosen were the fastest the Colonel had. They were like the galleys of a man-of-war, and were rowed with ten oars, or on occasion with twelve. The third was smaller and lighter, and was the swiftest of the three. Late in the afternoon, for till then nothing was touched, that there might be no sign of anything unusual, fifty rifles and pistols, cases of cartridges, and as many cutlasses and dirks, were distributed among the boats and laid in the bottom. Nets, ropes, and lines, were flung over them. The night promised to be dark—there would be no moon till three in the morning; they started out under cover of the dusk, and by their course they seemed to be making for the usual fishing ground behind the Island.

In half an hour the last of the daylight was gone. They could scarcely see the land themselves, and were in no danger at all of being seen from it. They then headed away for the lonely inlet of Adrigoole, which was half-way to the place of their destination. Adrigoole lay at the foot of Hungry Hill. In the afternoon Goring had sent a scout to the top of it to examine the horizon for signs of the *Doutelle*, and with orders to meet him there with the latest information. The scout brought word that he had distinctly seen her after sunset coming in towards the land. She was then outside the Durseys, and, if the breeze held, would soon be running up the Bay.

No doubt now remained. The wind was right from the westward; it was inclining to fall, but the *Doutelle*'s large canvas would draw her fast through the water so long as any air remained, and the ebbing tide would not delay her long. The night was hazy without either stars or moon; but at sea it is seldom absolutely dark, and before long they saw the spars and sails of Morty's vessel against the midnight sky as she swept slowly by. As the tide was out she would have to make a round to enter Glengariff harbour. By keeping to the west of the rocky islands at the mouth the boats would be there before her.

The landing cove was on the farther side, where the Bantry road approached the water's edge. So far, Goring had been concealed from observation by keeping under the cliff; but between him and the rocks which he designed to occupy there was now a stretch of open water, which it was necessary for him to cross. He had a double danger to guard against. He might be seen from the shore and seen from the *Doutelle*, and Morty's eyes would perhaps be helped by night glasses. He had no time to lose either, for the vessel was fast running up. He could reach the middle of the passage unobserved by manoeuvring behind the islands at the entrance. From there he had to dash boldly across, and there was a mile of dangerous water should any sharp eye be looking out. Beyond this he would be in the shelter of overhanging woods, and could reach the reef unobserved. Fortune peculiarly favoured him that night. No one saw or heard him. The ground swell was unusually loud, and drowned all other sounds.

At low tide the cove was a natural harbour, of which reefs on either side formed the piers, leaving a narrow opening between them. The depth of it from the mouth to the landing beach was two hundred yards, and inside was a completely sheltered pool, where boats could run in and be left unmoored. The reef was formed of two ridges running parallel, with a channel between them, and there boats could lie unseen either from the shore or from the water. There was depth sufficient for the largest of Goring's galleys to float, and two hands left in each would hold them ready for instant service. Into this channel they made their way; Goring, with the boatswain of the coastguard, crept to the top of the rock to reconnoitre.

The entrance to the cove was directly under them, and he could see faintly to the shingle and sand at the end of it. He made out, dimly, some half-dozen carts and horses standing in the road, and a few indistinct figures were seen moving about the sands.

The mist rose a few minutes after they had taken their positions, and the *Doutelle* was seen creeping into the bay. The breeze had fallen, and she was gliding through the water, rather with the motion which she had brought with her than from any force which was left in the wind. She went on till she had passed an island with an old castle upon it, designed for the protection of the anchorage, but now left by the general neglect to become a deserted ruin. Here she swung round. The canvas was taken in, and they heard the rattling of her chain-cable as the anchor was let go. The peak of the mainsail was dropped, her foresail furled, and her topsails lowered. In a few minutes she lay still and motionless.

A blaze of straw from the shore was answered by a blue light on her deck. Her largest boat had, the day before, been disabled by the fall of a spar, which had stove in the side of it; but she had two others, which she was towing at her stern, to be ready for immediate use, and a heavy turf barge of the country had been left moored at the spot where she was to bring up. This was brought alongside, and the creaking of blocks, and the running of ropes through the sheaves, announced that the chests were being lowered into it. Many hands were employed, the work was swiftly accomplished, and the silence which followed was again broken by the splash of oars.

The sound of oars now drew nearer every moment, and black forms began to show on the water, growing larger as they came nearer. At length, Goring made out two gigs, or long boats, with ten figures in each, beside the coxswain. They were towing the turf barge, which was loaded to the gunwale, and were advancing slowly in consequence. It was an unwieldy tub, which would not steer, and he could hear them cursing it. The minutes were like hours.

Nothing tries men's courage more than lying in ambush, and the hearts of the Dunboy men were in their throats. As the leading boat came into the mouth of the cove, the crew lay upon their oars, to see which way they were to turn—and Goring observed with satisfaction that they were strangers to the place. Shouts were raised on shore to direct them. They had just begun to move again, dragging at the weight behind, when they were startled by a sharp challenge, at a few fathoms' distance.

'What boats are those?' said a voice, which seemed to come from directly above their heads.

'What is that to you, whoever you are?' answered the coxswain, looking sharply up, and supposing that some one from the land had come out on the water and was playing the fool. But he saw his mistake in a moment.

'Your arms, men!' he cried. 'Here is treachery.' The oars were dropped, and there was a clash of iron, as each hand caught the musket that was nearest.

'What boats are those?' said the voice again. 'Speak, or we fire.'

The coxswain answered with a pistol shot, aimed in the direction from which the sound came, and the ball struck a stone which he had mistaken for the speaker's cap. A dozen rifles flashed in reply, from the crannies of the reef. With a loud cry, four of the *Doutelle*'s men reeled on their seats, and rolled over into the bottom of the boat; while another ball had passed through the coxswain's arm. Attacked thus suddenly by invisible assailants, they concluded that the Irish had betrayed them, and that they had fallen into a trap. They would have backed out into the open water, but they dropped upon the boat behind them and fouled the oars, and all was at once confusion. A second volley into the entangled mass was answered by fresh shrieks, which showed how the shots were telling.

Wild yells rose from the beach. A hundred dark figures came rushing down over the shingle, firing guns with as much danger to friend as foe. One man only—it was the young de Chaumont—rushed round to the farther side of the cove, plunged into the water and swam off to join his struggling comrades.

Goring's real danger was from the *Doutelle*. Morty Sullivan comprehended in a moment the whole situation. To lower his remaining boat and to fly to the help of his people was his instant impulse. But the fates were against him that night. The boat was on deck under repair. He had still men enough in plenty, but the best seamen were away in the two gigs, and those who were left were awkward and unhandy. When the boat was brought at last over the side, the after-tackle was let go with a run, and she fell stern foremost into the water and filled.

The rattle of the rifles and the cries of his own people told meanwhile how unequally the struggle was going on. There was now but one thing for Morty to do. The flashes showed him where the coastguard were lying. He brought his broadside to bear, and sent nine-pound shot flying about their ears, making the mountains echo to the roar of his artillery. Seldom or never had such a sound disturbed that quiet harbour. The shot struck the stones and sent the splinters flying. The Colonel's men dropped into the boats behind the outer ridge and were untouched.

Under cover of such a fire the smugglers' boats might have extricated themselves and renewed the fight to more advantage, but the reef lay in a line between the vessel and the landing-place. Shot after shot, flying high, fell among the crowd on the shore. The horses plunged and started off with their carts. Some were hit, and their dying screams struck fresh panic into the people, who fled in all directions. Morty found his mistake and stopped the fire, but he could do no more to help his own men.

He guessed instinctively that he had been again baffled by by his old enemy. More bitterly than ever he swore that one day he would have his revenge. But for all that he could tell, Goring might have a hundred men with him. The chance was gone of landing the cargo that night. The *Doutelle* could not move, for not a breath of air was stirring. She might herself be attacked next: he sent up a signal rocket for the boats to return to the vessel.

Goring, however, did not mean to let his prey escape so easily. The night was absolutely still. The *Doutelle* would have to lie still till the wind rose. Instantly that they saw the smugglers retreating, they dashed out after them, and in fifty strokes were alongside the turf boat. The smugglers, to gain freedom of movement, had to drop their tow line. Although outnumbered and encumbered with their wounded, they turned on their pursuers. The boats closed, and dark as it was there was light enough to fight by. Pistols, cutlasses, handspikes, stretchers, anything that came to hand, were snatched up on both sides. With the clashing of steel and the rattle of shot were mixed cries and curses, English, Irish, French and Spanish, from the motley desperadoes who formed Morty's company.

A party of the coastguard had taken possession of the barge. Half-a-dozen of the smugglers, with de Chaumont at their head, leapt on board and drove them off. The flashing of the pistols and the shouts of the combatants told their own tale to Morty; but he dared not use his guns by firing into a black mass where friend and enemy were locked together, and he could only pace his deck in fury. The fight was hand to hand. Again and again the cargo boat was carried with a rush; again and again it was recovered, and the assailants forced back.

At length superior numbers and the solid courage of the Dunboy men told decisively. The privateer's crew were embarrassed by their wounded comrades, whom they were trampling to death. They found that they would be either taken or killed themselves unless they could retreat under the guns of their vessel. The barge and its contents would have to be abandoned to its fate.

De Chaumont was the last to leave it. Slightly made, but agile as a panther, he had sustained the courage of his men to the last moment. Ordering them to clear the boats of the *mêlée*, he stood himself alone against the whole force of the attack, till he saw that they had extricated themselves. Then flashing his pistol at the match of a hand grenade, which he picked up to use at the last extremity, and rolling it down between the powder barrels, he sprang overboard, dived under the pike thrusts which were aimed at him, and joined his companions.

The engineer of the mines, who was in the nearest boat, saw his action. He leapt into the barge either to extinguish the shell before it could burst, or hurl it into the sea. But it lay flickering where he could not reach it. To linger would be destruction, not to himself only, but to half his comrades, who were fastening ropes to the prize which they supposed to be their own.

He darted back, shoved off the boat to which he belonged with a desperate effort, and called to the others to save themselves. They were barely clear when the grenade burst and blew in the head of the nearest powder cask. The flash of the explosion illuminated the whole harbour of Glengariff. The rocks, the woods, the old castle, the spars and hull of the anchored vessel, even the nearest mountains, were lighted up with the momentary splendour.

Morty's men believed for the instant that the Coastguard and their commander had been destroyed; and they sent up a shout of triumph. The cry was answered by a defiance as loud as their own. But the prize was gone. The barge and all that it contained had been blown to atoms.

After the sudden blaze the darkness was thicker than before, as the smoke settled down upon the water. When it cleared the engineer's boat was found to have been stove in, and her crew to be in the water, holding on to the broken timbers. In the other boat a man had been stunned by a splinter, and the Colonel was hurt in the leg. Several others had been wounded in the fight, but no one had been killed.

There would be no prize-money, but they had done their duty, and saved the neighbourhood from an imminent danger.

Taking the men from the lost boat into the two others, they gave a parting cheer, and pulled away out of gunshot from the *Doutelle*, which happily for them was chained to her place by the stillness of the night.

Chapter XIV

THE STORM

DESPOTIC as was the authority of the chief on board a privateer or corsair, permitted as he was to meet the first symptoms of mutiny or insolence with a pistol-shot, or a rope from the yard-arm, his power rested on his personal qualities and the consent and allowance of the general crew. Let a doubt, either of his ability or even his good fortune, once find an entrance among them, and the bond that held them together was dissolved.

Hitherto they had been well enough pleased with Morty. They thought him too distant, and too much of a fine gentleman, but he had done a handsome month's work with them off the Channel, and the Irish expedition they had put up with as an episode on their way to the West Indies. But the affair at Derreen, and their defeat at Glengariff had shaken their confidence altogether.

As long as the calm continued the *Doutelle* was fixed to her anchorage. Morty Sullivan, thinking nothing of the disaffection of the crew, but sore and exasperated, shut himself in his cabin, leaving the vessel in charge of Connell and de Chaumont, with orders to see to the wounded and to get under way with the first sign of wind.

Day broke at last. A few uncertain cats'-paws were rippling about the water. The smoke from a cabin on the land was rising straight in the morning air, but signs were about, which, to an experienced seaman, showed that the stillness would be of short duration. The swell from the ocean which had been moaning round the rocks the night before, was now breaking in great sheets of foam over the low point at the harbour mouth, an infallible symptom that a gale was blowing in the Atlantic, and was on its way from the sea. The rocks never roared as they were roaring then without a meaning, and wild weather would be on them before many hours were past. Unless they were to remain in shelter where they were and run the chance of being found there by a king's ship, not a moment was to be lost in clearing out. If the wind came from the westward, as it seemed likely to do, while they were still inside Mizen Head, the *Doutelle* herself, in spite of her weatherly qualities, would be unable to work out of the bay.

The orders were given to set the canvas and get the anchor in. Instead of obeying, the men stood at their quarters without moving, and the boatswain, a Creole from Martinique, desired to speak with the captain. Morty was ill to deal with when the black fit was on him. Connell and de Chaumont were both favourites with the company. They called the whole crew aft to hear what they had to say. The boatswain spoke for the rest.

There was a storm brewing up, he said. The blindest eye could see that. If a gale came on they would be on a lee shore on the most dangerous coast in the world. Their present anchorage was safe and landlocked. They had their many wounded, to whom, if they were caught in a tempest, it would be impossible to pay proper attention, but chiefly and essentially, and this was the real objection, they had their dead comrades to bury. There was ill luck in going to sea with dead men on board.

The tone was respectful, the language reasonable, the whole company unanimous. Threats would be useless, and violence fatal, for mutiny was in their eyes if their demand was not complied with, and to have called up Morty would have probably provoked a catastrophe.

Quietly, and expressing the strongest sympathy with them, Connell explained, on the other hand, the exact particulars of their situation. They were embayed in a deep estuary, from which, if the wind came heavily from the west, they could not work out. At that moment, however, he showed, pointing overhead, that the clouds were coming up from the south-west and by south. With the wind at this quarter they could hold their course down the bay, if they started immediately, and make an offing before the worst of the gale came on. They had cause to suppose that their being on the coast was known at Cork and that the same south-west wind would probably bring some frigate in search of them.

'We have lost faith in the captain, we tell you plainly. None but a fool would have brought us into such a situation. He has gone wrong on the brain, but if you and M. de Chaumont, there, will take the command—'

'Don't speak of "Ifs",' Connell said. 'You may cut us in pieces before we will let you lift a hand against the captain. I promise you this only, that you shall have your orders from me till you ask him yourself to take the command of ye again. If all goes well, I will bring you to Nantes before four days are out, and then you can do what you will.'

The possible arrival of a ship of war was a new feature of the case to most of them. They had no ambition to be hanged, and after a conversation among themselves they sulkily returned to their duty. The anchor was weighed. They towed the vessel off with their boats till they were clear of the harbour, and then, setting every stitch of canvas, down to their lightest studding-sail, they stood, closehauled, down the bay.

Morty came on deck as they passed off Dunboy. He walked slowly to and fro, watching the spot which had been torn from his ancestors because they had been true to their country and their creed. He said nothing. He must have been aware by this time of the temper of his company, but he did not choose to notice it. He merely observed that they were on their right course, and retired again to his cabin.

By the evening the wind, which had stood all day at south-west, drew into the west, and then to a point north; the *Doutelle* was bearing for Mizen Head. They counted that, when clear of it, she would have a free course to the eastward; but for this they required a steady breeze, and the wind, so far from being steady, blew only in occasional puffs with intervals of absolute calm.

The sea, meanwhile, grew higher every moment, and there is no point on the shores of the British Islands where, in such weather, there are higher or uglier waves than those which break on the headlands at the mouth of Bantry Bay. They sweep in, long, massive and unbroken, from the deep waters of the Atlantic till they reach the submerged rocks, the remnants of the abrasions of millions of years, which fringe the south-western Irish coast. But there are times, before and after a storm, when the wind falls, and the waves, wantoning at their own pleasure, are more distracted and distracting than ever. It was in one of these windless intervals that the *Doutelle* found herself, now rolling helpless with her canvas flapping, now caught by a sudden squall on the crest of a great roller when her helm had lost all power.

The sun went down green into the sea. The night was near upon them, and with the last of the light they perceived that they were losing the way that they had made, and were rolling in to leeward. It was too late (even if they could have got their vessel under command) to put back into Bantry Bay, for they were too far to the southward. The crew clustered in angry groups under the bulwarks. Their fears had proved true. The spirits of their own dead, who ought to have been sleeping in their graves, were abroad in the storm; and as they shuddered and muttered, the great green billows would come crashing over and breaking on the deck, and sending tons of water rushing from stem to stern.

At last the wind came, came like a West Indian hurricane, breaking off the crests of the billows and lashing them into foam. The ship's canvas had been reduced to receive the stroke of the gale. The mainsail had been reefed down to a sixth of its size. A staysail and a storm jib was all that was showing forward. The staysail flew to ribands with a crack like a gunshot, but Mr. Blake's ropes were sound and the rest held. After one reel, as if she was going under and for ever, the *Doutelle* rose, shook herself like a sea bird, flew into the wind, and there she lay, rising and falling in the swell, with the storm howling among her spars, but safe now, if only she had sufficient sea room, and was not driven in upon the shore.

In Morty's seamanship, at any rate, there was unbounded confidence. With the first distress he had resumed the command. The position was extremely precarious, and the men were gloomy and discontented. What was to be done next? Morty's opinion was strong as ever to hold on. No frigate would be out looking for them in such weather. They ought, therefore, to make the best of it to get away. The vessel was sound and seaworthy. They could lie to through the night and crawl off in the morning. So far they were in deep water, and the storm might do its worst.

But there was no crawling off from comrades' ghosts. Throw the bodies overboard they dared not, while they were all assured that the presence of them on board had brought the gale; and they demanded to know whether there was or was not any harbour now under their lee where they could run. Morty could not deny that Crookhaven was but a few miles from them, that they could approach it in daylight even in the present weather.

Wilder and wilder grew the night. It was impossible to get any way upon the *Doutelle*. She would have been instantly swamped had they tried. Her only security was to lie head to wind, and in that position slowly but surely drift to leeward.

In the whole ship's company there was but one exception to the opinion that with the first streak of dawn they must make for Crookhaven. That exception was the captain. Colonel Goring had threatened to bring a ship from Cork upon him; Colonel Goring had gained the advantage on every occasion when they had encountered; and the ill-luck was perhaps not yet exhausted. Ships, canvas, cordage, all were sound. The only fear was from the English cruisers; and as long as the storm lasted no cruiser would leave its moorings. He advised, therefore, that they should make the best of their time while the coast was clear.

But he could persuade no one to agree with him; it was new for one usually so daring to be frightened at an English man-of-war; they had come and gone; they had been chased, and had laughed at pursuit. To neglect a harbour of refuge in a tempest from a hypothetical danger of that kind was so unlike the confidence of Morty Sullivan that they thought again that his nerve had been overset. The seas were still washing over the bulwarks. Five bodies sewn in their hammocks lay below, waiting for burial. The wounded were suffering from the plunging of the vessel. Every single man was for running in. Even his two officers could not understand his obstinacy. To persist would, he saw, be useless. The crew would take the ship from him, and perhaps do worse. Since go in they would, he accepted their decision, and himself took the helm to pilot them through the channel at the entrance. No one knew it better than he. Every creek and corner from Kinsale to Dingle had been familiar to him in the expeditions in which he had been engaged in his boyhood.

As the night wore on the storm swept the clouds off the sky and the outlines of the land became gradually visible. As soon as they could see their way the *Doutelle* was brought round before the wind; she flew in on the crests of the seas—she shook herself into order as she smoothed her water under the shelter of Mizen Head; and before daylight had fairly established itself the scanty inhabitants of Crookhaven, when they rose to light their turf fires in the morning, saw a strange vessel with French colours riding quietly at anchor, the sole occupant of their secluded haven.

The visit of a French trader, though a breach of the Navigation Laws, was always welcome. Usually it meant brandy, it meant tobacco. It meant a market for the woolpacks and the salt fish. If the *Doutelle* had nothing to sell or buy, the hospitalities of the place were not the less freely offered. The rovers were open-handed, and spent their money freely, and thus had full liberty to remain in the land-locked harbour till the storm abated, while everything which the people could do for them was freely at their command. A priest was found who had been educated in France, and with his help the poor fellows who had been shot at Glengariff had honourable burial within the walls of an ancient abbey, their comrades firing volleys over their graves. When this solemn duty was discharged, and the hurts of the survivors looked to and dressed, there was still the *Doutelle* herself to be overhauled, boats repaired, broken rigging re-spliced, and the hundred damages made good which always grow out of a gale.

In these occupations two days passed away, and nothing had appeared to disturb or alarm them. On the land side no hint of their presence had got abroad. No official presented himself to learn who they were or whence they came. Seawards, not a sail was visible from the highest point of the barrier which covers the haven from the ocean.

On the second evening the weather began to take up. The wind fell to a moderate breeze, and the sea went down rapidly, showing that the gale was no longer blowing in the Atlantic. Morty, still impatient of delay, urged an immediate start; but his alarms had hitherto proved groundless; the horizon at sunset had been absolutely clear, only sky and water, and besides them nothing. They would have time enough in the morning; if the worst came and they were chased, what had they to fear? As long as the sea was smooth, they need not fear the fastest cruiser that ever came out of Portsmouth Harbour.

Thus sunrise found them still at anchor, but everything ready for a start. Their canvas was up. They had their whole mainsail set, foresail reefed, and jib-boom housed, on account of the swell, which, though no longer vicious was still considerable, large staysail, and storm jib ready to hoist when the anchor should be off the ground—fair cruising costume, suited to weather not yet completely settled. The *Doutelle* herself had been smartened up, her decks clean and white as in a man-of-war, the guns scoured bright, the brass binnacles—the brass-work everywhere—shining as if they were silver. They expected to be in the Loire in fifty hours, and privateers on coming into port always made a point of appearing in the same condition as their rivals in the regular service.

The morning was brilliant. The wind, having been in the north in the night, had fallen back in the morning to the west. But the sky was cloudless. The bay was flecked with green and white as the level rays of the sun shone through the curling crests of the still breaking waves. A few country boats followed them to the harbour's mouth, to see them off and wish them 'good luck and God speed'.

They stood out leisurely under the land, Morty having recovered his spirits when the vessel was under way, and almost wondering at the weakness, as he now deemed it, which he had allowed to overcome him. The deck of the *Doutelle* was flush fore and aft, with a clean walk from end to end between the guns. Abaft the mainmast it was sacred to the officers. Forward, the men were laughing and singing, their comrades now disposed of, bodies and spirits alike, themselves looking forward to the black girls in the Tortugas, and the wild life of licensed plunder which they were soon to be enjoying in the West Indies.

One doubt they still had, indeed, whether Morty Sullivan was a commander to their taste. They would have preferred some one who was less of a gentleman and luckier or more skilful in his enterprises; while Morty, on his side, after his experience of the condition of a privateer captain's tenure, felt entirely uncertain what his own course would be after reaching the Loire.

Chapter XV

A CHASE AT SEA

THE steward was getting breakfast ready in the cabin. The three officers were pacing the deck over his head, Morty Sullivan absorbed in thought and saying little. A seaman had been sent aloft to secure a loose end of rope which had been left flying, and had finished his work and begun to descend, when his eye seemed to be caught by some object which he could not clearly make out. Steadying himself with an arm round the topmast, and with the other hand shading the light from his eyes, he looked attentively for a minute or two, and then hastily descending he came aft and said, 'There is a sail on the horizon, sir, bearing S.S.E. I thought it might be the Fastnet Rock when I first observed it, but I saw the Fastnet distinct and inside. She is hull down, sir,' he continued as Morty looked and made out nothing, 'only her spars and upper canvas showing; but a ship it is, and, I think, a large one.'

A ship might mean a New England trader, something in their own line of business, to put them in heart again after their misadventures. Snatching a spy-glass from a rack, Morty sprang up the shrouds, twisted a leg in the main-rigging to secure himself, and anxiously studied the object which the seaman had described. Apparently he completely satisfied himself, for he slid down calmly and deliberately, and rejoined his officers. The weary listless look had gone out of his face. Mouth and eyes were set and firm, with a cynical smile in them.

'It is as I expected,' he said. 'There is an English frigate bearing directly down upon us. If she sees us, as of course she has or will, we shall be talking to each other in an hour or two. So much the better. There will be work at last fit for a gentleman.'

Fighting is the privateer's man's business, but he fights only when he cannot help it with an antagonist bigger than himself. Connell took the glass out of Morty's hand, went aloft, and took a long gaze. 'It is a ship, certainly,' he said, when he returned to the deck, 'and to appearance she is heading in towards us, but she is twelve miles at least, and for all I can see she may be a merchantman.'

'My dear Connell,' said Morty, 'no merchantman ever carried yards so broad as yonder vessel, or set up so taut and square. Trust me to know an English man-of-war when I see her. I have the list below of the frigates at Cork, and if this is the _Æolus_, as I think likely, she is the fastest craft we have yet tried our speed against. We are in for a fine race, any way, and perhaps for something besides. She is rated for thirty-eight guns, and I believe she carries forty; they are all small nine-pounders like ours; but we have a lively morning's work before us.'

'I hope that for once, sir, you are mistaken,' said Connell, 'but if it be as you say, the dog need not jump down the leopard's throat. We can hardly make her out against the sky line, and she cannot yet have seen us with the mountains right behind us. If we hold on as we are we shall run straight into her course. We have the sea open to us. Why not bear away under the shore behind Cape Clear Island? She will never follow us among those rocks.'

'For the best of all possible reasons we can do nothing of the kind, my friend. As the wind stands she could cut us off if she saw us try it, and they have as good eyes as we have. We can beat her, I believe, working to windward, and that is what I mean to try. That is,' he said, scornfully, 'if it pleases the ship's company to be commanded by me in this business. It is for them, I suppose, to choose.'

He blew his whistle. 'Call the men aft,' he said to the bot-swain. 'I will soon know.'

They were all on deck watching the stranger.

'My men,' said Morty to them. 'You have ill liked the work we have been after since we came on this coast. I have liked it ill myself, and I don't blame you for that. We may have better days before us—I trust we have; but meanwhile we have a morning's work cut out for us which will try what we are made of. A man-of-war from Cork is bearing down upon us as

fast as a ten-knot breeze can bring her along. I thought it
might be so, and for this reason I was unwilling to stay at
Crookhaven. You were not satisfied. You had your way, and
here she is. She carries twice as many guns as we do, and
three times as many men. You have out-sailed these cruisers
before, and you think you can do it again. On one point of
sailing, I believe you can; but I must understand first if you
mean to obey my orders.'

They were in a scrape, and a scrape of their own making.
They were willing enough to let Morty or any other person
get them out of it, but they had not yet taken in the actual
danger in which they were. They had never yet met a ship that
could catch the *Doutelle* in a stern chase. Like Connell, they
were for bearing away under Cape Clear, and trying what
speed would do for them.

Morty, for answer, spread a chart on the roof of the companion. The wind was westerly, with half a point to the north.
They were standing out close-hauled from Crookhaven, intending, after weathering the Fastnet Rock outside Cape Clear, to
ease away S.S.E. on their course home. The frigate lay exactly
in their track, and the two vessels were approaching on opposite tacks. But the frigate had the advantage of the situation.
If the *Doutelle* tried to pass through the sound behind Cape
Clear Island, she would find the frigate waiting for her as she
came out. To keep in shore among the rocks and islands would
have been dangerous in a calm, and certain destruction in the
swell which still continued. The chance of escape, in Morty's
opinion, was in the opposite direction round Dursey Head and
the Bull and Calf Rocks. Once there, the *Doutelle* would have
open water, and a free course for her own sailing qualities. But
to weather Dursey Head, as the wind stood, she must make an
offing of six or seven miles, and this she could hardly hope
to do without coming under the frigate's guns.

Whatever other doubts might have been entertained about
Morty Sullivan's qualifications, there were none about his
seamanship. Every man in the ship's company was easily
assured that what he said about the vessel's capabilities was
necessarily true. The daring character of the plan which he

proposed was infectious and touched and roused their spirits. If there had been fault, this time the fault was theirs, not his.

'You see, my men,' he said, 'we gave her the chance to find us, and she has taken it. We are not cowards to be frightened at the chance of a broadside. The boldest course is the safest. We can trust the rigging. Set everything that she will carry. Drive her through it, and let us see what she can do. Get the cartridge boxes up, and see all clear. Keep the guns lashed but ready when we want them, and let the aftermost starboard gun be trained over the stern. You will do your duty all of you. I see it in your eyes.'

With a cheer for the captain, the men flew about their different duties. Morty turned to Connell and de Chaumont. 'Gentlemen, breakfast has been waiting all this time. It is ill fighting on an empty stomach. By the time we have finished we shall see better what our friend here means to be after.'

Twenty minutes later, when they came on deck again, the aspect of matters was considerably clearer. In the first place, any doubt which might have remained, as to the character of the vessel outside, was removed once for all. Morty had judged her rightly at first sight. She was a long, low, powerful frigate, pierced for eighteen guns on a side, with bow and stern chasers. Her lofty spars were struck on account of the weather. She was taking things easy, with her lower canvas, and her topsails reefed, but the pace at which she was coming down showed what her speed would be, if she chose to exert herself.

The sea was rising again, and the wind freshening. She lay gracefully over as the squalls struck her, till her mainyard almost touched the water, and the white paint upon her bottom glittered in the morning sun. She seemed herself like a thing alive, so lightly and airily she lifted over the swell, and sent the foam in showers from off her bows. Morty himself, ugly customer as she was likely to prove, could not refuse his admiration for the most beautiful vessel of the kind which he had ever seen.

The frigate was by this time about five miles west of the Fastnet Rock, bearing N.N.W., and looking just outside the Calf, at the extreme point of the long Dursey promontory, which must be weathered by any vessel which was going away to the northward. The *Doutelle* was coming out from behind Mizen Head on the opposite tack. Staggering under a crowd of sail, an occasional sea washing along her decks, but, with her broad beam and hollow bows, for the most part lifting easily over the swell. She, too, was as near to the wind as she could go, her course being nearly south-west. The *Æolus*, for they could now read her name through their glasses, was slightly to windward, and if both vessels held upon their present course, would cross the *Doutelle*'s bows. But she intended apparently to use her advantage, bring the saucy rover, which had given so much trouble, to immediate close quarters, and either sink her or force her to strike.

With this purpose she kept slightly away as if to run the *Doutelle* down. Morty saw what she was after. He had himself taken the helm when he came on deck. He had been watching the relative sailing power of the two vessels, and as they had been on opposite tacks, he had not completely satisfied himself. Before he would allow his enemy to come within striking distance, it was necessary for him to ascertain exactly the conditions of the game.

The interval between them was every moment lessening, but he observed with satisfaction the frigate, in her eagerness to close, throwing away the superiority of her windward position. He held on till they were less than a mile apart, when it appeared as if the frigate was coming straight into him, and her men could be seen swarming about the guns. Suddenly he gave the order to go about. The *Doutelle* spun round. Notwithstanding the intensity of the excitement, the crew worked with the precision of a machine, doubt and disagreement all forgotten; everyone did his utmost and his best, and without losing her speed the smart little vessel was off in a few moments in a new direction.

The frigate and the privateer were now on the same tack. The *Æolus* had so far been out-manoeuvred. She had lost her advantage owing to her own impatience. She was as near as possible in the *Doutelle*'s wake, and a mile astern of her. The course of both was outside Dursey Head, the Calf Rock bear-

ing N.N.W. and fifteen miles distant. Had the water been
smooth they might have been able to weather it, but the set
of the sea drove them both to leeward, while the immediate
question was which of the two was gaining. If the *Doutelle*
could have increased her distance before she was obliged to
tack and reach out again, she might get round the point and
escape. The rate of sailing was so even, that for several minutes
it was difficult to tell which had the advantage.

But the privateer was doing her utmost. Her masts were
groaning under the sail which she was carrying. The frigate
had not shaken out a reef, and might add a knot to her speed
when she pleased. It appeared, too, when the chase had lasted
for a mile or two, that from her size and power she held up
better against the sea, and was regaining her position to windward. She had only therefore to hold on for an hour till they
came in with the land, and Morty must then either go about
and fall straight into her mouth, or run up into Bantry Bay
and be captured at leisure, or else be driven ashore and destroyed. The end seemed so inevitable, that the frigate made no
more attempts to close, but was content to wait the issue, which
could not be two hours distant.

Morty himself so little liked the look of things that, if the
frigate's great length had not promised that her superiority
would be still greater before the wind, he would have worn
round, taken the chance of a broadside, and run back to the
eastward. But there was no hope that way. At the worst he
could run the vessel ashore, land his crew, and blow her up.
But he still had an hour and a half before him to try what
better he could do.

Perhaps guessing what he might attempt, the *Æolus* hoisted
a signal ordering him to heave to. As he took no notice she
fired a shot from one of her bow guns; the ball fell short, and
so did a second with which she followed it. Morty, satisfied
that he had nothing more to do with than the old-fashioned
nine-pounders, called a seaman to the tiller, and bidding him
to hold on upon the same course, determined to try what he
could do with his own particular favourite, the long twelve-
pounder which Blake had made for him on his own design,

and was so constructed that it could be slewed over the stern. If he could but cut away a spar, or a few ropes, he might gain a precious half-hour.

A dancing target is easily missed from a dancing platform, but Morty had commanded an Austrian Artillery Company, and was a master of his art.

To find the range, he fired his first shot at the frigate's hull. The white splinters from the bulwarks told him what he desired to know. It was also evident that the shot had disturbed the equanimity of the frigate's company, who seemed to feel as some large mastiff might do who had felt the teeth of a bulldog. They were more astonished at the impudence than irritated at the damage done. But the officer in command thought again that it was time to end the business, and after the bow guns had been tried once more without effect, the reefs were shaken out of the topsails, and the ship began to quicken her speed through the water.

The frigate now came tearing along, as if she were alive herself, and was feeling the fever of the chase, with the men at quarters, and the mouths of the guns showing ominously at the open portholes. The *Doutelle*, which had been hitherto jammed up close to the wind, was allowed to fall off a point or a point and a half, which gave her additional speed, and enabled her to maintain her distance for a short time longer. The advantage which she gained in this way she would have to pay with interest when she came up with the land and had to tack. There were still however eight miles to be run first, and Morty's one chance was that some lucky hit might save him.

Aiming now at masts and yards, now at ropes and sails, he sent shot after shot through the frigate's tops. She with her short guns could make no reply, and he fired on with impunity, cutting sheets and halyards and sending chips flying, till she found that in this way she was exposing herself uselessly to a chance of serious damage, and that she had better wait at a safer distance for the inevitable catastrophe. Before any important spar had been injured therefore, or rope severed, she checked her way and drew out of range, and the two vessels plunged on, the frigate half a mile to windward and as far astern, till from the decks of the *Doutelle* could be seen the clear green of the great Atlantic billows as they swelled up against the rocks direct ahead and broke over them in thunder.

The promontory which divides the bays of Kenmare and Bantry terminates in an island three miles long, called Dursey, or including the rocks round it and outside it, the Durseys. From a distance this island appears like a continuation of the mainland, and is in fact divided from it only by a sound or strait a couple of miles wide and as many deep, which narrows at the bottom like the neck of a bottle and terminates in a passage, in places half a pistol-shot across, leading from one bay to another. Fishing boats use it, but, from the rocks at the most critical points and from the violent stream of tide which runs through, vessels of larger size never venture that way if they can help it, even in smooth water and with a fair wind; and no one at all can venture at any time without the most intimate local knowledge.

The basin of the sound itself before it draws in, is formed by Dursey Island on the west side, on the east by a long arm of land called Crow Head, a sort of natural pier or breakwater. Outside this Head, at a hundred fathoms distant, is a dangerous reef called the Catrock, the passage between the Catrock and Crow Head being held impassable in any weather from sunk rocks. Inside the sound, with a westerly wind, the water is calm, the island acting as a shelter. But everywhere else the waters roll in unchecked, breaking the whole line of the coast from Berehaven to Dursey, and it was at the middle of this line, at the point known as Black Ball Head, that the *Doutelle* was now coming up to the land.

At her first start across the bay she had looked outside Dursey Island. She had fallen off till she could barely fetch the Sound. To escape the frigate she had edged in still further, while the wind had drawn up a point further to the north; she had thus just weathered Black Ball Head, and had another half mile for which she could stand on between her and the shore.

It was no time for fighting now. The guns were secured, and Morty went again to the helm. As he had failed to touch the frigate in any way that would check her speed, his position now seemed desperate. Colonel Craig's settlement was but seven or eight miles off under his lee. He was tempted for a moment to dash the vessel on the beach there, and die, as became an O'Sullivan, in a last furious revenge upon his enemy. But there was still a chance of saving both ship and men, and he had no right to throw it away. No one spoke to him, for he had an ugly look in his face. With set lips and arms rigid, he clutched the tiller and watched the coast, as the *Doutelle* rushed in under the shadow of the cliffs.

The frigate herself lay half-way between him and Dursey Head. She supposed that the *Doutelle* must pass outside it; and that there was no occasion for her to run needless risks. She had but to wait, and the doomed vessel would fall into her hands if Morty did not plunge her desperately upon the breakers, as to appearance he seemed bent on doing.

On flew the *Doutelle*, till her bowsprit plunged into the spray which fell back from the cliff as the great rollers burst upon them. The officers on the deck of the *Æolus* were watching to see her run upon the rocks. They could not help a cry of admiring surprise when at the last moment they saw her sweep round like a racing cutter within her own length, her canvas fill on the other tack, and the vessel begin to move fast up the shore. The wind was, as Morty anticipated, blowing right off; all his canvas drew, and fiercely as the squalls came down he held his course straight up towards the outer mouth of Dursey Sound. The frigate filled on the same course a mile ahead, but being without the same advantage fell off towards the sea. The advantage would be but momentary, however, for off the Sound the *Doutelle* would again meet the true wind and the weight of the sea, and the *Æolus* would resume her superiority. The passage through into the Kenmare River was marked in her charts as only practicable for small boats and the end, though protracted for half-an-hour, was none the less assured.

It was beautiful to see the smaller vessel flying on, her lee gunwale buried to the water line, her tall masts bending like whips and her boom and the bottom of her mainsail dipping in the water as the waves rolled under her. The frigate was waiting for her half a mile off the land, with her fore canvas backed, and the distance between them was rapidly narrowing; but as long as the *Doutelle* had the wind from the land it was impossible for her antagonist to close with her; and for three miles Morty was able to hold his course before he reached Crow Head.

Here, however, the coast took a bend to the south-east, the wind followed it, and he was obliged, at last, as the English officers saw that he would be, to keep away to the sea and face them. By his knowledge of the coast and by admirable skill he had gained the weather-gauge, and would cross the *Æolus*'s bows, but at so short a distance that it seemed like madness to venture it. It would not be a single broadside which he would have to face, for as the *Doutelle* came up the foretopsails of the *Æolus* were filled, and she too began to fly through the water, tossing the spray over her bows, on a course exactly parallel to her intended victim's.

For Morty it seemed there was nothing for it but to stand on, with his great antagonist first a quarter of a mile and then but a hundred fathoms to leeward of him, over the five miles which still lay between them both and the point of the long headland round which lay the *Doutelle*'s chance of escape. The privateer crew were sent below, every one of them. The side of the vessel exposed to the frigate's guns being buried in the water, the deck might be swept and torn to splinters; but as long as she remained floating they would themselves be out of danger. It was no time for fighting. They had to trust to their seamanship.

Morty alone, of all the company, stood at the helm, his hair streaming in the wind as it escaped under the folds of a handkerchief. Firm as iron he held on, watching and avoiding each approaching wave, and heedless of the storm which he knew must in a moment descend upon him. So fine it was to see him, so daring and desperate with his enterprise, that on the *Æolus* they hesitated for a moment to fire upon him. They had made up their minds that the Rover which had caused them so much trouble should either sink or strike, but they would gladly have spared so beautiful a craft and so gallant a commander if he would only surrender.

Seeing, however, that there was no sign of lowering the flag, the frigate's broadside opened, gun after gun, first singly then all the guns upon a side together. At so short a distance every shot told. The decks of the *Doutelle* were ripped open, being entirely exposed as she lay over to the wind, and splinters flew from stem to stern. The marines from the frigate's tops poured in volleys of musketry, and the musket balls could be heard rattling when they struck. For five minutes the tempest lasted. No structure of oak and copper could bear another five of so pitiless a tornado. Yet the point of Dursey lay half an hour ahead of them, and no miracle could be looked for to save a crew of pirates. The spars and cordage of the *Doutelle* were so far untouched, as the fire had been directed upon the hull. Morty had not escaped entirely, a ball had torn his cheek open; but he was still erect, as if the storm had been pelting him had been but drops of rain. Still he held on, never looking at his enemy, glancing now at the sea and now at the land.

Rushing on together the two vessels thus reached Crow Head and could look into Dursey Sound. Half a mile in front was Catrock, rising black among the streams of foam which poured down its sides as the seas broke over it, and between Catrock and Crow Head were a line of reefs under water among which the great waves burst and thundered.

There, if anywhere on earth, lay the hopes of Morty Sullivan, for among those reefs there was a passage into the Sound, narrow, tortuous, perilous, through which he had himself once steered a smuggling lugger in a storm; and if he survived the hail that was rattling about him he believed that he could do it again. Impracticable though the officers of the *Æolus* supposed the passage to be from the Sound into the Kenmare River, they conjectured that Morty must be intending to try it; but beween the Catrock and the Head not one of them had any notion that it was possible to pass at all.

They were about to close with him and make an end, when there was a sudden call in the *Doutelle* of 'about ship'. Morty sent his helm down. The crew swarmed up from below and handled the sails. Round she came, no longer offering a broad-side mark to the *Æolus*, but turning her stern to her and rapidly leaving her, and dashing in direct upon the boiling cauldron. The frigate held on upon her course, believing that Morty was running purposely on shore, and herself unable to follow till she had weathered the Catrock. In another moment the privateer was in a turmoil of waters as wild as the Maelstrom.

But her pilot had not overrated the accuracy of his recollection. The blood dripped fast from his shattered cheek, but he never left the helm. On the gallant vessel passed, the dark rocks starting up all round her in the hollows of the waves; leaking badly in places, from the *Æolus*'s shot, for her starboard side was now under water, where she had been wounded by balls which had passed through her deck. Through she went, unscathed, and made her way into the quiet waters of the Sound.

He shook off his enemy, and by his bold manoeuvre gained a mile upon him. The cut into the Kenmare River was now but a mile from him. He might be wrecked in passing through, or he might be sunk from the holes which had been already made in him, but the *Æolus* did not mean if she could help it to let her prey get off. Astonished and mortified, Captain Elliot, for so her commander was named, stood on till he had passed the Catrock. Not believing that Morty could get through after all, he too then went about and followed him up the Sound as far as he dared.

Morty, whether he was to escape or perish, would not leave the friend which had stuck so close to him without a parting benediction. The crew were all busy stopping leaks with rags or clouts, or anything which came to hand. He himself, leaving the tiller to Connell, loaded his own favourite gun, which had fortunately escaped damage. The water in the Sound being still, there was no longer a rolling platform. With his bleeding cheek rested on the breech, and his eye steadied to the precision of an instrument, he covered the line of the frigate's masts as she came behind him. The shot sped upon its way. It caught the foot of the foretopmast. A squall came down at the same moment off the cliff, and Morty saw the tall spar bend, double over, and then fall, carrying down upon her decks a confused mass of rope and sail and splintered timber. The jib-boom snapped off, the frigate flew up into the wind, and there she lay, till the wreck could be cleared, at the mercy of the winds and waves.

Cool, but exulting as he had a right to be, Morty sprang upon the binnacle and waved his cap as a parting salute. The next moment the *Doutelle* and her Captain had passed out of sight round the end of the island, and entered the narrow channel. Both to him and to Connell every twist and turn of it was familiar. They passed through their second peril without misadventure, and were safe in the open waters of the Kenmare River. Never more would any member of the *Doutelle*'s company raise a question of the qualities of their commander. Morty, who had taken the danger upon himself, was the only one of them all who had been seriously injured.

But if the crew had escaped danger, such had not been the fortune of the *Doutelle*. The shot had torn through her deck, and started her timbers. The holes in her sides had been plugged, but the water was reported as rising in her hold, and unless she could be beached somewhere, and promptly, her escape from destruction might prove but a brief respite. Where to go in such a dilemma was a problem. Morty's own bay at Eyris was close by and safe, with level sand. But Colonel Goring would be but a few miles off, at Castlehaven. The *Æolus* it was likely would put in there to refit, and two hundred blue jackets might come down upon him over the hill while his ship was on the ground.

Eyris could not be thought of, but there was another spot not far from Connell's home at Darrynane, where for Connell's own sakes they would be certain of hospitality, if not demanded for too long. At the wildest point of Kerry, where the deep Bay of Ballinskelligs has been scooped out by the waves which have rolled in from the Atlantic for millions of years, a peninsula which has since parted from the mainland and become an island, still sheltered, as it had done for ages, a small haven. Tempted by the situation a colony of maritime monks who lived by fishing, had built an abbey on the shore, and had excavated an inner boat harbour for themselves. The monks were gone, the abbey lay in ruins. The sea had broken a passage behind the island, was tearing away the cemetery, and strewing the beach with fragments of bones and coffins. The neglected boat harbour was beginning to fill up. But the mouth of it was still available at spring tides, and happily it was just new moon.

Hither Morty carried his wounded *Doutelle*. Here, out of sight and out of ken (for great headlands and mountainous islands lay between him and the Sound, where he had left his pursuers), he took her in at high water, and laid her gently on the sands as she had deserved by her splendid behaviour. Here too we may leave him to repair his damages, replace his started planks, and finally make his way back to Nantes, which he reached successfully at the end of a fortnight.

Chapter XVI

AMENITIES OF GOVERNMENT

THE firing of heavy guns in Dursey Sound had been heard at Dunboy, and Goring's sanguine temperament had assured him that the work was being done effectively, and that they would hear no more of Morty Sullivan and his clipper. It was therefore with no small disappointment that he saw the crippled *Æolus* creeping in to the anchorage before his windows, and heard from Captain Elliot the unsuccessful result of the engagement.

In Ireland, as in all countries pervaded generally by disaffected feeling, news spread rapidly, no one knows how; and before two days were over, Elliot's expectation that, after all, perhaps the *Doutelle* had gone to the bottom, was proved to be baseless. She had been seen crossing the mouth of the Kenmare River, and disappearing among the islands. She had been beached in Ballinskelligs Bay. She had been repaired. She had suffered little or nothing. She had sailed for France again.

The failure filled the friends of the French and of Morty with a hardly concealed delight; and the shattered spars of the frigate were a witness of his daring, and a promise of future triumphs. The satisfaction was not too openly expressed, for the victory was by no means unqualified. If a king's ship had been baffled and beaten off, the fight at Glengariff, and the destruction of the cargo of arms, had inspired a wholesome fear of Goring's Protestant colonists.

But for this very reason, it was the more likely that the disordered bands in the mountains might make some desperate fight to destroy them. Morty himself might return and lend a hand, to revenge himself, as soon as the frigate was gone; and Elliot, considering that it would be neither safe for the public interest, nor fair to Colonel Goring, to leave him to control on his own resources a district so exposed, and so mutinous, thought it best to remain at Berehaven till he had communicated with the Government at Dublin.

Many years had passed since a ship of war had been seen in the harbour. The Irish had been encouraged by the apparent indifference to Goring's requests for assistance. Captain Elliot wrote at length, and Goring wrote. Often had Goring told the same story to deaf ears, but he was supported now by a distinguished officer, who had been specially directed to make enquiries.

For three weeks they waited for the reply. At length it came. The authorities at the Castle had taken time to deliberate, and they answered thus:

'His Excellency was not insensible of the service which Colonel Goring had rendered, in checking the enterprises of a dangerous privateer. The offence of smuggling, serious in itself, assumed a graver complexion when connected with the introduction of arms, the enlisting recruits for the enemy, and the encouragement of political disaffection. Supposing therefore the account which had been forwarded to be correct, a point on which his Excellency, for the present, offered no opinion, he had no fault to find with Colonel Goring's conduct.

'At the same time, he could not admit that the practices to which Colonel Goring had drawn attention, prevailed to the extent which both he and Captain Elliot assumed; his Excellency trusted that the lesson which the smugglers had received, would suffice to deter them for the future from a renewal of such enterprises; and, with respect to the request that one of his Majesty's vessels should be stationed at Dunboy, his Excellency regarded such a measure as unnecessary in itself, as an affront to the loyalty of his Majesty's good Catholic subjects in those districts, and as interfering with the important duties attaching to his Majesty's ships in other parts of the Empire.

'In conveying to Colonel Goring and his tenants and servants his appreciation of the courage and loyalty which he understood them to have displayed, his Excellency desired further to remind both him and them, that living as they were, surrounded by a population of a different race and religion, it was their duty to avoid, as far as possible, everything which might give reasonable offence. His Excellency thought it the more necessary to insist on this point, as he had learnt, to his regret, that the English families whom Colonel Goring had introduced upon his estate, did not conform to the Established Religion, but professed opinions which, in the judgment of the excellent Prelates to whom the spiritual care of the country had been committed, were not calculated to promote peace and good feeling.

'Trusting that nothing which had been said would be taken as reflecting upon the conduct of Colonel Goring, for whom he entertained the highest respect,

'He had the honour to be, etc.'

The same messenger brought an order for the instant return of the *Æolus* to Cork in terms which amounted to a reproof to the Captain for having been so long absent without orders.

It was too much. This was all the thanks then to Colonel Goring for five years of toil and danger. A qualified acknowledgment which was almost a rebuke, and a definite intimation that no help would be given him.

It was not, however, the refusal of support and the steady discouragement of his efforts which gave him the greatest anxiety. It was the animosity, visible in the letters and visible in the whole action of the authorities towards him, against the settlement itself which he had formed. He had built and endowed the church at Glengariff at his own expense, in the hope of conciliating the Bishop. But building the church had been made an excuse for the continued refusal of the registration license for the Independent chapel at Dunboy. He had appealed to the Bishop, and from the Bishop he was again referred to the Grand Jury of the county, of whom by the letter of the statute he seemed entitled to demand consent. But again the Grand Jury pretended that the Dunboy congregation professed opinions of the lawfulness of which they were not satisfied. The question was referred back to the Primate, and with the Primate it was left to be considered, and never was considered.

Goring was perfectly certain that unless they might serve

God after their own fashion, and bring up their children in their own prnciples, the best of his people would certainly refuse to remain with him.

As yet nothing serious had been done. The congregation had continued to meet. The Falmouth minister had preached and prayed, and the meddling of the clergyman in the school had been disarmed by judicious diplomacy. But this could not go on for ever. Recent events had drawn attention to the colony, and the power and usefulness of such a community in encountering disorder had been displayed in a remarkable way. Absurd as was the general administration of the country, Colonel Goring could not believe that wilfully and with their eyes open the Government could desire to destroy it.

He determined that he would go himself to Dublin, make his way into the presence of the great persons there, and learn what they really meant. He was a stranger to the ways of politicians. He had never moved in political circles, and his experience at a distance had not created any anxiety to be more intimately acquainted with them. But politicians he understood were human creatures, and even a superior kind of human creatures, and he was anxious to see what they could be like, and to learn the principles of their actions, which were leading to such unaccountable results.

Among the Fellows of Trinity College he had a near relative, a Mr. Fitzherbert, who would be his heir if he died without children. Fitzherbert was thirty-five years old; he moved in the highest society in the metropolis, and was a critic and a man of the world. He had not sought admittance to either of the learned professions. Though intimately acquainted with every member of the House of Commons, he had never invited the suffrages of a constituency, and had amused himself with watching the action from outside of the most corrupt assembly in the world.

He had often invited Goring to pay him a visit; and Goring on the other hand felt that no one would be better able than Fitzherbert to explain the situation to him. Parliament was to meet at the end of November. The session was to be an exciting one, and every person of consequence would be in Dublin for the occasion, even to the Viceroy, whose visits to Ireland were brief and rare as those of angels. A better opportunity could not be found. His kinsman welcomed his proposal with enthusiasm, and added an invitation from the Provost for the distinguished Colonel to be a guest at the College.

It was arranged that Mrs. Goring should spend the weeks that her husband might be absent with a friend at Cork. Dunboy was a wild place in mid-winter. The friend entreated, Colonel Goring approved. The Governor of Cork offered to send an escort to Bantry. The lady at least was in good hands and safe, and the Colonel went upon his way.

Irish country gentlemen in the middle of the eighteenth century made their journeys on horseback. Carriage roads were few, and being unmetalled were cut into ruts a foot deep. Men of business travelled in companies for protection. Lords and ladies were attended by retinues of servants heavily armed, for Rapparees and Tories were still on the prowl, Whiteboys had sprung out of the earth like the mystic warriors that grew out of the teeth of the dragon. Dissolute young spendthrifts, even out of the upper families, were not ashamed to mend their fortunes on the highway. Not in Kerry only but throughout the whole of Munster, the peasantry were busy tearing up the landlords' farms at night, or carding tithe proctors, or drilling to be ready for the landing of the French.

It was a wild scene in which those who could find a home elsewhere would not care to reside, and those who were obliged to reside in it might be expected to stir but rarely from under their own roofs. Habit, however, which inures us to everything, rendered life in such circumstances not tolerable only, but delightful. Irish society grew up in happy recklessness. Insecurity added zest to enjoyment, and the solid Saxon families which were spread over the soil under Cromwell and Charles the Second, finding themselves unprotected by law and left to their own resources, adapted themselves to their new element and lived for the day that was passing over them, leaving the morrow to care for itself. They had a charm about them, peculiarly their own, a charm of high refinement along with habits wild as a red Indian's. They were reckless, careless, infinitely hospitable and utterly extravagant, regardless of law, but graceful in the neglect of it, only too like in a new element to the original Celts among whom they had been planted.

Colonel Goring was passed along among them from mansion to mansion, no gentleman being allowed under penalties to go to an inn, when recommended under the universal rule from one host to another. He was entertained with boundless cordiality. To some he was known by reputation, with others from his service in the army he had a distant acquaintance. He was amused, he was horrified, he was occasionally interested. More and more he found himself speculating on what could be the political future of a country of which such light beings were the social chiefs. To him it seemed as if the English settled in Ireland were playing over the crust of a sleeping volcano, which they were themselves half aware of and tried to forget in light-heartedness. Many of them like himself were moving to Dublin for the season, and, if he had pleased he might have attached himself to one or other party for the entire journey. But he preferred his own society, and hurried forward under pretext of urgent business.

A November evening was closing in when, after encountering no particular adventure beyond a faction fight on market-day at Thurles, where a dozen people were killed, and no one thought anything about the matter, Colonel Goring found himself entering the Irish capital. He was almost a stranger there. His youth and early manhood had been spent with the army abroad. He had been some time in Galway with his friend Eyre; but to the Viceroy's Court and the smart circles about St. Stephen's Green he was an absolute stranger. Once or twice he had passed through Dublin on his way to or from England: that was all that he knew of it. His road lay beside the Liffey, along the broad, level, but ill-lighted causeway, which formed the margin of the river. Something seemed to be going on, for a steady stream of people was flowing eastward along the embankment, growing as it advanced, from fresh additions pouring in from adjoining streets and lanes.

The administration of Ireland, if inefficient, was at least

economical. If little was done, little was demanded of the people for doing it. There was neither police in city or country, nor systematic organization of any kind to make the law respected. If Ireland was ungoverned, there was no charge for neglecting to govern it; the revenue exceeded the expenditure; there was an annual surplus; and the Government in London and the Irish politicians could not agree as to which of them had a right to the disposition of it. No middle term being discoverable between views so opposite, and each side being obstinate, the Irish members had threatened that as soon as Parliament met they would refuse the supplies.

The Castle had tried to undermine the coalition against it by corruption. The success had, so far, fallen short of what was usual on such occasions, and there had been threats in consequence, both in London and among the supporters of the Castle in Dublin, to suppress the Irish Parliament altogether and either vote the taxes in the English Parliament, or else dispense with them and carry on the Government, which could hardly be more a shadow than it already was, with the part of the revenues which had been permanently settled on the Crown.

The session was to open on the day on which Colonel Goring arrived in Dublin. The Viceroy had landed a few days previously with the latest instructions from London, and an impression had gone abroad that a proposal was to be introduced for the modification of the Constitution, which certain members of both houses had been bribed into promising to support. A patriotic demonstration was in consequence about to be held at the doors of the Parliament House, and the crowds whom the Colonel had fallen in with, were streaming towards College Green for the purpose.

There had been heavy rain for the last few days. The Liffey was coming down in a brown flood. The streets were deep in mud, and through the yellow fog the link-boys could be seen running with their torches by the side of chairs and coaches, the occupants of which were either bound out to dinner, or were on the way themselves to the opening. The throng of vehicles was thickest at the gate of the Castle, where the Vice-

THE TWO CHIEFS OF DUNBOY

roy, it seemed, was entertaining some distinguished party.

Finding the crowd grew denser as he advanced, Goring left his horse with his servant, to follow at leisure to the College, and pursued his way on foot. From the talk of the people round him he gathered in fragments the cause of the excitement, of which as yet he had heard little or nothing.

'Ah, then,' said one, 'the bloody Saxons will be taking our Parliament away, and setting our necks under the feet of the soldiers. Bad cess to the race of them. 'Twas a black day for Ireland that brought the heretic divils among us.'

'It is the Parliament men themselves,' said another, 'that is selling the country for the pensions; they would sell their souls out of their bodies for King George's gold, if the divil hadn't a mortgage on them already.'

'Little good the Protestant Parliament ever did us,' said a third. 'We will have a Parliament of our own again as we had in King James's days, and those will be the boys that will make them skip. The French are coming, and the ould owners will be back upon the land.'

'If ye wait till the French come to help ye, ye will be waiting long in my thinking,' said a woman who was plunging along with a troop of Amazons about her, her snaky ringlets streaming out from under a tattered bonnet. 'Sure the gentry would be well enough if they knew how to behave themselves, the poor cratures. We will take possession of the Parliament House ourselves this night, to give them their instructions, and may be they will do better in time to come.'

'There may be two words to that bargain, Mary my lass,' said a man in a sailor's dress, who had just come up out of the 'liberties' with a party of seamen. 'There is a regiment of Dragoons in the Castle barracks, that will be breaking out upon ye before the night is much older.'

'Is it the Dragoons break out upon us?' exclaimed the woman. 'And who will be giving them the orders I wonder, and don't we know every mother's son of them, the darlings; and won't the girls here melt the hearts of them with the glances of their purty eyes?'

The mob assumed every moment a more formidable appearance. They were joined by compact bodies of men, armed with cutlasses, pikes, and pistols, and moving under orders with some form of discipline. They gathered steadily in volume till they reached the open space in front of the Houses of the Legislature, and proceeded to take military possession of the Green and its approaches. The iron railings surrounding the sanctuary of the Irish Constitution, were torn down. Strong detachments occupied the doors and the flights of steps which led up to them. Space in front was left sufficient to allow the members to drive up. As Peer or Commoner arrived, the door of his carriage was opened. His name was shouted out, and was greeted with applause if his patriotism was above suspicion, but more often with howls or derisive scorn and laughter. An oath to be true to Ireland and Irish liberty was then proposed to him. If he swallowed it, he was allowed to pass on. If he resisted or refused, his horses were quietly turned round and he was advised to go home, or worse might befall him.

Colonel Goring had by this time discovered that in leaving Bantry Bay he was in the same Ireland as before. Authority was as feeble in Dublin as in his own peninsula, and the sacred ark of Irish liberty was the centre of the fire. Most of it he understood but too well. Mr. Francis —, the Chancellor of the Exchequer, with one of his colleagues on the Board, had taken advantage of a full Treasury to set up a private Bank, using, so malicious rumours said, the public money for their capital. The Bank had failed, causing widespread ruin. The Exchequer accounts were unintelligible; but the estates of Mr Francis — and his friend were found to have been secured against the creditors, and also to have been cleared of their incumbrances.

Mr. Francis —'s name was a signal for a general yell, and he might have been roughly handled, had not the woman with the snaky hair, who had made her way to the front of the crowd, mockingly protected him.

'Arrah, then, Mr. Francis,' she cried, 'it's yourself that is the right boy for the place ye are holding; ye have been careful of the surplus, God bless ye, that them English would have been carrying away from us, and ye have put it safe into the Irish soil, where it will be for the redeeming of the dirty papers that ye set going upon us from your bank.'

'Ye'll be pleased to swear, sir, before we let ye pass,' said a big man, flourishing a sword over the unlucky official's head, 'that ye will give up that land of yours to the poor people that ye have swindled.'

Mr. Francis — mumbled, stuttered, protested, and looked about him, angry and helpless.

'Don't be spoiling the handsome face of ye that way, Mr. Francis,' said the woman. 'What are ye afraid of, man? Sure ye have sworn oaths enough in your life, and broken them too, that you are choking now when we are asking ye to be an honest man for once in your life. Swallow the words down, me honey, and ye'll be the better for it afterwards.'

The unlucky Mr. Francis — would have been forced to promise to disgorge his plunder, had not the attention of the people been called off by a more important arrival. Surrounded by servants and link-boys, there now drove up no less a person than the Irish Lord Chancellor. His attendants, who were accustomed to find their master treated with a respect second only to what was paid to the Viceroy, ordered the crowd imperiously to clear out of the way. Finding they did not immediately obey, the coachman flogged his horses, and struck a man across the face with a whip who had taken them by the head to prevent their plunging. The driver was dashed in a moment off his box; the servants were hustled and beaten; and a paving stone was flung through the carriage window as an intimation to the great man that he must come out.

The Chancellor, Lord B—, was an Englishman. He was supposed to have been put in possession of the seals for the express purpose of suppressing the constitution, and was thus the especial object of suspicion and animosity.

Seeing that it was useless to resist, Lord B— alighted, and stood fronting the mob with an eye which overawed them in spite of themselves.

'My Lord,' said one of the best mannered of the leaders, 'we are sorry to be rough with you, but we must require a promise of you this night on your oath. Ye will please to take an oath that ye will do nothing, either in your office or in your place in Parliament, against the Liberties of Ireland.'

'We don't know the rights of it, your honour,' said another, 'but they do say that the British nation is tired of quarrelling with the Parliament here, that they mean to make an end of it, and vote the taxes which they intend to take from us themselves.'

'It is a dream,' the Chancellor replied. 'The British nation have no such purpose. Emissaries from our enemies in France have been telling you lies about us. The British nation means only good to Ireland, and has never meant aught else but good.'

' 'Deed then,' said the man, 'if the intention is good, the performance falls mighty short of it. But if your Lordship spakes the truth, the oath won't harm ye. Ye have only to say the words as we will put them to ye.'

'I will not swear,' the Chancellor said. 'I will not degrade my office by taking an oath at the dictation of an armed rabble.'

'There is a ground apple to teach ye manners then, ye ugly-mouthed villain,' said one of the women, and she flung a stone at him which grazed his cheek. There would have been a general rush in another moment.

Colonel Goring, who had been standing a few yards off, seeing violence begun, was springing forward to help his countryman and save or fall with him, when the first speaker who had addressed the Chancellor, and appeared to exercise some authority, strode to his side with a pistol in each hand. 'Back with ye,' he said. 'Will ye dishonour the good cause by a cowardly murder? If any of ye dare lift a finger against this gintleman, by the blessed angels I will send his soul to Paradise.'

It was a scene for a picture—the fierce faces of the crowd lighted by the flaming torches, the proud old Chancellor standing pale and scornful, menaced with death, and the mob leader thrusting himself between them with set teeth and cocked pistol.

'My Lord,' he said, 'no hurt shall be done you; but unless you swear to be true to Ireland, you will not enter the Parliament House this night. Bid your men turn your horses; get into your

THE TWO CHIEFS OF DUNBOY

carriage and go home with ye, and give thanks to God that He has saved ye this time from worse.'

It was still doubtful whether he would have been allowed to retire uninjured, when a voice exclaimed:

'What will we be doing now then, as his Lordship has been plased to retrate? There is the good gentlemen and the great Lords and the like that swore as we told them, and they are just waiting in their places to begin the business of the night.'

'Business of the night is it?' said another. 'Sure the business is to hear what King George's deputy has to say to them, and who is to tell us what that will be?'

'Ah, then,' cried the sailor, addressing the woman to whom he had spoken on the road. ''Twas yourself that said it, Mary my darling. There shall be no message from King George this night, but there shall be a message from ould Ireland, and your own voice shall give it, with the Chancellor's big wig on the head of ye. Sure the jintlemen that have sworn the oath are good Irish, but they have the English cross in them, and it will do no harm for once to have a lady of the country to speak to them. Come along with ye, Mary, and we'll sate ye on your throne.'

With the mixed feeling—half of glory in the Parliament, as a national institution, half of contempt for it as Protestant and an English importation—the mob hurled themselves against the doors of the building, which the ushers vainly laboured to keep closed. They swayed along the passages, and poured into the upper chamber, where some fifty peers and half-a-dozen bishops who had passed the ordeal were expecting, in pallor and anxiety, what was next to follow. The people swarmed in among them, scrambling over the velvet and gold which covered the chairs and benches, jostling against scarlet robes and lawn sleeves—the potter's coarse clay against painted porcelain.

Mary Dogherty was conducted in state to the woolsack. The Chancellor's gown was thrown over her back, and the wig squeezed down upon her tattered bonnet.

'Light your pipe now, Mary,' said one. 'Ye will not be complete without the dudheem in the mouth of ye. When we have drawn a whiff or two to compose yourself, we'll go to business, and you shall give us your spache from the Throne.'

It would have, probably, been a speech as remarkable, and perhaps with as much sense in it as many which had been, and will be, delivered from similar places, but, unfortunately, it was not delivered after all. The interruption came from the source which Mary's sailor friend had first anticipated. She had finished her pipe, had flung off her wig and bonnet, and had stood up to begin, when a shout was heard from without of 'The Dragoons!' and the sound of the sharp trot of a body of horse. Rough work had still to be done before an Irish legislature could settle down under its new presidency to regenerate their country.

RIOT IN DUBLIN

COLONEL GORING, seeing that the rioters were in possession of the Houses of Parliament, and that no effort was being made by the authorities to restrain them, forced his way through the crowd to Trinity College. The gates were closed, but, on his explaining that he had come on a visit to one of the Fellows, he was admitted through a wicket. The quadrangle was thronged with students, who were clamouring to go out and act as extemporized policemen. Trinity College was proud of its loyalty. The present outbreak had been so sudden, and was so unusually violent, that the Provost had hesitated how to act. He had directed that the students should be kept within walls till the nature of the disturbance could be better ascertained, and he was himself in the middle of them, trying to moderate their impetuosity, when Goring arrived.

The Fellows were all assisting their Chief, and the Colonel had no difficulty in discovering among them his kinsman, Fitzherbert. Fitzherbert introduced him to the Provost, to whom his adventures at Derreen and Glengariff were already well known, having been the talk of Dublin.

There was no leisure for conventional politeness. The Provost shook his guest heartily by the hand, telling him that he was come at the right moment, and a rapid conversation followed as to what was best to be done. The Provost, after hearing Goring's description of what he had himself witnessed, decided that a couple of hundred students, whose courage and steadiness could be relied upon, should be allowed out under Goring's command. The Fellows would not be behind-hand, and half-a-dozen of them, Fitzherbert among the rest, eagerly joined the party. The gates were flung right open, and they filed out into the Green.

The scene was now wilder than ever. By the glare of torches

a vast mass of men were seen surging to and fro, agitated and excited by the presence of a company of dragoons, whom Colonel Goring was, for the moment, relieved to see had at last appeared. It became soon evident, however, that, although called out, they had received no orders what to do.

The Chancellor, on being turned back from the House of Lords, instead of going home had driven at once to the Castle, where the Viceroy had a large dinner party, and informed him of the condition of the city. Never was ruler more taken by surprise. He enquired anxiously where the Mayor was, and desired an *aide-de-camp* to go in search of him.

'You will have no difficulty in finding the Mayor,' said a gentleman who had just entered from the street. 'I left his worship at the Green five minutes ago. He was sitting on his horse, telling the mob how much he admired their patriotism, and asking them if they would be so good as to go home.'

'Mr. Mayor,' said the Viceroy, as the city functionary entered the dining-room, 'what is the meaning of this disturbance? You are the chief magistrate in this city. You are responsible for the keeping of the peace. I insist that this insolent contempt of authority be suppressed on the spot. Call up your constables, arrest the ringleaders, and bid the rest of the crowd return to their homes.'

'My lord,' said the Mayor, 'it is true some of the poor misguided cratures yonder are a little misbehaving themselves. But your lordship may believe me it is no harm they are meaning. They are only a little excited like and expressing their feelings. And why wouldn't they, for the matter of that? Sure they have feelings like the best of us.'

'Misguided people!' exclaimed the Viceroy indignantly. 'Innocents creatures over-excited, and expressing their feelings! And here is my Lord Chancellor nearly murdered among them, and the House of Peers in possession of armed ruffians. What language is this? Call out the city force, Mr. Mayor I repeat, and no more words about it.'

'Indeed, your lordship,' said the Mayor, 'I may call as ye tell me; but the force ye are spaking of is but a company of fifty or sixty old bedesmen that can just crawl the rounds, and where would be the use of sending the like of them into the streets this night? Surely every mother's son of them is stowed away safe in his own house between the blankets at this moment, out of sound of harm. And where better would they be?'

'This is intolerable,' cried the Viceroy. 'Tell the guards in attendance to get to horse,' he said to an orderly in waiting. 'Let a hundred men ride down at once to the Green.'

'That will be force sufficient to enable you to deal with the disturbance, Mr. Mayor,' he said, turning to the magistrate; 'and it concerns my honour and yours that the leaders in this business be arrested and punished. You will accompany the troops. You will read the Riot Act, and if the mob does not then disperse you will know what to do. Why do you stand hesitating?' he continued, as the city functionary showed no signs of complying. 'Do you not know that you are answerable for the peace of the city? Is the law to be obeyed, or is it to be broken with impunity?'

'Your lordship speaks of the law,' answered the Mayor; 'but the law is a quare thing, and it is well for us to know where we are before we meddle or make with it. I'm thinking your lordship doesn't rightly understand the law of this country. And no wonder, for your lordship is a stranger. You tell me to read the Riot Act, and you are not aware that we have no Riot Act at all among us, the paceable nation that we are. I have no more power to direct your troops to act than your lordship has; and if your lordship will have the poor people shot down for the privileges of Parliament, you may give the order yourself.'

The trampling in the court-yard and the clanking of sabres announced that the dragoons were mounting, though what they were to do was as far from being settled as ever. The Viceroy, with the fear of his masters at home upon him, was determined to take no responsibility upon himself if he could possibly help it. The Mayor was equally determined that the Executive Government should not throw off a duty upon him which really belonged to themselves. The Mayor had the best of the argument; and the unhappy Viceroy wrung his hands as the shouts came swaying up in the night air. As a middle course, the dragoons were directed to ride down to the Houses of Parliament, and then remain drawn up to see whether the mob would be frightened. There was just a hope that the sight of them would restore order.

'You are come to look at the show, then,' said a big man, who had been active in the attack upon the Chancellor. 'Mighty fine ye are in your lace and gold, and it is pleased we are to see ye on the people's side. And kindly welcome are you too, young gentleman,' he said, turning to the cornet in command, 'if it is not a woman that I am speaking to as it is like I may be, to judge by the down that's on the purty cheek of ye.'

He patted the officer's charger as he spoke. The young Englishman touched the horse with the spur, which sprang forward and trampled on the man's foot, making him howl with pain. Immediately a shower of stones rattled about the dragoons' helmets. Five or six of them were struck in the face; and galled by the blows and by the insulting cries which rose round them, they were handling the hilts of the sabres, when at the moment the corps from the College appeared on the scene and called off the attention of the mob.

Well led, and eager for a fight, the students struck in with a will. But the mob were ten to one, and for some reason were exceptionally determined. Many of them had cutlasses, and some had pistols; and Goring was forced to hold the students in hand, watching his opportunity, and noting scornfully the inaction of the military, too like what he was familiar with in Kerry, when a fresh party of horse, led by a distinguished-looking man in a General's uniform, dashed in upon the scene.

The commander-in-chief of the English garrison in Ireland was the celebrated Lord A—. He was one of the Viceroy's guests for the evening, and had listened with angry impatience to the useless argument. An officer, whom he had sent out to make enquiries, came back with the news that stones were still flying. One of the men had been struck from his horse, and it was feared had been killed. The rest were becoming ungovernable, and, if they were not to act, were demanding to be recalled. The Viceroy was still wrangling with the Mayor, who had entrenched himself and could not be moved.

'You will make nothing of this fellow, sir,' said Lord A—, with a look of contempt. 'The rascal only wants to gain time. In a few minutes the mob will be in possession of the whole town this side of the river, and we shall have them looking in upon us here. Give me orders, or let me act on my own responsibility. Unless this riot is stopped, the Castle will be on fire before the morning.'

'Go then, A—' acquiesced the poor Viceroy. 'Go. Do the best you can. Only be gentle. No unnecessary violence.'

'Never fear, my Lord,' answered the General. 'I will be gentle as a turtle-dove. Violence!' he muttered, as he rushed downstairs, and sprang on his horse, calling the remaining dragoons to follow him.

With drawn sabres, they galloped down to join their comrades, trampling on everyone that got in their way. The company which had been so long suffering under the stone-throwing, received them with a shout of relief. For one moment Lord A— paused. He seized a ringleader by the collar, dragged him back into his own ranks, and ordered a sergeant to pinion him. In a clear, high voice, which could be heard above the roar of the crowd, he gave them a last chance to disperse. He was answered by a paving stone which struck his corselet, and shook him in the saddle, and at once he gave the order to charge.

All was ended then. Shrieking, yelling, swearing, they wavered, they broke; they fled up the side streets, both detachments of dragoons hewing at them in full pursuit, and the students avenging their own broken heads on the scattering masses. The students' share in the punishment was a merciful one, for they had only their blackthorns to strike with. It must be allowed to the soldiers' credit, too, considering how they had been tried, that the women and the old and the young they touched only with the flat of their swords, reserving edge and point for those who had been active in mischief. A corporal, however, was unluckily killed by a bullet from a window, as he alighted to save an infant who had fallen among the horses' hoofs. Some rascal used the opportunity to take deliberate aim at him, and shot him dead. Furious after this, they gave little quarter. The narrow lanes were littered with bodies. The crowd had been so dense that it could not immediately get itself dispersed, and half-an-hour passed after the orders to the troops, before the last straggler had been cut down, or had disappeared into alley or doorway. Then the torches were quenched: the streets of Dublin became again dark and silent and deserted, the singular outbreak of the subterranean fire which startled even the great Pitt, in the midst of his imperial dreams, was for this time suppressed and driven in.

Chapter XVIII

PRIMATE STONE

'I have come to Dublin,' Colonel Goring said to his host, as they sat at breakfast the next morning in Fitzherbert's rooms at Trinity, 'to obtain help in keeping order in Bantry Bay. I might as well have stayed at home, and spared myself the journey. You have not enough of the article for your own consumption.'

'My dear cousin,' replied Fitzherbert, 'the thing called order, you ought to know at this time, is an exotic over here. It has been imported from England, but it will not grow. It suits neither soil nor climate. What we are to-day, we have been for a thousand years, neither worse nor better. What ailed the English to be meddling with us at all? We were here before Noah's flood. The breed survived it somehow. As we were before, so we continued, fighting, robbing, burning, breaking each other's heads. But we killed each other down, and nature never meant that there should be more than a few of us in the world; and you English must needs come and keep the peace as you call it, and now there are three millions of us.'

'Shame on you, Fitz, to speak so of God's creatures,' said the Colonel. 'But what set them wild last night? What has the Parliament been doing that they are all in such a rage? I thought the politicians were all going in for patriotism just now.'

'Patriotism? Yes! Patriotism of the Hibernian order. The country has been badly treated, and is poor and miserable. This is the patriot's stock in trade. Does he want it mended? Not he. His own occupation would be gone. They are suspected of being willing to sell the Parliament itself, and the good people in Dublin don't like it.'

'And they have got their heads broken for their pains,' Goring answered, 'and some twenty of them they tell me have been killed. The Lord help them! My business I fear, will speed but badly, when you can manage no better at your own doors; but I must do what I can. I can hardly, I suppose, hope to be admitted to the Viceroy.'

'It would do you no good, if you could. The Viceroy is seldom here for more than a fortnight in two years. Our real masters are the three Lords Justices, Lord Kildare, the Speaker of the House of Commons and the Primate. Kildare is shuffled aside by the other two. The Speaker and the Primate do not love each other, but they have come to terms for their mutual advantages. The Primate is the strongest and holds the reins. In spiritual matters he is despotic; in secular, nearly so; but he is checked by a fear of a possible coalition against him of the Speaker and Kildare.'

'My special business lies with the Primate,' Goring said, 'and I mean to call on him this morning. If I am to keep my Cornishmen about me at Dunboy, I must get a license for a chapel for them. It is no great indulgence. They are entitled to it by the law, and they have earned it by their services. If they cannot serve God in their own way, they will go to America or back to England, and if they leave me I cannot stay there myself. What is the character of this powerful gentleman?'

'They call him here the Beauty of Holiness,' said Fitzherbert. 'But that I am forbidden by high authority to speak evil of the rulers of the people, I would add, myself, that he was one of Swift's highwaymen. You will remember that the Dean of St. Patrick's said the Government appointed excellent persons to the Irish sees, but it always happened that on their way to Bristol they fell among thieves, who stole their Letters Patent, crossed to Dublin, and got installed in their places. George Stone never took the road, that I heard of, but if half the stories are true which are told of him, it was not because he he was more honestly employed. Our present Viceroy pushed him forward. He was pretty to look at when he was young. They called him the Duke's Ganymede.'

'I don't ask you what the world believes about him. I ask you how much of all this you believe?'

'Well, a man does not rise in these days to be an Archbishop and Lord Justice of Ireland with nothing more to recommend him than a Duke's patronage. George Stone's grandfather kept the gaol at Winchester, and grew rich, it was said, by extorting money out of the prisoners. The family fortunes were on the ascending scale. The son of the master of the gaol became a banker and advanced loans to spendthrift young lords. Connections which he thus formed behind the scenes enabled him to push his own son forward, who, among his other gifts, had a face of singular beauty.

'The youth made the most of his opportunities. He was clever, proud, ambitious, perhaps unprincipled, skilful in flattering the great and in making stepping-stones of those below him. He was put into the Church, as the readiest road to preferment, and he adopted the high, legal, Anglican uniform. They gave him an Irish living, and directly after a Secretary's place at the Castle. Being obsequious and useful, he rose next to a Deanery, and then a Bishopric, and when the last Archbishop of Armagh died, he was advanced, while still far below middle age, to the Primacy. To us in Dublin he is known as intriguing, arrogant and overbearing. He is lavish of money, grasping always at power and steadily devoted to the views of his masters in England, whatever those views may be. His chief pleasure is in corrupting patriots, in which he is remarkably successful. Religion he is supposed to have none, but to be unaware of his deficiency, since he does not know what it means. He may not believe in God, but he certainly believes in the Apostolic Succession.'

To the Colonel's inquiry whether this astonishing prelate would be likely to see him, Fitzherbert answered neither yes nor no; he could not tell: but at least the Colonel might try, and he let him go, with a few formal instructions, to make the experiment.

The great man's residence was a palatial building in St. Stephen's Green. It stood in the midst of a large court or garden, which was approached from the road through massive gates of bronze, while from the court to the house itself, was a broad flight of stairs. Heathen gods and goddesses standing on pedestals in the lightest costume indicated that the Arch-

PRIMATE STONE

bishop's tastes were rather sensual than spiritual; and the sentinels at the doors and at the gates kept guard for him more as Lord Justice than as Primate. About the household there was an air of disquiet. Officers in uniform were passing in and out; and mounted orderlies were bringing or taking messages. Colonel Goring had some difficulty in prevailing on a lackey to take in his name and the lackey was himself evidently surprised, when he brought back word that the Colonel was to be admitted.

The Lord Primate or the Lord Justice, whichever he preferred to be called, had but lately risen. He was sitting in a large, handsomely-furnished library, sipping his chocolate. Letters and reports lay open, scattered about his table. He was himself glancing through the morning newspaper. In his hand was the *Advertiser*, a new paper just brought out by Mr. Lucas, a popular tribune, while the *Citizen's Journal* lay on the hearthrug as if impatiently flung aside.

Though he had passed middle life, George Stone had not yet lost the traces of the beauty to which he owed his fortune, and his dress was evidently designed to make the most of what remained. His costume was a long, loose, robe of purple silk, lined with ermine, which set off his height. Round his neck was a gold chain, from which a cross was suspended of pearls and emeralds, and a ring, with one splendid diamond in it, glittered on his delicate hand. At his wrists were elaborate frills of Flemish lace, and on his feet purple silk stockings and satin shoes, with gold buckles and rosettes. He was fifty years old, but so well cared for that he might have been taken for twenty years younger. His complexion was pale. The grey in his hair, if grey streaks had yet appeared there, was concealed by the powder. His eyes were dark-brown and softly brilliant, and his voice when he spoke, was a flute-toned tenor.

He did not rise when Colonel Goring entered, but smiled as if he had expected to see him and know the purpose of his visit. He motioned him to a seat, as a god might motion a mortal who had strayed within the Palace at Olympus. 'Colonel Goring,' he said, 'I am glad to see you. I heard that you were in the town and I looked for a call from you. You come early—

earlier perhaps than I was prepared for—but no matter. I much wished to speak to you.'

The Colonel bowed. The Archbishop continued:

'I understand that you were a witness of the unhappy scene which occurred last night in front of the Houses of Parliament. I am at this moment, as you may easily suppose, intensely occupied with what has taken place. As an officer and a gentleman you will give me an impartial account of what you yourself saw. I may add that your reputation as an active and efficient magistrate in your own district has not escaped my notice either. I have been for some time anxious for a word with you about that incident with which you were concerned at Glengariff. You are staying, I think, at the College?'

'My Lord,' replied the Colonel, 'I arrived in Dublin last night only, on a visit to a relative who is one of the Fellows. It is quite true that I was a spectator of the riot to which you refer. I saw the beginning of it, and I saw the bloodshed in which it unfortunately ended. But how or why my presence was taken notice of, and so brought under your lordship's observation, I am at a loss to conjecture.'

'You do not know that you are a notorious person, Colonel Goring,' rejoined the prelate. 'More eyes are on you than you are aware of. Do you think that I am finding fault with you? It was by mere accident that your name came before me. The Provost mentioned it in a report which he has just sent in on the conduct of the students. But this and your own opportune call enables me to speak to you on a subject very serious always, and now of graver moment than ever.'

He paused for an instant, looking steadily in Goring's face, and then went on: 'Such scenes as that which you witnessed last night, are fortunately of rare occurrence in this city. Many years have passed since there has been any disturbance here which has required the interference of the military. We had no warning of what was coming. There was no discontent among the people that we knew of, yet some cause, of course, there must have been. We have been enquiring anxiously into what that cause was, and we believe that we have discovered it.

'It has been proved to us beyond a doubt that the most

162

violent section of the mob consisted of artizans from the Earl of Meath's Liberty. As you are not, perhaps, sufficiently acquainted with the city to understand the meaning of this, I must inform you that the workmen in that quarter are almost to a man what we call Swaddlers, Protestant Dissenters, whom we owe to those most mischievous of modern agitators, Wesley and Whitfield. Under pretence of preaching a purer gospel, those gentlemen have revived the rebellious and independent spirit which dishonoured the Reformation by its excesses and led in the last century to Revolution and Regicide. That the evil seed has been brought hither is a frightful addition to our other difficulties. It is fortunate, however, that the true character of this sect should have so early and evidently betrayed itself.

'I speak frankly, Colonel Goring. I do not conceal from you that you have yourself been reported to me as showing favour to these people in your own district. That you should be personally connected with such miscreants is of course impossible; as an officer and a county magistrate you are necessarily a communicant in the Established Church; you are a gentleman and a man of honour, and can have nothing in common with ignorant and vulgar fanatics. But I am told that you have introduced some of this very rabble out of England to work your mines and fisheries. You have even applied for a license for them, under the Toleration Act, to have their own preachers and form of worship. I trust that you will take warning from what you have seen and will send them back to their own country at your earliest opportunity.'

Colonel Goring had seen too much of life to be easily surprised; but the charge against the unfortunate Wesleyans took away his breath. Of all imaginable suggestions on the origin of the riot, that it could be connected with Protestant Dissent was the most wildly impossible. Finding, however, that the Archbishop was really in earnest, he said:

'My lord, not more than a few hours have passed since the disturbance was at its height. There has been little time for examination. May I ask what proof you have obtained of the guilt of the parties whom you mention? Your Grace began with asking me to tell you what I saw myself. Certainly nothing that I saw would bear out the view which you are now expressing.'

'Colonel Goring,' replied the Primate shortly, 'I am not accustomed to use words at random. It is enough that an active inquiry has been carried on during the night, and the information brought to me is uniformly of the same complexion. The riot originated in the Earl of Meath's Liberties, where these anarchists are known to congregate. My agents are perfectly trustworthy. The inhabitants of those streets are well known to them, and they cannot be mistaken. We are so satisfied that we are on the right track that my secretaries are already writing their report, and it will leave for England by the yacht this evening.'

'You may think it unbecoming my Lord, in such a person as myself, to question the propriety of so hasty a decision. Your Grace is better judge than I can be of what it is fit for you to do. But as a magistrate, I am not without experience in such matters. If the facts be as you say, your agents must be able to lay hands on some, at least, of the ringleaders. Would it not be right that they should be arrested and questioned? A good many persons were unfortunately killed. The bodies can surely be identified.'

'Further enquiry is not necessary,' answered the Primate impatiently. 'You say you have had experience. Then you know enough of the people of Ireland to be aware that the last thing which you can get from any of them is the truth. One will lie, and another will lie, till facts are all lost in lies. We are satisfied, and that is enough.'

Goring opened his eyes even wider than before. He admitted the general truth of the Archbishop's indictment, but he observed that it applied equally to the evidence which had been made the basis of the report. 'My Lord,' he said, 'I say frankly that I mistrust information so quickly collected, and at once so positive and so consistent. It savours to me of a preconceived conclusion. But I must not argue with your Grace. I will proceed, if you will allow me, to the particular business which has brought me to Dublin. Your Grace has yourself alluded to it in terms which I fear promise ill for my success. I will, however, be as brief as I can.'

'The briefer the better, Colonel Goring,' said the Primate, who, knowing what was coming, had intended his declamation against the Dissenters to be a reply to any favour which might be asked of him, and, provoked by the Colonel's incredulity, would have now closed the interview. 'The briefer the better, for I have a busy morning before me.'

'A few sentences will be sufficient,' he replied. 'My residence, as your Grace knows, is at Dunboy on Bantry Bay, and I have got under my charge a hundred miles of coast line. The Bay is a general haunt of smugglers, privateers, French recruiting officers and rebel agents and incendiaries. Half the people in the country are in league with them, and the other half, who wish for a quiet life and an unburnt roof over their heads, prefer not to meddle with them. My duty is to maintain the law, and to bring to justice those who violate it. The force allowed me is wholly inadequate. I have applied for an increase, and I have been answered that I cannot have it, and I must manage as well as I can with my own resources. This is what I have tried to do.'

The Primate turned over his letters, drummed with his fingers on the table, and gave other signs of unconcealed impatience. 'Colonel Goring,' he said. 'I have nothing to do with the Revenue Board. You must address yourself to the Speaker, or to the Commissioners of Customs. I have more important matters to attend to.'

'Pardon me, my Lord,' answered Goring. 'Most unwillingly do I intrude upon your Grace's time. But your Grace and no one else can assist me. You alluded to the Protestant families whom I have introduced upon my estate. They are the persons in whose behalf I have to trouble you, and in spite of the unfavourable opinion which you appear to have formed of the character of these poor people, I still hope that I may induce you to modify your judgment.

'When at the time that I succeeded to my property, I was also given the charge of the Bay, I found it would be impossible for me to do my duty there with only the ordinary

Water-guard. The coast was beset with smugglers and pirates. I asked for a small Revenue sloop, and for a few months a sloop was allowed me. It was then removed, and I was told that it would not return. On this I then went to work with my own means. I established a fishery. I opened a copper-mine. I introduced those families of whom your Grace was pleased to speak, Protestants from Cornwall and from Ulster. Your Grace distrusts them. They were selected for me by friends on whose judgment I could rely, and I have found them the very best of men that I have ever known, brave, faithful, loyal, industrious. They have taken root. They have opened out the wealth of land and sea. They have thriven and prospered. With their help I have checked the smugglers and almost suppressed them. I have restored order in the Bay. I have a body of men with me who can be entirely relied on in case of local disturbance or a French landing. Some of them are Calvinists from the North of Ireland. The rest I must admit are what your Grace terms Swaddlers. They are men who were recovered (I fear I shall fall under your Grace's censure in what I am about to say)—who were recovered from practical atheism by Wesley and Whitfield, and were brought under the influence of Christianity. They cannot live without their religious services, and they claim as they are entitled to do by law, the benefit of the Toleration Act. The Bishop of the diocese refuses to allow their chapel to be registered. The grand jury of the county refer me to your Grace, and I cannot believe that a request so reasonable will be refused. I must add that the concession is a condition of their remaining with me. If their petition is again rejected, they will emigrate to the American plantations.'

The listless indifference had passed out of the Archbishop's face while the Colonel was speaking. His eyes flashed, his lips quivered. He made not the least attempt to restrain or conceal his anger. 'Their petition is again rejected,' he said; 'and let *me* add that I am astonished at your presenting it. The benefit of the Toleration Act to which you refer is limited to those of whose loyalty to the Crown there is no suspicion, and of the loyalty of these God-fearing Christians of yours we have no assurance at all. From what I hear of them they are like the

Fifth Monarchy men of the Usurper. I am astonished that you, who call yourself a member of the Establishment—who have even built a church and endowed it, such is your consistency— should desire to retain such a set of hypocrites about you. Protestant Dissent, sir, from the first hours of its appearance, has been the nursery of sedition. To what it led in England I need not remind you. Of the effects of it in this country we have had too recent and too bitter experience.'

'I have heard it said, my lord,' answered Goring, 'that the Protestant Apprentices who defended Derry were not generally members of the Episcopal communion; but I must not presume to contradict your Grace on a question of history. There may be bad men in all communities, religious or civil. My own request is in behalf of a set of persons who are individually known to myself, for whose conduct and character I can myself answer, and who have stood by me in my difficult duties with courage and fidelity. I ask no more for them than has been allowed since the Revolution to Nonconformists in England, and which it was supposed that the recent Act of the Irish Parliament had conceded in this country.'

'You will answer?' said the Primate, flushing with displeasure, 'and who, sir, I am obliged to ask, will answer for yourself? We hear of you—you, an officer of the Crown— publicly fighting a duel. We hear of you parading your religious indifference by building a church in one place and a chapel in another. When you speak of those persons standing by you, you allude, I presume, to your late exploit at Glengariff. There are two versions of that story. We have been given to understand that the vessel which came into Glengariff harbour was a French trader under French colours, that her crew were sent on shore for water and provisions, that they were fired into by a party under your command, and that many lives were lost in consequence. Complaints have been made to us by the French Consul of this performance of yours. In the present critical relations between France and Great Britain, it is unfortunate, to use a light word, that a fresh occasion of dispute should have arisen. Your zeal, sir, in the suppression of smuggling is well known to us; but it is possible to be too busy even in the discharge of a duty.'

Colonel Goring smiled. 'If you have any charge to bring against me, my lord,' he said, 'let me be called to my answer. It might be enough to say that this same harmless trader, when overtaken by a King's ship, three days later, refused to give an account of herself and fired upon his Majesty's flag. She was not merely a smuggler—she was landing arms for an intended insurrection. I have my evidence to produce. If it is insufficient let the law punish me.'

'We do not want your evidence, sir,' retorted the Primate, 'or the bad blood which the production of it would raise. You may be right or you may be wrong about the character of the vessel which you meddled with. I decide neither for you nor against you. But at a time when the ill-feeling between the different classes of the population in this country is dying away, when we are receiving the most gratifying assurances of loyalty from the leading Roman Catholics, and his Majesty's Government is contemplating a relaxation of the penal laws, nothing can be worse timed or more to be deprecated than the breaking out of these petty local conflicts, and the parade of them before the world. For this reason, and for many other reasons which I need not enter upon, we deprecate also the re-establishment in the South of those Protestant colonies, which provoke irritation and violence, and keep alive angry memories. If these people of yours wish to remain in Ireland they must conform to the Church established by the law. You cannot have two laws in the same country, and you cannot have two religions.

'For myself, I regret all these concessions to Protestant sects. They are a legacy to us from unsettled times, which I hope in time may be withdrawn; but we endure them among us as long as they are politically harmless. But we do not tolerate, and we never will, the Anabaptists or Socinians, whose principles undermine the foundation of civil society. We do not tolerate the random congregations of paltry and illiterate upstarts, who imagine that they are competent to form a religion for themselves. Such sects as these are the spawn of the seed left behind by anarchy and regicide, and we regard them as

PRIMATE STONE

the worst, perhaps as the only serious, danger which now threatens the peace of Ireland.'

Colonel Goring listened calmly to this impetuous invective. Strongly tempted though he was to speak his mind, he restrained himself; and drawing two scrolls of paper from his pocket he said quietly:

'Again I must decline to follow your Grace across so wide a field. But you say that the Protestants scattered about Munster must attend the parish churches, and be content with the ministrations of the parish clergyman. Will your Grace be kind enough to glance over these schedules?'

Impatiently the Archbishop took the papers and ran his eyes over them. They contained lists of the Episcopal churches in the Counties of Cork and Kerry, with a description attached to each of its present condition. In the entire Diocese of Ross there were but five parish churches in sufficient repair to allow service to be carried on in them. The rest were roofless and in ruins. In the seventy-nine parishes in Kerry, in all of which were remains of churches where men and women had met and prayed together, all but eleven were going to pieces, roof and doors gone, and windows fallen out. In the eleven which were still weather-proof, there was service in only six. The rest were deserted.

'Your Grace will observe,' the Colonel said, 'that with the exception of the church which I built myself at Glengariff, there is not one where there is any service within twenty miles of me. Glengariff is a long day's journey for women and children, and in refusing to allow my people their chapel you are condemning the majority of them to live like heathens. Nor can it be said that there are no means of making better provision for them; for the tithes are extorted to the last corn-sheaf or potato sack, while the poor people who pay them have built a mass house in every parish and support a priest of their own.'

Something which resembled a blush did for the moment tint the Primate's cheek; but if blush it was, it was the blush of anger rather than shame.

'Colonel Goring,' he said haughtily, 'to what purpose is this?

169

Confident though you are in your own judgment, you do not, I presume, think yourself wiser than the Legislature which has decided on the Ecclesiastical organization adopted for this island? The Established Church of Ireland is the direct representative of the ancient Church of St. Patrick. It has been recognized and maintained in authority by the three estates of the Realm, and if the buildings have fallen out of repair, it is because the gentry have neglected their duties, and the old inhabitants have persisted in their ignorant attachment to the unreformed ritual. Meanwhile the tithes you speak of are the Church's property. If the peasantry refuse for the moment to avail themselves of the ministrations which the law provides, the excellent men whose services they reject find use for their talents elsewhere. The tithes of Munster are still applied to spiritual purposes, when they go to support learning and piety in other parts of Ireland or in the English cities. They are a tax upon the land, designed to maintain the Church as a corporate body in dignity and efficiency.'

This ingenious defence of pluralist canons and Irish rectors, resident at Bath and Cheltenham, was new to Goring. Crushing down his disposition to laugh, 'I wish,' he said, 'that I could either share your Grace's expectations for the future, or accept your defence of the present state of things. I can do neither. The peasantry, so far as my experience goes, do not understand the purposes to which the tithes are applied, nor would they appreciate them if they did. The Church as it stands, they regard as a mockery and an insult, and if the principles of the Reformation are to make way in this country, it will be through agencies unconnected with the demands of tithe proctors. It will be through the presence among them of self-supporting Protestant communities, whom I am sorry to see your Grace so little inclined to encourage.

'But I occupy your Grace's time I fear to no purpose. I came to request that a community of blameless and industrious men, who live on my estate on Bantry Bay, might be allowed freedom of worship, on the same terms as the Roman Catholics, the Presbyterians of Ulster, the Wesleyan Methodists and the the Quakers are severally allowed their own. You assume that they are disentitled by opinions or practices, which you are pleased to ascribe to them; you fall back on your discretionary powers, and I understand you to say that my demand is finally refused.'

'Your apprehension is correct, sir,' said the Primate. 'I expressed myself with so much explicitness at the beginning of our interview that I might have expected that you would have understood me even more readily. It would have spared us some unnecessary discussion. Enough, however, that you do understand me, and that you realize that my answer is final. One word only, in conclusion. You seem to argue that, because the Roman Catholics are tolerated, we ought to tolerate these people of yours. Let me tell you, sir, that we refuse to regard the adherents of a great and ancient institution, which is the main support of order on the Continent of Europe, as on a level with a congregation of vulgar, psalm-singing mechanics. And now I wish you good morning.'

Chapter XIX

THE SPEAKER SPEAKS HIS MIND

'THE Primate, I fear, will have sickened you of Castle officials,' said Fitzherbert, when his kinsman gave him the history of his reception. 'He is the most absurd, the most ridiculous—but, unhappily, the most influential—of all our politicians. He is put here to protect the English interest. Money and patronage will buy every public man in Ireland, soul and body; and this extraordinary successor of the Apostles has, unfortunately, the most of both to give away. What the Primate says the Viceroy will say, and Lord A. will say, and —alas! that it should be so—the Judges will say; and if you appeal to either of them, you will lose your time and perhaps your temper. But you must see the Speaker. He has his price, like the rest. He knows that you are here, and he wants to talk with you. You are a famous person, you know, since your duel at Derreen. You are to meet him at dinner to-morrow. Here is an invitation for you. I know what is in it, for Achmet told me.'

'Achmet!' said Goring. 'And who is Achmet, in Heaven's name?'

The letter, elaborately folded, was addressed with many flourishes, to his Excellency the Pasha Goring. The seal was a crescent, and round it was an Arabic inscription. Goring tore open the envelope, and read with wide eyes that Dr. Achmet Borumborad requested the honour of his company at a Parliamentary dinner, to be held on the following day, at the Turkish Baths, on the Liffey.

'What circumcised Philistine is this?' he said. 'Dr. Achmet Borumborad! Whoever heard of such a name? Is it a joke—or what is it? A Parliamentary dinner, and the twenty men not buried yet that were cut down in the streets last night!'

'No time so fit,' Fitzherbert answered. 'If we hadn't our little entertainments, there would be no living at all in this miserable country. This Achmet, as he calls himself, pretends to be a true Turk, and I suppose he is one. His beard is long enough, any way. He walks about in a blue silk pelisse, with a high-peaked cap, and a dagger in his belt, with a diamond in the hilt of it. We like novelties in Dublin, and we like Achmet.'

'But what does he do? Is he in Parliament? Have you sworn him on the Council in this most Christian land?'

'He appeared in this city a few years since. No one knows where he came from, and no one cares. He called himself a Hakim, or medicine man. He said that we were dirty, and that we were suffering from want of ablutions. He got into society and, being a sharp fellow, he found that in a place where there was no trade, and where we had nothing to occupy us but politics, the women wanted excitement, and the men wanted to be amused. He extended his premises, as the demand grew, adding a club-room and a dining-room, after the pattern of Bath and Cheltenham, which became a convenient lounge for our wits and orators. The rooms became a state institution; and when they were still insufficient for the members that crowded into them, Parliament proposed to use the surplus in the Treasury for their own diversions, and voted Achmet a grant. Last Session they gave him the most munificent of all as a reward for his services. He has laid it out in a great new swimming-bath, which is regularly filled by the tide. The bath is to be opened to the world to-morrow, and he gives a grand dinner on the occasion to his Parliamentary friends, to which he has done you and me the honour of inviting us.'

Colonel Goring had encountered many strange things in Dublin, but this was the strangest of all. 'Is it possible,' he said, 'that, with the country in its present condition, Parliament is voting away the public money on such an absurdity as Turkish Baths?'

'And why shouldn't we, I wonder?' said Fitzherbert. 'If we kept the money in the Treasury it would go to some German cousin of his Majesty. Or if we keep our expenses too low, they might make it an excuse for extinguishing us altogether, sending the Parliament about its business.'

'I have few acquaintances in Dublin,' said the Colonel. 'Whom shall I meet at this beautiful party?'

'Almost all the distinguished men will be there. Not the Chancellor, I suppose. He was too much flurried in the row yesterday. And Kildare and the Primate fly high and will not make themselves common. But you will find most of the Judges, the Attorney and Solicitor-General, all the barristers who are in the House of Commons—the best company in the world— and a dozen or two of the country gentlemen besides. Tisdale will be there, and old Fitz-Gibbon, and a showy Oxford youth they begin to talk about, called Henry Flood, and Hely Hutchinson and Malone and Ponsonby, all our shining lights in the Lower House and a sprinkling of stars from the Upper. I do not know but what you may meet a bishop.'

Achmet's establishment, the favourite lounge of Dublin in the third quarter of the last century, was an Orientalized imitation of the Bath Assembly Rooms. It stood on the bank of the Liffey, which, as the city was then innocent of drains, was free from pollution. Instead of the hot springs there was the fresh sea water which came up with the tide, and in winter was raised by a warming apparatus to an agreeable temperature. Saloons, dining-room and library were available for every kind of entertainment.

The contriver of all this delightful recreation was the favourite of society. His broken English passed for wit. As a master of ceremonies he was as accomplished as Beau Nash, with the addition of his eastern manners. A word to the head of the establishment had secured an exquisite little cabinet with a bow window overhanging the river. The air, though it was winter, was soft and warm. The sash was thrown up, and a light breeze blew in from the Pigeon House. Here, when Goring and his kinsman arrived, a couple of hours before dinner, they found the Speaker waiting for them.

Henry Boyle, better known as Lord Shannon, a rank to which he was on the point of being raised, was one of the triumvirs who, except on the rare occasions of the Viceroy's presence, administered as Lords Justices the Government of Ireland. Boyle, Kildare, and the Primate led the three parties into which the Irish Parliament was divided. Their objects were nominally different, and on the surface they were constantly quarrelling. But there was an understanding between them behind the scenes that their disagreement was not to be pushed to a point where it might become dangerous to the distribution of power. They were united in a resolution to keep the management of the country in their own hands, and resist the encroachments of the London Cabinet. The Primate represented the authority of the Established Church and, so far as his colleagues would allow, the English interest. Kildare represented the old Irish traditions, and Henry Boyle the constitutional patriotism which was to be the mother of Irish eloquence, and of its twin brother Irish corruption.

The Speaker was one of the wealthiest, and one of the most useful of the great Irish landowners. He was descended from the famous Earl of Cork. His magnificent domains were the best improved that were to be seen in Munster. He was adored by his tenantry, for he was the most munificent of masters, and when they applied for leases of his farms he never enquired into their creed. His estate was a cultivated oasis surrounded by desolation. In the House of Commons he had been raised to the chair by his genius, by his courtesy, and by his adroitness as a party leader. He was about to be a peer, and to receive a pension out of the public funds to meet the expenses of his new dignity. He was tall, handsome, polished, the finest of gentlemen in the eighteenth-century sense of the word, and was now in the meridian of his life and fame.

'Colonel Goring,' he said, warmly extending his hand, 'I am delighted to make your acquaintance. We have heard much of you in the last two years, and everything which we have heard has been to your honour. If more of the gentry were like you, Ireland would be a happier country to live in than you and I are likely to see it. But you have had a hard time of it, and I fear a dangerous one.'

'I am a soldier, sir,' said Goring, 'and soldiers must not complain of dangers. I have tried to be of some use in the district where I live. I wish I had more success to boast of.'

'Success never comes up to endeavour, even with the strongest of us,' the Speaker replied. 'Only the lower animals act out their nature completely. Man aims beyond his powers and so falls short. But it is better to aim high and partly fail, than to crawl contentedly on a lower level. I should be well satisfied if I could give as good an account of myself as you can do. But alas! our poor country is not a place for honourable ambitions. If you are ill off down in Bantry, we in Dublin are little better off, as you have had an opportunity of seeing. The poor Chancellor has not got over it yet. I was in the middle of the riot, too, and the rascals had hold of me, but they let me go when they ran off with their old lady to the woolsack. Bah! What would you have? England will not let us break the heads of our scoundrels; she will not break them herself; we are a free country, and must take the consequences.'

'The Irish make good soldiers, sir,' answered Goring, 'and no man can be a good soldier who has not fine qualities in him of some kind.'

'You are a philosopher, Colonel, as well as a soldier,' said the Speaker. 'Our countrymen are strange creatures, but if we begin discussing their qualities, we shall waste all our time. You saw the Primate yesterday?'

'I did.'

'You have settled a colony of Protestants at Dunboy. Most of them are Nonconformists, and you want a chapel and a minister for them. You asked for the Primate's consent, and he would not give it you. He hates Dissenters of all kinds. He is particularly sore against the Wesleyans, Swaddlers he calls them, because he has been obliged to tolerate the poor devils. He listens to any calumny against them. He told you that they made the riot. He does not believe it, but he tries to believe it; and he and the Viceroy will so represent matters across the water, because he wants the Swaddlers to be discouraged. The people that you have brought in belong to the other prophet, Whitfield I believe they call him. They are the old dangerous, fighting Protestants, like the men that Cromwell brought over, desperate fellows in the field, and very useful, I daresay, to you, but never well inclined to bishops. The Primate shudders at the thought of them. He knows very well that if a strong

Nonconformist interest grows up again over Ireland, it will go hard with him and his Church, and cleverer fellows than he have been of the same opinion.'

'To me,' said Goring, 'his Grace is acting like the clergyman who, when his house was on fire, allowed no one to fetch water who was not a communicant. Little can he know of the condition of the southern counties of Ireland. Fifty years ago there were Protestant settlements all over Munster. They are melting off like snow, and unless they can be revived all the old troubles will inevitably come back again.'

The Speaker was silent for some seconds, looking hesitatingly at Goring, as if there was something which he wished to say, yet doubted whether he could prudently say it.

'Colonel Goring,' he said at length, 'you complain of Irish anarchy; but even anarchy has its advantages. You asked the Archbishop's leave to have a chapel. That was a mistake on your part. You should have taken leave without asking. Build your chapel if you have not built it already, and call it a room. Set a few forms and desks at one end of it where the children can have their Bible lessons and be taught reading and writing. Nobody will meddle with you. You will receive some letter from your Bishop. Don't answer it. The Bishop will feel that he has done all that he was required to do, and will thank you in his heart for sparing him further trouble.

'You are surprised and hurt because we have been so languid, and because the gentry in your county have been so languid in supporting your efforts to suppress the contraband trade. Take a friend's advice, and do not for the future let your exertions go beyond the evident sense of the country. If the rogues are landing arms, like your acquaintance Morty Sullivan, or are taking recruits to the Brigade, or are engaged in pirating work, be down upon them as hard as you please. But as to the smuggling, it is the only refuge we have against the intolerable laws by which England has crushed our commerce. When ruling powers are unjust, nature reasserts her rights.'

'You are surely jesting with me,' Goring answered with a smile. 'Law is law, and we who are executive officers of the Government must at least try to make it obeyed. These contraband people are the cause of all the crime and disorder on the Irish Coast. Those who break one law break all. Murder, piracy, rebellion, they are ready for any of them. How can any country prosper when the people are taught from their cradles that laws are only made to be laughed at?'

'Nothing can be more true, my dear Colonel; but those are precisely the conditions under which it pleases our sovereign masters that the affairs of this country shall be administered. We live under a set of laws which we cannot repeal and are not allowed to execute. How is it with the Catholics? By law no priest may officiate who is not registered. Not one in fifty is registered, yet no one is ever punished. By law no Catholic bishop ought to be in Ireland. They reside openly in their palaces; they preach, they ordain, they rule their dioceses as effectively as our own prelates. Not only does no one call them to question, but we ourselves in the government use their help in keeping order. By the law no Catholic can own land or hold a lease for more than thirty years. The estates of Catholics are now as safe as those of Protestants. By law no Catholic can practise in the learned professions. Go, ask at the Four Courts how many Catholics are on the roll of attorneys. The laws are on our Statute Book. We do not try to enforce them, for England would interpose if we did. But the whole system that we live under is an instruction to us that laws are made to be disobeyed. By-and-bye, when they see their prohibitions cannot be carried out, the English consent to do us justice. Till then they never will.'

'God help Ireland then,' said the Colonel, sorrowfully. 'God help us all, and send us another Oliver.'

'Do not let the Primate hear you say so,' the Speaker answered, 'and in default of Oliver I recommend you to do as others do, and swim with the stream. High notions of duty are admissible when time and place suits them, but they will not work in Ireland in this age that we live in. You do not think me serious. I wish I was not. Oliver conquered this country. He drove the fighting Irish across the Shannon into Connaught. He partitioned the lands of the rebels among his own soldiers, or among Puritan colonists from England and

Scotland. He gave us Free Trade and a political union with Great Britain. Had he lived ten years longer the English race, the English law, the English character, would have been rooted as firmly in Leinster and Munster as the Scots are rooted in the North.

'Even as it was, so long as Oliver's foundations were left standing we had a chance of making something of the country. We had English farmers, English mechanics, English artisans in tens of thousands. France and Flanders sent us their Protestant refugees. We had our shipyards, and fifty vessels might be seen lying in the Liffey, where now there are but yonder half-dozen miserable coal brigs. We were so prosperous that England was jealous of us. They destroyed our shining industry by their Navigation Act. They closed our woollen mills, and all those busy hands that were employed in them were cast adrift, and sought more hospitable shores. Even of our fleeces, the best in Europe, they would not let us make our own market; they required them for themselves, and at such price as they were pleased themselves to fix.

'If we are robbed of our legitimate trade the people will, and must, open other channels for themselves. The very life of the country depends upon it. They order us to sell our wool in the English market. They have so tied us up that they think they can compel us to let them have it on their own terms, and they offer us a fourth part of what we can get for it at Nantes and Rochelle. They overreach themselves with their own avarice. You might as well try to stop the Shannon from running into the Atlantic as to prevent Irish wool from going to France when there is such a profit to be made upon it. Full two-thirds of our fleeces are taken there; and for that matter two-thirds of our salt beef, and bacon, and butter, and the rest of it. Every rank, every profession in Ireland is interested in maintaining the contraband runners. It is not only a point of honour and patriotism, but our very existence depends upon it.'

'And how long is such a state of things to last?' said Goring.

'That depends on the pleasure of the Parliament at Westminster; or on the power of the English to keep the seas and prevent the French from coming over. If a French force was once landed, we should have a pretty business here. It is of course possible that they may discover that they are cutting their own throats. It may be, though I confess I have small expectations of it, that they may have some prickings of conscience. But nature keeps an accurate account in such things. The longer a bill is left unpaid, the heavier the accumulation of interest. It will be sent in one day, and our sons and grandsons will have to settle it. For myself I see nothing but to live for the day that is passing over us.'

The ideas thus presented to Colonel Goring's mind were so bewildering that he had to collect himself before he could answer. He sat gazing mechanically out of the window at a coal barge which had drifted upon a broken pile, and was being slowly upset as the tide went back and left it. 'We are told,' he said at last, 'that a wise man mindeth his own matters, but a fool's eyes are in the ends of the earth. I am sure you will pardon me when I tell you that I cannot go along with you. No nation can prosper when the units composing it voluntarily neglect their duties; and if we are wronged we do not mend the matter by doing wrong ourselves. But what you say confirms me in a purpose which I had half formed before I came to Dublin. You have shown me that in struggling with the smugglers at Bantry I have undertaken an impossible task. As long as I am an officer of the revenue I must and will attempt to repress them; but there is no obligation on me to retain my commission. I have enough to do without it, and I can spend my time more usefully if I confine my attention to my own estate and my own people. Their disposition has been to live peaceably with their neighbours, and if trouble has risen it has been on account of the business in which I have had to employ them. We shall get on better together when all that is at an end. I shall therefore thank you if you will send down my successor and will leave me to my own affairs.'

'I believe you are right,' said the Speaker laughing. 'If you go on as you have been doing hitherto, you will inevitably get yourself killed; and how will the country be the better for that? Yes, yes. Stick to your colonists, and keep them to the mines and the fishing. Neither you nor they can thrive as

Ireland now is, if they are to do the work of a coastguard and a police. We ought not to have allowed you to try. We cannot relieve you at this moment. We are at war with France in reality, though the beggars won't declare it. The chances are that they will try a descent on our coast, and an officer of your experience cannot be spared.

'But we can let you off the Customs' work, and, my dear friend, make your mind easy about what the Archbishop said to you. I can't promise you a license, but I can promise you that you shall never be troubled for the want of it. You cannot live in Ireland without breaking laws on one side or another. *Pecca fortiter*, therefore, as your friend Luther said. Keep your chapel open. Preach there yourself if you like. I am told you do sometimes, and do it admirably well. Don't try to make converts; it will get you into trouble with the priests; and let your minister go on quietly attending to the school and the people.

'But Achmet calls us to dinner. The guests wait; we must go. Let me see you again at my own house to-morrow morning.'

Chapter XX

ADVENTURE AT THE TURKISH BATH

WHEN the Speaker with Goring and Fitzherbert joined the company, they found forty gentlemen collected in the hall which adjoined the dining saloon. Their infidel entertainer, magnificently dressed in silk and turban, received them with Oriental dignity, yet a dignity so tempered as to imply that he was accepting, rather than conferring a favour. Though he was the giver of the dinner, he professed himself too humble to preside, and he conducted the Speaker to the chair. In broken English he welcomed Goring, and thanked him for the honour of his presence. 'We know you Sir,' he said, 'if you not know us. We all hear how you shoot that leaf, and let go that dam rascal. We all grieve Sir you no kill him, but you brave man Sir, dam brave, and I shake your hand Sir, and is proud of your acquaintance.'

No accomplishment stood higher in Irish estimation than skill in the use of a pistol, as indeed was natural, for none was more required; and many an eye glanced curiously or admiringly on Goring as he took his place at the Speaker's right hand. The dinner was magnificent, the wine superb, and every one showed at his best. Judges left their dignity behind with their wigs and robes, and told stories, not always decent, which convulsed the room. Old Parliamentary hands tried the metal of young aspirants, by quoting and affecting to commend their absurdities. Irish barristers, concerned as they were each day of their lives with the misadventures or misdoings of the most amusing people in the world, related anecdote against anecdote, the genuine absurdities of which no fiction could improve.

Gradually, as the wine flowed freely, the rays of humour concentrated on the person of Achmet. It appeared that having succeeded in establishing a prosperous and growing business, he had been looking about him for some one who would share his fortunes with him. More than one he might not hope for, being in a Christian land, but one at least he might find who would forget his origin in consideration of his wealth and his good looks. And indeed no sooner was his purpose known, than the difficulty was to select among the competitors who were eager to be asked. He might have stocked a harem, had the laws allowed, the young ladies flocking about him like flies about a ripe peach. He had but to choose and be happy.

Fate, however, always perverse on these occasions, so ruled that Achmet, instead of taking, as he might have done, either maid or widow who would have been his and have made no conditions, fixed his affections in a quarter where there had arisen most complicated difficulties. The fair Miss Biddy Flanigan had no objection to Achmet himself. She thought him beautiful, she thought him charming. It would have been delightful to her to carry off a prize so much desired from so many rivals. But she had scruples of conscience. Achmet she thought must forsake his errors, shave his beard, and be baptized. She could not be the wife of an unbelieving Turk. Achmet pretended to a conscience also, and would not throw over Mahomet and the Koran unless he was certain of his reward; while, supposing all these intricacies could be disentangled, a further question had been raised about the good man's origin—Who and what was he, and where had he been living before he came to Dublin?

Matters were in this situation at the time of the dinner. Achmet's matrimonial prospects had already been discussed at every Dublin tea table. The present opportunity was too tempting to be neglected; one question led to another, and Miss Biddy's difficulties became the general talk of the party. It happened unfortunately that Miss Biddy herself was listening to all that was going on. She had expressed a wish to her lover to see the gentlemen at the banquet, and to hear their speeches. A gallery ran round the upper part of the dining and other public rooms. Here Miss Biddy, with half a dozen other girls, was installed behind a curtain, and not a word that was said escaped her.

The evening wore on. Champagne corks had crackled like

musketry fire. Claret of the finest flavour that had ever ripened
on the Garonne had flowed in streams, and loyal toasts had
been drunk, and disloyal also, for a hot Jacobite had proposed
the three P's, and no one had objected with more than a laugh.
The room began to swim; the night grew hot; and more than
one grave and learned counsellor unbuttoned his waistcoat and
loosened his neckcloth, while through the mask of his official
features, the wild Irish face came into focus, like the second
landscape in a dissolving view.

The wine which had been brought up was exhausted. The
elder guests began to think they had had enough, and Sir John
—, the Chief Justice, suggested an adjournment. Remon-
strances rose loud from the lower end of the table. There was
a cry for another dozen of Lafitte, and the proposal was caught
up with so much enthusiasm, that Achmet was dispatched to
the cellar with a basket.

Goring, who had drunk nothing, and had been excused as
a stranger, sat quietly by the Speaker watching what was going
on. Sir John — however, and one or two others, determined to
attempt an escape while their feet were still steady enough to
carry them. It was now dusk; daylight was almost gone, and
candles were not yet lighted. The door by which they had
entered was at the lower end of the saloon, and led into the
outer hall, from which there was an easy exit into the street.
Watching his opportunity, Sir John slid from his seat and was
half-way down the room before his flight was observed.

Free, however, as most things were in Ireland, there was no
freedom in the regulations of convivial assemblies. Guests on
such occasions were not allowed to shirk. A cry rose, 'Against
the rules.' The master of the Kildare foxhounds, who was
present, gave a 'View Halloa!' and with 'Yoicks! Forward!
Stole away!' started in pursuit, with half the company at his
heels. Sir John sped on, with the pack after him in full cry.
He dashed open what he believed to be the entrance door, and
plunged into the darkness beyond. Alas, for him! it was not
the door into the hall at all, but the door into the new bath
room, where the great basin stood brimming full, and the Chief
Justice shot head-foremost into the middle of it.

ADVENTURE AT THE TURKISH BATH

Close behind followed the pursuers, in heedless impetuosity. They could see nothing. They could not have stopped themselves if they had. Over went the first flight. Those behind dropped on the floor, but the crowd pressing on stumbled over them, and all went down together. There, amidst peals of laughter, and shouts for help, for the water was deep, the Legislature and Counsellors of Ireland were splashing, plunging, seizing hold of each other, unable to see anything, and such of them as could not swim running a chance of being drowned. Happily, ropes were hung from the roof at short intervals for the use of the legitimate bathers. Those who had their senses least disturbed caught hold, and gave a hand to the rest, while the seniors from the top of the table, with the Speaker and Goring, came in with candles, and threw light upon the extraordinary scene.

Achmet returning from the cellar with his basket, found the dining-room deserted, and, from the noise in the adjoining apartment, guessed too surely the catastrophe which had happened. Dropping the wine, tearing off his turban, and forgetting in his distraction who and what he was, he dashed into the confusion. 'Och, Thunder and Turf!' he shrieked. 'Nineteen members of Parliament squattering in the water like so many goslings, and my Lord Chief Justice like the ould gander at the head of them. Oh! wirra, wirra! what will we do now? Sure it is murdered for this I'll be, and that will be the laste of it.'

Wild as was the excitement, the whole party, wet and dry, were struck dumb by this astounding exclamation.

'A Murracle! a Murracle!' shouted a youthful senator, who was swimming leisurely about among his struggling companions. 'The Turk has turned Tipperary boy. I'll swear to the brogue. In with him, we'll baptize him on the spot.'

'No Turk,' shouted the self-detected Achmet. 'No Turk at all, at all. Sure, it is Pat Joyce from Kilkenny I am—no less— and as good a Christian as the Pope of Rome.'

Loud was the laughter, but louder yet was the shriek that rang from the gallery. On the rush of the guests into the bath room, Biddy and her companions had followed by the passage above, and she had arrived just in time to witness her lover's metamorphosis.

'Ah, ye false thief!' she screamed. 'And ye tould me it was a circumcised haythen that ye were, and ye'd the Sultan for your godfather, and that if I married ye, I'd be a Princess at the worse. It is tear your eyes out, I will, when I can catch ye, ye desaving villain.'

'Whisht, Biddy, and be asy with you,' answered her love. 'Don't be bothering the gintlemen till we get them out of the water.'

By this time, Sir John, very angry and half drowned, was on dry ground again. The Speaker, choking with laughter, said:

'This is a hanging business, Mr. Patrick, or whatever ye are. Ye have conspired against the lives of half the representatives of Ireland, and that is death by statute, Irish and English. You planned it yourself, you scoundrel, because some of us voted for cutting down your grants. But, Sir John will catch his death, shivering here in the wet. Bring some dry clothes, if you have any that a Christian can wear, and some brandy and mulled claret, and then we will put you on your trial—see what shall be done with you.'

Achmet's wardrobe had been furnished only for his assumed character. Silk robes, pelisses, shawls, huge bagged trousers, were hunted out and brought down. When the supply still fell short, the ladies' bathing dresses were drawn upon, and, one way or another, the whole party were furnished out and dried. Even Sir John recovered his amenity, when the mulled claret came, and warmed him back into good humour; and in wild spirits at the ridiculousness of the adventure, they formed themselves into a Court to try the offender, the Chief Justice presiding.

The offence was palpable; but the audacity of the imposition, and the skill with which it had been carried out, recommended the prisoner for pardon. It was remembered that his baths and his rooms would be none the worse because he was Patrick Joyce, and not the Sultan's barber. To prove his Christianity, he was sentenced to drink a pint of brandy on the spot, which he did without flinching. Other penalties were thought of. Henry Flood, who liked to show off his acquaintance with the East, proposed that Achmet, in Turkish costume, should ride a donkey through the streets with his face to the tail, and Pat Joyce pinned, in large letters, on his back. Hely Hutchinson suggested that the adventure should be entered in the Journals of the House of Commons, as a lesson against further grants in aid. But, after terrifying the unfortunate wretch with these and other more frightful suggestions, the Court agreed on a verdict of—Guilty, with good intentions; and they signed a Round Robin to the outraged Biddy recommending her suitor to mercy, on the ground that a decent lad, with a good Irish name to him, was a fitter mate for her than a Turk, and that Achmet had only been all along what she professed that she wanted to make him.

It was now midnight, and the party broke up. In sedan chairs and in coaches—where a wisp of straw had first been lighted, to warm them—Achmet's guests were carried to their homes in their parti-coloured apparel. Goring and Fitzherbert walked back to the College, the grave and earnest Colonel too much diverted with the incidents of the evening to be able to moralize over them. Ireland's fortunes might be committed to a singular set of legislators, but he had never met with more entertaining companions.*

* I am indebted for the adventure at the Turkish Bath to the *Personal Sketches* of Sir Jonah Barrington.

Chapter XXI

THE COLONEL'S RETURN

NO signs of the evening's adventure were to be seen in the Speaker's appearance, when Goring called upon him on the following morning. Whether a dozen or two of the City mob had been cut down in the streets, or the brightest ornaments of the Bench or the House of Commons had been half drowned in a bath, affected little the careless good-humour of Dublin society. The centre of gravity was always being disturbed by something, and casualties were only noticed as they furnished matter for amusement. The Speaker himself was as composed as if nothing had happened, nor did he make the least allusion either to the dinner or to what had occurred at it. He had been occupied since an early hour with serious business, for the English Mail had come in, and his table was covered with freshly-opened letters.

'There are news from London,' he said, 'and they will interest you. There is no declaration of war yet, but they are fighting everywhere. Young Howe is plucking the feathers from the French fleet on the American coast: he has taken another frigate; and the French are preparing at Brest, in earnest, for a descent on the Irish coast. We know not where it is to be; but your country, Colonel, is the likeliest point. You will have to get back to your post at once.'

'I am at my country's service,' said Goring. 'What you direct, I will do—or try to do. But I must remind you of what passed between us yesterday. I said that I must resign my post in the Revenue service—and you were good enough to approve.'

'Yes, yes,' said the Speaker, 'quite true—the Revenue service is no fit occupation for such as you. You must hold on, however, just at this moment; for all the correspondence with France is carried on through the smugglers—the rascals!—and they will want sharper looking after than ever. But we must not compromise your colonists down there. Well I know how precious they are, and how important it is that they should be kept together. You will judge how interested I am about it, when I tell you that I have already seen the Primate this morning. I had to pull him out of bed to come down to me, and he was in the worst of humours; but he was frightened out of his wits about a French invasion, and more tractable, on the whole, than I expected. I am sorry to say he was immovable about the license for your chapel and school. He hates Protestant settlements in the South, while I would encourage them. He does not like you very well. I don't know what you said to him.

'I told him that you made up a hundred and twenty fighting men, all to be thoroughly depended upon. You had shewn what you could do, and in the present state of things to discourage such a force, which was costing nothing, would be something like treason. His Grace started at this, so I followed it up by saying that I was writing to England, and might feel it my duty to mention the subject to the Cabinet. This finished him, for he is desperately afraid of being reported upon, so the sum of what we agreed on is this. Your chapel is not to be registered; but, for the present at least, no questions will be asked about it, and you will be on the same footing as most of the Catholic chapels. This, I suppose, will content you.

'Meanwhile our young engineering genius, General Vavasour, has been sent to Cork to see after the fortifications. We consider that Berehaven ought not to be left undefended either. The harbour is the largest and safest on the coast. At present the enemy's ships can run in and lie there as long as they please in perfect security, and the very presence of a French frigate will set the country wild. We intend, therefore, to have a fort on Bere Island, with a company of infantry and a few artillerymen, who are to be maintained there as long as the war lasts; and we have that confidence in yourself that we shall ask you to take the command.'

The warmest hopes which Goring had brought with him to Dublin were more than realized by a proposal so gratifying. A position of authority and command would give him the influence which he had hitherto wanted, and the additional security which would enable his wife to return to him with safety. The refusal of the registration of the chapel, however, carrying with it as it did a sentence upon his school, would be quite certain to wound and irritate his people. In this, Goring himself actively sympathized. Since his conversation with the Archbishop, he had doubted strongly whether he had any right to call himself a member of the Church of Ireland. For the sake of honesty and consistency he was tempted to sever the connection; he hesitated and he told the Speaker so, to accept another commission which would pledge him afresh to the Establishment.

He was listened to with impatience. He asked for time to deliberate. The Speaker, who was a man of the world, and had to deal with questions as they rose from a practical point of view, conceived these new scruples to be as absurd as they were unseasonable.

'As to yourself, my dear Colonel,' he said, 'I have every respect for scruples of conscience, but I would remind you that man has two duties; his duty to God, and his duty to his country. Conscience extends to both, and you have no right to disable yourself from serving your King by exaggerated conceptions of what your religious belief requires of you. I tell you again, you shall not be meddled with. So now God be with you. Vavasour shall have his orders, and the sooner you are back at Dunboy the better.

'By-the-bye, we have news of your friend Morty. After he escaped through Dursey Sound, he made his way to France, refitted at Blake's yard at Nantes, and went to sea again, they say, with a letter of marque in proper form. He is bound for the other side of the Atlantic, where, unless he is caught, we shall hear of him burning and plundering. If he can, he will raise the Irish in the Sugar Islands, and set them to murder the planters. On the second day that he was out, he robbed a Liverpool ship off Scilly, and sailed away with twenty thousand pounds and a dozen prisoners that he holds to ransom. Concieve the mischief that such a fellow will do before we can get him hanged. You see what you are responsible for in having let him go.'

Brief as had been Colonel Goring's stay in Dublin, a large
experience had been crowded into those few days. He had seen
the very shrine and temple of the amazing thing called the
Anglo-Irish Government, the functions of which, so far as he
could read them, were to do what ought not to be done and to
leave undone what ought to be done. The recklessness distressed him; the levity shocked him. He was no longer surprised at the indifference with which he had been left to
struggle unsupported in Bantry Bay. He was alive to the ridiculous side of it all as the wittiest Counsellor at Achmet's dinner.
But he did not care to prolong his visit.

On returning from his interview with the Speaker, he gave
his servant orders to prepare for immediate departure. He took
leave of the Provost, with a promise to return in better times.
Of his kinsman he did not take leave, for Fitzherbert, to his
extreme pleasure, asked to be allowed to accompany him.

They were nearly of the same age. They had been thrown
together as children, but had rarely met since. Goring had been
absent on service. Fitzherbert had followed a distinguished
career at school and college. He had won scholarships and gold
medals, and had for several years been a Fellow of Trinity.
Fitzherbert, being well provided for, had kept clear of the three
black Graces, neither of which (as Irish life was then constituted) had too good a reputation. He had a clear eye for men
and things, but he did not see that it was his business to mend
them, and he preferred the attitude of a spectator, amusing
himself with watching the chicaneries of political life. He distrusted enthusiasm, and his temperament inclined him to the
sceptical tendencies of the age.

To such a man, independent of their relationship, the character of Goring was an attractive study. When men talked of
duty and disinterested motives, Fitzherbert generally believed
them to be either fools or rogues. He used to say that on the
rare occasions when he had gone against his own interest to do
something which he thought right, he had found invariably
that he had better have left it alone. Once or twice he had gone

out of his way to be kind to people at his own cost. He had
always had his face scratched for it. They would take what he
gave, but they never forgave him for laying them under an
obligation.

With a mind so constituted Fitzherbert would naturally feel
little sympathy with his cousin's religious enthusiasm and
spiritual convictions. But he found them combined in Goring
with a simplicity and practical vigour unlike anything which
hitherto he had personally experienced, and he found himself
speculating on a problem which had often perplexed him.
Why was it that while in his own age the religious professors
were either charlatans, or at least unfit for the rough work of
the world, in the two preceding centuries they were another
order of beings? In the struggle of the Reformation the neutral
mass of the European nations would have acquiesced in any
decision which would have left them their properties and their
lives. Political liberty and freedom of conscience had been won
by fanatics, or by such persons as the world now called fanatics.
Every country had the same experience. In France it was the
Huguenots, in the Low Countries the Calvinists, in Scotland
the Covenanters, in England the Puritans, in Ireland the Boys
of Derry and Enniskillen. The brunt of the conflict everywhere
had been borne by men of strongly marked religious character,
who, so far from being unpractical, had achieved an extraordinary victory. Nor was it in war and politics only that their
distinguished qualities were shown. It was the same in the
common business of life. The best of the artisans, the most
successful merchants and manufacturers, the seamen who had
built up England's ocean empire, the successfully industrious
everywhere, had been men of the same type. What did it all
mean? What could be the explanation of the change?

Often Fitzherbert had asked himself and could find no
answer; and now this cousin of his had come across him as a
revenant from the old age. Here again was an ardent professor
of religion who was doing work of the same kind, and doing it
admirably well. He had begun by studying him as a curiosity.
A character so natural, so vigorous, so cheerful, so entirely indifferent to personal consequences, first puzzled him as con-

tradicting his theories, then won his respect, and finally his genuine admiration.

Goring, on the other hand, found under Fitzherbert's outward cynicism an essentially honourable nature, an acute intellect, and a knowledge of men and things incomparably greater than his own. His life at Dunboy had been lonely, and for his wife's sake, who had insisted on rejoining him, as well as for his own, he was delighted with the prospect of a visitor who would brighten them up when they were inclined to be out of spirits.

Among the gentlemen of the county he had many acquaintances, but hardly a friend. Most of them disliked him for an activity which they felt as a reproach to themselves. They might have fine qualities of their own, but the Colonel and they were so far apart that they failed to appreciate one another. With such a guest as Fitzherbert, with the promise of another visitor in the famous General Vavasour, and the prospects of an improved order of things which Vavasour was to introduce, he looked forward to his return home with better spirits than he had known since Lord Shelbourne's death and the failure of his hopes at Kilmakilloge.

His return was not a day too soon. He had been absent little more than three weeks, but doubt and distrust had begun to spread where hitherto there had been only unanimity and resolution. French agents were busy all over the South spreading disaffection. Once more the population were inflated with the hope which had so often betrayed them that a Catholic army would soon arrive for their deliverance. It showed itself in the insolence of their outward demeanour: It showed itself in acts of audacity and defiance which hitherto they had been too cowardly to venture on. The colonists, who had lately lived on tolerable terms with the people whom they employed at the mines, found their boats again injured, their nets cut, their cattle maimed, and their fences thrown down in the night. They were not men to submit patiently to injuries of this kind. There had been fights in which several of the Whiteboys had been hurt, one, it was supposed, mortally.

Thus, on the Colonel's arrival at home, instead of the peace

and improvement which he looked for, he found all in confusion, and the elders of his congregation in serious deliberation what they ought to do. There were difficulties at the mines
as well. The plan for the restoration of the furnaces on the
Shelbourne estate having failed, the ore had to be taken to
Swansea to be smelted; and as the communications became
irregular with the breaking out of the war trade had been
suspended and profits diminished. The colonists were of tough
material, and not easily discouraged; but they began to fear
that it was not the will of God that these Protestant settlements on the Irish coast should prosper.

In this disposition Colonel Goring found the congregation
with whom he had fought so many battles against fortune, just
at the moment when he was expecting that better days were
about to dawn. He had looked forward, perhaps with a shade
of vanity, to showing his kinsman a set of men the like of whom
he had never seen before, men who had the spirit of God in
them, of the same stuff and nature with those whom he had
read of and wondered at. He found them unchanged; but the
same temperament and beliefs which gave them their strength
and quality were now threatening the ruin of his hopes.

He had heard nothing to prepare him for what he was to
find. They arrived late. He was to meet his people in the
chapel in the morning, to hear what they had to say, and to
tell them in return the answer which he had brought back.

It was deep winter, and night had fallen before they reached
Dunboy, so that it was with some curiosity that Fitzherbert
opened his window and looked about him when he awoke in
the morning. A warm south-westerly wind was blowing in from
the Atlantic; a swell was breaking on the west end of Bere
Island, and the clouds hung low on Hungry Hill. But the sky
was open in the east, and the crests of the waves in the Bay
were sparkling in the sunshine; while mountains and woods
were steeped in the soft purple green which makes the winter
landscape in the south of Ireland so peculiarly beautiful. The
village was early astir. The boats had been hauled up on the
shingle; oars and sails had been stowed away, and the nets
spread to dry on the poles. A large concourse of people was

gathering about the house; men and women plainly but solidly dressed in broadcloth and home-spun woollens. Fresh groups continued to arrive while Fitzherbert watched, and he calculated at last that there could not be less than two hundred of them. A bell rang, and they filed into the chapel behind the house. He hastily completed his dressing and followed them.

If he had been struck by their appearance when seen at a distance, their faces impressed him the more remarkably when seen close at hand. They were of all ages, from grey-bearded seniors who had passed their three-score and ten, to youths just entering upon manhood; but in the features neither of old nor young was there anything of the strained austerity which Fitzherbert looked for. They were grave, as became the place where they were assembled; but they looked frank and open, and their creed, whatever it was, gave them no appearance of unreality. If there was any common expression belonging to them all it was of quiet unconscious steadiness. He was a little surprised when Mrs. Goring sang Ken's Morning Hymn, and the whole congregation joined, showing they were familiar with it. A prayer followed, and then Colonel Goring told his tale, or that part of it which the special anxiety was to hear.

There were two points on which their minds were most exercised; one was their chapel service, the other the education of their children. In both of these he had to say the Primate would make no concession. To the first they had a right under the statute, whether the Bishops approved or not, and he intended to appeal to the law. The second was less simple. The right of teaching was rigidly reserved by the statute to the clergy of the Establishment. But education they were naturally and properly extremely anxious about. Their children were in continual danger of being influenced by the Catholic population round them. On this subject, which was so very vital, he was sorry to inform them that no formal concession was to be looked for.

Goring's communication was coldly received. Towards himself the affection was unimpaired, but the news which he brought was evidently unwelcome. A venerable old man, the patriarch of the congregation, rose to reply.

It was no novelty, he said, that the elect should suffer for conscience sake. Their fathers had borne the cross when the nails had torn into their flesh. The trials to which they were called were of a milder kind, but at all times the portion of the saints had been to suffer, and so it would continue. They had come to Ireland as strangers into a strange land, remembering what God had done there by their hands in other days, and hoping it might be given to them to do Him service as their fathers had done. But they had cause to fear that they had mistaken His purpose.

They could only meet and pray together, and hear the Word, by evading or breaking the law, a course of action unbecoming in Christian men. Their young people could not be married by their own minister. They could not bury their own dead, but were obliged to lay them in the common graveyard among strangers. They had borne these hard terms, and would have continued to bear them, but they found now that they were not allowed to bring up their children according to their conscience, or if they chose to do so they must risk the indignity of being prosecuted as criminals under a statute which neither they nor their fathers had been able to endure. The providence of God had opened to them a land beyond the Atlantic where they could live in peace. They had taken counsel with Him, and it had been borne in upon them that they ought to go.

They loved and honoured Colonel Goring. They looked up to him as the commander set over them by God. Would not he remain their leader still, and himself conduct them to the land of promise? Let him shake off the dust of his feet against the inhospitable land, and accompany them to America, and they pledged themselves never to leave him.

A hum of assent rose from the whole congregation. The old man had expressed the universal feeling. Goring was touched by their affection for himself—touched by the readiness of a hundred families to break up their homes and leave behind them the fruits of years of industry. But his own duty was no less plain to him.

'I have hesitated,' he said, 'I have been tempted to return to my profession as a soldier, but my lot has been assigned me in this country, and here at my post I must stay till I am called away. On you there is no such obligation. You came hither with me at my own invitation, because it seemed to you that there was work for us to do. We have fought our battle together not unworthily. We have turned the bogs into green fields. We have gathered our harvests in the sea. We have dug our copper out of the hills, and in worldly goods you are all richer than when you came hither. We have succeeded mainly by our own strength in restraining the lawlessness which till we came pre-vailed in Bantry Bay. These are not signs that God has set His face against us. If trouble threaten us now, they may be no more than the clouds which gather over our mountains and pass away and leave them as they were. My friends, I cannot go with you to the New World, but I will ask no one to stay with me here against his will. Only this I will say. Decide nothing in haste. War with France has broken out, and there is danger here. If I know you, you will not choose this particu-lar moment to leave me.'

Gravely the old man replied. 'It may be, sir, as you say. We must weigh this matter before we act.'

'You must judge for yourselves,' said Colonel Goring. 'Whether you go or stay, I remain.'

The meeting broke up. It was agreed that, unless they were interfered with by force, they would wait six months before coming to a final resolution.

The intention of fortifying the island created a strong im-pression. If it was carried out, the difficulties with the people would be at an end. But they distrusted the promises of the Government, and could not fully believe in its sincerity till the work was done or was in progress. They resented the indignity with which they had been treated, and nothing would satisfy them short of a full concession of their rights. They dissolved into groups as they left the chapel, and dispersed in scattered parties to their homes.

Chapter XXII

AN ANTIQUARIAN GENERAL

MONTH after month went by, and Fitzherbert was still a guest at his cousin's house. He was occupied partly in studying the ways of the colony, partly in examining the old stones and circles, and monuments of the ancient race, which are strewed about the mountains and valleys. Winter turned to spring, and spring to early summer, and nothing more occurred to disturb the quiet of the settlement. The ill-wind which had risen among the Catholic population died away again. There were rumours of moonlight meetings, like that which Goring had witnessed at the Pocket, of the coming of the French, and of a contemplated general insurrection. But stories of this kind were always current in the South of Ireland. Loose powder lay about everywhere, but it was damp, and required fire to kindle it; and in spite of the French war the signs of active disturbance were lighter than usual.

News was heard occasionally of Morty Sullivan. He had been the terror of the Bahama Channel. He had made an insurrection among the Irish convicts at Montserrat, and had gorged himself and his crew with plunder. When last heard of, he was lying concealed somewhere among the Spanish Islands; but a couple of frigates had been sent in search of him, and it was thought that he could not long escape. Meanwhile, the coasts of Cork were less disturbed than they had been. The Swansea vessels came back again for the copper ore, and the mining work went on briskly again. The chief disappointment was that General Vavasour had not appeared to survey Bere Island. He was often coming, but business of some kind or another had detained him; and Goring's heart had begun to misgive him, that the Speaker's promises were after all no more than vapour, when, one afternoon in June, a revenue cutter came in from the sea, and brought up in the basin in front of

Dunboy. A boat came on shore from her, and the long-expected officer had arrived.

General Vavasour was the most distinguished of the rising officers in the English service. He was a person of the most varied accomplishments, and, as often happens, he valued himself highest for his knowledge of subjects on which he was no more than amateur, and was modestly unconscious of his merits where those merits were indisputable. As a scientific engineer he eclipsed all his contemporaries, but his pride was in the discoveries which he believed himself to have made in the history of the ancient Irish.

'It admits of no doubt whatever,' he would say. 'Those old legends of the Tuatha de Danans may be dreams, but the imagery of dreams is always drawn from reality. The Irish language is identical in structure with the Persian of the Zenda-vesta. The traditions run on the same lines. The name of Druid, which foolish persons have connected with Oak Groves, and supposed to be Greek, is as little Greek as it is Red Indian. It is the Persian Draoidh, the wise man of the East. The bon-fire which the Galway or the Killarney peasant passes his children through on St. John's Eve, is the fire of Moloch, which was denounced by the Jewish prophets. The Round Towers were Bel Tines built after the story of the Tower of Babel, when the sons of the survivors of the Deluge built their Temple to the visible Gods in the sky.'

Vavasour's acquaintances generally took flight when he brought out his hobby. The Speaker especially dreaded the sight of the beast. Fitzherbert, however, who knew him well, tempted him to mount on all occasions; professing always the deepest interest, and the greatest willingness to believe till some one equally learned proved exactly the opposite.

'No one can prove the opposite,' Vavasour would say, 'for, look you, the Tower of Babel was the first Temple ever built. Babel was Bel, Belus, or the Sun, and the symbol of him was the Bull, the Minotaur, the Apis of Egypt, the Golden Calf of Aaron; in the feminine, the heifer Baal, the cowfaced Juno, the transformed Io. Jupiter when he carried off Europa took the same form. And why this symbol? Because the Festival of the Sun was held at the Vernal Equinox, and five thousand years ago the Sun crossed the line six weeks later than it does now, exactly at the time when he entered the Constellation Taurus. We have thus the date fixed for us of the earliest of all religions. It was first pure. It then became idolatrous, and mankind were punished by the confusion of tongues, and by a miraculous dispersion. The Celtic branch was carried westward, and was deposited in Spain, and France, and the British Isles. They brought their creed and their knowledge along with them, and their monuments still survive among us.'

Fitzherbert would listen reverentially, only dropping here and there some uncomfortable objection, which would be imperiously dismissed. Fitzherbert, while admitting the possible truth of Vavasour's theories, dared on a single occasion to ask what all that had to do with Ireland?

'My dear friend,' Vavasour answered, 'it has everything to do with it. You observe, that as the Bull was the symbol of the Sun, so in the same theology the Serpent was the symbol of intellect. The serpent was the tempter in Paradise, who led our parents to the fatal Tree of Knowledge. The Serpent was the guardian of the golden apples. The Serpent lay wreathed under the altar of Pallas at Athens. The Serpent in Sanchoniathon was the type of Eternity. In shedding its skin it was supposed to renew its life for ever, and to be naturally immortal. Thus when we we read that St. Patrick banished the snakes out of Ireland, we are merely reading an allegory; the Christian Apostle was making an end of the ancient creed.'

After so luminous a reply, Fitzherbert would profess himself convinced, and Vavasour would flow on unrestrained.

Such was the officer who had come from Cork, as was supposed, to draw the plans for the Fort on the Island, and it was with no little satisfaction that his arrival was greeted at Dunboy. Goring thought that he was now to be relieved of the strain of anxiety and expectation. Fitzherbert was delighted to meet again a companion whose speculations amused him, and whom he respected for his accomplishments.

They met their visitor at the landing place.

'What an exquisite spot!' the General said as he stepped

ashore. 'Well for mankind that, amidst the vulgar occupations of common life, there are still places where it is possible to be reasonably happy. How can I sufficiently congratulate you, Colonel Goring, that one of the most beautiful of these has fallen to your lot?'

Charming as land and sea appeared in the summer sunshine, such an enthusiastic exclamation scarcely met the condition of Colonel Goring's feelings. He missed some allusion to the matter of which his mind was full. He observed merely that he hoped the General's visit would enable him to enjoy their blessings in more tranquillity.

'I trust it will be so,' the General said. 'All the knowledge which I possess will be at your service. I am sorry only that my stay can be but brief, too brief to exhaust a hundredth part of the interest which attaches to so remarkable a neighbourhood. I must leave you in three days; but we will turn to profit every hour of them. We will begin to-morrow—we will begin this instant, if you are disengaged.'

'You are a most zealous officer, General Vavasour,' Goring answered. 'Would that more were like you in the service! We have still some hours of daylight and, if you really wish it, a boat shall take us at once to the Island.'

The General looked puzzled. 'The Island!' he said. 'Is it possible that there, too, fresh treasures have been found? I had not heard of this.'

'I believe that an old gun has been turned up on the site of Carew's battery,' said Goring. 'I am sorry, however, that I must confess my carelessness. I have not even looked at it. The position you will see is unsuited for a modern fort which is to command the anchorage.'

'Carew's cannon!' replied the General. 'You do well to be indifferent to such worthless rubbish. But the fort—I know nothing of a fort. Oh! yes; by-the-bye, yes. When I told the Governor of Cork that I was coming here, he did ask me to take a glance at the Island, and see whether in case of necessity a gun or two could be mounted there. Any time will do for that, however. I must first see what you have to show me up these valleys of yours.'

To Goring, whose thoughts and hopes were fastened on the prospect which the Speaker had held out to him, General Vavasour's words were unintelligible. What else could there be in the neighbourhood which the General was so anxious about? After a moment's reflection, he concluded that the reputation of his Protestant garrison had reached the General's ears, and that he wanted to see what the men were like that he had about him. Most of his people, he said, were away at the mines, and the boats were on the Bay fishing; but they would walk through the village and see their families, and there should be a muster under arms the next morning.

'Gad! Goring,' said the General, 'they told me you were half mad with your Methodists, or whatever they are—a very irregular and disorderly set of rogues, from what I have heard of them. I hope they have done no mischief here. The Puritan scoundrels in England tore the abbeys down, and spoilt half the churches, Vandals that they were. I have known a cromlech in Cornwall split to pieces to mend a road. If your fellows have been at the same work here, I will never forgive them.'

'General Vavasour,' Goring coldly replied, 'I am gratified that you have done me the honour of visiting Dunboy. I confess, however, that I am somewhat at a loss. The Speaker of the House of Commons, Lord Shannon, I believe I must now call him, led me to expect your assistance in providing for the defence of the harbour here. I supposed your arrival to be connected with this undertaking.'

Fitzherbert, who had been struggling with his laughter, struck in to prevent further cross purposes.

'You do not know the treasures you are possessed of, Goring,' he said. 'Our little troubles down here are but the accidents of the moment. The General is occupied with the secrets of Irish national history, of which he believes the key to be in these mountains.'

'Of course,' cried the General, his eyes beaming at once with pleasure and good humour. 'Have you not within reach of an easy day's expedition the precious sandstone slab, which, if the engravings do not lie, is an ancient snake ring. Have you not a fort more precious than any which we could build, the most perfect now left in Northern Europe, which I expect will settle the question about Stonehenge?'

'I believe there are such things, sir,' Goring replied. 'I am a poor ignorant soldier and know nothing of them, but all I have is at your disposition. But we are at my house, excuse me for a few minutes. I must see that your rooms are ready for you.'

Fitzherbert meanwhile explained to the General how matters stood. Vavasour, who was really a kind-hearted man, and was a keen and shrewd officer when the antiquarian fit was off him, recognized at once how deep must be their friend's disappointment, and how real the dangers against which he had been contending single-handed, and how idly and carelessly he had been treated. It was a typical instance of Irish administration. Lord Shannon had meant what he said. A warning had reached him just at the time of a probable descent on the coast of Cork or Kerry, and he had sincerely intended that the harbour at Berehaven should be put in a state of defence. But the alarm passed off. The French seemed to be occupied elsewhere.

When Goring was in Dublin, Shannon was on doubtful terms with the Primate. But they had made up their differences. He had secured his Earldom and his pension, and preferred to let a subject drop which might have led to fresh questions between them. He sincerely wished Goring well, but he believed he was no longer in danger. Thus time had run on, and it was not till Vavasour had applied for a short summer's leave of absence, and had mentioned that he was going in search of antiquities to Dunboy, that he was told to take a look at Bere Island, and see whether anything could be made of it in case of necessity.

He was sorry on all accounts, sorry especially for the light tone in which he had himself spoken, and when they met again at dinner he was the soldier, the engineer, the brother officer. The Fire Towers and the Tuatha de Danans went forgotten; the French, the Whiteboys, the possible insurrection, and the means of dealing with it, appeared to be the only subjects with which his mind was occupied.

It was agreed before they parted for the night that the next day should be devoted to an elaborate survey of the Island, and the General undertook to report on the necessity of doing something or other to defend the harbour, whether the method before suggested should appear feasible or not.

Thus he almost succeeded in driving away the unpleasant impression which he had created on his first arrival, and restoring Goring's hopes and spirits. Almost, but not entirely, for the shock had been deep, and he knew too well that his position was at stake.

Chapter XXIII

AN EXCURSION

MORNING came blue and cloudless. The sun rose over Hungry Hill, flashing on the thousand tiny waves which rippled the grey waters of Bantry Bay. The boats had come in from the sea, and the miners and farmers off the Hill; and fishermen and landsmen mustered under arms for General Vavasour's inspection. There were a hundred and twenty of them, old and young, and the General found himself astonished into real admiration. In this army of Swaddlers, he saw before him a set of men whom he would be as well pleased to have behind him in the most dangerous service he could be sent upon, as he would have liked ill to find them in his front.

The day, as had been arranged, had been given to the Island. Sites were examined, rocks were tested, and measurements were accurately taken. The water supply question was gone into. Soundings were taken at the anchorage, and the range of guns calculated. Once launched upon the business of the profession, the General's enthusiasm warmed to the work. He was not contented with the Island. He examined different points upon the mainland. He made the men row him to Adrigoole, to see whether something could be made of that. He said little, but he sketched and made notes incessantly, and his silent eagerness was more satisfactory, a great deal, than a profusion of words would have been.

The morning following was spent in writing a report, which he gave Goring to read and make suggestions on. It set forth how, without difficulty, any French cruiser might take possession of the harbour, with the most dangerous effect upon the population. It contained a plan for the defence of the place, and advised that it should be carried out without delay. Knowing the habits of Dublin Castle, he said that his despatch should be forwarded to the English authorities, from whom there was better hope of attention.

Two days out of the three which the General could allow himself, having been thus consumed, the least which Goring could do was to let him have the third to himself, mount his hobby, and go in search of the antiquities.

General Vavasour, being slightly ashamed of his outburst on the day of his arrival, had felt a delicacy about suggesting it himself; but when Mrs. Goring appealed to him not to leave Dunboy without giving herself and her husband the benefit of his unrivalled knowledge, he eagerly consented.

The most important of the curiosities were in a valley some miles distant. The greater part of the way, they were to go by water. Mrs. Goring joined the party, and they set off together; cares and anxieties laid aside for an entire day of amusement and instruction. The sea was smooth; the Colonel's six-oared gig bore them rapidly across an arm of the bay; and they were landed at the mouth of a small river, from which point they were to walk. Summer was in the pride of its beauty; the air was scented with fresh-cut hay; the wild rose-bushes were covered with blossom, and the hill sides were pink with fox-gloves. The wet bogs shone with asphodel and orchids; and the large blue pinguicolas—loveliest of all the wild flowers of Ireland—luxuriated in the peat, where the water dripped on them off the rocks.

A couple of boatmen carried the luncheon-basket, and they proceeded for a mile up the course of the stream, till they came to a broad and shallow valley, full of rich grass, with high mountains rising on either side. To enter it, they had to pass over the projecting shoulder of one of the lower hills, on the top of which the soil had been long washed away. The red sandstone was spread out bare and flat, and some one at some time or other had smoothed and polished a few square yards of it. On this he had drawn a circle, enclosing it with a line, which was crossed and doubled as if to represent a twisted rope. Over the area, inside the circumference, were scattered a number of rings of various sizes, deeply cut in the stone, with central holes in each, and an occasional spot on the edge of the ring itself; while in and out among these circles were lines and strokes, appearing to mean something, from the regularity of their figures, but what the meaning could be, there was nothing to show.

This was their first object; and Vavasour sprang upon his prize, as a hawk upon a partridge. He produced an engraving, which he compared, point by point, with the original, and then flung it away in disgust.

'It is always so,' he muttered. 'The fools start with an idea, and then draw their own notions, and not what they see. They made me believe it was a snake-ring, with which it has not the faintest resemblance; but if not that—what is it, and who made it, and when?'

'That is for an expert, like you, to explain,' said Fitzherbert, 'I am no conjurer. Somebody has taken a great deal of trouble here; but whether it was a fortune-teller, or dealer in charms and spells, or whether some idle hand was making a board for the shepherd boys to play games upon, I cannot pretend to guess.'

'That is right,' said the General, 'never guess, unless you know. I am puzzled myself. The marks are not what I expected.'

He knelt upon the rock, counted the number of rings, measured the distance of one from the other, and of each from the centre, then examined the lines and scratches.

'I see what it may be,' he said, 'and though it disappoints me in one way, it may settle a curious point of history. But there ought to be a fort in the valley close by—Cahir Askill, I believe they call it. The fort and the stone will, surely, be in some way connected, and one will help us to understand the other.'

Cahir Askill was, in fact, not a quarter-of-a-mile from the engraved stone, and lay in the valley below the hill on which they were standing. Walking forward a hundred yards, they came in sight of a circular fort, as it was called; an enclosure, erected in the middle of an open meadow, a hundred and fifty feet in diameter, and surrounded by a thick wall, constructed so solidly that two-thirds of it were still in fair condition. The stones were large, and the more important of them had been rudely hewn. There was one distinct entrance; and signs of where another might have been, on the opposite side; while on the inner side of the wall there were stone staircases, leading to the top of it; and underneath each of these a chamber, large enough to hold ten or twelve men.

Tradition describes the place as an ancient Danish fortress. The least instructed eye could perceive that the hollow cellars under the steps were meant to contain human beings. The steps themselves gave access to the top of the walls, and the walls seemed as if they must have been meant for a defence of some kind; yet, as they all instantly observed, no building could have been contrived less capable of resisting a serious attack; the fortifications, if such they were, being low, and exposed on all sides, while within there was no shelter of any kind, or place of retreat, should the outer line be carried.

Fitzherbert waited to hear what the great authority would say. He had his own private doubts whether a building put together without mortar, and so loosely constructed, would have survived from such a high antiquity.

Goring, who had seen the place before, was not so prudent. He was no antiquarian. But he had sense to see plain objects and draw plain conclusions from them. He said that, in his opinion, the enclosure was nothing but a cattle pound.

The General listened languidly. With one side of his mind he recognized that Goring was possibly right. But he had formed large expectations of this Cahir Askill. It had been described to him as the most remarkable of all surviving Irish remains. It must have had some connection with the flat stone, and the flat stone could have had nothing to do with cattle stealing. Leaving Goring and his wife beside the luncheon basket, he walked round the building with Fitzherbert, examined the stones for inscriptions, of which he found none, looked carefully at the peaks of the different mountains which overhung the valley, and took their bearings with compass and quadrant.

It happened to be Midsummer Day, and high noon. Having a measuring rod with him, six feet long, he fixed it vertically in the centre of the enclosure.

AN EXCURSION

'Look here,' he said, and he pointed to the shadow of the rod upon the ground. 'You have here the earliest observation of the ancient astronomers. That stick is a gnomon. The direction and length of the shadow fixes the meridian for you. Today the sun is at its highest elevation for the whole year, and the shadow is, therefore, the shortest. It was here a few minutes ago,' he said, pointing to a scratch he had made in the clay. 'Now you see where it is, here. With this simple instrument the ancients fixed the time of the solstice, and each day the exact moment of noon. From the sun they passed to the moon and the stars, and the science of astronomy was begun.'

Fitzherbert's eyes glimmered. He could not guess what was coming, but he congratulated himself on his own forbearance. The gnomon must be leading up to the fort, but by what extraordinary route. He did venture to ask, however, whether the results which it gave depended on its situation, and whether it would not have yielded the same results if it had been set up anywhere else.

'I admit that it would, most sapient Fellow of Trinity. But now observe that large stone on the top of the wall, under the sun. At noon the sun was exactly over it, as we stand here at the centre. Look the other way, and you will see a corresponding stone under the North Star. Here are marks definitely pointing to the two poles.'

'And what then?' enquired Fitzherbert, eagerly.

'If you had read science at college, as you ought to have done, instead of wasting your time upon literature, you would not have required to ask, "what then?" Why then, finding sun, moon, and planets moving about among the stars, finding some stars rising and setting, others revolving about a point above the horizon, and the single North Star remaining fixed in its place, those old people, being men of lofty thoughts, determined to discover the law of those erratic bodies, and they measured their movements by watching how they bore towards fixed objects, which were always the same. Stonehenge had the same design. At sunrise on Midsummer morning the sun's rays touch the altar stone there. But the Druids of this island found instruments ready made for them in their own moun-

209

tains; and, unless my judgment deceives me, we are in the ancient lecture hall, where wise men conveyed by mouth the traditional lore of the stars which their fathers had brought with them, and illustrated their teaching directly from the objects themselves.'

'Brilliant!' said Fitzherbert, 'if your speculations had only a few facts in the middle of them. So far as I can see you have only a couple of stones which happen to stand north and south.'

The afternoon was hot. A pleasant patch of grass had been found by the side of the stream under the shelter of a rock, and once established there the party was in no haste to move. These luncheons amidst moors and mountains are among the bright incidents of our lives. Goring duly hoped that his distinguished guest had found something to interest him. Fitzherbert gravely repeated the astronomical theory; which they were permitted to laugh at, Vavasour laughing as loud as either of them.

Vavasour, alive as he was to the absurdities of many of his friends, and even of himself in his enthusiastic moments, would not leave his favourite pursuit undefended. There was proof, he said, in the language, in the old poetry, in the legends of the saints, in many of the less disputable monuments, that the Celtic Irish had once been an interesting people, full of energy, intellect, and high spirit. If they were to be raised again to a higher level, it could only be done by reminding them of the qualities of their forefathers, and waking up again the ancient genius of their race.

They rowed home together in the summer twilight; and so closed the last day of unclouded enjoyment which the family at Dunboy were to know.

The next morning the General departed. His report went home to the Horse Guards, and thence to the Admiralty. It was so emphatic in its language, it spoke so warmly of Golonel Goring's deservings, and so seriously of the danger of leaving so exposed a part of the coast without better protection, that it was not immediately thrown aside. It was referred to Dublin Castle, and thence back again to London. But no conclusion was arrived at, and in a few months the defences of Bantry

Bay were forgotten in the larger anxieties of the war.

About the same time that Goring's hopes on this side had died away, he was informed of the final decision which had been arrived at about his chapel and school. It had been ruled that the Protestant colony at Dunboy did not fall within the limits contemplated by the Toleration Act. Power had been reserved, when that Act was passed, to exclude from the benefit of it all bodies professing opinions dangerous to the established constitution. And the majority of the congregation at Dunboy were Independents, whose views were identical with those which in the preceding century had produced revolution and anarchy.

The Council of State had come to the conclusion that to grant formal toleration to a community of such a character would lead to the establishment of others of a similar kind. The growth of societies of Protestants in the Southern Provinces of Ireland could not fail to create irritation among the Catholic inhabitants, and disturb the improved feeling between the two races which the conciliatory policy of the British Government was tending to produce. For these reasons it was the unanimous opinion of the Judges that the registration could not be conceded. And the Council of State entertained no doubt that an officer of so high a character and reputation as Colonel Goring would comply at once with a resolution thus conveyed to him in a friendly manner, and would render unnecessary any further proceedings.

It was over. Colonel Goring had been too sanguine. It was plain to him that the colony must abandon its militant character. Among his tenants and workmen there was a mild and gentle minority, who were willing to remain with him on quiet terms. The Church at Glengariff would serve for him and for them. The rest he knew that it would be useless to try to persuade, and it would be equally undesirable to push any further his quarrel with the Government.

Out of the hundred families whom he had introduced upon the estate, sixty left him in the fall of the year, and took their passage at Cork for Rhode Island. With them the fighting strength of the community was departed. As in the clearing of a forest, when the great trees are felled, the wind rushes in and chills and blights the undergrowth, so after their brethren had passed away, the remaining members of the Dunboy settlement went about their business with languid hearts, no longer hoping. They took their quiet way on Sundays to Glengariff Church, but there was no longer any song of battle in them for the cause of the Lord. And they too, although for shame they could not yet propose to forsake the Colonel, yet felt themselves to be strangers in an enemy's land, and began to cast their eyes backwards across St. George's Channel to their old villages on the Cornish coast.

Chapter XXIV

THE BUCCANEER RETURNS

THE story now returns to Morty Sullivan, who was left repairing damages at Ballinskelligs, after his escape through Dursey Sound. A single tide sufficed for him to nail plates over the shot-holes in his hull and splice his damaged rigging. He made his way without further adventure to Nantes, where the *Doutelle* was overhauled and refitted. After the display which he had made of daring and seamanship, there were no more murmurs among the crew; the old hands were eager to sail with him, and he had his choice among the most desperate villains in the mouth of the Loire.

The loss of the arms at Glengariff was more than compensated, in the opinion of the French Government, by his defeat of an English frigate, and as there were not many officers in the French service who could boast of such an exploit, they were the more ready to trust him with a larger adventure. He had a letter of marque which would open the French harbours to him in all parts of the world; and in less than a month he was again at sea, and had captured a large vessel in the mouth of the Channel, which was sailing without a convoy, as the Speaker had informed Goring at Dublin. Thence he bore away to the West Indies, where his exploits for the next fourteen months made him as famous as Morgan or Kidd.

He took a score of prizes. He cut out a richly loaded barque from the roads at Bridgetown, under the guns of the fort. He raised a mutiny among the Irish at Montserrat, who sacked a dozen planters' houses, and set the town on fire. He laughed at the West Indian Squadron. He ran away from the frigates. He fought and beat the brigs and brigantines of his own size. His captives he sold at Martinique, or at New Orleans, or at any French port which he happened to be near. His headquarters were among the lagoons at Española, where, if he

213

was hard pressed, an inaccessible retreat was always open to him. Not Captain Daniel himself ever created such havoc, or excited such alarm in the English possessions in those seas, as Morty Sullivan, in a single year. Had he tempted fortune much longer, the end of him would probably have been like the end of most of his predecessors on the same road. The English looked upon him as a rebel and an outlaw. They would have taken him at last, and he and his followers would have swung on Gallows Point at Port Royal.

But the plot was thickening at home. The French were supposed to be meditating an invasion of England. They were really purposing the long-threatened attempt on Ireland, which had been talked of so long that nobody believed in it. Representations had been made to them from all parts of the country that the people were ready to rise. Ireland being the side where England was most vulnerable, a squadron was fitting out at Brest to make the experiment; but it was still undecided in what part of the Island the attempt should be made. It was necessary to be careful. Irish promises did not always become performance. Landings in Ireland by sympathizing Catholic foreigners had been many times tried, but had never yet prospered.

This time Louis and his advisers meant to be sure of their ground. It was from the South that they had received the strongest assurances; but they required the opinion of some one on whom they could entirely rely, as to what they might really expect, and for this purpose they cast their eyes on Morty Sullivan.

Thus some fourteen months after he had started on his raid among the West Indies, Morty Sullivan received a communication from the Governor at Port-au-Prince that his presence was required at home. The French Cabinet had a service of importance for him, and he was to repair to Nantes without loss of time. His ship's company and himself were equally willing to be gone. The men wished to enjoy the fruits of their adventures in Europe. Morty had always looked forward to changing his privateering for employment better suited for a gentleman. He took leave of his cruising ground, going off with flying colours, and laughing at the English cruisers which caught sight of him and chased him.

He made a swift passage across the Atlantic, and arrived at Nantes late in the same winter in which Colonel Goring's colony had begun to dissolve. At Nantes he found dispatches waiting for him. He was ordered to repair instantly to the coast of Kerry. The *Doutelle* and her crew were to be left behind. The vessel was known and would be recognized, and his presence in Ireland was to be kept an absolute secret, except from a few persons who could be trusted. Blake had fitted up for him one of the fast luggers, which were used in the ordinary fishing trade, and would pass unobserved by any English ships of war which might be on the look-out at the Land's End. His commission was to ascertain the actual state of readiness of the Southern Province, and what the French might count on in case they landed.

It was not without misgivings that Morty accepted the commission, for he saw that considerable expectations had been formed of the state of things in Ireland. The patriotic leaders had as usual so magnified their resources that Louis had asked in wonder why, if they were so strong and united, they had not driven the English into the sea. The lugger, however, was ready in the river. The wind was steady from the east. The weather promised well and Blake hurried him on board. Connell only went with him of his old comrades. They sailed under false names, and the skipper only knew them as agents whom the firm was employing upon secret business.

Bally Quoilach Bay is an estuary of the Kenmare River, lying between Ardgroom and Dursey Island, and immediately opposite to Darrynane. The entrance is covered by a long, flat-topped rocky island, ground smooth by glaciers, which forms a natural breakwater, while inside there are hidden shoals and reefs, through which there is but one passage, that twists and winds like a snake. Thus the approach is very dangerous. Large ships cannot venture in at all, nor vessel of any kind without a local pilot.

Inside, however, when these perils are all passed, there is

in one corner of the bay, a quiet basin, into which even the swell of the open ocean fails to penetrate, with a bottom of sand which slopes up gradually to a beach of powdered sea shell. At a little distance is the mouth of a small river, like that where Ulysses landed in Phœacia, and here too kings' daughters and their maidens may have washed their house linen and spread it to dry on the shingle, for the spot was the favourite haunt of sea rovers.

The valley which opens on the Bay is but one of the series of hollows through which the rain which falls on the mountain that divides Cork from Kerry finds its way into the sea. A horse track from Ardgroom passed through it over the hills to Dunboy. But the track was seldom used, for there was little intercourse between the two districts. Bally Quoilach, like Derreen, still remained, either by lease or otherwise, in possession of the O'Sullivans, and they clung to it with passionate tenacity.

Morty Sullivan's father had resided there, and had been in trouble more than once with the authorities for sheltering Rapparees and Tories. He had sent his son abroad to find employment better suited to his rank and birth; but he had continued to live there himself in friendly intercourse with his kinsman at Derreen. Out of the Rapparees, as the Revolution Settlement relapsed into Anarchy, had developed the smugglers and for many years an active contraband business was carried on in the Bay. On the old man's death, Morty ought to have succeeded, but the estate had fallen to the widowed sister whom Goring had removed from Dursey Island, and she with her son, a boy of seven years old, was now residing there, the chief or chieftainess of the relics of a clan as wild as the wildest of the Scotch Highlanders, and equally ready to do her bidding, lawful or unlawful. These fierce Caterans would have long since swept Goring out of Dunboy, and burnt his roof over his head, but for the wholesome fear in which they stood of his Protestant guard.

The river, in ordinary weather, was a mere brook, trickling innocently among the stones. In heavy rains it became a furious torrent. The floods had long since made it necessary to throw a bridge across the stream, for the use of cattle. A hundred yards below the bridge, protected by a rock at the back, and sheltered by a wall, stood the ancient baronial mansion of Eyris. In front was a rude garden, with the river beyond. The sea was a quarter-of-a-mile off.

The building itself, and the structure of it, told the tale of its history. It was quadrangular, with a court in the middle. the living-rooms were on the ground floor, with garrets in the roof, and the roof itself was thatched. The walls were of massive stone, and the timbers, which were of solid oak, had once formed the ribs and beams of a large ship. A dozen cabins now occupy the old site. The rafters of the O'Sullivan mansion can still be seen in them charred with fire, and the auger-holes which were bored in them when the ship was built.

The dimensions of the house were evidently considerable. It was not only the home of the chief, but the home of the crews of his vessels. It was a refuge for hunted outlaws, and was constructed to resist the attacks of a sheriff's party, should any sheriff be rash enough to pay a visit there. It was a magazine of ships' stores, and a warehouse of cargoes. There was a blacksmith's shop and a carpenter's shop. There were outbuildings filled with spare sails, coils of rope, spars, copper and iron bolts, anchors, chains, and all the necessaries for the repairing or fitting out vessels. The hall, or family sitting-room, was itself an arsenal, being hung round with muskets, blunderbusses, pistols, swords and pikes. It was curiously furnished, out of the spoils of ships' cabins; with sea chests, carved bureaus, couches, tables of oak or mahogany, each one of which had, probably, a story connected with the acquisition of it.

Here, since the early part of the century, the elder Morty had maintained his patriarchal rule, owning no jurisdiction save his own will and strength of hand. He had no neighbours to interfere with him. He escaped molestation from the county authorities, because no one was sufficiently interested in calling him to account. He filled the cellars of the county gentlemen; he supplied the ladies' wardrobes with silks and laces. In extremities, he used the wealth which he had acquired in making friends at the Four Courts and in Dublin Castle.

The Morty of our story, and his sister, had been born in this house. In it they had spent their childhood and youth, with the exception of occasional visits to their Derreen kinsman, who, being more exposed to the world's eye, kept himself a little further within the lines of civilization. As he grew to manhood, Morty's ambition rose above so squalid and lawless a life; and, having no opening at home, he carried his sword into the service of the Catholic powers abroad.

His sister, Ellen, married a Mahony, a son of the famous Donnell, who ruled Kerry for a generation with the help of four thousand 'fairies'. Her husband dying soon after—being drowned in some wild adventure—and Morty being far away, Ellen and her child had gone to live with her mother, at the old castle at Dursey, from which Goring, in consequence of their connection with the smugglers, found it necessary to remove them. The mother had died, it was alleged in consequence of exposure, at the time when they were expelled; and Ellen Mahony had gone back to her own house at Eyris, burning with resentment at the Saxon intruder at Dunboy, who had added a fresh injury to the crime of being the possessor of her ancestral home.

Morty's reappearance in the *Doutelle*, the fight at Derreen, and his defeat at Glengariff, were so many fresh scores in the accounts which were run up against Goring in the passionate lady's mind. Morty had gone again. Goring had left the Revenue service. Between the families at Eyris and Dunboy there was no communication. But Ellen Mahony brooded incessantly on her own and her brother's wrongs, and her one thought, sleeping and waking, was of revenge.

So matters stood with Morty's widowed sister, when one winter's day a French lugger swept into the Bay, bringing her brother and his friend. She rushed to the conclusion that this sudden arrival must be connected with the subject of which her own mind was so full. She found Morty indifferent and preoccupied. He was full of the mission with which he had been entrusted, and could think of nothing else. For a fortnight the emissaries of the secret societies of Munster were coming and going; but it proved as he expected, and he could find nothing satisfactory to go upon. There was the confident assertion that the people were ready to rise, and would rise when the French fleet came in sight. He was reproached for want of patriotism when he insisted on answers to inconvenient questions. Were the people armed? Were they drilled, and did they know their officers? At what points could they be collected, and in what numbers? Had they guns, or had they only pikes? Had the muskets and ammunition which had been sent from France been distributed, or were they still in hand, and where? Should a French force be thrown on shore, how many men could be counted on as ready to join at short notice? How were the French to be fed if they came, and what number of carts and carriages could be collected for the transport service?

To all such questions the answers were general and vague. Was not all Ireland ready to welcome their deliverers from English tyranny? Wouldn't they burn the houses of the gentry over their heads, and set the land in a flame from end to end? The Dublin boys would take the Castle. The Irish in the English regiments would shoot their officers and bring over half the army. All, in fact, was just as it was when Morty himself, as a lad, had attended the Whiteboy meetings. There was the same enthusiasm of the tongue, the same absence of solid preparation.

Weary and disgusted, he had despatched Connell across the water to meet a party of delegates at Derrynane who were to bring final information. Waiting anxiously for Connell's return, he was strolling on a soft winter's morning with his sister along the sandy shore. The tide was out. The lugger was high and dry on the beach. The men had brought her in at high water to clear her bottom of shell and weed. She would float off again with the flood, and they were busy scouring her with brooms and scrubbing brushes. The little boy, the heir of the valley and the chieftainship of the O'Sullivan's, was watching the men at their work with childish interest.

For how many ages had the bay and the rocks, and the mountains, looked exactly the same as they were looking then? How many generations had played their part on the same stage, eager and impassioned as if it had been created only for them! The half-naked fishermen of forgotten centuries who had earned a scanty living there; the monks from the Skelligs who had come in on highdays in their coracles to say mass for them, baptize the children or bury the dead; the Celtic chief, with saffron shirt and battle axe, driven from his richer lands by Norman or Saxon invaders, and keeping hold in this remote spot on his ragged independence; the Scandinavian pirates, the overflow of the Northern Fiords, looking for new soil where they could take root.

These had all played their brief parts there and were gone, and as many more would follow in the cycles of the years that were to come, yet the scene itself was unchanged and would not change. The same soil had fed those that were departed, and would feed the others that were to be. The same landscape had affected their imaginations with its beauty or awed them with its splendours; and each alike had yielded to the same delusion that the valley was theirs and was inseparably connected with themselves and their fortunes.

Morty's career had been a stormy one, and his actions such as weaker men might like ill to think of. He was an outlaw, and in his enemies' judgment a pirate and a freebooter, but he had done nothing which weighed on his conscience as a crime. He had been fighting all his life; but fighting chiefly against the oppressors of his country and his race. His mind was free to wander from his own concerns into the speculations which the scene suggested. He too had played as a child on the same shore where his nephew was playing now. He had kindled with his young enthusiasm at the tales which were told him of his forefathers. He had gone out into the world, and had battled and struggled in the holy cause, yet the cause was not advanced, and it was all nothing. He was about to leave the old place, probably for ever. Yet there it was, tranquil, calm, indifferent whether he came or went. What was he? What was any one? To what purpose the ineffectual strivings of short-lived humanity? Man's life was but the shadow of a dream, and his work was but the heaping of sand which the next tide would level flat again.

THE BUCCANEER RETURNS

So Morty mused as he strolled to and fro, glancing occasionally seawords for signs of Connell's return. His sister walked
at his side, gnawing her lip impatiently. In appearance she was
very like her brother. She had the same hard, clean-cut face,
the same sinewy figure, the same falcon eyes, dark, fierce, and
fearless. But Morty's larger experience of life had taught him
to govern his passions, and had given him wider views. She,
shut up on a promontory of Kerry occupied alternately with
her personal injuries and with the wrongs of her country, in
whose cause her family had been robbed of their inheritance,
could think of nothing beyond what was immediately close
to her. Ireland to her was all in all. To pray and plot for
revenge was her only interest.

Morty muttered something which did not please her. Flushing up, and grinding the sand under her boot, she said:

'It comes to this, then! After all you have done, and all you
have suffered, you mean to abandon the cause, to leave the
land you were born in, to leave your clansfolk, each man of
whom would lose the last drop of his blood for you, to leave
the last of your father's children, for you need not think that
I and that child will go with you!'

'What would you have?' he said bitterly. 'I tell you the
people cannot fight. The heart is not in them. They will bluster
and boast, but when the time comes for action, it will only be
which shall be first to betray the other. Come here, Dermot,'
he called to the boy who was struggling in the mud with a
sand-eel. 'Can you hit a mark yet? Let me see what you can
do with this,' and he drew a pistol from his belt.

The child's eyes glittered as he looked with delight at the
long, chased Spanish barrel. 'I shot a gull once, Uncle,' he
answered. 'Paddy O'Brien held the gun, but I aimed it, and I
pulled the trigger, and the bird tumbled off the rock into the
water, and Paddy swam in and brought it out in his mouth
like a dog, and he said the best shot in the Barony could not
have done it better.'

'Well then,' said Morty, 'now you shall hold the pistol yourself. You see that white mark on the stone yonder. Try if you
can put a ball into the middle of it.'

In both hands, for the pistol was too heavy for him to hold in one, the child grasped the butt, a little alarmed, but too proud to shew it. He clenched it firmly, levelled and fired. The pistol sprang out of his hand with the recoil, the guard cutting the middle finger to the bone, but he neither flinched nor cried, and the ball, more by chance than skill, went true to the centre of the spot.

'Well done, little fellow,' said his uncle. 'You shall have a pistol of your own, as a birthday present, and here is a King George's shilling for you.'

'I'll not touch a shilling of King George's,' cried the boy. 'Not if you never give me anything more in all your life, Uncle Morty.'

'You shouldn't bark, Dermot, before your teeth are grown. What would you like to do with yourself when you come to be a man?'

'I'll learn to shoot,' answered the boy, 'and I think I will take the shilling you give me. I'll set it up for a mark, and practise at the face that's on it; and when I'm big, I'll watch behind a wall and shoot the English Colonel that lives in the place that ought to belong to us.'

'God help the child,' said Morty. 'You have schooled him well, Ellen, and when he grows up he will be an honour to the family. So it is with us all. None are braver than we, when cows' tails are to be cut off, or the enemies of the country shot from a hiding place. But to stand up and fight the Saxon in an honourable field, as the Scots did with Bruce and Wallace, that is beyond us.'

'Shame on ye, Morty, once more,' said his sister, 'to speak evil of the land of your birth. What nation ever held out against oppression as we have done? For six hundred years the hoof of the stranger has been on our necks. He has torn our lands from us. If he could, he would have torn from us our faith and our God.'

'Constant! Yes, we have been constant. What were we when we had the island to ourselves? If we were again free, we should cut one another's throats in the old style. God knows I have no love for the English. I would put a ball through Goring's head to-morrow, and desire no better day's work. But it must be in fair fight, man to man; I have no taste for shooting from behind hedges.'

'Aye, Morty, you are for honourable ways. And to what honour are we bound, when the strong thief is in our homes, and our children are turned away from their own doors to starve? A fair fight in my mind is too much honour for the like of him. Take him in the front, if you have the chance to meet him in the front. Shoot him in the back as you would shoot a mad dog, if you have no better opportunity, and rid the earth of him any way.'

'Well, well, Ellen, we will not quarrel about it, but I'd be well pleased if I had never left the Emperor's service. By this time I might have been by the side of Lacy and O'Donnell at the head of armies, instead of dragging out a soiled existence, doing the dirty work of the Court of Versailles. What am I now? A desperate adventurer, who, if he fails and is taken, will be hanged as a felon and an outlaw. If I now tempt the French by false information to send an expedition here, it will end as all such enterprises have ended before. We call ourselves Patriots, and we have not the spirit to face our tyrants like men. I will have no more of it. The Austrians will take me back if I ask them. France, herself, has promised me employment by land or sea. I will go, and forget these last years as a miserable dream.'

'And leave your fine Colonel,' said she, 'in the home of your fathers, him that hunted you from Culloden field, and drove your mother from the roof that sheltered her, and gave you your own life at Derreen House—I wonder that you would take the gift at such a hand—and slaughtered your boat's crew at Glengariff, and brought the King's ship upon you after that. I would rather that ship had sunk you with her guns in Dursey Sound, or that you were now lying dead on the shore where you stand, than that you should go away and leave that man unpunished.'

'Ellen,' he answered, 'you will drive me to madness if you speak like that!'

He turned away to catch sight of a boat coming round the

rocks. Then, with a last fling: 'We shall hear now what is to be looked for. If, as I suppose, it is all froth and foam, I shall know what to do!'

Chapter XXV

MORTY'S CODE

THE boat which Morty had seen came in swiftly over the smooth water of the estuary. Four men were rowing, apparently fishermen. The boat itself was of the native build of the country—a light framework of ash covered with cow-hide, and held in shape by the keel and the cross benches which formed the seats of the rowers. It was frail to look at, but it was buoyant, and able to encounter seas when stouter vessels would have found their end.

Connell was steering, and two persons were sitting in the stern beside him, one of whom, as they stepped on shore, was seen to be old Sylvester O'Sullivan; the other was a stranger, and a note which Connell handed to Morty referred him to this gentleman for an answer to all enquiries which he had to make. Sylvester, it seemed, had been taken into counsel, and, affecting the ease and intimacy of relationship, he seized Morty's hand.

'Welcome home,' he said. 'Right glad are we to see ye once more among us! We are from Derrynane this morning, and this is Mr. —. But we will name no names. It is safest so. This is one of the best-born gentlemen in the province of Munster, who is honoured to make your acquaintance.'

The stranger was a tall man, with red hair and whiskers, blue eyes, and broad features. Morty glanced at him, and liked neither his look nor the mystery about him. Still less was he pleased at that moment to see his kinsman, whom he regarded as the chief cause of his having left the highways of life for the tortuous road into which he had fallen.

The stranger, who saw that Morty was out of humour at something, put on an easy air, and said:

'It is well pleased we are to see ye here, sir, and pleased at the cause which has brought you home among us. We have all heard what ye have done in the West Indies with our poor people that were working in chains there, and how ye fought the big frigate off Dursey yonder, and sent her home to Cork Haven slower than she came. If ye could hear how the country speaks of ye, ye would be a proud man this day!'

'The frigate was well handled, sir,' Morty answered coldly, 'and if we escaped it was more by luck than skill! But you have something to say to me, Mr. —? And I will be glad to hear it, for my time is short.'

'You may call me O'Brien, sir, for want of a worse name,' he stranger said. 'There is good blood among the O'Briens, anyway, and the best of it runs in my own veins. We mean you well, and we hope you will mean well by us, but you are rather short in your speech. Mr. Connell here brought us word from ye, that ye would like to know what we are prepared to do if the French ships at Brest should be seen in our waters. Well, I'll tell ye! Right welcome will be the sight of them! Not an Irish heart in the Four Counties but will feel the French are the best friends that are left to Ireland in all the world!'

'I can believe that,' replied Morty, 'but it is not what I have been sent to learn. It has been represented in Paris that if M. Thurot's squadron appears off this coast and lands two or three regiments, you have fifty thousand men ready to join at a day's notice. Is that so?'

'Indeed, and it is! It is not fifty thousand nor a hundred thousand. It is all Catholic Ireland that will join—every mother's son of them!'

'Every mother's son cannot be put in the field to fight. The English have twelve thousand red coats in the island, besides the gentry and their servants, and the Protestants in the North. Can you produce fifty thousand men, drilled, who, if Thurot lands, can march at once to support him?'

'We have, sir, and more! Who knows it better than King Louis, who has the Brigade with him? And didn't they beat the English at Fontenoy?'

'You mean that Thurot is to bring the Brigade with him?' Morty said.

'Sure, and of course that is what we mean,' answered the

stranger. 'And what else would we mean? Aren't they the flower of us all? And haven't we sent them over to learn their trade and be fit for fighting when the day comes for it? Our poor people at home are just peasants, and how would they be able to fight? They can make the country hot for the Protestant gentlemen, but that is all they are fit for. Let the King send the Brigade over, and twenty thousand Frenchmen at the back of them, and then he should see what we could do! There would not be a Protestant left alive in the Island a month after!'

'I can believe that, also, Mr. O'Brien, or whatever your name may be,' said Morty. 'But no such force is likely to be sent! They require to know, in case M. Thurot throws a small division of French troops on shore in Bantry Bay or the Kenmare River, what number of men the Irish can bring into line at once at immediate call? Arms have been sent. Officers have been sent. Money has been sent. What have you to show? Can you produce fifty thousand men? Can you produce five thousand men?—or five hundred?—or one hundred?'

'You are hard on me, Mr. O'Sullivan! You are one of ourselves, and you might know by this time that we have tried that way long enough, and that we find others answer better!'

'Too well I know that,' said Morty, 'and I know what has come of it. By no advice of mine shall French soldiers set foot on this soil. And though it is my own soil, and though I would live and die for it, I will not mislead those who trust me. Fight the battle your own way, and with your own weapons. I will meddle with you no more!'

'Sure it is joking you are, Morty,' Sylvester said, 'or the black dog has bitten you. You talked that way years past at Nantes, when Mr. Blake put the work on you, and may be you had reason then, with the peace and all. But now, with the war back again, and the old enemy with his hands full the world over, and the French on the seas and ready and willing to help —is it you, Morty, that will be hindering them? What hurt have the English been able to do to yourself for all their power? You slip through their hands like a merrow, and for each blow they give you, you give them two in return. In

Dublin Castle they are shaking as if the fit was on them. The light of the brightest day that ever dawned on Ireland is breaking over the hills, and would you be leaving us now, Morty, when if you will stay and lead the rising you will be ruling again before another summer in your own Castle at Dunboy, with the Colonel's head on a pike over the gateway.'

'So you go on,' said Morty. 'It is the old story which we have heard a thousand times. The light breaking on the hills! The better day that is dawning! I will tell you what the end will be of such a day. A few hundred wretched dupes will take up arms, believing the lies that are told them, and then some Cromwell will come and trample them into mud. The very schemers that lead them astray may be are selling them all the time to the Castle. You yourself, Mr. Sylvester, have played many parts before this, and who knows what part you are playing now?'

'No thanks to you, Morty, for your suspicions of an innocent man,' answered his cousin with a sinister twist in his face. 'You might have remembered who it was that spoilt the Colonel's game for him at Kilmakilloge, and brought Lord Kerry's orders to keep your kinsman at the old place. May be that day at Derreen is no pleasant recollection to ye, Morty Oge.'

Any allusion to Goring touched Morty to the quick.

'I tell ye,' he said, 'that only for the thought of that man I would never have seen Kerry more; and that you know yourself, Sylvester. There was a long score between us when he came to me, and there is a longer now. If I could be brought to meet him where none could come between us, I would not ask to live another day.'

'May be,' said the man who called himself O'Brien, 'we would be able, some of us, to help you to that same, and I had the purpose in my mind when I came to see you this morning. The gentlemen of the county are just wild about the Colonel bringing the Swaddlers here, and spoiling the trade and disturbing the quiet. Devil a frigate, devil a revenue officer would be plaguing the coast at all but for the Colonel. We don't like him, and that is the truth of it, and we would have found means among us to clear him out, but that he is not handy to fix a quarrel upon. The boys say there is not the equal of him with the sword in the four provinces, and what he can do with the pistol you know yourself, Mr. Morty. But you are as good a man as he any day, and I can tell ye that any one who would put the Colonel out of the world would have the thanks of every gentleman that wants claret for his cellar, and of every tenant that wants a market for his fleeces. When the Colonel is gone we may do as we will, and the coast will be our own from Cape Clear to Dingle.'

A savage look passed over Morty's face, which the stranger interpreted into encouragement. 'You are handy by,' he went on. 'You are not six miles over the hill from Dunboy, and you have lads here that will do your bidding. They say half the people he brought over have left him and gone to America. What can hinder ye to slip over the pass, catch the Colonel and the lave of them in their sleep, and make a nate end, and be off to sea by the morning? There are not many in Ireland, gentle or simple, but would say you were doing a good service in that same.'

'These gentlemen of Ireland that the English laws have set to reign over us seem an interesting set of beings,' replied Morty. 'There was a story on the Continent about a Danish treasure ship that was wrecked on the coast hereabouts. They said that squires, clergy and great ladies stole the cargo and shared the plunder. They asked me over there if these were the persons whom the English had put into Ireland to keep order, because we were not able to do it ourselves. And now you say they would like me to murder—to murder I say, for that is what you mean—this Colonel Goring, who, to give him his due, is one of the best of them, because he keeps their brandy cellars empty. Pretty rulers they—but, bad though they may be, I don't believe that of them. You are not speaking the truth.'

O'Brien flushed to the roots of his hair. 'Is it insulting me that you would be, Morty Oge?' he said, 'and me a better gentleman than the best O'Sullivan of the whole of ye.'

'I will quarrel with any man,' said Morty, 'who proposes to

me to assassinate a man in his bed. I am a soldier, sir, and not a cut-throat. You talk of your country, and all you want is the smuggling trade. If I were to do this precious piece of service, which you say would be well taken, who but you would be washing your hands at the door of the Castle, and pretending that a pirate had done it that came in from the sea. There would be a price on my head, and if I was not out of the way you would raise the country to take me and hang me. I am weary of the whole of you. The poor land is under a curse. The sun will never shine on a free Ireland till she has learnt to face her conquerors with better weapons than the murderer's knife.'

'You are sharp in your words, Morty, but I must not answer you back as I would if any spake so but yourself. You have lived so long away from us that you don't know your own people. We know what we are about. Sure the English would like nothing better than that we should face them as ye call it. That is not the way at all. We can't do it. But what we can do is to burn their houses and their farms and harry their cattle, and set the Whiteboys on them to scare them in their sleep. Yes, and for all ye say there is the knife and the pistol for them that plunder the poor with their tithes and their rack-rents. They daren't do as Cromwell did, for the world would cry shame on them, and we tire them out and make them sick of us, and then may be they will let us drop at last.'

'Go on your way then,' said Morty, 'but it was not the way of my fathers, and it is not mine. My ancestors held Dunboy against Carew's cannon. The bones of them lie buried under the walls, and cowardice and ferocity was never laid to their charge. You think you can do better for yourself by houghing sheep and cattle. Well then, try it, but don't ask me to go along with you, or to bring the French to help you. Any country may have its liberty, when there is manhood there that will live free or die, and no country, I believe, will get much good of its liberty when there is not. A brave people always wins in the end, for it costs more to hold them than to let them go.'

'Ye have fine words at your command, there is no denying

that, Mr. O'Sullivan, and I'll not say but ye can fight finely too, and welcome would be the day when we had need of your hand for that same. But if ye will help us with the Colonel, we'll ask no more of ye for this time. A dale of blood would be running before we could drive the red coats out, and a dale more would run among ourselves when we had seen the last of them and the land was our own. Maybe we see our way to what would be good for us better than yourself. I'll not quarrel with ye, anyway. Only well I know ye would like to clear your account with the Colonel yonder, and your friend, Mr. Blake, will be a glad man the day he hears that the Colonel is under the ground. Sure if ye wouldn't go in the dark ye might take the mountain boys, and we'd provide ye with a score of Wild-geese, and ye might just go in the blessed sunlight and have it out in the fair fight that you are so fond of. Ye will find but a sprinkling of them left to deal with and you owe them a turn for that night's work at Glengariff.'

'That would be a brave day,' said Sylvester, 'and well would I like to see the dawning of it. But you must mind what you are about with thim English. They will take a deal from us, and never seem to heed what we do, but if we go a step too far they are just wild, as Phelan O'Neil found to his sorrow. No, no; a house may be burnt, and a man that is under the displeasure of high and low may get his deservings, and it will be the talk for a week or two, and no more about it, but you must respect the customs of the country.'

'I tell you,' said Morty, 'I will have none of your customs. You have ruffians enough of your own to do your devil's work without coming to me. Bring Colonel Goring and me where none can interfere with us, and I will thank any of ye. We can then settle our differences once for all, and there will be an end. But if I challenge him he will only send word to Cork that I am here, and every frigate on the station will be out to seize me. Goring gave me my life once, and it shall never be said that I took him at a disadvantage.'

'Indeed then, it's mighty particular you are, Morty Oge,' said Sylvester, 'and it is little like an honourable man the Colonel would be if he refused the challenge of a gentleman that is better born than he is. You forget what is due to yourself, kinsman, to be condescending that way with a thief that has stolen the land that belongs to ye. But we love ye the more for it, and maybe we will find the means to help you to your wish. The Colonel is a trusting gentleman, and easily believes any tale that is brought to him. Leave it to me, and I'll fetch him where there shall be none but your two selves as ye say, unless Mr. Connell and I might be in the neighbourhood to see fair play.'

Chapter XXVI

A STRANGE SUMMONS

THE world had not mended with Colonel Goring since his people began to drift away from him, and it seemed as if circumstances would do his enemies' work, and force him out of the country, without further stir on their part. The peasantry of the neighbourhood, agitated by rumours of a French landing, grew unruly and insolent. Encouraged by the reduction of the numbers of the settlers, they renewed the attacks on their property. Cattle were again mutilated and fences broken down, and corn stacks set on fire. The smuggling enterprises revived on a larger scale than ever, and the colonists, harassed and dispirited, were less willing to lend their help in making seizures.

The seceders who had departed first had been those who were most strongly under religious impressions. Their example and their influence being removed, the rest fell off from the austere habits which had distinguished them all at the beginning. How they thought and felt might be perceived in a fragment of a conversation between a party of them one evening after work.

'Well, master,' said a big miner from Liskeard, named Treherne, 'I don't know how it strikes you, but for my part I don't like the look of things, and I shall clear out before long. I have saved a little money, and I shall take the wife and the young ones home, before worse comes of it. We have had no luck since the rest went off, and in my mind we shall not mend.'

'True enough,' said a young fisherman, 'things are not as they were, and I don't rightly know the meaning of it. But the Colonel and his lady have been good friends to me and mine, and I will not leave the ship at the first touch of bad weather. He is a good man, is the Colonel. He tries to do his duty to his Master, and I will do mine to him.'

THE TWO CHIEFS OF DUNBOY

'And get your head broken for your pains, as you did last year at Glengariff,' sneered the miner. 'We came here to get a living by our work. What had we to do with fighting and quarrelling, and making the people hate us? If they chose to run a keg or two of brandy to keep their stomachs warm in this precious climate, it is no more than the lads do at home.'

'You came here with your eyes open, Dick,' said another. ''Twas part of the bargain you signed with the Colonel, to help him in the revenue work. You have made a good bit of money out of the mine; you don't deny that, and you must take the rough with the smooth. For my part, I would stay willingly enough, if they had not shut the school up. I don't want children of mine to grow up ignorant heathens, or Papists, which is worse.'

'No fear of that,' answered Treherne. 'The last of us will be gone out of this place before any child of yours or mine will lose his soul among these savages. The Colonel thinks he can make them mend their ways. What was the first thing I saw this morning? Tom Pollen's red cow roaring about the field with her tail sheared off at the stump, and the white heifer lying on the grass with the sinews of her hind legs cut through. Things can't go on in this way. I would shoot the skulking rascals like so much vermin, if the Colonel would allow it. But he won't. Well, then live and let live. He can't stand by himself, and the Government won't stand by him, nor anybody else that I see. The whole of us had better clear out.'

More clearly than any of his people, Goring himself saw whither he was drifting. Fitzherbert, after staying half-a-year with him, had gone at last. He had done his best to persuade him to abandon a hopeless enterprise, and to leave the country. But to this, Goring would answer that God had placed him there, and that he must remain at his post till he was relieved; and there was no more to be said.

Only many an anxious conversation passed between him and the companion of his life on their changing outlook. No clamorous peasants any longer brought their complaints to his hall-door in the mornings; no children with scalded legs were brought to the house for the mistress to mend them. The greetings on the roads which used to be kindly, were exchanged for a look of unfriendly recognition, while the nightly outrages shewed that the worst spirit was abroad. The Colonel still went about unarmed. To carry pistols, he said, would not diminish any danger which there might be, and he had an objection to shooting people himself, which perhaps he might do if he was attacked. But he also felt that he could not keep English families about him whom he could not protect, while he could not allow them to take the law into their own hands.

Specially he felt that Dunboy was no longer a fit place for women, and he proposed to send his wife away to Cork again. To this she had answered, that if it was not a fit place for her, it was not fit for the families of the miners and fishermen. Enthusiastic as her husband, but with clearer judgment, she saw that their experiment had failed, or, as the first seceders expressed themselves, that it was not God's will that it should prosper.

'If you stay, and the rest stay, I must stay, too,' she said. 'But surely we have done enough. Let us go home together. We have fought a good fight, and if we have not succeeded, the fault is not with us or with our people. Why persist in useless efforts to improve a race which will not be improved on our pattern, or to serve a Government which neither helps nor thanks you?'

To these arguments constantly repeated, the Colonel could but answer as he had answered Fitzherbert, that God had put him where he was, and had given him a duty to do. If, as he hoped, he was one of God's servants, he must take the work which was allotted to him. Absenteeism had been the curse of Ireland. Providence had given him an estate there, and he must reside upon it, come what would.

One Saturday at the beginning of March, when the week's work was over, he called his people together to address them on the situation. Since the failure of his appeal to the Dublin Courts, the chapel at the house had been closed. The congregation had chosen one of themselves to read and explain the Bible to them, and they met at each other's houses, out of sight and below the notice of any one inclined to inform against them. On this occasion he invited them all to meet him at the old place. The bell woke from its long silence. The hall, for it was but a hall after all, soon filled to overflowing, for the hearts of the people were full, and they knew that the master himself meant to speak to them.

Every member of the little colony that could be spared from home was present, men, women, and children, well-dressed, decent, and respectful, even the discontented among them, like old Treherne, for all loved the Colonel.

The link which held the Colonel and his people together was in their common faith. He knew that many of the best and simplest of them were perplexed at the withholding of the help from Providence for which they thought that they might have looked, and to this very natural feeling he wished to address himself. When they were all collected, he came forward on the platform and said:

'You and I, my friends, believe with all our hearts that God is a living God. He is no idol, but the actual living ruler of this world. This is the basis on which we build our own lives. Yet Psalmists and Prophets—and not they only, but perhaps every man and woman who has tried to do God's will—have been staggered by His apparent indifference, and have cried out in their perplexity—"where is God? *We* have never seen Him—we have seen no signs of Him. Oh, that He would but shew Himself for one moment, and assure us by definite proof that He is really there". The soldier, on a campaign, loses his heart, if his General hides himself in his tent. One, greater than the saints, cried out upon the cross, that He was forsaken. And this is the feeling of all persons, in the bottom of their hearts, who have been trying hard to do right, and find circumstances too strong for them. They are apt to fancy that if God was really on our side, it could not be so. They will allow it to be true that God has never promised success—that is, outward and worldly success—to those who give themselves up to His service. He has promised them rather mortification and suffering, and apparent failure. But no one entirely believes that, in his own case. He can understand the misfortunes of other people. He feels no surprise when he reads what has

happened to saints and martyrs. But when the trial comes
home to himself, he is generally puzzled and distressed.

'Something of this kind is very likely passing through the
minds of many of you who are listening to me. You came to
Ireland at my invitation, to work with me on an estate which
I had not sought, which God's Providence gave to me. We have
taken nothing from any man; we have cultivated land which
was lying barren; we have caught fish which, but for us, would
have been left in the sea; we have raised metals, which were
lying untouched in the earth; we have brought wealth where
before there was poverty; we have introduced order and law;
we have set an example of industry. We have helped all who
would take help at our hands—yet no one has stood by us, no
one has encouraged us. Those who ought to have been our
friends will have nothing to do with us; we have enemies all
round, and we cannot go about our daily labour without
danger.

'You will naturally ask yourselves why you ought to per-
severe any longer in a thankless struggle? Last year, it was
borne in upon many of our number, that they had a call elsewhere, and their letters tell us that they are prosperous and
happy in the new land that they have chosen. You have stayed
by me, and I have been touched with your affection and fidelity.

'But have I a right to ask you to remain any longer? I myself
have no choice. God has placed me here, and here I must continue till I am called away. You have no such call. To you it is
open to choose whether you will face the dangers, which I do
not conceal from you that I believe to be increasing, or whether
you will go home, or will follow your friends to New England.

'Here, you are an unprotected outpost in an enemy's
country. The Government does not support us—we are left
to remain, if we please, on our own risk and responsibility.
For me, I have an assurance within me that I am where I
ought to be—doing, or trying to do, what my conscience orders
me. I may lose my life. To be ready to face death, is a condition
of a soldier's service, and I cannot find a more honourable end.
But this does not apply to you; and, if you choose to stick by
me, it must be with your eyes open.

'Go, then, you who prefer to go and follow your friends—
and stay, you that will stay. The Lord can save by few, as well
as by many. Three hundred men alone were left to Gideon to
encounter the Midianites, but the three hundred were enough.
Those were days of miracles, and there are no miracles now.
But we know, what Gideon did not know, of how little consequence is anything which may befall us in this world. I cannot
prophesy what may happen to you or to me. But, well assured
I am, that no honest work which we may do in this world is
lost in the end—and that nothing which we suffer will be
thrown away. The battles of the Lord are but as other battles.
The bravest and best may fall, but their lives are the price of
victory.'

So spoke Colonel Goring: the enthusiasm of faith being
tempered, in him, into quiet and calm conviction. But he did
not expect heroic virtues from miners and fishermen. Emotion
may lift even the commonest men, for moments, into self-
forgetfulness; and conscience, and shame and pride may hold
them up where the voice of duty is plain. But instinct tells
every child of Adam to withdraw himself, and those dear to
him, out of the way of perils which he may think that he is
not called upon to face. Doubtless, many of those who heard
him did feel that they would gladly be out of the scrape, and
home in Cornwall again.

Personal admiration for their Chief, however, determined
them—at least for the moment—to continue to share his fortunes. They could not believe that, after all which it had cost
England to plant Protestant colonies in Ireland, they would
be deliberately sacrificed. Those who, like Treherne, were disaffected, found it prudent to be silent; not a single family con-
fessed to irresolution; and when the assembly broke up, there
was an unusual display of animation and affection. Their spirit
rose. That some sixty Englishmen, well armed and drilled
should be in personal danger from a rabble of savages whom
they despised, was absurd and incredible.

So talking among themselves they went their several ways, a
few loiterers only being left who had special communications
to make or questions to ask. A stranger who had been in the

chapel, came up to Goring, as he was standing at the door, and said:

'The Lord bless your honour this day, and a good day it is for Ireland to see your honour and the likes of ye in the midst of us! The Lord prosper ye, and grant ye long life, yourself and your good lady, to reign in Dunboy! It is cutting our own throats we'd be, or starving for hunger, if ye were taken away! And if your honour is tould that there is any here that would do ye hurt—barring a few skulking villains that we'll have out of this, or know the reason for it—don't believe them, your honour! They are telling ye a lie!'

Such effusive expressions from a person whom he could not recall that he had ever seen before, struck the Colonel as excessive. He knew Ireland by this time, and knew what such vehement protestations were worth. Some request or other usually followed, and it seemed to him that there was to be something of the same kind in this case. The man professed to have a communication to make to him of an urgent kind, and begged for a private interview.

Colonel Goring reserved his Saturday evenings for himself as a preparation for Sunday, and was besides affected by the scene which he had just passed through. He required to know on the spot what the business was. The stranger would say nothing, save that it was an affair of life and death. It was necessary for him to see some magistrate at once, and the Colonel was the only magistrate within reach.

Some caution was observed in admitting persons who were not known. The man was introduced into the hall, and two of the water-guard were directed to stand outside at the door. Colonel Goring then looked at his visitor more particularly. He was a man advanced in years, dressed in the grey, coarse frieze of the country, with the common expression of innocent helplessness, which is not always a true indication of the character behind it. His coat was in holes; his breeches were untied at the knees; his stockings were torn, and his shoes stringless. His hair was matted and grey, and he had green wandering eyes, which looked everywhere save at the person to whom he was speaking.

'Well, man,' said Goring, 'you say that you have business with me? Who are you? And what do you want?'

The stranger rubbed his head, glanced vacantly round the hall, and dangled his hat in his hand. 'I'm a poor boy, your honour, from beyant Bantry towards Dunmanway, if your honour would be pleased to give me a help!'

'Give you a help?' the Colonel said. 'There are boys enough, and men and women too, for that matter, that want help, and some deserve it and some don't. But you told me you had come on a matter of life and death—whose life and whose death?'

'It is hard to know your honour who is living and who is dead in this distracted country, and in some parts there is little to choose between them, and a short step from one to the other. There has been wild work up yonder with the proctors and the rest of it!'

'A tithe riot again?' said the Colonel, whose attention was caught in a moment by his recollection of the scene on the mountains. 'But why do you come to me, five and twenty miles away? Why didn't you go to Mr. White at Bantry? He has charge of the district, and has the force of the county with him. What are you yourself, and what have you to do with it?'

'Sure, your honour, Mr. White is not in the country at all. He is gone to England they say, and there is none but yourself that we have to look to, more by token that your honour is a good Protestant, and there is mighty few of us that way in this land!'

'A Protestant are you?' said Goring, looking again sharply at him. 'You don't seem a credit to your profession. But speak out! Tell me what has happened!'

'Your honour is a good friend to the poor, and there is no wonder if ye care to hear as little as ye can of thim proctors. But it is not them that does the wrong that feels the worst smart of it. When the childer are starving the fathers are just mad. My poor master that has the church on the way from Bantry to Dunmanway—the Lord be good to him!—he is just destroyed entirely, and the Lord knows whether the life is in him at this hour, and he as poor as the worst of them! No food better than the potatoes and the milk has crossed the lips of

him this twelvemonth! 'Tis truth I am telling your honour,
and the Lord knows it!'

'I can make nothing of this,' said the Colonel, growing im-
paient. 'Sit down, man, and tell me your story from the beginning. Some crime has been committed. The curate at the Cross
Roads, my friend Mr. Dudgeon, has been injured, I suppose.
But how, and why, and when?'

'It is the same good gentleman that your honour speaks of;
and it is I that am all the servant that he has to look after the
cow and the bit of garden and ring the church bell on Sundays!
It is but two shillings a week he gives me for that same, and
he can afford no more, with his children running about without shoes to their feet, and his own clothes hanging in rags
upon him!'

'Tell your story your own way, my good fellow,' said the
Colonel, 'only tell it. I can do nothing till I know what is the
matter.'

'Well, then, I'll tell your honour, and no more words about
it. Your honour knows we are a poor people up there. Papists
and Protestants are poor enough for that matter, all Ireland
over, and we have hard masters upon us. Your honour has
learnt by now how many pounds the acre they take for our
bits of land for the potatoes. There is the agent, and the leaseholder, and the leaseholder that is beyond him, and another
below, or may be two, and the poor boy that works the ground
must keep the whole of them, with my lord that lives in
England besides them all. The divil knows how they part it
among themselves, but the boys must find it, and how are they
and their families to live at all, your honour, let alone the
pigs? And that is not the worst, for when the rint is paid, the
rector of the parish must have his tenth bag of potatoes, and
the tenth sheep, and the tenth of the pig's litter. The rector
himself is the Dane of the Cathedral with the roof off the top
of it, and he has six other parishes besides, and never a
church in any one of the seven save the little chapel at the
Cross Roads, and never a curate but Mr. Dudgeon, that has
twenty pounds a year from him, and mighty generous he thinks
he is for that same. He is a fine preacher in London, they say,

and he keeps a proctor in each of his parishes, and five shillings by the year he gives them, and they squeeze the rest of their living out of the poor people, who have to keep their own priest besides, for fear the divil get them at the last day.'

There was a scornful tone in the account of the rector and his London occupations, which did not suit exactly with the account which the man had given of himself or with his abject appearance. Again Colonel Goring examined his face, and for a moment fancied that he had seen it somewhere before; but his recollections failed him; the impression passed off, and the vacant look returned. But he was as far away from the point as ever.

'All this may be true my man,' he said, 'but what has this to do with the story you have come to tell me? What has been done at the Cross Ways?'

'Is it not telling your honour that I am, as fast as my tongue can out with it? Your honour knows that last year was a short harvest, and the landlords and the agents all the country over, barring your honour's self, would abate nothing, and would have the last farthing, or the tenants should be out on the road; and the poor people didn't know where to turn, the little ones crying for food and none to give them. Then came up lawyers from Cork for the clergy, and they cleared away the lave of the male and the potatoes. So the people went clane mad, and the Whiteboys were out to find the villains, and they could find none of them, for sure they had gone away with what they had got as if the divil was at the heels of them. So the boys came to Mr. Dudgeon's house, who had done no harm to mother's son. But what did the bloody-minded ruffians care for that? They said if he hadn't done it, them as he served had done it.

'So they up with him out of his bed, your honour, his wife lying by the side of him, and she screeching, and the boys swearing they would make an end of her if she didn't hould her tongue, and they stripped off Mr. Dudgeon's shirt and laid him on his face on the floor naked as he was. They tied his arms and his legs. They brought a great Tom cat and set it on the back of him, and they dragged the baste up and down by his tail, the cat scratching, and spitting, and driving the claws of him into the poor gintleman's flesh till it was all as if they had drawn a harrow over him. Some of them thought this enough, and would have spared him more. But the black hearts was in the most of them, and they said they would have his life before they gave up. So they took him out into the bog and dug a pit, and laid the bottom of it with thorns, and flung him in naked as he was on the top of them. Thin for fear he should catch could, as they said, they heaped in more briars and faggots round him, just leaving his head out and no more. They trampled them all in till he neither spoke nor stirred. This done, they locked the rest of us in the house and swore we should all die if we looked out before the morning. So they left us and went their ways.

'When the day broke we went out and we found the master. We thought he was gone, for he was covered over with blood, and he spoke never a word. But there was life in him yet, and we put him in his bed, and the lady, she crying and beside herself like, bade me go to your honour and tell you how it was, and to pray your honour if it was likely you would be at Glengariff Church the next morning to ride on to the Cross Ways, and do what you could to help them.'

Goring was acquainted with the spot and the neighbourhood, and slightly with Mr. Dudgeon himself, who was a hard-working and half-starved curate. Other magistrates lived nearer to the scene of the outrage than himself; but some, he was aware, were absent, and the one or two that were resident exerted themselves as little as possible in the interests of the poorer clergy. The information was so explicit that he felt that he ought not to neglect it. His habit was to go to Glengariff for service on Sunday morning, with as many of his people as would accompany him, and Glengariff was on the way, and more than half the distance. Should the story be true, and he had no reason to suppose it false, he would never forgive himself should the unfortunate man be dead, as was too likely, and if he had neglected to go to the help of the unhappy widow and her children.

Nothing could be done that night. They usually went to

Glengariff by water, as the easiest and quickest mode of getting there, but he would require a horse for the rest of the
way. The service being at twelve too, he reflected that if he
waited till it was over he would not have time to reach the
Cross Roads and return before nightfall. He therefore decided
that he would ride forward early and alone. At Glengariff he
would hear further particulars. If nothing was known at Glengariff, he would then attend church as usual, and return.

The man, having walked all day, as he said, professed to be
tired, and required a few hours' rest. Colonel Goring offered
him supper, but he declined to eat, having been well fed, as
he alleged, at a cabin on the road-side. He desired only to be
allowed to lie down for a bit. A bed of straw in the loft over
the stable would answer him well, and he could be off on his
way before daybreak without disturbing the family.

It all seemed straightforward, and yet Goring knew that the
Irish were the best actors in the world. There was something
about the man not satisfactory to him; nor could he shake off
the impression that somewhere under some circumstances he
had seen that face before. He was not of a nature, however, to
be deterred from doing what he thought right by vague misgivings. He would not alarm his wife by a horrible story. He
told her merely that he was obliged to be early at Glengariff
the next morning. He would ride forward, and she could
follow with the rest in the boat. The horse was ordered. The
stranger was given his straw bed in the stable; the Colonel's
habit also was to go to rest early; but the frightful character
of the country in which his lot was cast had been freshly
brought home to him, and disinclined him to sleep.

He sat long gazing out of his window on the sea, his eyes
following, half unconsciously, the patches of moonlight between the shadows of the clouds. His rule on Saturday evenings
was to touch no worldly business, and to spend an hour or two
always in meditation. But his thoughts wandered. He could
not fix his attention as he desired. Either mechanically, or because he wished to occupy himself, he arranged his papers,
made a few notes, and wrote replies to letters which needed
answers. He lay down at length to toss uneasily through the

midnight hours, to fall at last into broken snatches of slumber, and to dream that he was at Culloden again.

When he awoke, the sun was shining over the crest of Hungry Hill. It was later than he expected. He hurried on his clothes, snatched a hasty breakfast, mounted his horse and rode away.

Chapter XXVII

FOUL PLAY AT THE FORGE

ON the road to Glengariff, near the sea, and at no very great distance from the gate of the avenue which led to Dunboy, there stood a blacksmith's shop. The blacksmith himself, Minahan by name, was a tenant on the estate. He was a native of the place, and a Catholic; but he was a good workman when he cared to be industrious; and Colonel Goring had provided him with so much employment that he was seldom idle. He mended chains, forged anchors, made ring-bolts and cleets for the boats, repaired carts, hammered picks and crowbars for the miners, and helped the engineers when the machinery fell out of order. His manner was sullen. He seldom asked a question, and when he was questioned himself he answered no more than was necessary. Goring on the whole liked him because he neither lied nor cringed, and because he did his work satisfactorily. If he showed no good-will, however, he showed no malice. If silent, he was never disrespectful. As a tenant he paid his rent regularly, and if he wanted repairs or improvements at his house or forge, the Colonel was always ready to execute them. He was a tall, lean man, strong and sinewy, with dark matted hair, face and hands scarred and seamed by sparks from the anvil, and his left eye injured through the same cause.

Before daylight, on the morning which followed the events related in the last chapter, a fishing lugger came round Dursey Island, and ran up into Bantry Bay. Under Fair Head she reduced her canvas, and brought up behind the hill. With the first streak of dawn a six-oared cutter, which she had towed astern, left her side and pulled in towards the island. In the dress of her crew there was nothing particular to attract attention; they rowed well and shewed that they understood their business; but except that it was unusual for a boat to be out at that hour on a Sunday morning, they might have passed for local fishermen. There was no one, however, to ask what they were, or even to see them.

At Dunboy all was quiet; the herring boats were drawn up on the shingle, their owners with their families sleeping late on the one holiday of the week. The strangers, whoever they might be, knew the habits of the place, for they pulled across the mouth of the bay, and entered a creek covered by a ledge of rocks, a short walk from Minahan's forge.

Two men wrapped in boat cloaks who had been sitting in the stern rose as they touched ground, and stepped ashore. One was slight and of middle height, the other tall and powerfully built. Under their cloaks it could be seen that both of them were armed. They had their swords, skenes at their belts, and pistols handsomely mounted, with barrels chased and inlaid. The shorter of the two ordered one man to stay in the boat and the rest to follow him. They then went on together to the road.

The sun was still below the horizon, and no one was abroad. The forge had been closed for the night, but the blacksmith himself was stirring. He had thrown back one of the shutters, and the door was ajar which led from the outside shed into the workshop. He showed no surprise at the appearance of his visitors, whom he evidently expected.

'Is Sylvester here?' the short man asked.

Minahan nodded, and pointed to the open door. They entered, and found there, waiting for them, the so-called servant of the curate at the Cross Ways.

'Welcome are ye, Morty Oge,' said Sylvester to Sullivan. 'It's in fine time ye are. The Colonel will not be here for an hour yet, but ye'll see him at the end of it; and he will be stopping here of himself at the forge, if there is faith in a nail and a horse's sore foot.'

'And what was the need of hurting a dumb beast?' said Morty. 'Ye are always after some devilry or other. You told me, as it was Sunday morning, he would be going by to his church; and what would be easier than for the boys with me to bring him to a halt?'

'I couldn't chance it,' said Sylvester. 'I'd be sorry anything went wrong, and yourself going away, and this the last occasion ye'd have. You may place the boys behind a rock that's there a few yards down, if it should so be that he rides by; but he will not, Devil fear it. Ye see I couldn't trust to the church-going. One time he goes by water, and another by the land—and if he goes by the land he has always a parcel of the Swaddlers about him, so I thought I'd take a surer way with him. The Colonel is of a free nature if any story is brought him of some one that wants his help. So I made up a tale of how the Dunmanway boys were out about the tithes, and how they had carded the curate beyont, and left him for half dead, and how the wife was crying out for his honour to come and save the poor cratur's life if any life was in him.'

'You are a treacherous villain, Sylvester. I mean the Colonel no wrong. He shall have fair play as a gentleman, and that is all that he has a right to ask for. Are you sure he did not recognize you?'

'Troth, and he did not. He never saw me but onst, the day at Derreen, you'll remember. I'll tell you how it was,' Sylvester said. 'But I'll just place the boys behind the rock I spoke of, for fear he might pass.'

'And tell them,' said Morty, 'that they are to stop him, and no more; and tell them, too, that they are to stay where they are till I come for them. It shall never be said that I took unfair advantage.'

Sylvester muttered an unwilling assent. He went out, and in a few minutes returned, and went on with his story.

'Ye'd not have known me yourself in these old rags, and it is odd if I could not desave an Englishman; let alone the Colonel, that is the simplest of the whole of them. He will be on the road by the time the sun is over the hill. He will come to a halt at this door, or I know nothing of farriery, and devil a servant he will have behind him either, or so much as a pistol to defend himself.'

'You may set so many traps that you will be caught yourself one day, Sylvester. How do you know that he will be unarmed? How do you know that he will have no one with him? How do you know that he will ride at all with the tide flowing and the water smooth?'

'How do I know?' Sylvester answered. 'It has been my business to mark the Colonel since he came into this country. He will be unarmed, because he goes unarmed always. I suppose he cut down so many poor creatures at Culloden that he is feared at the sight of blood. He don't like to shoot any man, as ye have experienced yourself, Morty Oge. He will have none with him, because he will never take a servant out on the "Sabbath Day", as thim Swaddlers call it; and as to the boats they are to go later with the lady, and the Colonel will ride.

'They put me for the night into the stable, and I got talking with the groom that was there. He showed me the horses, as I knew he would, and I just asked him which of them it was that the master rode when he went upon his arrants of mercy. What did the innocent cratur say but that it was sometimes one and sometimes another. It would be the grey, however, that he'd ride in the morning, for that was the horse he had ordered. So when all was shut up, and the key turned in the stable door, I just slipped down the ladder out of the garret above. There was a bit of candle left in the lantern, and I had all I needed in the pocket of me. I drew a nail from the shoe of the near hind foot and slipped in a longer one in the place of it. The point will have run into the quick before the Colonel has been half a mile on the road. He will see Minahan standing at the door here, and he will want to know what is the matter. Devil a step further will his purty grey go with him till the nail is out.'

'Well, well,' said Morty, 'such doings may seem fair in this accursed country. We were a brave people once, and did not stoop to cowardly tricks, that would suit better with forgers and footpads. Colonel Goring is the worst foe I have; yet I would give a finger off my right hand at this moment had no lies been told to bring him here to meet me. On my soul I hate you for what you have done, Sylvester. There is a stain on my honour this day which all the waters of ocean will not wash off. Any way, this shall be the last of such things. This English

Colonel and I have our quarrel to fight out, and one or other of us will not leave this place alive.'

Morty was savage at finding that he could not even fight a personal enemy in his unfortunate country, without being dragged into treachery that he hated the thought of. As little, however, did it occur to him that he ought not to use an opportunity which had been dishonestly brought about for him.

In the midst of his excitement, his ear was caught by a voice outside in the road. Colonel Goring was before the door of the smithy. His horse was dead lame. The nail in the foot had been driven home, as Sylvester intended, and the poor beast, having limped for a quarter of a mile, had come to a stand at a place where it knew that the hurt could be looked to.

Minahan was leaning against the post of the outer shed. 'Good morning,' said the Colonel, 'I am lucky at finding you at home. Your fire will be out, but perhaps there will be no need of it. My horse here is dead lame. I am sorry to ask you to touch work on Sunday. I should not be out myself, but that it is matter of necessity. Look and see what is the matter.'

'Pleased I'll be to serve your honour, any day of the week,' said the blacksmith, 'and indeed there is Gospel order to take care of the poor animals on the Sunday.'

The Colonel alighted. Minahan lifted and examined the foot. 'Begorrah!' he said, 'it is little the lad knew of his work that fitted this shoe on. Shame on the awkward hand of him, he has driven a nail into the quick, and the dumb baste is complaining of it in the only way that he can speak. I'll have it out in five minutes, but I'd advise your honour to take the horse no further this day, for the wound is sore, and maybe he'd be the worse for the journey.'

'I cannot stop,' the Colonel said, 'but if ye have a gossoon about, who would run back to the house, and tell the groom to bring me another and take the grey home when you have seen to the hurt, I'd thank you kindly. Meantime it is cold, standing out here. The air is raw this morning. I will step in, and ask how the mistress is.'

'Thanks, your honour,' said Minahan. 'The mistress is not

at home. She is away over the hill; and I'm thinking,' he muttered, dropping his voice, 'it might be better if your honour would let the business ye are after just wait over till to-morrow, and go back to your own house. There are strangers inside, that maybe ye would not be well pleased to see.'

'Strangers?' enquired the Colonel. 'What stranger can be here at such an hour as this?'

'Indeed, it is more than I know,' said the smith. 'There is three of them come in from the sea, any way, to hear mass at the chapel they say. They just asked me to let them rest here till the bell rings, and that is all I can tell you.'

'Not all that you might tell me, if you chose to speak, my good fellow. They will be some of my old acquaintances, come for once on an honest errand. If they had never come on a worse, they and I would not have fallen out together.'

The smith muttered something, which was neither assent nor denial. He had led the horse, while they were speaking, out of earshot of the forge. In a low, but clear and earnest voice, he said, 'If ye will take a poor man's counsel, ye will be off at your best speed, and never stop till ye reach your own door. The gossoon shall bring your horse behind ye.'

Mistaking what was intended for a friendly warning, the Colonel conceived that there was someone in the forge whom the smith wanted to conceal.

'I may return or not,' he said, 'but I must first have a word with these strangers of yours. We can meet as friends for once, with nothing to dispute over.'

Minahan made no further attempt to prevent him from going in. If gentlemen chose to have their quarrels, he muttered between his teeth, it was no business of his.

Goring pushed open the door and entered. By the dim light, for the shutter that had been thrown back had been closed again, and the only light came from a window in the roof, he made out three figures standing together at the further end of the forge, in one of whom, though he tried to conceal himself, he instantly recognized his visitor of the previous evening.

'You here, my man?' he said. 'You left my house two hours ago. Why are you not on your way home?'

Sylvester, seeing he was discovered, turned his face full round, and in a voice quietly insolent, replied, 'I fell in with some friends of mine on the road. We had a little business together, and it is good luck that has brought your honour to us while we are talking, for the jintlemen here have a word or two they would like to be saying to ye, Colonel, before ye leave them.'

'To me!' said Goring, turning from Sylvester to the two figures, whose faces were still covered by their cloaks. 'If these gentlemen are what I suppose them to be, I am glad to meet them, and will hear willingly what they may have to say.'

'Perhaps less willingly than you think, Colonel Goring,' said the taller of the two, who rose and stepped behind him to the door, which he closed and barred. Goring, looking at him with some surprise, saw that he was the person whom he had met on the mountains, and had afterwards seen at the funeral at Derreen.

The third man rose from a bench on which he had been leaning, lifted his cap, and said, 'There is an old proverb, sir, that short accounts make long friends. There can be no friendship between you and me, but the account between us is of very old standing. I have returned to Ireland only for a short stay; I am about to leave it, never to come back. A gentleman and a soldier, like yourself cannot wish that I should go while that account is still unsettled. Our fortunate meeting here this morning provides us with an opportunity.'

It was Morty's voice that he heard, and Morty's face that he saw as he became accustomed to the gloom. He looked again at the pretended messenger from the carded curate, and he then remembered the old Sylvester who had brought the note from Lord Fitzmaurice to the agent from Kenmare. In an instant the meaning of the whole situation flashed across him. It was no casual re-encounter. He had been enticed into the place where he found himself with some sinister, and perhaps deadly, purpose.

A strange fatality had forced him again and again into collision with the man of whose ancestral lands he had come into possession. Once more, by a deliberate and treacherous contrivance, he and the Chief of the O'Sullivans had been brought face to face together, and he was alone, without a friend within call of him, unless his tenant, who as he could now see had intended to give him warning, would interfere further in his defence.

He supposed that they intended to murder him. The door, at which he involuntarily glanced, was fastened by this time with iron bolts. He was a man of great personal strength and activity, but in such a situation neither would be likely to avail him. Long inured to danger, and ready at all moments to meet whatever peril might threaten him, he calmly faced his adversary and said:

'This meeting is not accidental, as you would have me believe. You have contrived it. Explain yourself further.'

'Colonel Goring,' said Morty Sullivan, 'you will recall the circumstances under which we last parted. Enemy as you are and always have been to me and mine, I will do you the justice to say that on that occasion you behaved like a gentleman and a man of courage. But our quarrel was not fought out. Persons present interfered between us. We are now alone, and can complete what was then left unfinished.'

'Whether I did well or ill, sir,' the Colonel answered, 'in giving you the satisfaction which you demanded of me at the time you speak of, I will not now say. But I tell you that the only relations which can exist between us at present are those between a magistrate and a criminal who has forfeited his life. If you mean to murder me, you can do it; you have me at advantage. You can thus add one more to the list of villainies with which you have stained an honourable name. If you mean that I owe you a reparation for personal injuries, such as the customs of Ireland allow one gentleman to require from another, this, as you well know, is not the way to ask for it. But I acknowledge no such right. When I last encountered you I but partly knew you. I now know you altogether. You have been a pirate on the high seas. Your letters of marque do not cover you, for you are a subject of the King, and have broken your allegiance. Such as you are, you stand outside the pale of honourable men, and I should degrade the uniform I wear if

I were to stoop to measure arms with you.'

The sallow olive of Morty's cheek turned livid. He clutched the bench before him, till the muscles of his hands stood out like knots of rope.

'You are in my power, Colonel,' he said, 'do not tempt me too far. If my sins have been many, my wrongs are more. It must be this or worse. One word from me and you are a dead man.'

He laid four pistols on the smith's tool chest. 'Take a pair of them,' he said. 'They are loaded alike. Take which you please. Let us stand on the opposite sides of this hovel, and so make an end. If I fall, I swear on my soul you shall have no hurt from any of my people. My friend Connell is an officer of mine, but he holds a commission besides in the Irish Brigade. There is no better-born gentleman in Kerry. His presence here is your sufficient security. You shall return to Dunboy as safe from harm as if you had the Viceroy's body-guard about you, or your own boat's crew that shot down my poor fellows at Glengariff. To this I pledge you my honour.'

'Your honour!' said Goring. 'Your honour! And you tempted me here by a lying tale, sent by the lips of yonder skulking rascal. That alone, sir, were there nothing else, would have sufficed to show what you are.'

A significant click caught the ear of both the speakers. Looking round, they saw Sylvester had cocked a pistol.

'Drop that,' said Morty, 'or by God! kinsman of mine though you are, I will drive a bullet through the brain of you. Enough of this, sir,' he said, turning to Goring. 'Time passes, and this scene must end. I would have arranged it otherwise, but you yourself know that by this way alone I could have brought you to the meeting. Take the pistols I say, or by the bones of my ancestors that lie buried under Dunboy Castle yonder, I will call in my men from outside, and they shall strip you bare, and score such marks on you as the quarter-master leaves on the slaves that you hire to fight your battles. Prince Charles will laugh when I tell him in Paris how I served one at least of the hounds that chased him at Culloden.'

The forge in which this scene was going on was perfectly

familiar to Goring, for he had himself designed it and built it. There was the ordinary broad, open front to the road, constructed of timber, which was completely shut. The rest of the building was of stone, and in the wall at the back there was a small door leading into a field, and thence into the country. Could this door be opened there was a chance, though but a faint one, of escape. A bar lay across, but of no great thickness. The staple into which it ran was slight. A vigorous blow might shatter both.

Sylvester caught the direction of Goring's eye, caught its meaning, and threw himself in the way. The Colonel snatched a heavy hammer which stood against the wall. With the suddenness of an electric flash he struck Sylvester on the shoulder, broke his collar-bone, and hurled him back senseless, doubled over the anvil. A second stroke catching the bar in the middle shattered it in two, and the door hung upon the latch. Morty and Connell, neither of whom had intended foul play, hesitated, and in another moment Goring would have been free and away.

Connell, recovering himself, sprang forward and closed with him. The Colonel, who had been the most accomplished wrestler of his regiment, whirled him round, flung him with a heavy fall on the floor, and had his hand on the latch, when, half stunned as he was, Connell recovered his feet, drew a skene, and rushed at Colonel Goring again. Wrenching the skene out of Connell's hands, and with the hot spirit of battle in him, Colonel Goring was on the point of driving it into his assailant's side. 'Shoot, Morty! shoot, or I am a dead man!' Connell cried.

Morty, startled and uncertain what to do, had mechanically snatched up a pistol when Sylvester was struck down. He raised his hand at Connell's cry. It shook with excitement, and, locked together as the two figures were, he was as likely to hit friend as foe. Again Connell called, and Morty fired and missed, and the mark of the bullet is still shown in the wall of the smithy as a sacred reminiscence of a fight for Irish liberty. The second shot went true to its mark. Connell had been beaten down, though unwounded, and Goring's tall form stood out above him in clear view. This time Morty's hand did not fail him. A shiver passed through Goring's limbs. His arms dropped. He staggered back against the door, the door yielded, and he fell upon the ground outside. But it was not to rise and fly. The ball had struck him clean above the ear, and buried itself in the brain.

Only a few seconds had passed since the first blow was given, before all was over. Fiercely cursing the fate which had made him a murderer, in spite of himself, Morty flung down the smoking pistol. There was no time to lose, for the people passing to church had discovered the boatmen behind the rock, and some others, drawn by the noise, had gathered before the smithy. His crew, in spite of his orders, found their way in.

'Take up that carrion,' he said, spurning Sylvester's body with his foot, as if he could fling off the burden of his crime on the miserable wretch; 'take him up and carry him to the boat.' As the wounded man showed signs of life, they rolled him in a cloak and bore him carefully to the waterside. Morty Sullivan and Connell strode behind, no one daring to interfere with them, and in a few minutes the galley had shot out across the harbour and disappeared behind the point of the island.

Chapter XXVIII

NINE DAYS' WONDER

THE murder of a revenue officer in Ireland was, like a duel, of so ordinary occurrence that in the common course of events it would have attracted small attention. Colonel Goring's predecessor had been shot by the smugglers. That he should be shot himself was no more than might have been expected. But men of exceptionally high character, though inconvenient to deal with when alive, are regretted ostentatiously when they are gone.

In the counties of Cork and Kerry, and even within the sacred precincts of Dublin Castle, the assassination of Colonel Goring, almost at his own door and among his own people, created a sense of shame strong enough to last even for a few hours, and an alarm which lasted as many days.

The story was published in the *Court Gazette*, in all its details, and called out a burst of penitent anger which was almost genuine, and compelled the Government to exert itself. The gentry of the county called meetings and passed resolutions. They had hesitated at first, being unwilling, for reasons of their own, that there should be too curious an enquiry into smuggling transactions. But they recovered courage when it was ascertained that Morty had escaped to France, and was not expected to re-appear in Ireland. The murder was represented as unconnected with the contraband business, and as having arisen out of a personal feud. They were, therefore, able to denounce it with unanimity, and to exert themselves in prosecuting an investigation which could lead to no more than was already known.

The *Garland* frigate came up from Kinsale to the Kenmare River, as far as the entrance of Bally Quoilach, and came away again after this bold display of energy. There was an odd influence in the Castle executive, which paralysed all attempts at dealing with popular delinquents as long as their efforts had a chance of being successful. They could only afford to be active when they knew the criminal to be beyond their reach. In the present instance there was a sense of relief, unavowed, but most real, that an unnecessarily zealous public servant had been put out of the way. Morty Sullivan was gone from Ireland, and there need be no more anxiety about him or his conspiracies.

Thus relieved of the necessity of doing anything, since they supposed there was nothing to be done, the authorities had only to be profuse with compliments to the merits of their murdered officer, with regrets that he had been lost to his country, and with polite condolences to his family. In this part of their duty they were honourably energetic, and they displayed agreeably the interest felt by the British rulers of Ireland in the fortunes of their servants. The Secretary in Dublin wrote a despatch to the Secretary of State in London. The Secretary of State in London replied with courtesy and dignity. The highest person in the realm sent a gracious message to Mrs. Goring to soften the poignancy of her loss.

Thus, after a decent demonstration, the nine days' wonder was over, and the waters of oblivion closed over the last victim of official incompetence. Colonel Goring had been killed at the beginning of March. By the end of the month Press and Government had delivered their funeral eulogies, and completed their easy and ineffectual efforts to punish the crime.

Colonel Goring's personal friends, his brother officers who had not forgotten him in his Irish exile, his relations and his immediate family, were unable to bear what had befallen him with equal indifference. No serious attempt had been made to discover the accomplices in the crime. It was assumed that they had fled, and even Eyris had been left unvisited. Fitzherbert had been left sole executor; his cousin's fortune was ample, and had been improved, notwithstanding his profuse generosity, by the success which had attended his enterprises in the years during which he had been able to pursue them.

Since the Catholic population had turned against him, he had been himself the only link which had held his colony together. He had provided in his will to send them all home if they wished it. After his death, Ireland and all to do with it, became hateful to them, and they hastened to be gone. The cottages were deserted, the mine shafts closed, the wheels broken, the boats gathered together and burnt upon the strand, and before the spring grass had begun to turn green, and the latest primrose had ceased to blow among the ruins of Dunboy, the settlement which had promised at one time to mature into a community that might have changed the history of the south-western counties, was left to the winds and the rain.

As long as there was anything to be done, Fitzherbert controlled his own feelings. He had anticipated always how his cousin's enterprise would end. The longer he had watched the working of it, the less hopeful he had been. He understood better than Goring the spirit of the age.

But the more he felt that the Colonel's success was impossible, the more he admired the simplicity and the devotion of his kinsman's personal character, the more indignant he was at the practical negligence with which the murder had been passed over. The widow, as soon as she had recovered sufficiently from the shock to be able to move, he conducted to England, and left her there with her own friends. The business of the administration obliged him to return immediately, and detained him in Cork.

General Vavasour was still busy there with the fortifications of Spike Island. The Governor being absent on protracted leave, Vavasour was in command of the forces, and in him Fitzherbert found a sympathizer who could share his wrath at the wilful indifference which could leave the noblest and best man in the country to be sacrificed with absolute impunity. Vavasour had studied Goring's character more carefully than he seemed to have done during his stay at Dunboy. The more he saw, the more, like Fitzherbert, he admired.

'Consider too,' he said, 'what Goring might have done, if he could have held his ground, for Irish history, surrounded as he was by the most curious relics of antiquity. He was not learned, but he had a good eye for fact. He was more right than you or I in the explanation which he gave of the Danish fort. He showed his sense, too, in his readiness to listen to what I could tell him. It is really dreadful to me to think of such opportunities thrown away. Like enough, he might have found on his own property the key to the Round Towers. Yes, yes; he was a splendid fellow! And I cannot yet feel certain that we have heard the last of the story. The villain that shot him will soon be at his old tricks again. Elliot came in with the *Æolus* last night. He would not be sorry to have a second chance at him; and as for me, if I hear of Master Morty on the coast, I shall act on my own judgment, without wasting time in writing to Dublin.'

Chapter XXIX

MORTY'S HONOUR

I F at any time during the week which followed the murder a careful search had been made at Eyris and in the neighbourhood, Sylvester O'Sullivan could not have escaped discovery. Morty's intention had been to sail immediately for France after his meeting with Goring, but Sylvester had been so badly hurt that he could ill bear removing. Morty hated the sight of him, and determined to put him on shore. The lugger returned through the Sound to Bally Quoilach. Morty sullen and silent, and Connell supporting the wounded wretch who was struggling back to pain and consciousness.

It so happened, that if a sufficient force had been sent to Eyris the instant the murder was known, Morty might have been captured himself. He had meant to sail again immediately, but the lugger had touched a rock in coming through the Sound, and had started a plank, and two days' work had to be done upon her before she was fit for sea again. Morty all the time spoke to no one, but moodily paced the shore. Of Sylvester he entertained a kind of horror, as the cause of all that had gone wrong with him, and the miserable old man was stowed away out of his sight in a cabin where he was least likely to be looked for.

It had been Morty's long settled purpose that his sister and her child should leave Ireland. He was passionately anxious that the last representative of the old house should grow up with more favourable surroundings than the half-savage neighbourhood of the Kenmare River. He thought of carrying them off along with him, but he was in no condition as yet to form plans for the future. He might not linger, for, with all his experience of persons in authority in Ireland, he could not anticipate that the sensation on Colonel Goring's death would pass off in words. This time, he assured himself that both he and Connell would be sharply sought for, and that they must escape at the earliest moment. If they were out of the way, his sister would not be interfered with; and whether Sylvester was caught or not was a matter of indifference to him.

Wretched as he was, too, he had his duties to discharge to the French Government; and thus the moment that the lugger's wounded plank was refitted, he and Connell sailed for Nantes, where their coming was anxiously looked for. During his absence in the West Indies his friend Blake's trade with the old country had been as active as ever, and the reports brought to Blake from his own correspondents as to the state of preparation for a rising in the Southern Provinces had been so much more favourable than the impressions formed by Morty, that in reliance upon them the French were seriously thinking of landing five thousand men at Bantry and marching upon Cork without delay. The French Government was only waiting for Morty's return. His opinion, if favourable, was to be decisive.

Thus, day after day, Mr. Blake paced his terrace, impatiently sweeping the horizon with his spy-glass. Other vessels came in from the Irish coast. Why was Morty delaying so long? At length the brown sails of the lugger were seen slowly drawing up the river; slowly, for the tide was falling and the breeze was light. She crawled along at a snail's pace. When she brought up at last, her crew were so long in lowering the boat that Walsh ordered his own in his impatience that he might go off and see what was the matter. The lugger's boat, however, put off at last, with O'Sullivan and Connell in the stern sheets, and he hurried to the stairs to meet them. Morty, when it came alongside, rose languidly and, with his arm on Connell's shoulders, came feebly up the steps. He barely touched his cap to Blake, and, when he reached the terrace, stood looking round him with weary indifference.

'The Lord be praised for your safe arrival,' said Blake. 'We thought some ill had come by ye, you were so long on the way. Welcome, anyway. But ye look as I never saw ye! Are ye ill, man, or what is it?'

'My friend Blake,' said Morty, 'I brought you back your ship from the West Indies, and you will not say but I did my duty to you and your house while she was under my command. There she floats, sound and watertight, for all the shot the English guns sent through the bottom of her! Your lugger, too —no hurt has come to her. You have her there as you trusted her to me. And now I must tell you I am tired of this work, and I will have no more of it!'

'I'll not believe that,' answered Blake. 'You have brought back yourself, and ship and lugger might have gone to the bottom for aught I should have cared, sooner than anything but good should have come to you. But what word do you bring? They are waiting for you at Paris. Each day brings me a post to ask if you are returned. Tired of the work? But what is it? Let us hear what has befallen ye that ye look like Father O'Brien's ghost when he came back to tell the bishop that he was kept in purgatory for want of being rightly absolved.'

'The only absolution which would be of use to me,' growled Morty, 'would be a bullet through the brain of me, and that relief I shall go and look for in my old service. We will part friends, Blake, but part we must. I'll be with the Austrians in Bohemia before the world is many weeks older. Fool that I was to leave them.'

'Don't be questioning Morty just now, while the fit is on him,' said Connell, pulling Blake aside. 'He had a misfortune before he came away. No great matter to my mind, but he rages when he thinks of it as if the divil was inside him.'

'If there is bad luck in the world there is good luck along with it,' said Blake. 'There was a sloop came in last night from Crookhaven that brought word that the revenue officer at Dunboy had got his death; he that was at Culloden and that Morty had the quarrel with. That is no misfortune, anyway, the ill-mannered villain that he was.'

'Hist!' whispered Connell, 'he'll hear ye; that is the very thing. 'Twas Morty killed him, and me standing by when it was done. Morty wanted the Colonel to fight him and the Colonel wouldn't, and gave him bad words instead. There was a bit of a struggle then. Old Sylvester, that you'll find, got a rap with a hammer from the Colonel, that nearly put the life out of him, and knives were drawn, and Morty's temper got up and he shot the Colonel through the head, and he has been cursing himself ever since for having done it.'

'And what ailed the cowardly rascal,' said Blake, 'that he would not fight a gentleman who was condescending to provide him with an opportunity?'

'Cowardly Colonel Goring was not,' said Morty, who caught the words and understood to what they referred. 'Cowardly he was not, and rascal he was not. I'll do him that justice though he crossed me at so many turns. God knows I prayed him to take the pistols and defend himself, and you can witness yourself, Connell, he knew how to use them. My hand fired the shot that killed him; my hand did it; but not I. I would give the best blood in my body that he was alive at this moment.'

'Indeed then,' said Connell, ''twas well for me that your hand was readier than yourself. The skene would have found a sheath in my heart else, and as to his being alive again, it is my opinion that he is better where he is.'

'I can ill understand ye both,' said Blake, 'or what it is that has happened at all; but from what ye say, Mr. Connell, there was the Sylvester creature half murdered, and yourself, but that Morty there came to your help, was murdered entirely. What would that be but a fair fight, and what is the use of crying when a drop of blood has been spilt, specially the blood of thim divils of Saxons? Why, you are a soldier, Morty Oge, and killing is your trade. The Colonel ye speak of was the worst enemy ye had. I have heard ye say so a dozen times. Have ye turned woman that ye are so chicken-hearted?'

'Aye, chicken-hearted,' said Morty bitterly, 'or it maybe it's a a hypocrite ye are thinking me. And what am I to think of myself? When I came here to you three years back I had been in many a battle. Fighting was my trade, as you say, but it was at the side of honourable men, and in an honourable cause. I had been named in despatches; I had won fame; I had promotion and rank within reach of me. I could carry my head as proudly as the best of them. No action could be charged against Morty Sullivan that he need blush to hear of, and you, Blake, made me a pirate, an associate of ruffians whose trade was plunder. Had I been taken I should have swung on the gallows, and now, because I have added another crime to the list, you are astonished that I give a second thought to it.'

'Morty Oge,' said Blake, 'what is done is done, and to whine over what cannot be recalled is weak and womanish. I called the man a rascal. Whether he was a rascal or not, in the world's sense, I neither know nor care, but he was an Englishman, and between England and Ireland there runs a river of blood which will cease to flow only when the accursed English flag no longer waves on Irish soil.'

'You may gloss it over as you will with your wars between the races,' answered Morty, 'and war there is and ever will be till one or other of them is out of that island. But the quarrel between that man and me was our own. He was a soldier, as I am, and a brave one. It is ended. He is dead; gone out of the world beyond my reach, and the balance is with him and not with me. If he had not been an Englishman I would say I envied him, and would rather have fallen as he fell, than live as I must live. On a fair field and by fair means I would fight the English while I could hold sword or level cannon; but as to your methods, neither to fight nor to yield, to have the form of peace, but to recognize no duty rising out of it, to plot and to murder and to burn, to put on a lying appearance of sub-mission, to fawn and flatter with hatred in the heart, for that is what your method means—I will have none of it.

'I saw the leaders of the Army of Insurrection, as they call it. They said what you say. They were not an army. They could not fight. But they could make the country ungovernable and keep an English army occupied in watching them. They pre-tended that if the French were once on land among them they would then rise. I don't believe it. If Louis trusts their promises, they will treat him as they have treated everyone who has been weak enough to depend on them. They will sit still and leave him to fight his own battle. That is my opinion of my countrymen. They prefer the methods to which they have been accustomed. If the French choose to encourage them on these terms, it is their own affair. For myself, I have a good record with the Austrians. The war with Prussia has broken out again, and there will be employment enough. In that service even an Irishman can earn an honourable name, or, if the luck be with him,' he added sadly, 'an honourable end.'

'It cannot be,' Blake said. 'France cannot spare you, and your country cannot spare you. They trust you in Paris as they trust none else, and your own people trust you, all the more since ye cleared your home of the Saxon. Thurot is ready at Brest, and to Ireland he is to go. Whether North or South is undecided, but surely to one or the other. It is not yourself that will be failing at such a time.'

'The old story,' Morty replied. 'The French are coming, and the Saxons are to be hurled out, and Ireland is to be free at last. One of two things always happens. Either the French do not come after all, and our poor fools in the expectation of them murder a landlord or two, and burn their houses, and then, when no help appears, betray one another, and a few score are hanged. Or else they do come, but in too small force to do the work alone, and nobody joins them, and they are lucky if they get out undestroyed. No invading army can be landed in Ireland in strength sufficient to drive the English out, unless the people rise at their side, and the people have not the heart for it. They never had. They never will. Nothing can come of this present project but fresh wretchedness. I at least will have no concern with it.'

'You will find the French are in earnest this time, Morty. You will see they are; and they will make it worth your while to lend them your hand. They mean to fight for India and America at England's own back door.'

'And if they do,' said Morty, 'what will that come to? Suppose Thurot takes Cork and keeps it; suppose he takes Dublin too, for that matter, do you think his master would find Ireland such a precious acquisition that he would stay and take care of it? The French will hold what they can get as a pawn in the game, and when peace is made they will go out again and leave us to the English hangman.'

Nothing that Blake could say, nothing that the trained emissary of the ministry at Versailles could say, availed to shake Morty's resolution. He persisted that, however sincere the present purpose of the French Government might be, however immediately successful the intended Irish expedition might be, Ireland would be sacrificed when the time came to purchase better terms for Dupleix and Montcalm. But he was confident also, he said, that the expedition could not be successful, and he refused to encourage idle hopes. Appeals to his ambition, to his interest, to his pride and patriotism, were equally vain.

If he could not pardon himself for Goring's death, yet as time passed on and he could think coolly, his conduct did not seem to him of so dark a kind that it need spoil and embitter his remaining existence. He had not designed any foul play. He had not allowed Sylvester's treachery. Goring's scornful words, which had blistered his skin like drops of melted metal, were not entirely deserved. There had been a fight—even to himself he could hardly say a fair one, but still a fight—and he had fired only to save his friend's life. His remorse was deep, but he could hope that it need not be eternal.

On one point only he yielded. When he went over to communicate with the patriot leaders, he had been entrusted with negotiations for the landing and distribution of fresh arms, and with important business arrangements for Blake's firm. In the haste in which he had come away he had left his work unfinished; and no one else could be found to take it up without his assistance on the spot. So at least the matter was represented to him by Blake, who insisted that he ought not to desert him in a matter of serious consequence. Morty, who was sensitive on a point of honour, felt the force of the argument, and another motive came in at the same time to increase the strength of it. He had sent word to his sister to come over and join him with her boy. She, to whom Goring's death had brought only joy and triumph, could think only of her country's approaching deliverance. She refused to go to him, and she reproached him with the desertion of the cause. Obstinate and violent as he had experienced her to be, he believed that he could persuade her if he could be in person on the spot to bring her away.

With these objects, and no companion save the faithful Connell, who had attended him in all his adventures, Morty

Sullivan sailed in the disguise of a common seaman in a Valentia hooker, and at the end of April he was again at Eyris under his own roof.

To his surprise and disgust, the first person who came smiling to welcome him, was his kinsman, Sylvester. Having recovered from his wound, Sylvester had established himself there as Ellen Mahony's guest; as he was known to have been at the murder, and had been named in the proclamation, his presence in the house was compromising her safety as well as his own. Already Morty had come to look at him with feelings for which detestation would be too mild a word. He spoke savagely and bitterly to him, and spurned him away. He bade him leave Eyris instantly and hide himself where he could among the mountains. He believed that he had done with him for ever. He had yet to learn that the dog-like affection of the follower for his chief turns to fury if it is scorned and rejected.

Chapter XXX

AN INFORMER'S REVENGE

GORING'S affairs had been left in good order. His dis-
positions were simple. His widow was removed to England.
The Dunboy settlers had been taken home. Only a few legal
details remained to be arranged with the Colonel's solicitor in
Cork; Fitzherbert could then wind up his duties as executor,
and a curious and interesting chapter in his own life would be
brought to a close.

During the last few days of his stay at Cork, he was the guest
of his friend General Vavasour at Government House, and
long and anxious conversations went on between them on
Ireland's condition, past, present, and prospective. Vavasour
insisted that the faults of the Irish rose from the supercilious
scorn with which England had treated them. He discovered in
the neglected race the elements of graces and talents which
the English themselves were without; and he insisted elo-
quently on the intellectual achievements of their ancestors,
among whom the lamp of learning and poetry burnt clear like
the evening star, when the rest of Europe was in darkness.

Fitzherbert, with less concern in these speculations and with
imperfect belief in the soundness of them, was provoked to see
an officer in high position and of high abilities wandering after
theories which, even if true, had no bearing on present prob-
lems. He liked Vavasour too well to contradict him, and he
knew the uselessness of it. 'I believe! I believe!' he cried, at the
end of a fresh demonstration that the Round Towers had been
built by Fire-worshippers. 'Not a word more I beseech you; but
how are we the better for knowing that two thousand years ago
our forefathers raised Temples to the Devil?'

If, as often happened, Fitzherbert alluded to the tragedy at
Dunboy, Vavasour would dismount from his hobby on the
instant. 'Forgive me, my dear friend,' he would say, 'none feels

269

it more bitterly than I do. I suppose I did not exert myself as much as I ought. He was too good for us. He was a Christian hero, and the modern world is not made for Christian heroes. Their existence is a reproach to the rest of us. They come to a rude end, and we breathe more freely when they are gone.'

At the end of one of these conversations, which had been more than usually discursive, Vavasour took a soiled note out of a portfolio.

'You talk of the state of the country, Fitzherbert,' he said. 'If I may believe the anonymous communications which are dropped here every day, my Celtic sympathies will not protect even myself. One morning I found a paper pinned on my dressing table with a coffin on it, and my name duly inscribed. Yesterday, the post brought me a letter, which told me that my time was up, and my soul was to be consigned to the "Sulphurous Flames of Puriphlegethon". What desperately long words the rascals use! Here is another which I got to-day, rather different. Probably it is a trap to tempt me into a place where they can put a knife into me, but I don't know. Look it through, and see if anything strikes you.'

In a large round, and evidently disguised handwriting, were these words:

'If your honour will give an assurance for my life, and will consider the service which I am willing to do for my country, I will put ye on the track of one that ye will be pleased to have holt on. I will take your promise if ye will give it, and will ask no more till ye have him in hand. If ye will walk this night alone at eleven o'clock on the Ould Quay, I'll see ye there and speak with ye.

'FROM *One* WHO WAS AT THE BLACKSMITH'S FORGE.'

Fitzherbert read and read again. 'Some villainy of course,' he said. 'It may be an informer who wishes to sell a comrade, or perhaps, as you suggest, it may be a design on yourself. The point is in the last words. He seems to think you will understand them.'

'My first impression,' Vavasour said, 'was to give the letter to the head constable, and set him to catch the fellow. But ten to one he would find it out and wouldn't show. You will observe that it was at a blacksmith's shop that your cousin was killed.'

'I did observe it, and I suppose that is the allusion. But who can the *one* be? The murderers are out of the country, and will take care how they shew themselves again just yet. Do you think of doing anything?'

Vavasour was as fond of adventures as the Caliph of Baghdad. 'Well,' he said, 'I thought of slipping on a cloak and strolling down at the time the man names, just to see whether there is anything in it. It is but a mile or so, and I can note what is going on in the town at those late hours.'

'The Ould Quay is no place for you, Vavasour. The lanes opening on it are the nests of all the crimps and blackguards in the town. You are a public person, and have no right to expose yourself. Let me go.'

Vavasour objected that the letter had been sent tỏ him, and that the man would speak to no one else. It was quite possible, however, that foul play was intended; and for the Governor of the town to be attacked at such a spot, would lead to questions how he came to be there, which could not be satisfactorily answered. Fitzherbert was a stranger. No one would recognize him, no one could have any object in doing him hurt. Vavasour, to whom the excitement of the thing had been the chief temptation, gave way at last, and consented that Fitzherbert should go.

It was now the first week of May. The days were lengthening. The sun did not set till after seven. By ten, however, little light would be left, and this particular evening promised to be unusually dark. An easterly wind had brought in a fog from the sea which shut out the sky, rested on the roofs of the houses, and spread over the city. The oil lamps at the street corners could not be seen at more than a few feet off. Decent people had closed their doors for the night and gone to rest. The streets themselves were deserted, and the only sounds which broke the stillness were the voices of the watchmen calling the hours or the cries of sailors on the river hauling ropes or heaving at a capstan.

Fitzherbert made his way with some difficulty through the lumber with which the wharves were littered. The few figures that he encountered avoided him as he avoided them. The lamps as he advanced along the embankment failed altogether. A few lines only of shimmering light came from ships anchored in the tide-way, by the help of which could be seen buoys floating on the water, or boats at their moorings. From the narrow alleys leading to the harbour were heard occasional sounds of revelry or of voices high in quarrel; but as he approached the appointed spot not a moving form was to be seen anywhere, and he passed on, shuddering in spite of himself at the thought of the evil things which might be going on close at his hand.

More than once he was tempted to turn back. He was well aware that no good will was borne to Vavasour by the lawless population of the lower town. The probability was that the letter really was a snare, and if so he might find a dagger in him at any moment that had been designed for the acting Governor. But he reflected that he was taller than Vavasour by a head, and could not be mistaken for him. He had undertaken to penetrate the mystery, and it would be cowardly to flinch. He went forward, and as the city clock tolled eleven he was at the spot which the letter had indicated.

It was a remnant of the old town, now deserted by everyone who cared for a decent reputation, the haunt of smugglers, thieves and prostitutes, an ugly place, suggestive of evil deeds. He found no one, and to appearance was entirely alone. He could see nothing save the outline of gables and chimneys against the fog. A hundred ruffians, however, might be skulking under the walls, and he kept near the water side, that he might spring in and swim for it if he was attacked. For some minutes he strolled to and fro on the edge of the jetty, neither hearing nor seeing anything. But someone must have seen him, for suddenly he became conscious of a figure directly in front of him which might have risen out of the pavement. That it was a man he could distinguish, but nothing besides.

'You walk late,' said a voice, 'and it is a dark night for exercise, scarce a darker I ever saw. May be you have business, that you are here at such an hour.'

'I might say the same to yourself,' answered Fitzherbert; 'but if I have business I do not speak of it to a stranger.'

'You are a gentleman by the speech of you; but you are not the gentleman I was looking for. You are taller like. Take advice from one who wishes you no ill and choose some other ground for your strolling. Here is no place for the like of yourself if you are an honest man. Be off out of this.'

'The Quay is open to me as to you,' said Fitzherbert, 'and where I please to walk depends on no one but myself. I, too, expected to meet some one here, honest or dishonest I know not, and for all I can tell you may be the man, if you come from the blacksmith's shop.'

The fellow hesitated, took a step backwards, and seemed inclined to slip away. 'You shall not leave me either,' Fitzherbert said, seizing him by the arm, 'till I know whether you are he or not.'

'Hands off!' said the man, lowering his voice to a whisper. 'Hands off, I tell you; or by the Lord, with one call on this whistle I'll bring them on ye that will lay ye on the harbour's bottom with as little thought as if ye were a bag of ballast. Who are ye, and what do ye mean by the words ye spake just now?'

'If you are the person I suppose you to be,' replied Fitzherbert, 'you have something to communicate of consequence to the state. I come to hear it.'

'Speak lower, man, if ye would leave this without a knife in the body of you. Who are ye, I say? I looked for another.'

'He you looked for does not walk about the quays of Cork at midnight to meet strangers who pretend they have secrets for him. It is enough that I am here in his place. I have seen your letter. I come to learn what you have to say.'

'I asked ye who ye were, and ye have not tould me. D'ye think I'd be speaking the word that might be a rope to hang me if it fell into the wrong ears? Unless you are plain with me, begorra I'll set them on ye that will have the mask off your face, whoever ye are.'

Fitzherbert hesitated. A disturbance might bring the watch, and he did not want the world to know that he met ruffians at night in the purlieus of Cork. But he had the right man before him. He was sure of that. And he would learn nothing unless he could satisfy the fellow that the secret might be safely confided to him.

'I am the friend of him to whom you wrote,' he said. 'I am to engage for him that what you may tell shall be no hurt to yourself, and that if you tell truth you shall have a reward. You will believe me the better when I inform you that I know what you mean about the blacksmith's place. I am the near kinsman to him that was killed there.'

'Hist, hist!' whispered the man. 'The stones can hear in these quarters. I know all about ye now. Ye'll be—but we'll speak no names, neither yours nor mine. If I tould ye that, ye'd be wanting me for the witness-box; and how many days do ye think I'd be living in this world if it was known I had helped to hang him that you think is beyond the seas. Ye will understand my meaning. I'll not tell ye who I am, but I can teach ye where ye may have him if ye will; for I tell ye I've sworn revenge upon him, and I'll have it. I risked my life for him, and I risked my soul for him. My soul I'll lose any way, for devil a priest in Ireland will give me his pardon for what I'm doing now; but I'll have my revenge, I say. After all I done for him, and me of his own blood! He drove me from his roof, he spurned me with his foot. He swore I'd brought a curse on him, and that shall be true for him any way. Will ye give me your promise? Will ye undertake on your honour that if I put ye in the way to capture him we speak of, ye will give me twice the published reward at such time and place as I'll tell ye of?'

'That is fair enough,' said Fitzherbert. 'Unless we take him the bargain is off. If we do take him you shall have what you ask. If we don't know you we can't send for you as a witness, and you can keep your own counsel. Yes, I engage for that.'

'Well, then,' the man hissed in his ear. 'Ye think he is away in France. I tell ye he has come back, and is at this day in the ould place at Eyris.'

'That cannot be,' said Fitzherbert. 'The coast has been watched. If brig, barque, or sloop had crossed from Nantes in the last six weeks, it could not have escaped.'

AN INFORMER'S REVENGE

'You will need sharper eyes,' said the man, 'than belong to your sea captains to see all vessels that pass between the French coast and ours. He slipped through where you would never think in a fishing boat of the Widow Crosbie's at Port Magee. He has been in Eyris for a week. He will stay another week, and then if ye miss your chance he will be gone. He has none with him but Connell and the boys of the place. If ye will send a company of red-coats over the hill at Dunboy in the dark, and let a cutter go round and stop the mouth of his hole, you may trap him like a wolf. Ye will do it if ye are the men I take ye for. And now God speed ye. It would be ill for us both to be found talking together.'

As he spoke he was gone, disappearing, as silently as he had come, into some smugglers' den. With difficulty, and with occasional anxious glances over his shoulder as the echo of his own feet made him fear that he was followed, Fitzherbert made his way back to the castle and reported his interview to the General.

Vavasour was not afraid of responsibilities. A rising easterly wind was blowing fair along the coast. Morty Sullivan was proclaimed, and loyal subjects had been called on to capture him anywhere and by any means. Two regiments stationed in the town were under Vavasour's immediate command, and although he had no authority over the King's ships in the river, he had a Revenue Cutter, well armed and manned, which had been commissioned for his personal use. There was a sloop besides in the harbour, which had been hired by Fitzherbert to transport Colonel Goring's furniture and books from Dunboy to England. She had made one trip, and had returned, and was waiting further directions with all hands on board.

Orders were sent to both cutter and sloop to be ready to sail at dawn, and a note was despatched to the barracks for a company of men with a couple of officers, whom Vavasour named for special service.

They were divided between the two vessels, Fitzherbert went in his own as a volunteer, and nothing was to be said of their destination till they were outside the lighthouse, and communication with the town was cut off. Thus it was that by noon on the following day, twelve hours after Fitzherbert had parted from his nameless informant, a hundred men were being carried up the coast with a fair wind between Kinsale and Galley Head. The instruction had been to select only English. It turned out that among them all there was one Irishman, and he a Sullivan, from the very district for which they were bound. Fitzherbert was to act as guide. The intention was to keep the sea till nightfall, and not to approach Bantry Bay till daylight was gone.

The weather was wild. The wind blew hard all day, with heavy rain and mist, which covered the vessels from inquisitive eyes on shore. They made a rapid passage, and before sunset they were off Crookhaven. No flight of predatory rooks on a new-sown corn field, are more swift to take alarm than the Irish of the coast at the sight of a British cruiser. On the least suspicion, warnings would be signalled from headland to headland, and, thick as it was, the sloop and cutter separated at the Fastnet, and stood off to sea as if they were on a fishing cruise.

At dusk, when ten miles from land, they drew together again, and made in for the Bay. At midnight the soldiers were put on shore in the Colonel's boat-harbour in front of his now desolate house. The Protestant community had departed, not a single straggler of them being left. The cottages were empty, the Catholic Irish having, as yet, avoided the neighbourhood. Thus shore and village were utterly solitary, not even a dog remaining to give notice of the approach of strangers. The sloop brought up at her usual anchorage, that, if by accident anyone caught sight of her, it might be supposed that she had returned for a second cargo of the Colonel's property. The cutter bore away round Dursey and the Bull Rock, with orders to haul her wind when she had passed the point, and bear up for the entrance of Bally Quoilach.

Chapter XXXI

THE END OF DUNBOY

WILDER and wilder grew the night. The wind howled among the cliffs, and tore to pieces the flowers which were blooming as if nothing had happened in the Colonel's desolate garden. The rain fell in slanting streams, making pools about the beach and turning lane and track into brown rivulets. Fitzherbert, to whom every object was mournfully familiar, led the party by an unfrequented path to the west, which had been the short cut from Dunboy to the mines. Skirting the deserted cottages of the colony, they ascended the hillside, without having been seen or heard. The single sign of life was a light burning in the back window of Goring's house, where an old servant still kept guard on the remnants of his property. After marching cautiously for half-a-mile they came out upon the regular track which led over the mountain gap to Eyris, and those among them who knew the country, understood now that it was to Eyris that they were going.

It has been mentioned that by accident there was an Irish private in the detachment. With ready instinct he saw that his own people were the object of the expedition. He bolted at a turn of the road, and dodged among the rocks. But he missed his footing in the dark, he was caught and handcuffed to a comrade, and the column passed on.

As they came up into the gap, the tempest increased in fury. They had been in partial shelter as they ascended. In the level brow, the wind had blown the peat stacks flat; the sheep had huddled away among the big pits; the raindrops pelted like hail. The very elements had conspired to ensure the completeness of the surprise. With the wind behind them, the soldiers moved the quicker; on such a night no human creature would be stirring abroad; and as they descended into the valley, and had to pass an occasional cabin, they were still unnoticed.

Even the curs were lying in-doors for shelter, and let them go by unheard. Had eye seen them, or ear caught the sound of the military tramp, the warning cry would have rung from house to house, a hundred lads would have started like hares from their forms and have sped over the moss-hags to give the alarm. But all eyes were closed in sleep, and all ears were closed by the storm.

Thus unobserved they went on. Dawn was beginning to break as they approached their destination; and the low lines of Morty's dwelling could be just discerned in the growing light, when a shot was fired from the middle of their ranks, which might have disconcerted all their precautions. The hand-cuffed Sullivan, careless of himself, and desperate at the thought of what might be coming, had contrived, in spite of his irons, to grasp and fire his comrade's musket. He was shot himself afterwards, for his ineffectual treason. His heroism had been thrown away. A gust of wind tore the sound to pieces, and scattered it in the war of the elements.

In the house at Eyris too, the inmates were all sleeping at last; but two of them had watched late, and had gone to rest only with the approach of daylight. Under the roof were some twenty of the river smugglers, who remained on guard there while Morty was in the country. These, and the faithful Connell along with them, had been slumbering the night through in their hammocks, or stretched on straw in the garrets, amidst spars, and casks, and rope coils. The boy, the heir of Morty's name and of his hereditary rights, lay gathered in his cot, dreaming of what he would do when he was a man.

Morty was engaged preparatory for his departure, in making up the accounts of various contraband transactions which he had undertaken for Blake before his flight to the West Indies. They were complicated by the secrecy with which the business had been carried on. Besides his ledgers he had piles of letters, some of which he had been burning, while he made notes from others, that he might leave everything in proper order. Ellen Mahony had been watching out the hours at his side over her spinning-wheel, and crooning out old Irish songs, saddest, sweetest and most hopeless of human melodies.

278

THE END OF DUNBOY

'There,' Morty said, pushing his books from him at last, and leaning back in his carved oak chair: 'there stand the names of more than a score of the gentry who now rule in these two counties. God knows whether our own ancestors were any better, but worse they could hardly be. Why, I have actually letters here from some of them, hinting how good a job they would think it if Goring was put out of the way, for spoiling the trade. Aye, aye! It is well for us that Goring has not left his like behind him.'

'And for what will ye be for ever thinking of that man, Morty?' said his sister. 'He was an ill friend to me, and a worse to the mother that bore us both. He is gone now. The Lord forgive him his sins. I will wish him that grace, at any rate, though he little deserves it at my hand. Ye are tired, Morty, and worn out. To bed with ye, and sleep. Sure the morning light is coming through the curtains. Hark, how the wind roars. It is an awful night. The Lord be gracious to us! What is that?'

She had risen to look out. At that moment something fluttered past the window which, to her strained senses, was like a draped woman's figure. It paused, and seemed to look at her; a long arm stretched out from under the cloak, and a skinny finger pointed into the room. The apparition lasted for half-a-dozen seconds, and then melted off, with a wailing cry, like a note struck by a passing gust from the strings of an Æolian harp.

The form might have been a phantom of imagination—but the sound disturbed a wolf-hound on the hearth, who raised his head and answered with a half-uttered howl. 'Oh God!' Ellen Mahony said. 'It is the Banshee. She came the night our mother died—and now she comes again. One of us in this room will never see another sunrise.'

Morty shuddered, in spite of himself. The dog sank back and turned uneasily over, as if he had been dreaming in his sleep. 'Tush, Ellen,' he said. 'It is but the moaning of the gale, and the sheets of rain gleaming in the half-light of dawn. You, too, are worn and weary, and fancy is playing pranks with you. We should both be asleep. A few more days, and our native soil will know us no more. The past is gone, a new life will begin for us in happier lands, and that boy of yours shall have a better fortune than his father.'

He rose and joined his sister at the window. The rain was rushing down in torrents. The swollen river was roaring along its channel beyond the garden in a yellow flood, and was brimming over the banks. Some sound caught Morty's ear. He started, and listened. 'That was strangely like a musket-shot,' he said. 'But, ah, no! We are the fools of our fears to-night. Some boulder was started from its bed by the river. It is time we were in ours. Good-night, dear Ellen. You have had a hard life in this land, and I am glad that you have agreed to leave it. The future shall make amends for all.'

Morty's ears had been truer than his judgment. What he had heard was the shot fired by his poor clansman, who had forfeited his life to save him. But the hound did not move again; and there were no further sounds but the raving of the storm and the noise of the water. Sleep had closed the eyes of Ellen Mahoney. Morty had flung himself wearily on his bed and was sinking into unconsciousness, when he was roused again by the fierce barking of a dozen dogs who were chained in the yard. To spring to his feet, seize a blunderbuss and rush to the door, was the work of a moment. Through a slit in the wall he saw that the house was surrounded. Yielding to his first impulse, he fired, but fired wildly, and the shot took no effect. It was otherwise with the fire from the windows, His men, roused, like himself, by the dogs, had bounded up, snatched their carbines, and poured out a destructive volley. One of the soldiers was killed, three were wounded. Captain N— sheltered his party among the rocks and walls, where they could be less easily hit, and so disposed them as to make escape from the house impossible. His orders were to take Morty alive, and he summoned him to surrender.

To resist, seemed a wanton sacrifice of life. The house, being thatched, could be easily set on fire. No relief could be looked for from outside; and, if he defied Captain N—, and forced him to storm the place, Morty knew that his poor followers would never desert him, and would all be killed at his side. He had his sister to think for also, and the child; and local

legend says, that, seeing the case was hopeless, he was unwill
ing to fire any more on the English soldiers—'He was too proud
to shoot the shilling-a-day men.' Probably he would not have
been too proud to shoot them, every one, if he could have
escaped by doing it; but he ordered the firing from the windows
to cease, he demanded a parley, and requested the English
officer to take charge of his sister, with the boy. To this Captain
N——, of course, consented; and Ellen Mahony, desperate, but
helpless, and almost unconscious, was passed out with the child
in her arms.

Morty then bade his men shift for themselves, and eighteen
of them started singly from various bolting holes to make for
the sea or the mountains. They were all caught, and each of
them had perhaps a dozen crimes to answer for. But the object
of the expedition was to capture those who had been concerned
in the murder at Dunboy, and the rest, who were found not to
belong to them, were let go.

Inside the house there were now five left. Morty himself,
Connell, and three more who had been in the boat at Dunboy
with them. If they allowed themselves to be taken alive, they
had nothing before them but an ignominious execution. If
they could reach the flooded river, it would either drown them
or take them down to the sea, where there would still be hope.

Again they were required to surrender, and they returned
no answer. The doors and windows were too strong to be
forced by ordinary implements. There was no spare powder to
make bursting charges. And thus to Fitzherbert's regret, for he
was anxious that Morty's papers should not be injured, it was
determined to set the house on fire.

Even this was found less easy than was looked for. The
thatch was soaked with the night's rain, and would not kindle.
Some one quicker than the rest tore off the damp layer of the
outside straw, and thrust in balls of wild fire. Then the flames
caught the dry rafters. The lofts were, as if laid for conflagra-
tion, full of tarred hemp, and spars, and brandy barrels, and
when these were once alight, the whole house was in a blaze,
the roof fell in, and through the sparks and eddying smoke
wreaths, Morty Sullivan and his four companions made a last

rush for life. Two were shot down within the walls, and were consumed in the fire. Connell, and 'little John Sullivan', who had been the coxswain of the boat which had brought Morty to Dunboy on the fatal Sunday morning, were seized and pinioned. Morty himself bounded over the flames into the garden; at the end of it was a clump of elder bushes, and beyond the elders there was a steep pitch down into the river. Could he reach the water alive, there was still a chance for him.

But he never reached it. A dozen muskets rattled out as he sprang through the branches. He fell dead, shot through the heart.

The house was so full of combustible materials, that although the rain helped to extinguish the fire, some hours had to pass before the ruins could be searched. It was supposed that there were powder barrels on the premises, and there was a fear of explosion. At last it was considered safe to examine the place. Nine-tenths of it had been completely gutted. The hall or sitting-room, however, being walled with stone and roofed with solid beams of oak, had almost escaped injury. The bills and ledgers were found in an iron chest as Morty had left them. Of the correspondence much had been destroyed by himself; but enough remained of so compromising import that the details of it were never revealed.

Perhaps if Morty himself had escaped he might not have been too curiously enquired after. But he had gone beyond the tolerated limits. Besides his smuggling offences and his Scotch adventure he had fluttered the dove-cotes in the West Indies. The blood of an English officer who had been a truer friend to Ireland than any Sullivan who had ever reigned from Glanarought to Iveragh was red upon his hand. By the law of England, by the law of all civilized nations, he had fallen as a felon, and as a felon only could he be regarded. The cutter had come round into the bay, and the body was given in charge to the crew to be carried to Cork. They lashed a rope round the neck and shoulders and made it fast behind the cutter's stern, and in this ignominious fashion they towed behind them all that was left of Morty through the waters of which he had been the glory and the terror. At Cork, when they arrived there, the trunk was quartered and the sea-washed head was set on the castle battlements. His comrades who were taken when he was killed had a short shrift, and the bloody drama was ended.

Connell, on the night before he was himself executed, wrote in Irish a last tribute to the friend whom he had so faithfully followed. The inflation of style may be more apparent than real, and may be due to the contemporary translator.

'Morty, my dear and loved master, you carried the sway for strength and generosity. It is my endless grief and sorrow that your fair head should be gazed at as a show upon a pike and that your noble frame is lifeless. I have travelled with you in foreign lands. You moved with kings in the Royal Prince's army. The great God is good and merciful. I ask His pardon and remission for I am to be hanged to-morrow at dawn. May the Lord have mercy on my master! It is for his sake I am now in their power. Men of Kerry pray for us; our heads will be high on a pike under the cold snow of night and the burning sun of summer. May our souls be joined to-morrow in rays of eternal glory.'*

* See Gibson's 'History of Cork', vol. ii, p. 524.